A

Nathan Dylan Goodwin is ⸺⸺⸺⸺⸺⸺⸺ educator. He was born and raised in Hastings, East Sussex. Schooled in the town, he then completed a Bachelor of Arts degree in Radio, Film and Television Studies, followed by a Master of Arts degree in Creative Writing at Canterbury Christ Church University. A member of the Society of Authors, he has completed a number of local history books about Hastings, as well as several works of fiction, including the acclaimed Forensic Genealogist series. His other interests include theatre, reading, photography, running, skiing, travelling and, of course, genealogy. He is a qualified teacher, member of the Guild of One-Name Studies and the Society of Genealogists, as well as being a member of the Sussex Family History Group, the Norfolk Family History Society and the Kent Family History Society. He lives in Kent with his husband, son, dog and chickens.

By the same author

The Suffragette's Secret
by
Nathan Dylan Goodwin

I would like to dedicate this short story to all my wonderful readers; your enthusiasm and keenness for Morton and his adventures is both humbling and motivating. Thank you.
In particular, I should like to mention those whose regular witty interactions help to brighten my day:
Connie Parrott, Karen Clark Cresswell and Gail Ann Pippin

Chapter One

Morton Farrier was pleased. He had found the grave. The effects of time and forty-seven years of passing seasons had tainted the headstone surprisingly little. Perhaps its remarkable condition was owing to its position within the protective lee of the church nave or perhaps it was owing to the permanence of the chosen material: deep burgundy marble. Crouching onto the freshly cut grass, he read the inscription: *'In Memory of a dear husband and father Cecil W. Barwise, died 18th December 1958 aged 74. At rest. Also beloved wife and mother Grace Barwise, died 15th August 1970 aged 94. Reunited.'*

Morton pulled out his mobile and took several shots of the grave. 'It's here,' he called out.

'Brilliant,' came the flat, sarcastic response.

He grinned. 'Come over and see.'

With a grunt and a sigh, his heavily pregnant wife, Juliette heaved herself up from a bench on the church's perimeter and ambled slowly towards him. 'I'm freezing and miserable—this can't be good for the baby,' she moaned. She reached the grave and took a long breath in. 'Cecil and Grace Barwise. Amazing. Can we go, now?' she asked, rotating back towards the car.

'Sure, let's go and get a hot drink from…' Morton started. His words faltered when he saw Juliette wince and reach down to her protruding belly. 'What's the matter?'

She turned, lifted up her coat and revealed a dark stain travelling down the legs of her light-blue maternity jeans. 'I think my waters have just broken,' she said, her face contorting into a grimace. 'I think the boy is on his way.'

'But he's two weeks early,' Morton said.

Juliette rubbed the sides of her stomach. 'I don't think Albert wants to wait any longer; I think I'm in labour.'

'Is it hurting?'

Juliette nodded. 'Yes,' she replied curtly. 'We need to get to the Conquest—now.'

'But…it's thirty-odd miles away—we might not make it,' Morton replied. 'We need to go to the nearest maternity hospital.'

Juliette looked horrified. 'But my birth plan…'

Morton shrugged. 'I think the water birth, soothing music and dimmed lights have just gone out the window. Come on, let's go—I'm not delivering Albert in a churchyard.' He took Juliette's arm and began back towards the car, all the while fumbling on his phone to locate the nearest hospital. 'William Harvey.'

'What?' Juliette snapped, pausing to bend over as a spasm hit her abdomen.

'The nearest maternity hospital—it's not far away, thank God. Okay?'

Juliette nodded, stood up and continued across the churchyard.

Finally, they reached the car and Morton programmed the hospital's location into the Satnav.

'Think you need to put your foot down,' Juliette gasped.

'I'll go as fast as I can,' he answered, zipping out of the church car park.

'Is it disrespectful for your waters to break on someone's grave? Do you think Cecil and Grace Barwise will be offended?' Juliette asked, a wry smile turning into a wince, as she clutched her stomach.

'I doubt it; they're your great grandparents.'

Chapter Two

Morton and Juliette, with one hand each clutching onto the handle of the baby car seat, passed through the exit of the William Harvey Hospital. The closing of the automatic doors behind them rocked them with reality. Simultaneously, they peered down at the tiny creature sleeping soundly between them.

A bewildered grin crept onto Morton's face. 'Is that it?' he asked, swivelling his head to look back at the hospital, half-expecting someone to come rushing out and to declare that a mistake had been made— that they weren't anywhere near ready to venture out into the world unsupervised with a baby.

'Yep, that's it. It's just the three of us now,' Juliette confirmed with an uncertain smile on her face.

'But…' Morton began, looking back at the doors, shocked at the simplicity of their discharge. She had only given birth last night. Nobody had even asked if they were prepared. 'How will we know what to do?'

Juliette laughed. 'A combination of instinct, advice from friends and relatives and the abundance of baby books we've got at home. Failing that, there's always Google if things get really desperate.'

'Right,' Morton said, not liking the sound of any of those options. For someone who had spent most of his adult life resolutely vowing never to have children, he wasn't sure his usually excellent instincts should be trusted. 'Come on, let's get it home.'

'*It?*' Juliette begged, as they crossed the car park. 'That's our child you're referring to.'

'What do you want me to say?' Morton asked. '*Albert?*'

Juliette rolled her eyes. 'No, obviously not.'

Albert had emerged as the favourite name, following the twenty-week scan in which a nurse had said that she was 'pretty sure' that they were expecting a boy, but that she couldn't be completely certain. A profusion of baby name books was subsequently dredged, resulting in a short list of five. Having decorated the nursery in various shades of blue, Morton and Juliette had begun to refer to the room and its contents as belonging to Albert. But now Albert didn't quite fit the child to which Juliette had given birth. 'It's a girl!' the midwife had declared, following a short labour. She couldn't understand their baffled faces.

'Are you... *sure?*' Morton had pressed.

'If, after twenty-two years in the job, there's one thing I can safely say I can do well, it's to tell the sex of a baby,' she had answered.

'Oh,' Morton had responded.

'It really isn't *that* bad,' the midwife had replied, her tone suggesting offence.

'No, I know,' Morton had begun, realising how his reaction was coming across. 'I'm very happy—it's just a surprise, is all.'

The midwife had shrugged and left them alone with their new-born daughter.

They reached the car and Morton carefully set the seat in place, the baby bedecked with an oversized pastel-blue knitted coat. Morton stared at his daughter, a surge of overwhelming pride moistening his eyes. 'Alberta?' he suggested, climbing into the driver's seat.

Juliette shot him an incredulous look.

'We need to draw up a new short list,' he said, starting the car.

Juliette closed her eyes and tilted her head back into the headrest. 'I can't face it; you can do that,' she muttered. 'I need to rest.'

Thirty-five minutes later, Morton, Juliette and the newest member of the Farrier family entered their home on Mermaid Street in Rye. It felt to Morton as though they had been absent for several weeks, rather than just two days.

'Home sweet home,' Juliette breathed, collapsing down into the welcome embrace of the sofa. 'I'm sleeping. Wake me up in time for *the child's* first birthday...'

'I'd better start ringing around and letting everyone know the news,' he said. The first person whom he wanted to tell was his newly discovered biological father, Jack. Pleasure and pride rose inside him at the thought of informing Jack that he was now a grandfather. Since meeting him for the first time in Boston last summer, they had spoken at least once a week on the phone and had met up once more when Jack had been in London on business. In recent weeks, as they shared the stories and memories from the past that had been denied them, their relationship had felt increasingly like that of a normal father and son. He'd felt guilty at first and would often find himself in a sombre mood following their phone conversations, feeling that he was somehow betraying the memory of his deceased adoptive dad. Long discussions with Juliette had helped and now he embraced the relationship and its accompanying feelings wholly.

He picked up the phone and started a video call. When Jack answered, Morton held the phone above the baby. 'Meet your new granddaughter,' he announced.

'Grand*daughter*?' Jack questioned.

'Long story.'

With the baby asleep in the Moses basket—*Albert's* Moses basket, Morton noted with a dry smile—and with Juliette curled into a ball under a blanket, he tiptoed up to his study.

The only wall in the room not to be covered in floor-to-ceiling bookshelves was the wall upon which Morton would usually attach the paper trail of his current genealogical investigations. For the past week, he had been working on a special project: creating a book charting the lives of Juliette's direct ancestors. He realised, now that he was looking at the complex pedigree charts fixed to the wall, that his idea of providing a fleshed-out account of several generations of her family was an enormous task and his hope of presenting it to her shortly after the birth was impossible now that Albert...*the child* had arrived two weeks prematurely. His daughter had evidently inherited her mother's wilful nature.

The name 'Albert' was written on a single sheet of paper attached to the bottom of the wall. Morton bent down, scribbled out the word, replaced it with 'Miss Farrier' and moved his eyes up the inverted-pyramid-like pedigree chart, the number of pieces of paper doubling with each new generation. At the very top of the wall were sixteen sheets. Some of them—place holders for ancestors as yet undiscovered—were blank. The others contained the names of his and Juliette's great grandparents.

Reaching up, Morton added the burial location of Grace Barwise—the current focus of his investigations. So far, all that he knew about her came from her birth, marriage and death certificates. Now, it was time to put some flesh onto her bones.

Knowing from her birth certificate that she had been born in Brighton on 8th July 1876, Morton ran a search for her under her maiden name in the 1881 census. The only result to match his enquiry was at the top of the list: *Grace Emmerson, inmate, born 1876, Brighton.* He clicked to see the original image and a long list of children's names appeared onscreen—residents of the Brighton Union Workhouse.

Could it be her? he wondered, returning to the search results. After some time of scouring, amending his parameters and checking the results, he came to the sad conclusion that yes, it was Juliette's great grandmother who had been living in the workhouse quite alone among strangers, aged four.

He switched his focus to the 1891 census. Despite not knowing the circumstances of her time there, Morton was saddened to see that Grace—now aged 14—continued to be an inmate there. He printed the document and jumped forward another decade.

He was relieved to see that by 1901 Grace had escaped the confines of the workhouse, being listed as a twenty-four-year-old unmarried domestic servant, employed by a large farming family by the name of Smith outside of Brighton. As Morton ran his eyes down the household, he spotted another familiar name among the servants: Cecil Barwise—the man who would later become Grace's husband. Now Morton knew the likely place at which Juliette's great grandparents had met. He smiled, printed the sheet out and moved on to the final census available to him: 1911.

He found her easily, living in Brighton with three other women at Sea View, 13-14 Victoria Road. At least, once again, he *thought* that it was her. Her age was given as zero. Her birth place and her marital status, written in a different colour by a different person, were stated to be 'unknown'. Her occupation—just like the other three women residing there—was 'Militant Suffragette.'

'Well,' Morton said, grinning at the screen. Juliette and her mother weren't the only headstrong women in their family after all, then. 'How interesting.' He wondered if being a militant suffragette might mean that she had been arrested for her protestations. He typed Grace's name into Ancestry's Suffragettes Arrested register—a document created in August 1914 at the outbreak of the First World War, when more than one thousand suffrage prisoners were granted amnesty in response to a suspension of militant activities. The search yielded one result, which Morton clicked. A scanned, ochre-coloured copy of the original record loaded onscreen. Grace's name appeared with no identifying information.

Emmerson, Grace
Brighton 1/8/10 – 177.568
Brighton 29/12/10– 183.189
Bow Street 22/2/11 – 200.455

Morton looked at the sheet, slightly baffled. This woman had evidently been arrested three times within six months. Even though there was no age, address or occupation given, he felt sure that the two references to Brighton indicated that the woman's record in front of him probably was Juliette's great grandmother—he just needed to prove it. The seemingly random collection of numbers at the end of each line was going to be the key.

Logging on at The National Archives website, Morton entered the first of the three numbers, preceded by the letters HO. He made a note of a new reference number, which pointed to a Home Office document. Entering the other two numbers, he received similar references, the documents for which, he was disappointed to read, could only be seen by paying for a search to be conducted, or by visiting the archives in person. *Now was not a good time to be scuttling off to The National Archives*, he thought.

He printed out the page and stuck it to the wall, then typed Grace's name into FindmyPast's newspaper collection. He grinned at the first result, headed *Suffragette's Violent Speeches*. He clicked to read the report and, just as it loaded onscreen, his daughter, with impeccable timing, began to wail downstairs.

Morton bounded down to the lounge. Juliette, her hair strung in every direction, was cradling the baby, trying to soothe her. Morton leant over and looked at her tiny pink face, screwed up and contorted through her screams. 'Poor little Albert,' Morton said, 'maybe he's hungry.'

Juliette scowled at him.

Chapter Three

Grace Emmerson gazed at the languid white smudges that blotted an otherwise perfect duck-egg-blue sky. Under her nightdress her stomach tingled with a tremor of nervousness that had been immediately present upon waking this morning. As she gazed out of her bedroom window, high on the fourth floor of the chunky Victorian house, she half-hoped that those flossy clouds might miraculously turn leaden and render today's proposed meeting rained-off. But the day was ripening to be exactly as they had wished: bright and warm. Anyway, it was time for her to conquer the fear within. Otherwise, what would she be? The precise embodiment of the view that they were opposing: a weaker, diffident, second-class citizen.

'Grace, we shall be leaving in thirty minutes,' a voice called from the hallway. It was Minnie Turner.

'I'll be ready,' Grace shouted through the closed door. Her lodgings here at Sea View on Victoria Road were small and simple. The floor was bare boards and on the walls was hung a plain green paper. Her rent, which provided her with a single bed, wardrobe and chest of drawers, was the lowest of all the guests. The best bedrooms were reserved for visiting holidaymakers—mostly fellow suffragettes. Of the two remaining bedrooms, one was occupied by her friend Olivia and the other by Minnie, the owner of the house and a prominent figure of the Brighton branch of the Women's Social and Political Union.

She needed to stop dithering. Pulling her nightdress over her head, she slipped on a floor-length, wine-coloured, two-piece walking dress that the other women in the house had presented to her for her first public speaking event. She styled her light-brown hair into a simple rounded pompadour, then carefully placed her straw hat upon her head. Lastly, she pulled on a pair of white lace gloves. She was ready.

Imitating a confidence which she had observed in the other women, Grace opened her bedroom door and descended the stairs to the sitting room.

'Well!' Minnie cried, leaping up from her chair and clapping. 'You really look quite the part, Grace.'

'Very sophisticated,' Olivia chimed in. She was herself dressed in her best clothes and her black hair was styled in a similar fashion to Grace's, revealing her somewhat harsh facial features.

Their reaction, although inflated, drew a calmness to Grace's breathing and a smile to her face.

'Are you ready?' Minnie asked, taking Grace's left hand in hers. 'My goodness, you're shaking.'

'I'm just a little chilly, that's all. I need to get my cold bones out into that glorious sunshine,' she replied brightly.

'Let's put these on, then we can leave,' Minnie said, holding aloft three freshly pressed tri-coloured sashes bearing the words 'VOTES FOR WOMEN'.

They placed the sashes over their heads and flattened them to their bodies. Olivia picked up a plain wooden box, Minnie collected a bag of leaflets and a small placard, then they made their way out of the house. In unison, the three women raised their parasols against the high heat of the summer sun, crossed the road and walked down Victoria Street, which ran perpendicular to the house. In the near distance, the sea sparkled hypnotically; there was little doubt that thousands would today be drawn to the town by its bewitching allure. The promenade would be packed.

The closer they got to the seafront, the more breathless Grace became. The sensation in her tummy had grown into a dull, uncomfortable ache. She wished that she had drunk some gripe water prior to leaving, but it was too late now.

Slowly and sedately they walked towards the seafront, as though they were on a leisurely Sunday afternoon stroll. The closer they drew to their destination, the more the crowds increased in number. Stares, glares, frowns, but also nods of approval, came from the men and women whom they passed. Some muttered their displeasure. Others vocalised their support. An elderly crone, being pushed along the pavement in a bath chair, barked her disgust at them.

'Thank you, Madam, for sharing your troglodytic views,' Minnie responded, with an extravagant wave of her hand.

The solemnity of Grace's face cracked into a light chuckle. Minnie was an old hat at this and such altercations were easily batted off with a pithy comment and a smile; she had endured much worse.

They arrived at the promenade and Grace's resolve curdled as they waited for a line of three horses and carriages to pass. Before them was the long, thin Palace Pier, jutting out almost two thousand feet over the cold English Channel. She raised her hand to her stomach and began to dig her fingers into the gripe.

Minnie reached for Grace's hand and pulled it down. 'You'll be wonderful,' she whispered, as they crossed the road. A warm smile spread across her soft round face.

When they had reached the other side, close to the entrance onto the pier, Grace looked about uncertainly and asked: 'Whereabouts should I stand?'

'Wherever you like—let the people come to you. *You* are in charge.'

'Here,' Olivia answered decisively, dropping the box down onto a random spot in the centre of the promenade. She stepped back and held her open hand aloft, waiting.

Grace drew in an extraordinarily long breath, placed her left hand in Olivia's and stepped up onto the box. She cleared her throat and tried to remember the opening lines of her speech, but the thinking space in her mind was knotted up with intangible threads and by the faces of passing strangers. Scowling. Snarling. Smiling. Smirking.

'Ladies, gentlemen—our good and kindly friends,' Minnie shouted, hoisting her placard above her head. 'The esteemed Brighton branch of the Women's Social and Political Union is delighted to present—for her very first public oration—Miss Grace Emmerson.'

Olivia reached into the bag and pulled out a handful of leaflets, poised and ready to pass them out to members of the public.

Not a single, solitary person stopped.

'Thank you,' Grace murmured.

'Louder,' Olivia urged.

Grace coughed, trying to dislodge the gritty blockage in her throat. 'Thank you,' she repeated, indeed more loudly this time. 'People of Brighton, I stand humbly here before you as one of your fellow citizens, entreating the charity of just a few moments of your time.'

Two ladies—charwomen, Grace judged by their outfits—stopped to listen.

'Our town is not a fair town. Our country is not a fair country,' Grace continued.

'Life ain't never fair, love—better get used to it,' one of the charwomen jeered. 'It ain't fair that I 'ave to work me ruddy fingers to the bone and the likes of you lot get to stand all 'oity-toity on the promenade in ya Sunday best.'

'Ours is not...' Grace stumbled, the words of the charwoman jarring her thoughts back to the unspeakable years in the Brighton

Union Workhouse. If only these women could have known of her upbringing…

A group of young lads and a well-to-do woman paused, curious.

'Ours is not…' Her words were stuck. The charwomen sneered. The young lads whispered and giggled.

'…a fair government,' Minnie hinted quietly.

'Our government—Asquith—is not fair,' Grace stammered. 'It's…it's…' More people began to gather.

'It's time you learnt to speak proper, miss,' one of the lads taunted.

'Leave her alone and she might be able to,' someone said from the back of the crowd. A male voice, which Grace thought that she recognised.

'It's…' she said, searching for the man who had decried her antagonist. But she couldn't see familiarity among the people—just hostility and derision.

More women joined the thronging semi-circle around her. She paused and searched her mind for the speech that she had diligently written, practised and rehearsed for hours on end. The jumbled words began to reassemble in her mind, slowly forming complete sentences. 'It's high time that we women rose up—together—women of all social backgrounds—young and old, workers, the privileged, married and single; uncommon in so many ways, yet *superbly* united in our inequality and our societal disadvantage.'

Grace eyed the crowd: she held the attention of each and every one of them now. And yet more were coming. Confidence elevated her stature, furnishing her voice with a new vigour and strength. 'Your fellow women around the country have written tens of thousands of letters to the dishonourable gentlemen running this land—and what for? All for nothing! They simply *are not* listening. If they won't listen to us with welcoming ears, then we must jolly well *make* them listen to us. Our time is now! And it is a time for action—*deeds not words.*'

'What good's a vote to me?' a bedraggled woman in her late thirties shouted. She was surrounded by a barrage of scrawny and unkempt children with bare feet. 'I need work. I need money. I need a proper place to live. What I *don't* need is a bloody vote.'

The woman's words were met with nods and murmurings of approval. One man clapped.

'But don't you see?' Grace answered. 'If you had a vote and you used it wisely, then you might be helped towards changing those other things. Do you think a female Member of Parliament would stand by and watch such social injustices?'

The crowd burst into laughter.

'What poppycock!' a different woman spat. 'You need locking up in the Hellingly asylum.'

Grace dropped her speech and directed her attention towards the woman, who was now walking away. 'Madam—do you hold regular employment?'

'Yes, I do, actually,' she answered indignantly.

'I trust, therefore, that you are contented that in this respect the government treats you as an equal to men—to tax you, to take your money and spend it as they, the representatives of the male population see fit? That sits right with you, does it, Madam?'

The woman had no answer.

Grace was on a roll. 'And are you, Madam,' she continued, before widening her gestures to the rest of the crowd, 'and the rest of you women out there, required to abide by this country's laws?'

'Course we are!' several women chanted.

'What a stupid question,' another chipped in.

'And yet you have absolutely no say in what those laws mandate!' Grace cried. 'Written *by* men *for* men. What if this government introduces a law that says women must dress in a certain way, or behave in a certain way? Who shall stop them?'

'Right,' a voice boomed, 'I've heard quite enough of this.' Two bulky policemen barged their way through the crowd. One of them grabbed Grace's hand and pulled her down from the box. 'On the subject of laws—real laws—not your fancy made up ones, I'd like you to explain what you mean by *deeds not words*, because it sounds to my ear suspiciously like incitement, for which you would be arrested.'

Some of the crowd booed at this latest drama, but most simply dissolved back into the passing throng. A small handful took from Olivia's proffered leaflets.

'Arrest me, please,' Minnie entreated, offering him her hands. She turned her head to the parting crowds and shouted, 'Deeds not words, ladies! Burn down their offices! Smash their windows! Make your voices heard!'

'Right, you're coming with us,' the policeman said, his fat hairy hand reaching around Minnie's upper arm.

'Deeds not words!' Olivia chanted. 'Deeds not words!'

'Olivia, no,' Minnie called. 'Just me—you come back here tomorrow and carry on. Votes for women! Deeds not words! Burn their buildings until they start to listen!'

Minnie made herself a dead weight and the two policemen, taking an arm each, dragged her along the promenade. All the while, she repeated her call: 'Votes for women! Deeds not words! Join the WSPU now! Votes for women! End the tyranny!'

From a crowd that had peaked at nigh on forty, there was now just Grace and Olivia—standing stones among a sea of promenaders.

'Well done, Grace,' Olivia said, throwing her arms around her. 'You were amazing—really amazing.'

Grace shook her head, a hollow feeling now occupying the space where the griping nervousness had taken root before. She had not been amazing. She had been heckled, forgotten her words, then when the test came and the police had arrived, she had stood silently whilst her friend had been dragged away. 'Let's just go home,' she said quietly.

'I thought you were really amazing, too,' a voice said. That same male voice which had urged the crowd to listen to her.

Grace turned and smiled. 'Cecil Barwise. What a surprise.' She rushed over to him, quite forgetting herself. She reached him and offered her hand, which he shook vigorously. He was dressed well—at least for a man of his station—and his dark hair was oiled from a side-parting. His upper lip protruded out slightly and he reminded Grace, as he had used to, of a pouting duck.

'I must say, it was a wonder to see little Grace Emmerson up there like that, standing up for herself,' Cecil said with a grin.

'Why?' Olivia barked. 'Because she's a woman?'

Cecil's face fell. 'No, not at all—because when I knew her she was… she was just ever so quiet, that's all.'

'Calm down, Olivia,' Grace urged. 'Cecil's a decent chap—we worked in the same house a few years ago.'

'And his views on women's suffrage?' Olivia demanded to Grace, her voice barbed.

Cecil turned his trouser pockets inside out. 'I am not eligible to vote. I don't own anything, never mind property.' He shrugged. 'My views are simple: I think all women *and* men—regardless of how wealthy they are, or whether or not they own property—should be able to vote. It's as simple as that. I hope as much as you to one day see female Members of Parliament.'

'Hmm,' Olivia mumbled.

'Are you still working for the Smiths?' Grace asked.

Cecil shook his head. 'No, I left the winter after you. I'm Head Groom over at Linden Grove now. I'm actually…'

Grace cut him short. 'Linden Grove?'

Cecil nodded.

'That place needs fire-bombing if anywhere does,' Grace said. Hearing the name again brought cruel flashes of the past into her mind.

'Never heard of it,' Olivia chipped in. 'Can we go now, Grace? We ought rather to be going to the police station to find out what charges have been brought against Minnie.'

'Yes, we ought,' Grace agreed, more than happy to shift the conversation on.

'Oh,' Cecil said. 'I was rather hoping that we might get to go to the Lyons tearoom together.'

'No time for that,' Olivia declared. 'Come along, Grace. We've got planning to do. *Deeds not words.* Or, in your case, *action not cake.*'

'Another time, Cecil,' Grace said. 'Good day.'

Cecil nodded his head. 'Good day.'

Grace and Olivia gathered up their things and moved off.

'Presumptuous fellow,' Olivia mumbled, as they crossed the road. 'Who does he think he is?'

'He's harmless enough,' Grace replied with a smile. 'Now, I don't think turning up at the police station with all this', she indicated the box and placard, 'will do us many favours. Let's return it all home first. Minnie might even have been discharged; it wouldn't be the first time the police have done that just to break up our meetings.'

'Well, she didn't actually *do* anything, did she?' Olivia said.

'No, but it's high time we did. We're preaching to the public about *deeds not words*, yet we're not doing anything ourselves.'

'What are you thinking of?' Olivia asked.

'Something that actually warrants getting arrested.'

Chapter Four

Grace Emmerson marched haughtily towards the exit of the Magistrate's Court. Her fourth speech in as many weeks on Brighton promenade had seen her get arrested by an oafish bobby for incitement. Her speeches had become more confident and she had quickly learned how to handle hecklers and jeerers. As the crowds had grown, so too had the violent rhetoric of her words.

She opened the doors and stepped out into a cold and cloudy morning.

'You're out!' Olivia said, flinging her arms around Grace, as she exited the doors of the court.

'I know, but did you hear what I had to agree to in order to get out?' Grace asked, unsure if she had done the right thing. She was riddled with an acute feeling of shame at what had just happened.

'Yes, I was in the public gallery,' Olivia confirmed. 'You did right— you're more use to us out here than inside prison.

'Yes, but I've had to agree to making no further inflammatory speeches.'

'There are plenty more of us waiting in the wings, don't you worry.'

They walked in silence for a short way, Grace replaying over and over her first court appearance. She felt as though she had failed yet again. *Should she have refused to agree to silence and taken a custodial sentence?* Women around the country were enduring much greater suffering than that. Hunger strikes for suffragettes serving prison sentences was actively encouraged in order to highlight the fact that the women's crimes were not being treated as political acts.

'Where are we going?' Grace asked, suddenly realising that she had no clue where they were headed.

'Home,' Olivia replied with a smile. 'Some Sea View relaxation is what you need.'

Grace stopped and looked at Olivia. 'It most certainly is *not* what I need. We're going…at least, *I'm* going to the headquarters.'

'Whatever for?'

'To plan what I'm going to do next.'

Olivia laughed. 'You know what, Grace. I used to wonder if you were actually up to all this.'

'Really?'

Olivia nodded. 'But look at you, now: Mrs Pankhurst herself would be proud.'

'*Mrs Pankhurst* wouldn't have ducked out of a prison sentence,' Grace countered.

'She would have, were it for the greater good of the cause; she's different—she's famous—her actions make the national papers because of who she is.'

'*I'll* make the national papers, just you wait and see,' Grace promised with a chuckle.

A few minutes later, they arrived at the Brighton branch of the WSPU. Their office was above the Singer Sewing Machine shop, on the busy junction of North Street and West Street in the town centre.

As usual, the door was locked. Grace knocked firmly and waited.

Moments later, the door crept open before being snagged back by a metal chain. Through the narrow gap appeared Minnie Turner's distrustful face.

'Ah! Grace, Olivia!' she beamed, briefly closing the door to release the chain before pulling it wide and bidding them to enter. 'How wonderful to have you back. You're just in time for a planning meeting.'

A *planning meeting* was the nebulous description of what upcoming actions the branch would be orchestrating.

Grace closed the door, ready to voice her desired actions.

Hours of fervent, passionate discussion had followed at the headquarters, with more than two dozen women proposing and arguing the merits of a variety of local and national militant actions. For three days, the heated debates had continued, stalking Grace from the office to her lodgings at Sea View, where they had continued unabated.

On the next day, Grace left the office prepared for her forthcoming duties. She closed the door and stepped out into the cool caress of the breeze blowing up from the sea.

'*In consequence of inflammatory speeches made by Miss Grace Emmerson a vast amount of damage to property had been done within the last two months in and around Brighton,*' a voice suddenly boomed from behind, startling her.

She turned to see the most recent edition of the *Brighton Argus* being held up, covering the man's face, as he read.

Grace rolled her eyes and pushed down the newspaper to see Cecil's grinning face.

'*The condition of things,*' he continued in a mock-upper-class voice, '*that was brought about by Miss Emmerson was such that the defendant, who had uttered some very violent speeches, should be brought before a magistrate in order that she should be put under sureties to be of good behaviour for the future.*' Cecil cocked one eyebrow and stared at Grace. '*Are* you being good, Miss Emmerson?'

'Only an angel could be more righteous,' she answered.

'I'm sure,' Cecil said, folding up the newspaper and tucking it under his arm. 'Now, how about that cup of tea you promised me?'

Grace furrowed her brow. 'I'm not sure I recall *promising* you anything.' She glanced up at the clock tower. The Lyons Tea Room was just a stone's throw from the WSPU headquarters. One cup wouldn't hurt. 'Alright.'

They crossed the street together and stopped at the windows of the Lyons Tea Room, which were filled with a multitude of different cakes.

'Tempted?' Cecil asked, watching Grace lingering beside the windows. 'That Victoria Sponge looks nice.'

'I'd better not,' she replied. 'I've got a busy day today.'

'More inflammatory speeches, Miss Emmerson?' Cecil asked, leading them inside.

'Something like that, yes,' she answered. Grace cast her eyes around the tearoom. The sounds of working-class chatter muddled in the cool air around her.

A waitress in a black uniform, white cap and apron approached them with a smile. 'Table for two? she asked in a bawdy East London accent.

'Yes, please,' Grace replied.

They were led to a round table with two chairs close to the front window.

'What can I get ya?'

'Just a cup of tea for me, please,' Grace ordered.

'Same for me—thank you.'

'Sure I can't tempt ya to one of me delicious cakes?' she asked, pointing at the window displays. 'All freshly made on the premises.'

'No, thank you,' Grace said.

'Right you are,' the waitress conceded, as she trotted off.

'So, what have you been up to lately?' Cecil asked her, placing his elbows on the table and leaning closer.

Grace tapped his newspaper. 'Haven't you read this?'

'Yes, but what *else* have you been doing—not work to do with the WSPU, I mean.'

'What else is there?' she asked defensively. 'It's the only thing that matters right now.'

'And when it's all over? When everyone has the vote—then what?'

'Maybe I'll become an MP, then Prime Minister.' Grace shrugged and laughed.

Cecil mirrored her good humour, but his fixed smile belied the seriousness underneath his question.

'What about you?' she asked. 'What has life got in store for Cecil Barwise?'

He inhaled and thought for an inordinately long time before answering. 'I expect I'll stay on at Linden Grove for the foreseeable future, then keep a lookout for a post somewhere with bigger stables.'

"ere we go,' the waitress said brightly, setting a tray down on the immaculate white tablecloth. She carefully lifted off and set out the teapot, two tea cups and saucers, a small jug of milk and a bowl of sugar. 'Not changed your mind about me cakes, have ya?'

'No, thank you,' Grace insisted politely.

'Right you are. Enjoy.'

'Grace—last time I mentioned Linden Grove you said that it deserved to be fire-bombed and then, just now when I said it again, you tensed up. Do you know of the place?'

Now, there was a question. She busied herself pouring the tea as she considered her answer. 'I knew it once—a very long time ago—so long, in fact, that it's almost like a dream. Tell me, is Mister Wild still the master of the house?'

Cecil nodded. 'Yes.'

'And how do you find him?' she asked, pouring the tea.

Cecil shifted in his chair, looked about the room, then lowered his voice. 'Like most of his sort: a devil as a husband, indifferent as a father and a tyrant as an employer.'

'A remarkably apt description,' Grace murmured. 'And his wife?'

'She does what's expected of a woman of her station. She usually treats me and the other servants alright, most of the time.' Cecil eyed her suspiciously. 'Did you once work there?'

'I was there for a very short time,' she answered with a heavy sigh. In the gap that opened up in their conversation, Grace realised that her palms had become moist and her fists clenched. She tried to relax.

'Why do you not speak of your past at these meetings you do on the promenade? Tell those poor souls that you weren't born with a silver spoon in your mouth like they think.'

He was referring, of course, to her years as a child in the Brighton Union Workhouse. It was a past that tormented her and that she would now rather forget. When preparing the notes for her third speech, Olivia had visited her bedroom and suggested the very same thing as Cecil was now mooting. But she couldn't do it. It was now, thankfully, a long time ago. She shook her head and drank some tea. 'I don't want the sympathy.'

'But these women see you as something you're not—or at least weren't—they think you're better than they are. If they knew you grew up in the workhouse…'

Grace shrugged. 'I want to look forwards, Cecil, not backwards.'

More silence followed as Grace finished her tea. She caught the attention of the waitress and waved her over. 'One piece of your Victoria Sponge, please.'

'I knew you'd come 'round!' the waitress sang.

Grace placed 4d down on the table and stood up. 'Well, it was lovely to catch up with you, Cecil. But now I must leave.'

Cecil looked surprised at the abruptness of her departure. 'But I haven't even finished my tea, yet,' he complained.

'You stay here and enjoy the tea and cake—I insist.' She shook his hand and turned to leave.

'Can we go out again sometime?' Cecil called.

'Maybe,' she replied, without turning around.

Chapter Five

Morton was in the land of the living dead. He had no concept of what time it was, nor what day it was. Every muscle in his body begged him for sleep. It had been, what, five days now since they had brought the baby home and, since that moment, he and Juliette could count the number of hours' sleep that they had had on two hands. Yesterday, after they had both inadvertently fallen asleep at the kitchen table, they had decided to devise a sleep rota. Now, it was supposed to be his turn to sleep. Except that the banshee wail, emanating from his daughter's lungs downstairs, penetrated the closed bedroom door, through the pillow placed over his head, before finally breaching the set of ear plugs that he had rushed into town this morning to buy.

Dragging the duvet and pillow off the bed, Morton left the bedroom, climbed the stairs to his study and shut the door. Collapsing into a heap on the floor, he listened carefully. Nope, he could still hear her. In fact, the whole of Rye must be able to hear her, he decided.

With a sigh, he closed his eyes and tried to settle his mind. He needed to imagine that he was somewhere else, lying on a deserted beach. Isn't that what people did to try and relax? The beach that popped into his mind was Chatham Lighthouse Beach on Cape Cod—one of the places that they had visited on their honeymoon last summer. Warm, perfect sand. Gentle waves breaking on the shoreline. He was almost there. His breathing was beginning to slow and the extraneous sounds were subsiding. He was back there, Juliette sunbathing beside him. As sleep lured him in, so his thoughts began to tear and fact became tangled with fantasy until he slipped into the enveloping darkness.

The sound woke him instantly. He tried to sit up but struggled to raise his forehead from the damp pillow. He was hot, sweating and his pulse was racing faster than if he had just completed a marathon. His eyes flicked open to try and determine the source of the noise. It was the house phone, he realised, disorientation messing with his mind. He was in his study and the phone was ringing.

Grappling up to his desk, Morton knocked the phone to the floor, then picked it up to answer. He spoke: 'Hello?' but nothing except a croak came out.

'Is that you, Morton?'

He cleared his throat, then tried again. 'Hi, yes.'

'It's Margot here.'

Oh, joy, Morton thought. Juliette's mother, the living embodiment of the interfering mother-in-law. 'Hi, Margot. How are you?' he asked, trying to pull his splintered thoughts back together.

'I'm okay,' she answered. 'How's my daughter and granddaughter? Have you got a name for her, yet? Everyone's asking.'

'They're good, thanks. We've chosen Ethel. Like it?'

There was a short pause on the other end of the line. 'Are you joking?'

'Yes,' Morton replied.

'Right,' she said flatly. 'I take it that's a no, then. Listen, is there anything I need to bring tomorrow?'

Morton outwardly groaned when he realised that she was coming to stay for a few days, then quickly turned it into a cough. 'Excuse me, Margot. Erm, no I don't think you need to bring anything…unless you can supply sleep in pill form?'

'Right, only I've got…' She continued blithering on about gifts from neighbours and cousins, but his addled brain had stopped listening. His eyes settled on Margot's name on the pedigree chart on the wall in front of him. He traced the line of ascendancy up through her mother, then on to Grace Emmerson.

'Actually,' he said, interrupting her mid-flow. 'Do you have anything at home about your grandmother, Grace?'

'What?' Margot stammered.

Morton repeated his request.

Margot blew out a puff of air. 'I'll have to have a look. I know I've got some photos and maybe some jewellery somewhere. I'll have a think. So, what about Sue's fruit scones, then?'

He had no idea to what she was referring. 'Yes, lovely—thanks.'

'What?' Margot demanded.

'Sorry—got to go—Albert's crying.'

'Who's Albert?'

Morton ended the call, placed the phone back into its cradle and rubbed his face. How long had he been asleep? It could have been minutes, hours, days or weeks for all he knew. One thing was certain, though, and that was that he felt no better for it. And now, thanks to Margot's call, he was wide awake. He glanced at the clock. Seventeen minutes he'd been asleep. Seventeen. Brilliant. He craved coffee—desperately—but considered the veritable orchestra of creaks and groans that would inevitably accompany his journey downstairs. No, he needed to stay put for the time being.

His thoughts turned back to Grace Emmerson. He had achieved absolutely nothing more on his research into her life and, in fact, couldn't now recall where he had even got up to. He opened his laptop lid and was presented with the newspaper report which he had found but not yet read, entitled *Suffragette's Violent Speeches*. Now he remembered.

'Miss Grace Emmerson, a prominent local suffragette, was yesterday afternoon arrested outside the Brighton branch of the Women's Social and Political Union building. She was taken to Brighton Magistrate's Court, where she was remanded until this morning. The warrant on which she was arrested, and which was granted yesterday afternoon set forth: 'For that she is a disturber of the peace and is an inciter to others to commit diverse crimes and misdemeanours. In consequence of inflammatory speeches made by Miss Grace Emmerson, a vast amount of damage to property had been done within the last two months in and around Brighton.'

Morton couldn't help but grin at the thought of Juliette's great grandmother causing havoc in the genteel seaside town. And these were just the crimes that she had been caught committing. Goodness only knew what else she had got up to. He continued reading the legalities contained in the article: Grace had been released on condition that she ceased her inflammatory speeches. Judging by the other newspaper reports, she had satisfied this criterion but had progressed on to more violent acts. *She certainly was a character*, Morton thought, convinced that, had the same social inequalities persisted to this day, Juliette would readily switch her career in the police force for a life of campaigning on the other side of the law.

Printing the article, Morton clicked back to the set of results. The headline of the next offered an enticing read: *Brighton Suffragettes on the Warpath* but it would have to wait. Juliette was shouting his name up the stairs. He supposed this was how it was going to be for the foreseeable future.

In the lounge he found a haggard, exhausted version of his wife sitting on the sofa, elbows on her knees, hands supporting her head. 'She's just been fed and changed,' Juliette muttered, barely able to look up. The baby was lying in her Moses basket, enthralled by the colourful toys that dangled down above her face.

'Do you want anything—food, drink?' Morton asked, stroking her wild hair.

'Just sleep,' she answered. 'Who was on the phone earlier?'

'Oh, yes—it was your mum. Wanted to know if we needed her to bring anything. I said we didn't.'

Juliette nodded and made for the door.

'Do you think when she arrives I could do a little work—I'm getting a bit behind?'

She paused in the doorway and turned, an eyebrow cocked in the way that implied suspicion. 'Is that just because my mum's coming and you want to escape?'

'I like your mum,' Morton defended.

'I didn't say you didn't,' she said pointedly.

'I just think it'll be good for you—three girls together, plus I get to catch up on a bit of work.'

Juliette waved her hand dismissively and left the room. 'Sleep…'

Morton crouched down to the basket and kissed the baby on the forehead. He marvelled at how it was possible to love so deeply, profoundly and instantaneously. How far he had come. Just five years ago he was single, resolutely childless and hauling around the chronic bitter burden of his adoption. He realised now that from the ignorance of his biological parents' identity had grown a rancorous mental cancer that, were it not for having met Juliette, would have swollen inside of him, eventually taking him over.

'I love you,' he whispered, taking her tiny hand in his.

She stopped playing and squeezed his finger, her sparkling brown eyes meeting his.

She was true perfection.

She held his gaze for some time, then switched her focus back to the stripy lion above her.

On the coffee table beside Morton was the baby name book, *60,001 Best Baby Names*. With a sigh, he opened the book at the girl's section and began to scan down the long lists. *Aaliyah, Aamori, Aarika, Aarionne, Aaronita…Addison?* According to the book it meant awesome. No. He continued. *Alessia?* Italian for nice. Nice Farrier. Maybe not. *Auburne?* American for tough-minded. One tough-minded woman was enough in his life. Next. *Audrey?* English for strong and regal. He leant over the baby's face. 'Audrey?' Then he shook his head. Definitely not Audrey. *Bahama? Barcelona?* Did they want to be one of those couples that copied the obscure names which celebrities saddled their kids with for the rest of their entire lives? Barcelona Farrier. Nobody would ever forget that name. Next. *Beatrice?* Latin for blessed woman. Yes, he liked that name and made a note of it, the first to make the list. Beatrice

Farrier. Morton smiled then carried on reading. *Blake?* English for dark—not a good sign. Plus, she would sound like a (male) private detective. Blake Farrier at your service. Nope. *Burgundy?* French for red wine. He added it to the list, just to see Juliette's reaction. *Catherine?* Greek for pure. Traditional, historical; he liked it.

The baby began to cry in her *zero-to-a-thousand-decibels-in-under-two-seconds* way.

Morton scooped her up and cradled her to his chest, lightly bouncing around the lounge.

It took ten minutes and she was asleep in his arms. He gently laid her back down in the Moses basket, pulled the curtains and crept from the room.

In the kitchen, he made himself a strong coffee and opened up his laptop to read the next newspaper report into Grace Emmerson's activities. *'29ᵗʰ December 1910. Brighton Suffragettes on the Warpath. Two Bottles of Dye Emptied into Pillar Box. Brighton suffragettes were out on the warpath last night. Some of the sisterhood placed two uncorked bottles containing a dark fluid in a pillar letter-box, spoiling and besmearing several letters that the postal authorities have been unable to decipher. The letter-box attacked is that situated on Queen's Road in the town centre. A collection of letters took place shortly after six o'clock, and at that time the contents were all correct. When a postman went to clear the box at seven o'clock, he was astonished to find that a large number of the letters and postcards were covered in a brownish fluid. A well-known local suffragette, Miss Grace Emmerson was apprehended at the scene, shouting a tirade of suffragist propaganda at the arresting police officers. She was detained in police custody overnight and will go before magistrate's tomorrow.'*

The next article was brief, summarising Grace's court case. She was sentenced to two months' hard labour for her actions. *Poor woman*, Morton thought, *but very admirable and courageous.* According to the newspaper indexes, her next arrest came just two months after her release from prison.

'22ⁿᵈ February 1911. Suffragette Raid on Downing Street. Ministers Assaulted—Windows Smashed. Mr Asquith's statement in the House of Commons on Tuesday, regarding the facilities the Government were prepared to give next session to the Women's Suffrage Bill, raised the wrath of the militants. A meeting of suffragettes was being held in Caxton Hall when the terms of the Prime Minister's announcement were made known. The meeting refused to accept them as satisfactory and Mrs Pankhurst announced that she would go herself to Downing Street, and the whole body of women, armed with banners on bamboo pole, set out to march to the Premier's House. On arrival there they found only three or four

policemen on duty, and thinking they had at last outwitted the powers of Cannon Row, they raised a cheer. Their victory, however, appeared to be more apparent than real. The constables on duty at once did their best to check the invading women, and in response to their whistles, a special force was despatched from Cannon Row. This force marched along Charles Street and through the Foreign Office quadrangle, emerging right opposite to the residence of the First Lord of the Treasury. The suffragettes threw themselves upon the police. For some minutes a bitter struggle prevailed, and then the police were forced back, and a shrieking, hysterical mass of men and women poured into Downing Street. For some moments a scene of pandemonium reigned. Policemen's helmets were knocked off with bamboo poles, and suffragettes kicked their legs. Mr Asquith was crossing Parliament Square, apparently on his way to Downing Street, when he stumbled right into the midst of the deputation. He was quickly surrounded by the women, and one of them, Miss Grace Emmerson, approached him and struck him, saying, 'You tax women as heavily as men, and yet not one woman is represented.' Half a dozen policemen surrounded Mr Asquith, whistles were blown, a taxi-cab was driven up, and the Premier was hustled into it. As the cab was driven away Miss Emmerson shouted 'Traitor, coward,' and then put her fist through the small pane of glass at the back of the cab. Arrest after arrest was made and soon Downing Street was cleared.'

Morton sat back and rubbed his tired temples. 'Wow,' he said. *What a feisty woman, accosting the Prime Minister like that. Amazing.* Having read the report once more and printed it out, he cross-referenced the date of the account with the information on Ancestry's Suffragettes Arrested register. Bow Street 22/2/11 – 200.455. The same incident. Clearly, a visit to The National Archives would be in order.

Having exhausted the newspaper articles on Grace, Morton turned his attention back to her childhood and to trying to understand the reason for her decade-long incarceration in Brighton Union Workhouse.

He typed the names of Grace's mother, Eliza Emmerson, into the 1881 census, followed by that of her father, Ebenezer. Although he didn't know enough about Grace's parents to be absolutely certain, he was fairly sure that they did not show up in the results. There were several possibilities for this, but the most likely being that they had died soon after Grace's birth in 1876.

He switched to the 1871 census and quickly found Ebenezer, an unmarried solicitor's clerk living in Brighton. He also found twenty-six-year-old spinster Eliza—under her maiden name of Hodgson—living with her solicitor father and mother in a house on the outskirts of Brighton. *But what, then, had happened in the intervening decade?* Ebenezer and Eliza had met—most likely under circumstances concerned with her father's and Ebenezer's shared legal work; they had married in 1875 in the Brighton district and, one year later, Grace had been born. According to the birth indexes on the General Register Office website, there had been no further children to the marriage.

Morton ran a search between 1871 and 1881 for their deaths and found them. Ebenezer had died in the Brighton district in 1877 and Eliza in the same district in 1880.

Poor girl, Morton thought, *an orphan before the age of four.* It certainly explained the extended incarceration in the workhouse.

'I can't sleep,' Juliette announced, suddenly appearing at the door. 'I think I'm hungry. When did we last eat anything healthy?'

Morton had no idea. Most of their meals had either been takeaways, something quick from the freezer or else skipped entirely. He shrugged. 'Before Miss Farrier made an appearance, I guess. I'll make us something. What do you fancy?'

'Surprise me.'

'Okay,' Morton agreed, opening the fridge door. 'Right. Let me think what I can make with milk, strawberry jam, three limp carrots, two out-of-date eggs and some red nail varnish. I think I'd better get down to Jempson's.' Morton kissed her on the lips and headed for the door. 'Oh, carry on with this list.' He handed Juliette the baby name book and the names which he had liked.

'Beatrice, *Burgundy* and Catherine. Is that it?'

'So far.'

Juliette huffed and glanced down at the book. '*Chinadoll?* Really! *Chickadee? Christmas?* I don't think I'm of sound-enough mind to do this—I'll end up picking a name at random and scarring the poor girl for life.'

Morton laughed, pulled on his shoes and opened the front door.

'Cinderella—there you go!' Juliette shouted. 'Done.'

Cinderella Farrier: his little princess. It certainly had a ring to it.

Chapter Six

The traffic had been horrendous. It was kind of his own fault for driving to Kew, on the outskirts of London, during rush-hour. What had he expected? Under a mackerel sky, he parked up and switched off the engine. He yawned, stretched and sighed, then grabbed his bag from the passenger seat and strode towards The National Archives. The building—ostensibly a monstrous block of uninspiring concrete—was reflected in a lake over which it presided, like an aloof monarch. A flock of Canada Geese flew low overhead, landing noisily in the still waters beside him.

Morton entered the building and, having had a security guard rifle through his bag, removed his notepad and pencil and placed his bag in a locker, before bounding up the stairs to the first floor. Guarding the entrance to the Document Reading Room were two further blue-jacketed security guards. Morton swiped his card and entered the room with a smile on his face; he loved coming here. Over one thousand years of British history—much of it unexplored and untouched in the vaults for decades—could be in his hands at the click of a few buttons.

He was like the proverbial child in a sweetshop; but he needed to focus. He had just a few hours here to find out as much as he could about Juliette's great grandmother, Grace Emmerson. He had escaped the house this morning just before the anticipated arrival of Juliette's highly-strung mother, Margot. She would undoubtedly arrive in a whirlwind of Mary Poppins' good intentions: cooking, cleaning and reorganising their home. The first thing, about which she would complain, would undoubtedly be the baby's not yet having a name. They had reached 'F' in the book, so technically they were almost a quarter of the way there. Cleo, Dakota, Eden, Eve, Felicity and Flora had made the shortlist. Just at least another 24,000 names to sift through and they should have a decent shortlist.

Having abandoned the baby name book late last night, Morton had pre-ordered six documents to be ready for his arrival this morning, and so he headed directly to a bank of lockers with translucent orange doors. On each door was a number etched in white which corresponded to a designated seat number. 10B, that was Morton's seat of choice and habit. Pulling open the locker door, he selected the first document: MEPO 3/203—Suffragettes' Complaints against Police.

He carried the thick file into the main search room and sat down at seat 10B. The room was vast, containing thirty-six tables, each offering eight places, plus a run of ten camera tables close to the windows, again each with eight spaces. Today, the room was around half-full.

Morton unbound the file and turned to the first page. It was headed 'Metropolitan Police, Bow Street, E Division' and was an account from the side of the police about the incident at Downing Street: '*I, with three sergeants and thirty constables proceeded to Cannon Row Police Station for reserve duty. Shortly after arrival we were sent to Downing Street where we found a large crowd of people, chiefly women, endeavouring to force their way into the Premier's residence. By threading our way through the people close to the building we were able to get in front of the crowd and assist in clearing the street. The women were very excited and time and again made concerted rushes at police, but after great difficulty they were driven back into Parliament Street. Two cordons of police were then drawn across Downing Street to prevent the crowd from reforming. The women, however, repeatedly hurled themselves at police and endeavoured to break through the lines until overcome by sheer exhaustion. During the whole time I saw no undue violence used by police of any kind. Neither was any complaint made to me by any person and had such conduct occurred as alleged by complainants, I could not have failed to observe it. Respectfully Chief Inspector John Millings.*'

Morton photographed the police's version of events, which was supported by several pages of junior ranking officers, all of whom strenuously denied any wrong-doing. The subsequent pages—more than equal in number—were filled with complaint after complaint from men and women accusing the police of using undue and severe violence. Morton took time to read and photograph each account. A bleak picture of viciousness on the part of the police was forming. Among the statements was one from G. Emmerson: '*On Wednesday 22nd February 1911, I was repeatedly thumped in the back. My arms were twisted and also my fingers. The police purposely trod on my feet while trying to take my hands off the railings. The policeman held me by the breast and I told him to take his hands off me. For an answer, he struck me in the mouth, making my lips bleed. I was then dragged along the pavement by three policemen who had torn off my hat and thrown away my hatpins. One of the policemen took off his helmet and hit me in the leg with it three times in a most violent manner. Some of the terrible injuries inflicted upon me that day have yet still to improve. I now walk with a cane—a situation my doctor informs me may never change.*'

After more than an hour of reading, Morton reached the end of the file and exhaled noisily. The countless suffragette complaints, identifying specific officers by their numbered epaulettes, were dismissed; hard labour custodial sentences of varying degrees were metered out by an unsympathetic Magistrate. Morton closed the folder, rebound it and handed it in to the Document Returns desk. He then selected another file from the locker: HO 144/1106/200455—the first of the three Home Office records referred to on the Ancestry Suffragette register.

He carried the grey cardboard file, wrapped in a white cord, back to his desk. He sat down, carefully untied it and opened it up. It contained a collection of loosely bound papers, aged and discoloured by time. The first page comprised the criminal case of one Nellie Godfrey, arrested for throwing a missile into Winston Churchill's motor-car. The next pertained to the case details of Sarah Carwin, convicted of breaking windows at the Board of Trade. Her file also included a petition to be classified as a political prisoner, a theme which Morton found continued throughout the documents of the convicted suffragettes. He was almost half-way through the file when he first encountered Grace's name. It was an off-blue sheet, date stamped by the Home Office 4th March 1911 and entitled: PETITION.

Name: Grace Emmerson
Age on conviction: 35
Conduct in prison: Bad
Offence: Assault, damage to property
Prison: H.M. Holloway

*To the Right Honourable His Majesty's Principal Secretary of State for the Home Department. The ~~petition~~ demand of the above-named prisoner ~~humbly sheweth:~~-
...'*

Before he even went on to read Grace's personal statement, he could tell by the way that she had crossed out *petition* and replaced it with *demand* and had obliterated the words *humbly sheweth* that it was going to make for a very interesting read.

'...that I am a political prisoner and demand to be placed in the First Division. Men, when they are convicted of political acts are allowed to wear their own clothes and various other privileges and I claim the right to the same treatment. I understand that all suffrage prisoners are entitled to certain privileges under Mr Churchill's regulations, viz to write and receive letters, to see visitors once a fortnight,

to have our own books and needlework, to exercise twice daily and talk freely during exercise time. This treatment has been refused us. I shall decline to keep the rules of the prison until this claim is granted, no matter what the punishment might be. Grace Emmerson.'

Morton ran his finger over Grace's original signature, his admiration for her growing with each new record that offered a glimpse into her life. He was far from an expert on suffragettes, but he was aware of the brutal treatment and force-feeding that had taken place in prisons.

Next came a report from the Governor of Holloway Prison, James Scott, which Morton read with interest. *'As I reported to you yesterday verbally, the 14 suffragettes, mutinous since reception, all broke their cell windows yesterday. They were left in the same cells. Some of them were singing loudly, and they all continued insubordinate in conduct. In the forenoon today they became very disorderly. They continued to sing and shout. Some of them waved their sashes through the broken panes. Some of their friends had secured a room in the neighbourhood, and spoke to them through a megaphone, made various signals, etc. The Police were referred to, and they inform me, as the result of their enquiries, that the room occupied by the outside suffragettes was secured by Cecil Barwise, of Linden Grove in Brighton, who is said to be a groom there.'*

Morton stopped reading and stared at the page. Cecil Barwise—the man who would later become Grace's husband—had taken a room opposite the prison. Had it been to be nearer to Grace? Or simply to assist with the suffragette cause? Perhaps both.

He returned to the document: *'The committee met at 4pm, having been reported to them under Rule 82, paras 3 and 5. They tried the 14 prisoners separately. All of them admitted the charges and gloried in their offences. Not one of them would promise amendment. Some of them were impertinent, noisy, and violent. One of them declared that she would not eat any food in prison. One of them bit a wardress so severely in the hand, that she has been put on the sick-list. One of them threw her loaf at an Officer, and also threw her hot cocoa over her, burning her and spoiling her uniform. Some of them made so much noise in their cells, singing, knocking, ringing bells, etc during the trials that the Magistrates had difficulty in proceeding at times. The Magistrates had no difficulty in deciding that the prisoners must all be punished. They were all, after sentence, placed in different cells to those they occupied before trial. Eight of them have been put in the special cells. James Scott.'*

Special cells, Morton thought. An ominous-sounding, camouflage term that smacked of institutional abuses.

It took him the best part of two hours to complete the file. Although there were no further mentions of Grace by name, the documents continued to provide an illuminating account of the suffragettes' incarcerations. It saddened Morton to think that Grace, having spent her childhood in the Brighton Union Workhouse, had, as an adult, exchanged one draconian institution for another.

The next file contained more complaints, letters written by suffragettes to the Home Office protesting at their treatment in prison. Several pages in, Morton discovered a letter written by Grace following her release.

'*The Right Honourable H. Gladstone. Dear Sir, In reference to your replies in the House Wednesday night as to the cells in which we suffragettes were placed, I should like to say that I think it is a pity that a man in your high position should not be more cognisant of the real facts as they exist. Having been brutalised and injured by the police whilst protesting at Downing Street, I was held in Holloway one month and during the whole of that time I was kept in close confinement for protesting against being put in the 2nd Division. For the same protest I was put into a punishment cell which was dark, foul and most insanitary. The place had been washed just previously to my incarceration and did not properly dry all night. The bed which was fastened to the wall was very damp and I was unable to take my clothes off but sat wrapped in a blanket the whole of that night. The cell in question is wholly unfit for human inhabitation. I have seen several of my colleagues since my release, all of whom were placed in similar disgusting cells and who suffered in the same way. The cells in question are below the level of the ground. Your cowardly allusion to "when prisoners refuse food they are hardly fit subjects for exercise" does not apply as I had been in close confinement for a week before I started the hunger-strike which was only resorted to as a final protest at being placed in the 2nd Division. Do you not think it would be more dignified when quoting facts to stick to the truth? I think the time has come for us to show that we no longer intend to lightly undergo the insults and contumely that we have patiently allowed to be heaped upon us in the past. Yours indignantly, Grace Emmerson.*'

Morton photographed the account, then turned the page. He was surprised to see that the women's complaints had resulted in an assessment of the cells at Holloway by H.M. Inspector of Factories. His report, which tested for air quality, ventilation and carbonic acid stated that the cell, D.I.12 which had '*previously been occupied by Miss Emmerson was a 'special cell', situated in the building at such a height that the ceilings of the cells are about 3 inches above the level of the pavement outside. The windows are constructed of very thick glass, which excludes a large part of the light, so that the illumination is inferior to that of the ordinary cells. Each cell measures about 12ft x 7ft with an air inlet consisting of a grating measuring 16x5 inches situated above the door.'* The report concluded: *'It is probable that any sense of oppression or discomfort felt in these cells is of psychological origin, due to the feeling of close confinement affecting a person unaccustomed to it.'*

Morton pondered the statement *'of psychological origin'*, another whitewash term that could be used to cover up any effect of any type of harsh prison treatment. His growing fears about the conditions of the prison and Grace's incarceration persisted when he turned to the next page—a further series of reports on the suffragettes at Holloway. Among them, he found Grace.

Daily Report on: Grace Emmerson
What is the physical and mental condition of the prisoner? Both satisfactory. She strenuously tries to make any examination impossible by wriggling. She will not be weighed jumping all the time on the scales.
Is the prisoner taking food voluntarily? No
If not, is the prisoner refusing both a) food b) water, and what sorts of food have been offered to the prisoner? Refuses a) and b) coffee, milk, cocoa and anything else
General conduct? Fair
General remarks in the case of a prisoner refusing food? Forcibly fed by means of the oesophageal tube twice daily with milk, eggs, Valentine juice and Benger's food. Dr W. Hilton-Parry assisting.

Awful, Morton thought, as he stared at the sheet. To go to prison for your beliefs was one thing, but to be held in a sub-standard cell and force-fed twice a day was quite another.

He worked his way through to the end of the file, finding no further mention of Grace, but plenty of additional mistreatment of other suffragettes. The succeeding pages made for uncomfortable reading: letters between prisons and the Home Office seeking confirmation on the force-feeding of suffragette prisoners on hunger strike. Young women. Old women. Pregnant women. Sick women. This was the ugly underbelly of the lauded, banner-carrying marches that history liked to recall. Morton's eyes glazed over and he thought of his daughter. His brain, befuddled from the horrendous details which he had been reading all morning, began to superimpose her in the position of these women. Her face was blurred, but inside, he knew that it was her.

A tannoy announcement joggled him out of his reverie. Even though he pushed the absurd notion from his mind and looked back down at the file on the desk in front of him, his heart continued to feel doughy, as though he had just had a premonition into the future.

He needed a break. He looked at his mobile—lunchtime already.

Heading back out through a security check, Morton descended to the ground floor, where he purchased a large coffee and a tuna mayonnaise sandwich. He sat alone at a small round table that overlooked the entrance to the archives and the lake. He wanted to phone Juliette, just to hear her voice and to know that they were both okay. The uncomfortable feelings which he had felt upstairs lingered in his gut, accentuated by an enhanced sense of his separation from wife and daughter. He sent her a text message instead, polished off his coffee and sandwich, then headed back up to the Document Reading Room.

He spent some time completing the file, increasingly understanding more about the plight of the suffragettes. In 1913, in response to growing public disapproval of force-feeding prisoners, the government changed tack by introducing a new law. Force-feeding desisted. Instead, when the women became dangerously ill from being on hunger-strike, they would be released from prison and re-arrested the moment that they became well again. *The Cat and Mouse Act*, as it became known.

Morton swapped the file for the one containing details of Grace's first arrest. The folder was thick, yet the mention of Grace was thin, adding nothing more about her arrest for incitement than that which he had gleaned from the online newspaper report. The third of the Ancestry-referred documents was as scant as the previous. It detailed Grace's conviction, which included identifying personal details and the sentencing for pouring ink into the pillar boxes, but offered no other new information.

He switched to another Home Office document that referred to the Brighton branch of the WSPU, but, after more than an hour's searching, had found no specific references to Grace. It was the same in the next two folders. By the time document-ordering had ceased for the day, Morton had found nothing more of her. It was curious that following her release from Holloway in 1911, someone as militant and defiant as Grace should suddenly became a model citizen with no further arrests. *Perhaps*, he thought, *she had continued but simply not been caught.*

33

Just getting into his own house was like a scene from the *Mission: Impossible* films. Having managed first to avoid the clanking metallic symphony from his absurdly large bunch of keys, he successfully pushed the door open so slowly as to eschew the mournful groan that usually accompanied anything resembling normal door-opening speed. Then, just as he was ready to step inside, a gaggle of noisy teenage girls appeared at the bottom of Mermaid Street and he had to pull the door shut and start again. Ultimately, he entered the house, set his bag down and carefully closed the door. The house was silent and he wondered if they had all gone out. He tiptoed into the lounge. Margot was sitting on the sofa, reading a magazine. 'Hi,' he whispered.

Margot gave a yelp. 'Oh my word! Where did you spring from?' she gasped, throwing a hand to her chest. 'You've almost given me a coronary.'

'Sorry,' Morton murmured. 'Wasn't sure who might be asleep.'

'Both of them,' she answered with a smile, standing up and pulling Morton into a tight squeeze. 'It's lovely to be here, Morton.' She had put on a little weight since he had last seen her, but had yet to update her wardrobe accordingly; her light jeans and white blouse revealed more of her lumps and bumps than she had probably intended. She'd had her hair styled recently by the look of it and dyed a chestnut brown.

'Nice to have you,' he responded, not entirely truthfully. Glancing around the room, he caught sight of some subtle changes which he knew to be Margot's handiwork. 'How's the baby been today?'

Margot closed her eyes and clasped her hands together, as if recalling some amazing exotic holiday. 'A treasure—an absolute treasure. And, we think we've come up with a name! You'll love it!'

'What is it?' he asked cautiously, not liking having been excluded from the process.

Margot lowered her voice. 'Don't tell Juliette I told you, will you?'

Morton shook his head, though of course he was going to tell her.

'Matilda!' she exulted.

'Matilda?' Morton repeated, looking around the room for the baby name book. They couldn't possibly have finished it all today in his absence. Matilda Farrier. He didn't *not* like it, but he just wasn't sure it suited her. 'Matilda.'

'Lovely, isn't it,' Margot breathed. 'It's German for powerful fighter.'

'I see,' Morton said, not particularly enjoying the mental image that his brain was conjuring up of his daughter's face on a centurion's body. 'Where did my shortlist go?'

Margot waved her hand. 'I threw it away—lot of old nonsense. What were you thinking?' she asked, delving her hand into the bin and pulling out a scrunched-up piece of paper.

This wasn't going to help.

'*Cloud, Cookie, Countess, Day, Diamond, Dragana, Ecstasy, Elton and Fudge?* Really?'

'They were joke ones,' he answered.

'Very amusing,' Margot replied, tearing the paper into pieces and tossing them back into the bin. 'Now, would you like some dinner? I've just cooked up a batch of shepherd's pie and potted them up in individual portions for the freezer. Would you like one?'

'Yes, please—thanks,' Morton said, his mind still evaluating the name that his mother-in-law seemed to have bestowed upon his daughter. Matilda. He wasn't sure. All he could think of was the Roald Dahl book. From what he could recall from his primary school days when he had last read it, she was a nice enough character. Maybe the name would grow on him.

'Here you go,' Margot said, presenting him with a plateful of pie. 'Enjoy.'

'Thanks,' he said, watching her float from the room. Evidently, she had other more important things to be getting on with, which suited him fine. He pulled out his mobile and began to scroll through the photographs which he had taken at The National Archives.

Then Margot unexpectedly reappeared, plopping a supermarket hessian jute bag down onto the table in front of him. 'A present.'

Morton looked at her quizzically.

'My grandmother's bits and pieces—that's the lot, I'm afraid. The contents of this bag have come down through the women of the family—from gran to my mother to me. Juliette then Matilda will have it.'

Morton's eyes suddenly lit up. 'Oh, wow!' He set down his knife and fork, pushed the plate to one side, then pulled the bag closer. He felt like Grace was one of his own close family now and he was eager to delve into the contents of the bag.

The first thing that he pulled out was an old photo album. Morton opened it to see that the first picture was of a middle-aged man and lady, smiling at the camera behind a large white cake. Below it, the caption read, 'The Silver Wedding Anniversary of Cecil and Grace Barwise, 1936.'

It was the first time that he had seen Grace—or Cecil, for that matter. She wasn't how he had imagined her to be. The lady in the photograph, with small round spectacles, was elegantly dressed with a delicate, gentle face and warm smile; she looked the polar opposite of a woman who had struck the Prime Minister before being dragged off by police and locked up in Holloway where she had to be force-fed.

Cecil, moustached with dark oiled hair seemed stolid, statesmanlike.

Margot leant over his shoulder. 'Ah, my lovely grandparents.'

'What do you remember about them?' he asked, turning the page to see more snaps of the gathering.

'Well, I was quite young…maybe around ten when grandad died, so my memory of him is a little sketchy. He was very quiet…would spend most of his time pottering down his allotment or messing about in the garden. He liked an ale or two down the local with his mates. Granny, I think, died when I was in my early twenties, so I've got a better recollection of her. They both doted on my mum. She was their only child, then, when my brothers and I came along, they fawned over us, too. After grandad died she came to stay for long holidays, Christmases…that kind of thing.'

'What was Grace like as a person?' Morton enquired.

Margot smiled at whatever thoughts were being brought to mind. 'Just lovely. Very caring, attentive. We never disobeyed her: there was something about her that commanded respect without her ever having to ask for it. I don't once recall her raising her voice or telling us off and yet we were good as gold for her.'

'Did she ever talk about her younger years?'

'Not too often. I remember her talking about the war—the Second World War—she was retired by then but they called her back to the railways. There she was in her early sixties driving trains to and from London. She told me a few tales about being dive-bombed by Messerschmitts and the like—I'll have to get my thinking cap on if you want exact details. Apparently, she was one of the first female train drivers in the country. Or county, I forget which. And she loved her baking and sewing—she was always knitting or making cushions, blankets.'

'Anything about being a suffragette?' he probed.

'I know she definitely was one because the moment I reached eighteen she drummed it into me that I absolutely *had to* vote. She didn't care who for—just that I went down and put an 'X' in one of the boxes.' Margot laughed. 'I remember replying that there wasn't any point; the ones I wanted stood no chance of getting in and she actually got upset. For the first time that I could recall, she cried. Then she sat me down and talked about some of the things she and her friends had to do to get the vote.'

'Like what?'

'Oh, the usual: marches, speeches, posting leaflets through doors. That sort of thing. All pretty tame by today's standards.'

Morton laughed. 'Not pouring ink into letter boxes, hitting the Prime Minister, getting arrested and put into Holloway and force-fed, then?'

Margot looked at him strangely then laughed. 'No, she wasn't *that* type of a lady.'

She's in for a shock once I've completed my research, Morton thought.

'So, anyway, I've always remembered that and have voted in every election since. I've switched sides a few times, but always voted one way or the other. What's with the sudden fascination with my gran, anyway?'

It was an interesting question. Given the amount of work which he had put into merely fleshing out Grace's life, his grand plan of documenting the lives of all of Juliette's recent ancestors now seemed a ridiculous prospect. 'She enthrals me,' he answered honestly.

'Oh, right.'

He flicked through the entire album, planning on photographing it at a later point, then, setting the album to one side, Morton delved into the jute bag and retrieved something that put a smile on his face: Grace's silk sash. Given its age, it was still in remarkable condition. The words VOTES FOR WOMEN were in bold black letters on a white background, bordered within two stripes, the inner one green and the outer purple. 'Wow,' Morton said again, holding it up. In one corner was sewn in small lettering, 'Miss Emmerson'.

The image of Grace in his mind was now complete. He could see her right now, outside Downing Street wearing this sash, her face resolute and determined as she accosted Asquith.

Margot reached into the bag, pulled out a framed photograph and passed to Morton. It was clearly Grace, although taken many years before her silver wedding anniversary. She was young, with short 1920s-style hair and a dark feather boa draped over her shoulders. At the neckline was a small brooch that looked like a grid with spikes on the bottom. Morton had some recollection of seeing this type somewhere before. 'Do you know anything about that brooch?' he asked.

'Well, it's in here, actually,' Margot said. She withdrew a very old yellow tin from the bag.

'Keen's Genuine Imperial Mustard,' Morton observed. 'That must be a good hundred years old.'

'Never mind the tin, it's what's inside,' she said, prising off the lid. 'Here we go.' She handed Morton the exact same brooch that Grace was wearing in the photograph. It was silver; well made. Now that he had it in his hands, he could see that it was clearly a portcullis. In the centre was an upward-facing arrow comprised of three parts, each part one of the colours of the suffragette's cause. He grabbed his mobile and quickly Googled the brooch.

'*Designed by Sylvia Pankhurst, the brooch was awarded to members of the WSPU who had been imprisoned. Described as 'the Victoria Cross of the Union' the design is of the Portcullis symbol of the House of Commons, the gate and hanging chains are in silver, and the superimposed broad arrow (the conflict symbol) is in purple, white and green enamel.*' Morton read.

'Imprisoned?' Margot questioned. 'Surely not?'

'I'll tell you more later—Grace is who I've been researching today at The National Archives—but briefly, yes, she was arrested. Several times.'

Margot seemed genuinely shocked. 'I just can't believe it of Granny. She was so quiet and unassuming. Golly. Well, you're the expert, so if you say so.'

Morton nodded. 'I've got pages of documents that prove it. I'm going to present it all to Juliette once it's finished.'

'That's a lovely idea,' Margot said, taking a gold locket from the tin and passing it to Morton. 'Grace's parents are trapped inside, whom I know nothing about whatsoever, before you ask. They look quite well-to-do, though, wouldn't you say?'

Morton took the locket and levered it open. In the left-hand oval was a painted miniature portrait of a lady gazing out to the left. She was well dressed with dark hair and dark eyes, bearing a stark resemblance to Grace. In the opposite oval was the painted portrait of a gentleman wearing a black jacket and high-necked white shirt. He was young, handsome and was looking straight out, his blue eyes meeting Morton's. 'Grace's parents, you say?'

'So my mum told me, yes,' Margot confirmed.

Something didn't quite fit with the portraits, but he couldn't put his finger on the problem.

'Last of all,' Margot announced, 'is this clipping.' She slid a neatly cut, sepia newspaper cutting across the table.

Morton read it aloud: '*Barwise-Emmerson. On 18th November 1911, Cecil Barwise, second son of Mr Walter Barwise of Brighton, to Grace Emmerson, only child of the late Mr and Mrs Ebenezer Emmerson of Brighton.*'

The top of the paper drew Morton's attention. '*Argus*' The cuttings were taken from the *Brighton Argus*, which, he realised now, were not online. The other stories which he had read about Grace's exploits had been from other county newspapers. *What else might the Brighton papers contain about Grace?* he wondered. Given that he already wanted to look into the suffragette goings-on at Sea View in Victoria Road, Brighton, a trip to East Sussex Record Office was now a necessity. 'Can I keep hold of these bits for a while?' he asked.

Margot took a moment to answer. 'Maybe now's a good time to pass them on to Juliette. I know they'll be well looked after, here.' She smiled and clasped her hands together. 'Yes, *this* is their new home.'

'We certainly will cherish them,' he answered sincerely.

'Then one day they'll belong to little Matilda,' Margot said.

'Yes,' Morton replied, still not sure that he wanted to give his daughter that name. 'Just out of interest, Margot, where did you put the *60,001 Best Baby Names* book?'

'One of the bookshelves in your study. I had a bit of a tidy up in there—hell of a mess—I don't know how you get anything done.'

Morton inwardly groaned.

Chapter Seven

Grace noticed the figure walking up Victoria Street towards the house. She was certain that it was him. She released the net curtain that was bunched in her hand, allowing it to fall back over her bedroom window. Her view now partly obscured, she leant closer and squinted hard. Yes, it was certainly him: Cecil—returned to check up on her again. She smiled at his persistence as he drew closer to the house. Then she noticed the bunch of flowers that he was holding and her smile widened and lit her eyes.

She moved away from the window and checked herself in the mirror. There was no rush to get downstairs, as there had once been when he had come to visit. Olivia and Minnie's initial misgivings about him had dissolved and he had won them over after taking the lodging room opposite Holloway Prison. They had been delighted to have a window from which they could, night and day, shout messages of solidarity through a megaphone to the imprisoned suffragettes. It was not the taking of the room, though, that had endeared him to Grace, as it had the other women, it was his motives. 'I know it'll be tough in there,' he had shouted up to her cell window. 'I just wanted you to have a friendly face nearby—to know that whatever happens, I'll be just across the street. Every night there'll always be a light on for you.' His kind-heartedness had made her cry more than any of the harsh treatments that had been metered out during her sentence; as much as she searched her past, she failed to find a single recollection of anyone doing anything as compassionate for her before. And, he had been true to his word: a light had remained on each night in his room for the entirety of her incarceration.

Grace picked up her walking cane and calmly left her bedroom. The injury sustained to her right leg on Downing Street had still to heal and navigating the three flights of stairs was a painful undertaking.

'Grace, Cecil's here for you!' Olivia yelled up.

'I'm on my way,' she called back. 'Tell him to pop back in a few hours, by which time I'll be there.'

She reached the final flight of stairs and saw him waiting at the bottom, cradling the red roses.

'Hello, Grace. How are you?' he asked.

'Better, thank you,' she answered. 'I won't be joining the circus acrobatics team anytime soon, though.'

'I got you these from the market,' he said, offering the flowers.

'Thank you,' she said, touched. It was another first for her—nobody had ever bought her flowers before. 'I'll put them in water. Tea?'

'If it's not too much trouble. Do you need a hand?'

Grace nodded. 'Thank you.'

Under Grace's guidance, Cecil placed the flowers in a vase of water and made two cups of tea, which he carried out to the terrace at the rear of the house.

Outside, the sun was high and hot, beating down onto the large parasol raised above a white cast-iron table and set of four chairs. Cecil pulled one of the chairs out for Grace to sit upon.

She nodded her gratitude, simultaneously hating feeling like an invalid but all the while grateful for the assistance. Cecil sat opposite her and perched his elbows on the table.

'Is the leg getting any better?' he asked.

'Slowly,' she answered. 'The doctor is hopeful that I'll eventually make a full recovery. How are you?'

Cecil shrugged. 'I'm still trying to find a new job.'

Grace frowned as she poured the tea. 'You really shouldn't have resigned on my account, Cecil—but thank you.'

'It was the least I could do,' he said. 'I hope it helped.'

More than you can know, she thought, sipping her tea. *Much more.* 'It was very good of you—it did indeed help to know that there was a friend just a stone's throw away.'

'Are you ready to talk about it, yet?' he asked. 'Prison, I mean.'

She hadn't spoken to anyone about it in any detail—she couldn't. To retell it would be like revisiting an awful, dark, atrocious nightmare. At night-time, her brain seemed to delight in scavenging through the bones of her memories, replaying the most harrowing parts of her time there over and over, like a vivid projection from a Victorian magic lantern. When people had enquired about what had happened she had tended to gloss over the prison sentence and regale them with tales of the Downing Street escapade. She drank more tea and placed down the cup. As she did so, she caught the earnestness in his face; he wasn't asking for the tittle-tattle, he was asking so that he understood her, fully, completely. Could she trust him with everything—her whole past?

41

'You don't have to talk about it,' he added upon seeing her reticence. 'Only if you want to—it might help?'

'It was hard,' she began. 'The cells were small, dark and ill-ventilated. There were lice on the damp mattress. We were forcibly searched, weighed and medically-examined at the whim of the wardress and doctor. We were allowed little exercise and nothing to read nor to occupy our minds. We tried singing and telling stories to keep our spirits up. And of course, we were *absolutely* starving hungry. Do you know what it takes to refuse a mug of cocoa and some bread and cheese when you haven't eaten a single thing in two days and it's placed down on the cell floor in front of you? Just the smell of it…'

It was a rhetorical question but Cecil shook his head. 'I can't imagine,' he mumbled.

'It was my own choice, of course: I could have eaten it and, on several occasions nearly did, but at that point it felt like running a race and giving up just before the finish line. We'd done so much. We made the national press,' she said with a wry smile. 'I knocked on Number 10 Downing Street and hit the Prime Minister: not many women from the workhouse can say that, now, can they?'

Cecil returned her smile. 'No, I don't suppose they can.'

'Being force-fed was…' She couldn't quite find the words: '…it was inhumane, barbaric, mediaeval…torture, really. Having a doctor shove a rubber tube down your throat—a tube not washed or sanitised from the last person—was just…'

Cecil leant over and touched her arm. 'You don't need to carry on, Grace. Maybe it's better forgotten?'

'I'll never forget it; not ever,' she said, touching his hand with hers. 'Do you know what the worst part was, though?'

He shook his head.

'The special cells. Dark, damp and cold. The singing stopped. A single day felt like a month. Hours and hours were spent staring at the walls. By the end of it, I came to know the lines, contours and cracks of each and every brick like those of my own palms. Loneliness and despair came hand-in-hand. The one thing that helped me through it, that made me believe that it would all be worth it in the end, was the light across the street.'

Cecil was taken aback and his eyes moistened.

'Even when I was moved and could no longer see it, it was there in my mind. You were there—not banging drums and shouting propaganda—just waiting for me. Thank you.'

42

Cecil wiped his eyes. 'Goodness, you're making me look a complete sissy.'

Grace laughed and squeezed his hand.

'Will you carry on?' he asked.

'Until my leg improves, I'm limited to letter-writing and speeches. I'm back on the promenade next Saturday if you want to come and listen.'

'I might just do that,' he grinned. 'Have you heard about the big meeting tomorrow night at the Brighton Pavilion?'

Grace shook her head and frowned. 'Tomorrow? Are you sure? Minnie or someone from the WSPU would surely have said something. I don't know anything about it.'

'No, it's an *anti*-suffrage meeting: the Brighton branch of the National League for Opposing Women's Suffrage. There's to be a march to the Pavilion where Mrs Wild is going to speak.'

'Oh, golly!' Grace muttered, sitting bolt upright. She had to be at that meeting. 'That awful man's wife.'

'Why do you hate him so, Grace?' Cecil asked.

'The way he treats women,' she answered. 'Every woman in his life—family, servants and in his big factory—they're all treated like third class citizens. He needs bringing down a peg or two. Will you come to the meeting with me tomorrow?'

'Of course, I will.'

Grace sighed and squeezed his hand again. Inside her heart an unknown warm sensation began to smoulder. 'Perhaps afterwards we could have a walk and a cup of tea?'

'I'd like that very much,' he replied. 'Maybe this time you'll stay long enough to let me finish my drink?'

'Don't push your luck, Cecil Barwise.'

A deep rage gathered inside Grace, as she used her walking cane to step out of the taxi motor-car. A large crowd—maybe up to one hundred people, predominantly men—was gathering under the clock tower, just across the street from the WSPU office in the town centre. The gall of it! Their appearances revealed them to have largely come from the working classes. *Didn't they know better?* Grace questioned. *They, too would benefit from universal suffrage.* The anger began to bubble up at the stupidity of what she was seeing. Someone on the other side of the crowd, out of Grace's sight, began to corral the men into lines. A brass band struck up with the opening bars of an unfamiliar tune.

The taxi pulled away and Grace was left alone on the pavement, feeling decidedly vulnerable. She straightened her sash around her and raised the wooden placard. 'Votes for women!' she shouted.

A sea of choleric faces turned in her direction. The jeers began.

'Votes for women!' Grace shouted. 'Votes for all!'

'Votes for dogs!' one of the men shouted back. 'Votes for cats!'

'Votes for flour!' one of them laughed, rushing up to Grace and emptying a bag of flour over her head.

She swung her placard round to swipe the juvenile delinquent but he was too fast and ducked down before scurrying back to the pack of laughing men.

Grace shook herself down like a wet dog, then combed her fingers through her hair to pull some of the flour free. Two hair pins tumbled to the ground, bringing with them a lock of hair from her previously neat pompadour.

Something hard suddenly struck her on the right temple. She yelped and dropped the placard, realising, as she raised her hand to touch the point of impact, that it had been a rotten egg, its green viscous contents now dribbling down the side of her face.

'Anyone got any milk? Turn her into a cake!' one of them yelled.

'Votes for cakes!' another called.

'How utterly moronic and cowardly,' Grace shouted. 'With bovine men like you lot running this country, it's little wonder we're such a backward-looking nation. Our empire is built on the stupidity of idiots like you.'

The men sneered but appeared to have lost interest in her now; they were being galvanised, ready to march along North Road towards the Pavilion.

Pulling out a handkerchief, Grace wiped as much of the egg from her face as she could. The foul stench of decay, however, remained like a malodourous tattoo. Inside, she was trembling with anger, but the last thing that she was going to do was give up. She crossed the street just as the march began and stood directly in their path, holding her placard high. 'Votes for women!' she yelled, as the band guided the baying group towards her.

Another egg struck her on the chin.

'Votes for women!'

The band were level with her, the pumping brass tones juddering in her ears.

Another bag of flour was emptied over her head, gluing to the foul egg trails that coursed down her face and dress.

'Votes for women! Votes for *all*—even the working men!' she chanted.

As the group surged past her, elbows were rammed into her side. Someone punched her in the stomach, sending her to the ground. Grace pulled herself into the foetal position, as the men stepped over her. She yelped out in pain when a heavy boot crushed down on the ankle of her bad leg. She looked up and saw the perpetrator, Mr Francis Wild standing over her with his arms folded, continuing to hold his boot on her ankle. He laughed, removed his foot and continued marching.

Within seconds, the crowd had passed: the jeering, the shouts and the noisy band were fading behind her. She sat herself up and glanced around. Her placard was destroyed but her walking cane had survived.

'Do you want a hand, lady?' a young lad asked from the pavement. 'You'll get hit by a carriage, if you ain't careful.'

Fearful of where his allegiances lay, Grace shook her head.

The lad shrugged and walked away. 'Suit yourself.'

Pulling herself up onto her cane, she hobbled to the side of the road and examined her ankle. It was red, swollen and painful. 'Damn that bastard man,' she seethed. He would get what was coming to him. She shook off as much of the egg and flour as she could before straightening herself out and standing tall again.

Slowly, Grace ambled down North Road, the distant sound of brass guiding her forwards. She walked as fast as her bad leg—and now bad ankle—would carry her. But it was slow progress. At this rate, the meeting would be all over and done with by the time she got there.

At last, the distinctive grand minarets of the Brighton Pavilion came into view. The building was in the Indo-Saracenic style and, with its pendentive decorations, balconies and arches, always appeared to Grace so incongruous with the rest of the town's buildings. She would never have imagined such a building being constructed in Brighton, but rather plucked from some exotic Arabian land and dropped into the centre of the town.

Grace hobbled on towards the entrance. A short line of diversely attired men and women fed in through the open doors. She spotted Cecil standing outside, his eyes anxiously searching the crowds. He saw her.

'What on earth's happened to you?' he begged, running over to her, his eyes running up and down the length of her body.

'The latest fashion,' Grace answered with a smile, as she ruffled her hair, sending a veil of flour down in front of her face. 'Did you not get the telegram that you had to come covered in half the ingredients of a Victoria sponge?'

Cecil was unsmiling. 'It's not funny. Let me get you a taxi back home.'

Grace shook her head. 'After the meeting—by all means—that would be much appreciated. But, right now, I'm going inside there,' she said, raising her cane to the entrance.

Cecil sighed, threaded his arm through hers and together they joined the end of the line of people queueing to enter the building. The line moved quickly and they found themselves at the doors of the Banqueting Room, where a fat policeman extended his arm in front of them.

'Not going to have any trouble, are we?' he bellowed at Grace.

She smiled sweetly and touched her hair, dusting her shoulders sending up another cloud of white powder. 'Heavens above, no.'

He nodded and they proceeded inside. The policeman shut the street doors behind them.

Grace gasped at the spectacle. The room was dramatic, elaborately decorated like a royal palace: rich colours, domes, canopies and canvases showing Chinese domestic scenes adorned every wall. Dominating the room, though, was the thirty-feet-high central chandelier which hung from the claws of a silver dragon.

'Could they have chosen anywhere more ostentatious?' Grace mumbled, glancing around the room at the assembled crowd, whose number she guessed to be more than one hundred. There was little room left in which to stand. 'What have they all come to hear, for goodness' sake?'

'Damned if I know,' Cecil answered. 'But I'm guessing we're about to find out.'

Appearing on a raised stage at one end of the room, was a well-dressed gentleman with a thick white moustache. The murmuring crowd fell into a still silence as he reached the centre of the stage. The man drew in a lengthy breath and took his time to survey the packed room.

'Who's he?' Grace whispered.

'Sir Theodore Angier, some local shipping magnate,' Cecil replied.

'Ladies and Gentlemen, I warmly welcome you to this meeting of the National League for Opposing Women's Suffrage.'

The cheers and applause from around the room squashed the few dissenting voices.

'Tonight, you will hear an auspicious range of voices—fervent and passionate in their opposition to women's suffrage. But now is not the time to merely listen passively; now is the time to act. A man, if he is a man at all, must start with all his prejudices in favour of the sex we love. But he must study his reason as well. If we adopt that course, there will be few supporters for the female vote. To give women the vote would be to make a revolution, damaging to the State, to the Empire and the family.'

'Hear, hear!' Grace shouted. 'The Empire will surely collapse!'

Sir Theodore Angier smiled in her direction. 'Thank you, Madam. And I bid a warm welcome to our opponents. We are pleased to live in a society where mature, adult debate can occur.' He paused amid indecipherable murmurings. 'Our first speaker tonight is Mrs Francis Wild. Please would you join me in welcoming her to the stage.'

A polite round of applause rose from the crowd and onto the stage glided an elegant middle-aged lady in a floor-length blue dress.

Grace watched her intently, not even wanting to blink. So, this was she, Mrs Francis Wild. She was beautiful, for her age, yet there was something about her face that appeared hard and cold.

Mrs Wild reached the centre and raised her hand to subdue the clapping. 'Things,' she began, once she had achieved silence, 'are at a critical time. Our opponents are demonstrating in the streets and hoping to accomplish by smashing windows what they cannot do by argument. This idea of any number from three to eight million women voters would be a vast change, altering at a blow the system on which the civilized world has acted. It can bring no corresponding advantage to women; it can bring only danger and disadvantage.'

'Rubbish!' Grace called. 'Coward!'

Hers was not the only opposing voice. Mrs Wild, however, persisted without pause. 'If,' she continued, 'any measure for women's suffrage passes into law, then the first step will be taken in the decline of England, and the first suffering of ideals, in the true and fruitful powers of her life, will be the *women* of England...'

A volley of cheers and applause rang around the Banqueting Room.

Grace's attention was snapped from Mrs Wild's absurd rantings by a set of fat fingers digging sharply into her upper arm. She turned to see the policeman. 'Anymore interruptions and you're out on your ear. Do you understand, love?'

'Perfectly,' Grace said, shaking off his grip.

Cecil rolled his eyes at her then whispered, 'Behave, Grace, or you'll get us thrown out.'

'Women—since the days of Adam and Eve—have had special duties to perform as wife and mother; duties that no man could ever assume, however much women may encroach upon the special tasks and duties of men.'

'What about working women?' a lady shouted from the other side of the room. 'Our derisory pay is set by the men!'

Mrs Wild shook her head impatiently, as if the person asking the question were an imbecile. 'Economic conditions govern wages, my dear,' she enunciated. 'Do you really think a group of men sit in a room deciding the pay of laundresses, then house keepers, then domestic maids? It's absurd. All the improvements that have been made in the treatment of women and in their education have been made by men, without women having the vote. Women have gained today what the suffragists said sixty years ago could not be gained without the vote. Ladies and gentlemen, it really comes down to this: England and our Empire governed by women cannot hold her own against states governed by men, and must surely decay. If the Empire is not to decay, we must insist upon the sex distinction in the parliamentary sphere, upon the absolute necessity that the supreme executive power shall rest upon the physical force and political experience of men.'

'You've not met my wife, then,' one man jested, receiving a reply of laughter, predominantly from the men in the room.

Grace looked at the policeman, who was chuckling at the heckler's apparent wit. She stood up. 'What utter nonsense! There are few—if indeed any—jobs that a woman can't do equally as well as a man. I'm sure if women were running the country, our beloved Empire might be viewed much more favourably by the rest of the world.'

Two women stood up and clapped.

'Yes!' one of them called.

'And less war!' the other added.

'Right, that's enough,' the policeman said, reaching in and grabbing Grace by the arm. 'Time to go back to your fantasy land. Out.'

'Ouch, you're hurting me,' Grace protested, trying to prise off his fingers, as he dragged her towards the door.

48

'Let go of her!' Cecil shouted. 'Everyone—you're witness to this—officer 503 is manhandling my friend and hurting her.'

The pressure on Grace's arm continued, as she was dragged unceremoniously towards the door.

'Out!' the policeman repeated. 'If I see you at any more of these meetings, I'll have you arrested.'

Grace smiled sweetly and curtseyed, before taking Cecil by the arm and limping to the pavement.

'That went well,' Cecil commented.

'God, I hate those two people,' Grace seethed, rubbing the sore underside of her arm.

'Which two?'

'Who do you think? Mr and Mrs Wild!'

Cecil positioned himself in front of Grace and met her fiery stare. 'What is it about them that affects you so much? Of all the people in this country, in this county, in this *town*, who are set against the cause, why do you get so bothered by them? What are you hiding, Grace?'

Grace could sense his desire to understand, but now was not the right time. Now was the time for action. 'I know you no longer work there but do you think you could get me inside Linden Grove?'

His eyes narrowed and took a moment before nodding his head. 'What are you thinking?'

'Revenge.'

Chapter Eight

Nothing. She could see nothing at all. Grace stopped, cursing her right leg, weakened significantly by the police attack eight months ago. She reached down and rubbed her calf, discovering as she did an abundance of fresh scratches. The tips of her fingers met with the syrupy wetness of fresh blood. Her long coat and dress had been torn and ruined by the indomitable knots and tendrils of bramble that reached across to block the path in front of her. But there was no path, that was the trouble: she was fighting her way through dense woodland; private woodland.

She looked up again and inwardly cursed, failing to locate any trace of the moon through the oak canopy above. A solid ceiling of elephant-grey cloud had wrapped and concealed what should have been a full moon. It was a truly imprudent night to undertake what she was about to do, but what choice did she have, now? Having already been postponed for the past two nights owing to biblical proportions of rain saturating the county, the family would be arriving back from their week's pheasant-shooting trip tomorrow. It was tonight or not at all.

She picked the bag up very carefully. Mrs Paine, the chemist's wife who had supplied the nitro-glycerine, had warned that the oily liquid slushing around in the three tins was liable to explode from exposure to heat, flame or shock. She continued picking a path through the almost-impenetrable ground foliage until, after what seemed an age, she finally reached the low stone wall that demarcated the boundary of Linden Grove. She climbed it and was relieved to finally step down onto a well-kept lawn. As she did so, the clouds tore apart and the moon illuminated the house, like the opening scene of a stage play.

She gasped as she took in the enormity of the place, and an uncontrollable shudder nipped down the length of her spine. It was bigger than she recalled. So much bigger.

As expected, the dozen windows on this western side of the building were in darkness. The rooms were empty, the curtains drawn.

Grace swallowed hard against the peculiar sensation that seemed to be rising from the pit of her stomach and stinging the back of her throat. It was, she realised, as she began towards the house, an uncomfortable fusion of past and present. Traces of a forgotten life flashed like a photographer's bulb into her mind—images so short and nebulous as to defy firm definition.

The house was close now.

She stepped onto the gravel path that edged the house.

'You took your time,' a voice whispered from the shadows.

Grace flinched but quickly calmed when Cecil stepped forward. Behind him was the open door to the kitchens, scantly lit by a lone candle.

'Come in, quickly,' he said in an unnecessarily low voice.

'There's nobody home, is there?' Grace asked, following his instruction.

'Just me, but even so,' he replied. He closed the door then reached for Grace's hand. 'Listen, are you sure about this?'

'Very,' Grace answered, holding up the bag. She caught the reluctance in his eyes. 'Listen, you don't have to do this, Cecil. I do. I know I haven't told you everything but believe me, I need to go through with this. I'm being sincere when I say that you can leave now—I'll think no less of you—truthfully. It won't affect our...closeness.'

Cecil gazed at the door through which she had just entered, as if deliberating his options. He looked back at Grace. 'But what if you get caught?'

Grace shrugged. 'Back to prison.'

'It means that much to you?'

'Yes.'

'Then I'm with you,' he assured her. 'I believe you must have your reasons and I want to help you.'

'Thank you,' she said, touching his hand.

'Have you got everything you need?' Cecil asked.

'Yes. Mrs Paine has given me three tins' worth—enough to take down the Brighton Dome, she said.'

'My goodness. Where are you going to put them?'

'Mr Wild's bedroom,' she declared. 'Let's go.'

Cecil picked up the candlestick and led them out of the room, along a dark low-ceilinged servants' corridor to a narrow circular staircase.

The groaning echo of the wooden steps, coupled with the ethereal dance of the shadows created by the candlelight, gave rise to a rash of goosebumps on Grace's limbs. The air was stale and damp-smelling.

51

She suddenly felt cold and pulled her coat more tightly around herself. She would have done it alone, without Cecil's help, but the truth of the matter was that she was glad that he was there.

They reached the top of the stairs. Grace stretched out for Cecil's free hand, as she took in the magnificence of the hallway. A vaulted, ornately decorated ceiling rose a good forty feet above them, the centre of which was dominated by an opulent chandelier. On the walls lavish Turkish rugs were interspersed with oil portraits of Linden Grove's long-dead residents.

Another lightbulb flash of recognition, as vagueness became replaced by certainty when she turned to see the staircase. It was stunning, mahogany, winding its way elegantly to the first floor. She recalled with clarity descending those very stairs. Voices from behind her, encouraging her down, praising her.

The memory was amorphous and its haziness left Grace feeling hollow and empty, as she placed her right foot down on the first step.

'Are you all right?' Cecil asked, squeezing her hand.

Grace nodded, taking another step in the shadow of her past.

They crept up the stairs, as though they were trying not to wake the entire house.

'It's this way,' Cecil breathed.

But she knew that already. They were going to head along the corridor to the room at the end, with its views across the lake and to the arboretum beyond.

Cecil paused at the door, listening, then he slowly turned the handle and the door swung open noiselessly. He stood back and ushered her inside. 'Here we are. Mr Wild's bedroom.'

The fabric of the room—the walls, the window and the floor—corresponded with her memories, only the furnishings had changed.

'Come on, let's get on with it,' Cecil said.

Grace nodded, placed the bag on the floor and opened it up. Warily, she removed one of the large yellow tins of Keen's Genuine Imperial Mustard and placed it in the centre of the room. *Deeds not words*, she thought, as she took out a canister of petrol and poured from the tin a trail out of the room and along the corridor to the top of the stairs.

Cecil picked up the bag and moved towards the door. 'Come on, let's get the other one ready and get out of here.'

'Calm down,' Grace snapped, spotting something on the far side of the bedroom. A dresser. Hurrying over to it, she pulled open the drawers. 'Come over here with that light.'

'No—it's too dangerous. One spark from this and they'll be finding us in pieces,' he protested. 'What are you doing? *Stealing*?'

'Oh, for goodness' sake,' Grace retorted, snatching the candlestick from him. She thumped it down on the dresser and used the weak amber light to search among the jewellery. Necklaces, brooches and rings.

'I didn't think you were like that, Grace,' Cecil commented.

'Like what?' she demanded, her eyes fiery. 'A lowly criminal from the workhouse? Have you forgotten my time in prison?'

'That was different—it was for the cause,' he answered. 'This isn't.'

She went to reply but she had found what she was looking for: a simple gold locket. A great deal of time had elapsed but she recognised it with certitude. Unlatching the clasp, she opened it up and received the final confirmation.

Her heart suddenly felt heavy, and her memories began to unspool inside her mind.

She faltered as she stared at the images encased in the locket. Was she really about to do the right thing? Legally, clearly not. But morally? Her previous resolve faltered.

'Grace?' Cecil uttered.

She held the locket up to the candlelight. 'These are my parents,' she murmured.

'What? Why's it here, then?' he begged.

The reason for the locket's being there was inextricably linked to *her* reason for being there. 'I'll tell you another time,' she replied, picking up the candlestick. 'Let's get another tin ready.'

Grace limped along the corridor behind Cecil, the stench of petrol guiding their way. He pushed the door open and they entered the room. She placed the second tin of nitro-glycerine on a plush rug and unscrewed the cap of the petrol canister.

'Wait!' he shouted, hurrying over to the window. 'Oh, God!'

'What is it?' Grace asked, rushing over to him. Then she saw it: two synchronised yellow lights, moving towards the house, probing the dark night sky.

'It's Mr Wild's Wolseley,' Cecil gasped, blowing out the candle. 'He's home.'

The car came to a stop below them and the lights extinguished.

'We've got to get out of here,' Cecil yelled. 'Come on.'

Grace ran into the hallway and pulled out the box of matches.

'There's no time for that,' Cecil exclaimed. 'We've got to get out.'

'I'm not leaving until I've seen his bedroom blown apart,' Grace rebutted, fumbling with the matches.

The first refused to strike.

'Come on, come on,' she said urgently.

The second refused to strike.

A loud bang of a door closing downstairs reverberated through the still house, making her jump.

'He's here!' Cecil called. '*Inside!*'

The third match caught light and, without hesitation, Grace dropped it to the floor, watching briefly as it ignited the snaking line of petrol along the corridor. 'Run!' she yelled.

Her injured leg hampered her progress; they had managed just five stairs before the explosion came.

For one tin of nitro-glycerine, the effect was remarkable. The blast punched out of the room and along the corridor, ripping Grace and Cecil from their feet and shoving them down the stairs in what sounded to Grace like the collision of several steam trains running at one another at full pelt.

She was on her back, her feet angled up the stairs. Her senses were overwhelmed. She could hear nothing but a metallic ringing which drowned everything else out that was surely making noise around her. She could see nothing but light-grey smoke and tiny pieces of debris falling around her like snow.

Cecil! Where was he?

She turned awkwardly and saw him, a few stairs below her, folded over, extricating his limbs from underneath himself like a new-born foal.

Grace ran her tongue over her dry lips and tasted blood.

Their eyes met and, despite their stunned looks, she could see that they would be alright. But they needed to move. The heat and smoke behind them was increasing dramatically. It could only be a matter of moments until the other tin would also be ignited.

She sat up and shook off a rind of dust and attempted to stand. Her legs gave way and she buckled down next to Cecil. As she righted herself, she saw Francis Wild, running up the stairs towards them. He was shouting something but Grace couldn't hear. Then he was standing over her and his look of shock changed to something else. Anger. She tried to read his lips: '...you at the march...' was all she could comprehend.

He had recognised her from the anti-suffrage march, which spoke volumes to Grace and confirmed in her mind that yes, she was morally right to have done what she had.

Mr Wild slapped her hard around the face, kicked Cecil in the back and then raced down the stairs out of sight.

Cecil picked himself up again and offered her his hand.

She took it and stood awkwardly, her body aching all over.

He led her down the debris-strewn staircase and from there they saw Mr Wild, trying to rip a huge painting down from the wall.

Cecil spoke but Grace couldn't hear him. She held his hand, as he led her out through the open front door.

Once clear of the gravel drive, they instinctively collapsed onto the lawn, breathing deeply.

'Are you alright?' he shouted.

Her mouth was so very dry that she struggled to speak. 'Yes, I think so,' she managed to answer, not really certain if she was alright or not.

Grace sat up and stared at the burning building. Giant curls of angry red and orange flames unfurled through the bedroom window and that of the two rooms adjacent. The fire was spreading quickly.

From out of the front door suddenly burst Mr Wild, wrestling with the over-sized portrait. She watched intently as he carefully set it down on the stone drive, then ran back inside the house.

She smiled at the thought of him hastening through the crumbling rooms of Linden Grove, attempting to save his precious possessions. But at what cost? Mr Wild had clearly identified them. Arrest and a lengthy prison sentence for both her and Cecil was now unavoidable. Yet still she smiled, pulling out the locket and squeezing it in her hands.

She exhaled steadily, then lent over and pulled Cecil into an embrace. 'We did it,' she breathed.

'*You* did it,' Cecil said, his hand gently caressing her back.

Grace sat back in mock displeasure. 'Is that what you're going to tell the police when they catch up with us?'

Cecil laughed. 'Of course not—you know what I mean. I wouldn't do that to you... I couldn't... I think I'm...'

Grace studied his face as his words ran dry with whatever it was that he had been about to say. She noticed then that their mouths and eyes were somehow in perfect synchronisation, wholly tuned to one another.

'I think I'm in love with you,' he finally managed.

Grace leant towards him, their faces drawing closer to each other. 'Me, too,' she whispered. Their dry lips brushed lightly at first, then she pushed herself closer to him with a fervency that rose suddenly from within her, taking her by surprise. For those few seconds in his arms, the various aches and pains around her body vanished.

Cecil shifted closer, pulling their bodies tighter, his hand tenderly stroking the length of her spine. Then, he broke away. 'Grace Emmerson—will you marry me?'

His words were hurried and, with the explosion continuing to ring in her ears, she failed to hear him. 'What?' she said, cupping her ear. 'I can't hear you.'

'Will you marry me?' he repeated, more loudly.

Her heart sang with his question. 'What?' she teased with a smile. 'I can't hear you.'

'I said, will you marry me?' he shouted.

Grace nodded. 'Yes.'

They kissed again for several seconds until the spell was broken by the agonising groan of part of the house collapsing. They looked over just in time to see the wing in which Mr Wild had his bedroom crumple to the ground.

Then, the man himself came running out again, this time carrying a chest of some kind.

'Let's not just sit around and wait for the police to get here. Come on,' Cecil said, offering her his hand.

Leaving the remaining tin of nitro-glycerine behind, she stood up, took one final glance at Linden Grove, then hobbled hand-in-hand with Cecil back towards the woods from where she had entered the estate.

From behind them, another explosion ripped through the house, as the second tin of nitro-glycerine ignited.

By the morning, Linden Grove would be nothing more than a pile of smouldering rubble.

Chapter Nine

'Here you go,' Juliette said, placing a mug of coffee down beside him.

He knew that it was a coffee by the smell but he couldn't actually open his eyes to see. He tried to mumble an acknowledgement but his mouth wouldn't work, either. In this other-world existence that he now occupied there was no amount of coffee that could get him ever to speak again. Less than two hours' sleep he had had last night.

'What are your plans today?' Juliette asked, sitting down on the bed beside him. 'Mum and I are going to take Matil...the baby to visit my uncle. Do you want to come?'

He tried to speak but a low grunt came out of his mouth instead.

'Morton,' Juliette said, impatience woven through the two syllables.

He opened his eyes, surely enough of an achievement for the day.

'Do you want to come with us because we'll be leaving in about twenty minutes.'

He shook his head. Visiting Juliette's mad uncle was about as appealing to him right now as having his legs amputated without anaesthetic.

'Well...do something constructive with your day,' she pleaded. 'Don't just stay in bed.'

Finding his way back to the land of the living surely had to be considered constructive.

With a slight huff of annoyance, Juliette kissed him on the forehead and left the room.

His eyes shut instantly and his mind went black.

He jolted upright, hearing a baby crying. His daughter. It was time for a feed and nappy change. He swung his legs out of bed, took a deep breath and stood up. He padded across the room, pulled open the bedroom door and listened. Silence. Then, he remembered that Juliette and Margot had taken the baby to see her uncle. Had they not gone? Or were they back?

'Hello?' he called down.

Nothing.

Either the cry had come from outside the house, or his mind was playing a cruel trick on him. Either way, he was wide awake now.

He picked up the coffee that Juliette had made for him: cold and undrinkable.

He looked around the room, not enjoying this perpetual state of bewildered disorientation. *Focus*, he told himself. What was the time? Just gone eleven. He needed to be productive, to take advantage of this time. A shower and some breakfast and he would be fine. But first, coffee. And lots of it. Maybe then he could continue working on Grace Emmerson.

In his heart Morton cried. On the document collection and returns desk in the Reference Room of The Keep—the name for the building housing all of the archives for East Sussex—was his nemesis, Miss Deidre Latimer. She was dressed in a hideous tartan skirt and some kind of loose-fitting blue blouse. They had never got on and yet, Morton had no real idea why. He was never in the mood for interaction with her. Today, however, he was in the kind of mood where he might well kill her.

He drew a deep breath and approached the counter.

A thin smile cracked her wrinkled veneer. Never a good sign. It usually indicated that a barrage of sarcasm was heading his way.

'Good morning,' she said brightly, removing her glasses.

'Morning,' he replied curtly. 'I've got some documents pre-ordered. I don't mind which first.'

She smiled again, unnerving him. 'I hear from our mutual friend, Jenny Greenwood, that you've a new addition to your household.'

'That's right,' he said, unsure where this was leading. She stood with her arms folded, making absolutely no attempt to go to the room behind the counter for his documents.

'Well, come on, show me a picture,' Miss Latimer said.

Now Morton was completely knocked sideways. 'Er...' he muttered, fumbling for his mobile. He unlocked the phone and looked up at her, waiting for her to say that she was joking and of course she didn't want to see a picture of his baby. But she didn't. She just waited. He scrolled past the photos taken yesterday at The National Archives to the abundance of pictures of his daughter. He selected a good one and passed the phone across the counter.

Her smile widened to a point that Morton had never seen before. What had happened to the miserable old hag that had blighted his life for the past goodness knows how many years?

'Oh, he's just adorable. Look at him!'

'Her actually,' Morton corrected. 'Long story as to why she's head-to-toe in blue, but she's definitely a girl.'

Miss Latimer nodded uncertainly. 'Well, *she's* adorable. Have you got a name yet?'

Morton went to say 'Matilda' but then he remembered back to first thing this morning. Juliette had faltered when she had gone to say it. Perhaps she wasn't overly struck on it, either. 'No, not yet. We're still making lists at the moment.'

'You've only got forty-two days legally,' she said, returning his phone to him. 'Right, let's go and get your documents, then.'

She disappeared into the back room, leaving Morton astounded. Miss Deidre Latimer might actually be human.

'Here we go,' she said, presenting him with a file. 'I'm afraid that some of the documents you ordered are unavailable, although they have been scanned and can be viewed on the computers in the Reading Room.' Another warm smile.

'Thank you,' he said, wondering if his sleep-deprived brain was misrepresenting reality, sparing him the pain of his usual exchanges with her.

Unnerved, Morton took a seat at one of the long tables. Today, there were half-a-dozen researchers quietly poring over the documents which were in front of them.

He opened his laptop and accessed his user account. The records that were unavailable, but which had been digitised, were photographs pertaining to one of the prominent members of the Brighton WSPU: Minnie Turner. According to the online index, the photos included her residence, Sea View in Brighton, where Grace had been living at the time of the 1911 census. In front of him now was a thinly bound packet containing Minnie Turner's correspondence.

The first item inside it was a letter, dated 12th April 1910, the writer expressing their condolences for the loss of Minnie's mother. The next four letters, from different authors continued this theme. Then he read a letter from 1947—an invite from the Suffragette Fellowship in London, inviting Minnie to visit their new museum. Next was a short undated notelet from a lady thanking her for a 'most wonderful seaside holiday in the company of like-minded women'.

Morton turned the page to see the final piece of correspondence: a discoloured pencil-written note that immediately aroused his interest, as, from a short way down the page, the words *Linden Grove* jumped out at him. He returned to the top and read: '*8th October 1911. Dear Minnie, It is done. I have destroyed Linden Grove. Given what has happened, I shall not be returning for the immediate future. With love & warm wishes.*'

Morton studied the words for some time, something niggling inside him about the letter. *I have destroyed Linden Grove.* The letter was unsigned, the anonymous author evidently known to Minnie. Was it a coincidence that this was where Cecil Barwise had been employed as a groom, just months prior to its apparent destruction?

He typed 'Linden Grove' into The Keep's search form. Zero results. *Perhaps it had made the local papers,* he wondered, making a note on his pad to check.

But there was something else about the letter that was bothering him. The handwriting. The elegance and precision of the descenders and ascenders were vaguely familiar. He studied the lettering carefully; the closer he looked at the grey pencil words, the more convinced he became that they had been written by Grace. Pulling out his mobile phone, he scrolled through his camera roll to the letter that Grace had written to Herbert Gladstone, complaining of her treatment in Holloway Prison. Identical.

Morton photographed the short letter, wildly curious about what had happened at Linden Grove. First, though, he needed to finish looking through the other document that he had pre-ordered.

He closed the file and carried it over to the desk.

Miss Latimer smiled. 'Ready for the next one?'

'Ye…yes,' he stammered.

Briefly heading out the back, she returned holding a tan-coloured file, entitled *Militant Suffragettes 1913.* 'Here we are.'

'Thank you,' he responded, returning to his seat, wondering if he had entered a parallel universe. He wasn't sure which version of Miss Latimer he preferred; this one unsettled him tremendously.

Turning the first page, Morton was greeted with a typed preface from the Criminal Investigation Department of New Scotland Yard: '*In view of the large number of disturbances and outrages committed by suffragettes in the Provinces, the Assistant Commissioner thinks it desirable to furnish Forces with portraits and descriptions of persons connected with the movement who may be likely at any time to engage in militancy. They should be kept entirely confidential.*'

Morton couldn't help but grin, completely certain that he would find Grace among the subsequent pages, which were filled with dozens of names and photos of ordinary women who took part in suffragette militancy.

Mary Richardson, age 31, height 5ft 5in, complexion pale, hair and eyes brown, nose rather long and hooked. Calls herself a journalist. This woman has been convicted several times of wilfully damaging the windows of public buildings, etc. Her last conviction was for damaging, with a chopper, the 'Rokeby Venus' at the National Gallery.

Catherine Wilson, age 31, height 5ft 1in, complexion fair, hair brown, eyes grey. Has been twice convicted of wilfully damaging plate glass windows and once being found on enclosed premises for an unlawful purpose, i.e. she was found in the House of Commons in male attire with a riding whip in her coat pocket.

Mary Lindsay, age about 24, height 5ft 6in, complexion pale, hair brown, eyes blue. Has been convicted of assault; she assaulted Lord Weardale with a dog-whip. Rides as Joan of Arc in suffragette processions.

Freda Graham, age about 26, height 5ft 6in, complexion fresh, hair and eyes brown. Has been convicted of assault and was concerned in the outrage at the National Gallery when she damaged five pictures. She has also thrown a bag of flour over a Cabinet Minister. During her last imprisonment she is believed to have taken drugs to cause sickness and so procure her release, and her health is now suffering from the results of an overdose.

Batten Poole, age about 23, height 5ft 5in, complexion fair, hair dark, eyes grey, slim build. In close touch with the leaders of the Movement and took a leading part in the Deputation to Buckingham Palace. She has undergone a course of Ju-Jitsu and teaches it to members of Mrs Pankhurst's 'bodyguard'.

And then she appeared.

Grace Emmerson, age about 37, height 5ft 4in, complexion fresh, hair light brown, eyes brown. Lived with the leaders of the Brighton WSPU and was active locally. Convicted of assaulting the Prime Minister during the 1911 incursion on Downing Street. Has not been seen actively since February 1911.

The photograph which accompanied her description was not a particularly flattering one. She looked thin and pasty and was being supported by the arm of an unseen woman to her left. The brick wall behind her, and the fact that she seemed unaware that she was being photographed, led Morton to believe that it had been taken surreptitiously during her time in Holloway.

He re-read the entry, curious again as to why she seemed to have suddenly ceased her militant activity in 1911. *Could it have been connected to whatever happened at Linden Grove?* he wondered.

Morton photographed the page then continued flicking through to the end.

He returned the document to Miss Latimer's outstretched hand.

'Thank you,' he said, making his way quickly towards the glass door.

'See you again soon,' Miss Latimer called after him. 'Good luck with the baby. You could always call her Deidre.'

He turned and nodded nervously. 'Bye.'

Never ever, ever, ever would he blight his daughter with the cursed named of Deidre. Never.

He was definitely suffering from some sleep-related problem, he decided, as he took a seat at one of the computer terminals, of which at least fifty were in the room. He navigated his way through to the digitised photographs of Minnie Turner.

The first picture—a posed black-and-white image—was of Minnie facing to the side as she tended to a vase of flowers. She appeared to be around thirty years of age, with a smart white shirt and dark dress. Her face, looking down at the flowers, was mournful, sad.

The next image was a sepia head-and-shoulder shot, taken several years later with Minnie gazing sternly into the camera. She reminded Morton of a tough Victorian school mistress. Zooming more closely into the image, he spotted that she was wearing the portcullis brooch which signified that she had been imprisoned for the cause.

Another sepia image followed. It was taken outside of Sea View, with the house name clearly visible on the two pillars and between which stood Minnie Turner. She looked to be in her mid-forties.

Clicking on to the next photo, Morton saw the front of the house in its entirety. In the bottom right-hand corner was written in black ink, 'Miss Turner WSPU'. In the bottom left was written '*Sea View, Brighton, 1911*', the very time when Grace had been living with her.

Morton smiled as he photographed the image. In his mind he could clearly see Grace walking up the short flight of steps inside the tall Victorian property—a house bubbling with the rhetoric and ideals of suffragettes, both permanent and transitory. He imagined the excited conversations, plotting and planning that must have occurred within those walls.

The final two images were of Minnie Turner's Votes for Women sash and a close-up colour photograph of her portcullis brooch, beside which was a piece of card with the words: '*Spent four months in prison for throwing a brick through a window at the Home Office.*'

Morton closed the folder down, gathered up his things and moved to one of the four digital microfilm readers. Walking the short distance to the run of metal filing cabinets, he selected Film 47: Brighton Argus 1911 and carried it back to the reader. He threaded it through the machine, then fast-forwarded to October, the month during which Linden Grove had been destroyed.

He found the story quickly under the headline, '*Palatial Mansion House Burned to the Ground.*' Splaying his fingers on the screen, he magnified the story, then began to read with great interest: '*The mansion of Mr Francis Wild was burned out during the early hours of this morning. The mansion was a beautiful residence, situated in the best part of the town, and was fitted out at great cost by Mr Wild, a well-known local factory owner. The Fire Brigade was called about three o'clock but the firemen were still at work six hours later, by which time the mansion was completely destroyed. The damage is estimated at many thousands of pounds. It is stated that the fire is the work of suffragettes, and the matter is being investigated. The family were away at the time and Mr Wild could not be reached for comment on the matter. No doubt this outrage will have the effect of alienating a large number of local people from sympathy with the movement. This seems to be the common result of militancy, and it is amazing that suffragists do not recognise the fact, and in consequence adopt a policy less likely to put off the day when the vote will be given to women. But whether the militant suffragists take this course or continue to pursue their mad career of crime, they will, in any case, soon be made to realise that the general public are disgusted with the present state of affairs and it will not tolerate it much longer.*'

Grace had burned down Linden Grove. *But why?* Morton wondered, photographing the newspaper entry. *What had Francis Wild done?* He pushed on to the following week, to see if the story had been followed up. And it had. '*Mr Francis Wild killed in Linden Grove arson*', shouted the headline. '*It has been confirmed by the Fire Brigade that local businessman, Mr Francis Wild was killed in the devastating fire at his home of Linden Grove last week, which destroyed the ancient mansion. Mr Wild's body was discovered in the wreckage of the building several days after the fire. It is believed that he had been attempting to rescue precious items from the house and became trapped inside. The incident is still being investigated as an arson attack caused by suffragettes. It is reported that two tins of explosives were detonated inside the house. A third tin of Keen's Genuine Imperial Mustard was removed from the scene by P.S. Lenehan, Special Branch, and taken to the Bomb-Proof House, Duck Island in St James' Park. Upon analysis, the tin was proved to contain pure nitroglycerine. The funeral arrangements for Mr Wild will be announced shortly.'*

So many thoughts were suddenly bouncing around Morton's brain, each vying for attention. *A tin of Keen's Genuine Imperial Mustard?* Wasn't that the same tin that Margot had handed Morton containing the portcullis brooch? *Francis Wild killed in the attack?* It was little wonder that Grace had ceased her activism if a man had died, albeit partially his own fault for trying to save his possessions. But still the main question persisted: *why target him?* He hoped that the ensuing pages of the newspaper might hold the answer.

Forwarding the newspaper on to the following week, Morton began to search for any mention of the incident or Francis Wild. Two weeks after the fire, the details of his funeral were printed: a lavish affair involving half the town and several motorcars. The report recapped the details of the fire, only adding that 'no arrests had been made' and that Mr Wild was 'staunchly anti-suffragist'. *Was that the reason that Grace had burned down his house?* Morton pondered. It seemed pretty thin, given that so many members of the public were against the cause. *Could it have been something to do with his factory?* Little had been mentioned of it in the newspapers.

Morton sat back and rubbed his temples. Time was slipping away. He only had two more hours left before the archives closed. He needed to understand more about Francis Wild, his home, personal life and business. But first, Morton needed to keep trawling the newspapers to find out if anybody had been arrested for the Linden Grove attack.

It took him over an hour and a quarter to find a report, in July 1912 that effectively said that the investigation into the fire at Linden Grove had been closed. It was arson, believed to have been perpetrated by suffragettes. Morton was smugly satisfied that Grace had escaped conviction and what would have certainly amounted to a lengthy prison sentence.

With just forty minutes left until closing, he decided to shift his attention to Francis Wild, first pulling up the reference to his death to ascertain his age: 45.

Switching to the GRO birth index, Morton typed in Francis Wild's name.

His mother's maiden name shocked him.

He quickly returned to the 1871 census, berating himself for having missed something so obvious.

Chapter Ten

18th November 1911, Wye, Kent

Grace cursed her injured leg as she descended the staircase. Using her walking cane, whilst clutching the small posy of white roses, was damned difficult. Apart from the wretchedly steep stairs, she loved the place. It was a quaint old railway-worker's cottage, located on the outskirts of the sleepy Kent village, which she and Cecil had rented shortly after fleeing the fire at Linden Grove. Believing that the police would turn up to arrest them at any moment, they had lied to the old widow who owned the cottage, telling her that they were married and in need of a place to rent for a short time. But the police hadn't come and, as the days had drawn on, so the likelihood of them losing their freedom had diminished.

Grace entered the sitting room and watched Cecil's face light up, as he stood from the armchair. His lips pursed into a whistle, as he eyed her up and down. 'Stunning.'

'You look quite the ticket yourself, Mr Barwise,' Grace commented, noting his best suit and freshly oiled hair.

'The car isn't here yet,' he informed her, leaning in to kiss her on the lips.

'Good,' Grace replied. 'Before we go, I want to explain myself to you…'

'Really, there's no need,' Cecil interrupted.

'But there is,' Grace countered, meeting his warm eyes. She knew before she spoke a single word that he would accept and forgive anything which she had to say. 'A man died because of me—you need to understand.'

Cecil nodded and sat back in his chair.

Grace sat beside him and thought for a moment. 'Twelve years I spent in the workhouse. Twelve of the worst years of my life—worse even than Holloway. I left in 1892, when I was sixteen, with nothing at all to my name but the clothes I stood up in. I was lucky to get a few domestic jobs, including, of course, the one with the Smith family.'

'Where you met me,' Cecil chipped in.

Grace smiled. 'Yes, exactly: life has improved by increment for me ever since. Minnie Turner took me in and improved my education and…well, here I am. For better or worse.'

Cecil placed his hand on hers, his eyes anticipating her making some connection to Linden Grove.

She knew from the way in which he had spoken in the past that he had assumed that she had once been employed there. 'You know where I spent my childhood, don't you?'

He nodded. 'The workhouse.'

'Yes, I was sent there when I was four years old. Do you know where I lived prior to that?'

'No.'

'Linden Grove,' she stated.

'What?' he asked, clearly taken by surprise. 'How?'

'For many generations, it belonged to my mother's family, the Hodgsons, passing down the family through the eldest male. All those grand portraits, which Mr Wild was trying to save from the fire, were my ancestors.'

'Are you teasing me, Grace?'

'No, I'm not. As I said, the house and all its contents passed down through the eldest male but then, when it got to my grandfather, there was no male heir, as he only had two daughters. My mother, being the eldest, inherited it all. She lived there with her younger sister until she met and married my father and then *they* made Linden Grove their home. I came along in 1876, born in the very bedroom where we set the first explosion.'

'I don't understand...' Cecil muttered, utter confusion imprinted on his face.

'Unfortunately,' Grace continued, 'my father died the year after I was born. I have no memory of him whatsoever. My mother had plenty of help in raising me and the few memories that I have of this time are happy. We were happy. Then she died unexpectedly when I was four—just dropped down dead one day, leaving me an orphan.'

'Oh, my goodness. Why didn't you tell me all this?' Cecil asked.

Grace shrugged. 'I haven't ever spoken about it to anybody—not even Olivia or Minnie know the truth. To be honest, I've tried to forget about it. What's the point in remembering?'

The revelation had muted him.

'Within a week of my mother's death, I was sent to the workhouse.'

'But Linden Grove?' he asked incredulously, this next piece of information freeing his tongue. 'Surely it passed to you as their only child?'

'If possible, it had to pass to a male heir and…there was one. So, it skipped me and went to my aunt's son. It stayed in his care ever since…'

'Oh God, no,' Cecil groaned. 'Not Francis Wild?'

Grace's eyes filled with the collision of memories in her mind. 'Yes…that's my secret.'

'Golly. But that's so unfair.'

'Yes,' she concurred.

'Why didn't he at least look after you in the house?'

'Because he's a monster, a greedy monster. He never once asked after me or visited or sent anything. In fact, I had no real idea what had gone on there until I was much older. I was a child, so I just did as I was told.'

'Well, I for one am glad he's dead—he finally got what was coming to him.'

Grace drew her fingers along her lower eyelids. She wanted to say that she agreed with him, but she couldn't. Despite all that had happened to her and even in her darkest days at the workhouse, she had never wished Francis Wild dead. Her anger had initially manifested itself against the bricks and mortar of Linden Grove, then, over time, whilst living at Sea View, towards the gross unfairness of the system. 'I hated what he represented,' she said. 'I wanted to do something about it—to change the system. That's how I got in with Olivia and she introduced me to Minnie Turner. After a few meetings at the WSPU, she invited me to live with her and, to all intents and purposes, make the cause my full-time job. I thought I could change things by delivering leaflets, going on marches and giving speeches but then, after that awful meeting at the Pavilion, something triggered inside me and I knew what I had to do.'

'I understand, Grace, I really do. But now what?' Cecil asked quietly.

Grace stood up and smiled. 'I should like to forget everything that occurred before this very second and to start again. Let's go and get married.'

With impeccable timing, the motor taxi pulled up outside the cottage, ready to take them to Ashford Register Office.

Cecil smiled, took Grace by the hand and led the way to the car.

Chapter Eleven

Juliette and Margot were sitting beside each other in the lounge, whilst the baby slept. Morton was almost through what had become a grand presentation on the life of Grace Emmerson. Having pulled all of his research into one file, he had unhurriedly worked through her life, starting with her time in the Brighton Union Workhouse, which was met with suitable mutterings and expressions of sympathy. He had progressed through her work as a domestic servant, where she had met her future husband, Cecil Barwise. 'Ah, Grandad,' Margot had said wistfully. Then Morton had reached the exciting and turbulent suffragette years. He showed every photograph and read every document. 'Sorry, this was my quiet wouldn't-say-boo-to-a-goose granny?' Margot had implored. '*Really*? Are you sure you haven't got the wrong woman?'

Juliette, not knowing her great grandmother very well, had uttered her absolute admiration throughout. 'What an amazing woman,' she had said, rapidly blinking to avoid showing that the information had touched her.

Morton had smiled and moved on to the arson attack on Linden Grove. He had shown images of the fire, read the accounts, then, to his wide-eyed audience, delivered the revelation that the fire had been started by none other than Grace Emmerson.

'No!' Margot had gasped.

'My God, she was a vandal!' Juliette had laughed, then felt the need to support her great grandmother's criminality. 'She was standing up for what she believed in; good on her. But,' she had begun, 'why target Linden Grove? From what you've said the suffragettes seemed to have targeted government or public buildings that would draw attention to the cause. Why hit a factory owner, who nobody outside of Brighton would ever have heard of?'

'Very good, Constable Farrier,' Morton had grinned. 'She was born there.'

'What?' Margot and Juliette chimed together.

'She was born there,' he repeated. 'Which is why Grace's mother and father appear quite well-to-do in the locket portraits—because they were.' He held aloft a print-out from the 1871 census, showing Grace's unmarried mother, Eliza at the property. In the top left-hand corner, in tiny scribbled letters were the words that he had overlooked when he had first been researching Grace's life: *Linden Grove.*

'So why did she then destroy the home of her birth?' Margot questioned.

'Because it should have been hers,' Morton answered. 'Male primogeniture. As a woman, she wasn't allowed to inherit the house if a male heir was to be found, and so it passed to her cousin, Francis Wild, and Grace got nothing. Wild threw her out on her ear and that's how she ended up in the workhouse, aged four.'

'What a horrible man,' Margot muttered. 'Disgraceful—he had what was coming to him.'

'That would explain her militancy,' Juliette said. 'Thank goodness I don't have to uphold such archaic laws anymore.'

'Precisely,' Morton agreed. 'After the fire, things calmed down a bit for Grace. No convictions were made.'

'She got away with it,' Juliette said triumphantly. 'Good woman!'

'Should you be saying that?' Margot muttered.

'Damn right,' Juliette answered.

'Grace and Cecil married and then along came a baby.'

'My mother,' Margot chipped in.

'After that—probably *because* of that—she gave up her militancy.'

'Wow,' Margot said. 'I'm very impressed, Morton.' She stood up and patted him on the shoulder, as she left the room. 'I didn't really think that genealogy was a proper job before now.'

Juliette's mouth opened in a silent grin and Morton rolled his eyes.

'Anyone for a cup of tea?' Margot called from the kitchen. 'Before Matilda wakes up?'

'Coffee, please,' Morton called. Then he lowered his voice: 'Do you like Matilda?'

'Do I *like* my new-born daughter?'

'You know what I mean. Do you like the name, Matilda?'

Juliette took a moment to answer. 'Yeah, I think so.'

'That's kind of how I feel about it. Shouldn't we be a bit more…passionate about it? Shouldn't we *love* it?'

Juliette shrugged. 'Come up with something better,' she challenged.

And so, Morton headed upstairs to his impossibly tidy study and searched the shelves for the copy of *60,001 Best Baby Names.*

Two days later, having registered the baby's birth at Hastings Register Office, Morton and Juliette were sprawled out on a picnic blanket, the sun beating down on the large golfing umbrella above them. Two plates contained the crummy remnants of their lunch.

'This is a fantastically inappropriate place to have a picnic,' Juliette said with a smile. 'But I love it.' She kissed Morton on the lips. 'Thank you.' Her gaze shifted beside them and Morton could see the awe, admiration and pride on her face.

He shrugged as his eyes fell to where she was looking. The burgundy marble headstone, which Morton had paid to be cleaned and restored, glinted in the sunlight, as though placed there only hours before. '*In Memory of a dear husband and father Cecil W. Barwise, died 18th December 1958 aged 74. At rest. Also beloved wife and mother Grace Barwise, died 15th August 1970 aged 94. Reunited.*'

Juliette bent down, picked up the baby under her armpits and held her aloft. She turned and addressed the headstone. 'Grace Emmerson, meet your great-great-granddaughter, Grace Matilda Farrier.'

Epilogue

28th August 1914, Wye, Kent

Grace couldn't bring herself to open the letter. It had just landed on the doormat, with a clear identification stamp on the envelope. HOME OFFICE. Those two words made her shudder with cold fear. Her mind raced, as she held the letter in her hands. *Why would the Home Office be writing to her? Had something happened to Cecil already?* The newspapers had been full of the British Expeditionary Force's battles in and around Mons these last days, with many soldiers killed. Surely, she would have received a telegram, if something had happened to him. Her thoughts jumped back to Linden Grove. Perhaps they had finally caught up with her. But would the Home Office be writing to her? Clearly not—the police would be knocking on the door.

She had no choice but to open it. She carried it into the sitting room and sat down.

Without thinking any further, she tore it open and removed the letter. '*Dear Mrs Barwise. You are receiving this letter as a person convicted of crimes committed in the name of suffragism. Owing to the suspension of militant tactics by the WSPU, among several other organisations, the Home Office is granting amnesty to all suffrage prisoners. This amnesty will take immediate effect.*'

Grace set the letter to one side, unsure of the implications. There was some relief, she supposed, at being freed from her crimes, but they were crimes that she had committed because of her beliefs; beliefs which she still vehemently held. She was angry, that was how she felt. War had come, a patronising pardon had been granted but nothing had changed. Universal suffrage was as far away today as it had been the day that she joined the WSPU.

She stood up, suddenly filled with energy, and marched to the bottom of the stairs. 'Minnie!' she called. 'Minnie! We're going out! Come down here and get your shoes on.'

Minnie, her two-year-old daughter, appeared at the top of the stairs with a sulky frown on her face. 'Where we going?'

'To the station,' Grace replied. 'Come on.'

Minnie beamed widely. 'On a train!'

'Well no, not quite. We're going to see the stationmaster. At least two of the guards have gone off to fight in the last few days and they'll be in need of some help.'

Minnie looked at Grace, bewildered.

'We'll show them that we're as good as they are,' Grace said to herself. 'Better, even.'

She took Minnie by the hand and led her outside into the hot late-summer sunshine.

'Deeds not words,' she said to Minnie with a wry smile.

Historical Information

Much of the source material, records and archives, and indeed some of the people featured in this short story are real. All of the records that Morton uses in his research are genuine, but with (mostly) fictitious content.

Minnie Turner was a well-known member of the Brighton WSPU. She lived at Sea View, 13-14 Victoria Road in Brighton, a house which was used by suffragettes recovering from stints in prison and also as holiday accommodation. In the 1911 census, she gave very little information about herself and the enumerator was forced to write 'Miss Turner and probably 11 others. Further information refused' on her entry. She was a militant suffragette and was sent to prison for four months for throwing a brick through a window at the Home Office. The information that Morton finds on her at The Keep is all real, with the exception of the letter confirming the destruction of Linden Grove.

As happened in many towns and cities, women were arrested for making speeches which incited violence. Arrests were also made in Brighton and elsewhere when pillar boxes full of post were targeted by the suffragettes. Protestations at Downing Street occurred on several occasions, including on 22nd February 1911. I have reproduced, almost word for word, the accounts of both the police and suffragettes in this story. The newspaper report is recounted virtually verbatim from an incident which took place there on 22nd November 1910, when Miss Henrietta Williams was arrested for hitting the Prime Minister and smashing a window in his car, as he tried to escape.

Grace's petition to the Governor of Holloway at not being placed in the first division was an amalgamation of several such documents held at The National Archives, most notably that of Sarah Carwin who had been arrested for causing damage to property and obstructing police.

The report by the Governor of Holloway, Mr James Scott on the conditions of the prison cells is also based on fact. Scott wrote the report following the complaints of several suffragettes about the conditions of the cells. H.M. Inspector of Factories investigated the claims, finding that *It is probable that any sense of oppression or discomfort felt in these cells is of psychological origin…*'

From 1909 many suffragette prisoners began to go on hunger strike, leading the authorities to force-feed them. The records of such incidents as presented in this story are sadly true and documented at The National Archives. In April 1913 the Government introduced 'The Cat and Mouse Act', whereby women, who became dangerously ill through hunger-strike, were released from prison then rearrested when sufficiently recovered. The women of the WSPU, who served prison sentences, received a portcullis brooch as a recognition of their action.

The reports of the anti-suffrage movement in Brighton are also based in fact. The 25th November 1911 edition of *The Brighton Herald* reported that Mrs Humphrey Ward had delivered a speech to the Brighton Branch of the National League for Opposing Women's Suffrage. It was held in the Brighton Pavilion and chaired by Sir Theodore Angier. Most of Mrs Francis Wild's speech in this story can be attributed to Mrs Humphrey Ward.

The Militant Suffragette file held at The Keep and the women (with the exception of Grace Emmerson) mentioned in the document are all real.

Linden Grove is a fictitious location, but one which I based on a house in Hastings, called Levetleigh. It was owned by the local MP, Arthur du Cros, a man who was against women's suffrage. On 15th April 1913 the house was burnt down and, although nobody was arrested for the arson attack, material found at the property led the police to point the finger of blame at local suffragettes.

Until the Married Women's Property Act of 1882 was enacted, women would, upon marriage, become one person with their husband under the law. Any property owned by the woman automatically passed to her husband. One such case, which inspired this storyline, was that of the large country estate, Knole in Sevenoaks, Kent. The house had been in the Sackville-West family for hundreds of years and, when Lionel Edward Sackville-West died in 1928, the house did not pass to his only child—his daughter, Vita—but instead to his male nephew.

Most, if not all of the unfair issues, which the suffragettes campaigned against, have since been rectified and amended in law. In 1918 the Representation of the People Act enfranchised women over the age of 30 who owned property, meaning that around 8.4 million women were eligible to vote. Later that year women became eligible to be elected to Parliament. The Act was amended again in 1928, extending the vote to all men and women over the age of 21, regardless of property-holding. The first female Member of Parliament to take her seat was Nancy Astor in 1919. The first female Prime Minster was Margaret Thatcher, elected in 1979.

The Wicked Trade
by
Nathan Dylan Goodwin

To Clair, Ciaran,
Poppy, Noah, Milo & Luna

Author's Note

This novel is set against the backdrop of a real moment and period in history: smuggling on the Kent and Sussex border in England in the 1820s.

Many real locations, characters and events have been used in this book. It is, however, largely a work of fiction.

As with one of my previous novels, *The America Ground*, this book revives some wonderful regional dialect, which is sadly now almost completely out of use.

Sacred
to the memory of
RICHARD MORGAN
First-Rate Quartermaster of HMS *Ramillies*, who was unfortunately
killed in the execution of his duties on the Blockade Service, 30th July,
1826
Aged 34 years
Left surviving Mary his wife

Stay, Reader, stay, incline your ear
to know who this is buried here.
A husband dear, a brother kind
a friend to all the well-inclined.
In doing duty he hath gained
the threat of some malicious men;
but those who serve their God and King
care not for men or worldly things.
His death was sudden, but we trust
in Jesus' arms he's now at rest.
No more in this vain world will he be toss'd
though many friends are left to mourn his loss.

Headstone in St Martin's Church, Dover, Kent

Prologue

7th July 1963, the Bell Inn, Hythe, Kent

'You ready for a drink, yet?'

Paul Major was standing awkwardly in the open fireplace, sweating profusely. He paused, the club hammer in his right hand ready to strike the back of the bolster chisel. Turning, he saw the grinning face of Ian Austen, the landlord of the pub in which he was working, peering under the horizontal beam of the inglenook fireplace.

'Drink?' he repeated.

'Is it too early for a beer?' Paul asked, setting the tools down on the pile of old bricks by his feet.

Ian took a glance at his watch. 'Is nine o'clock in the morning too early for you?'

'Na—that'd be great,' he grinned, running his shirt sleeve across his gritty, damp forehead.

'Is it going okay?'

Paul looked at the partially demolished wall beside him. 'Yeah, fine—the mortar between the bricks is like breadcrumbs—they're practically falling out by themselves.'

'So, not long until it's down, then?' Ian asked hopefully.

'Well, I don't think it will be ready for lunchtime like I said it would, actually.'

Ian groaned. 'Why's that?'

'Well, I expected to find a single course of bricks running up the middle of the chimney, dividing the two fireplaces, which would have taken a couple of hours to knock down and another couple to clear up.'

'But..?' Ian pre-empted.

Paul sniffed. 'There are *two* courses of bricks, not one.'

'So, double the work-time, then?' Ian mumbled.

'Possibly more. It's a weird one—the two courses have got about a foot's gap between them with a brick lid on the top—completely sealed up, it was.'

Ian frowned. 'Is that normal when one open fireplace has been divided into two?'

'I've never seen it before.'

'Well, just do your best and I'll have to hope we don't get a rush of customers coming in for lunch. I had a coachload of pensioners from Gravesend arrive unannounced yesterday.'

'Sorry,' Paul muttered, picking up the club hammer and bolster chisel. Turning to the side, he began hammering out another row of old bricks. The wall, now being just below head height, allowed him to peer inside the enclosure. Through the fine cloud of brick dust choking the air, Paul caught a glimpse of something. Material? A bag, perhaps? He pushed his head further into the cavity and squinted, but the conspiracy of darkness and grimy air prevented further clarity. Stepping out of the fireplace, he began to rummage in his tool-bag.

'Here you go, mate,' Ian said, returning with a pint of beer.

'Oh, lovely—cheers,' Paul said, reaching for the cold glass and taking a long glug. 'Nope—definitely not too early for that! I was just looking for a torch—looks like there might be something between the walls.'

'Tell me it was glistening and golden,' Ian quipped.

'Afraid not,' Paul answered, returning to his tool-bag. 'More like a bunch of old rags.' He found the torch—not a particularly powerful one, but it would do. He took another swig of beer, set it down on the nearest table then ventured back inside the fireplace.

'Well?' Ian asked.

'Give me half a chance!' Paul returned, angling himself so that he could get both his head and hand inside the cavity. He switched on the torch. The muted yellow light pushed through the granular air, settling on a rounded grey object. It took a moment for his brain to decipher what he was seeing. 'Oh, Christ!'

'What is it?' Ian demanded.

Paul shifted the beam of light to another similar object, protruding from the material that he had seen earlier—clothes. Specifically, two uniforms. Containing two skeletons. 'I think you need to phone the police.'

Chapter One

11th February 1821, Romney Marsh, Kent

It was shortly after two o'clock in the morning at Camber, on the westerly edge of Romney Marsh on the Kent and Sussex border, that the receding tide brushed the hull of the nameless galley for the final time, releasing it to the wet shingle beach. The boat—ten oars, thirty feet in length and painted stark white—could scarcely be seen on this cold, moonless night. Beside the galley queued the last dregs of the men, whose original number had been nigh on two hundred. The men had been quarried for their bestial strength from the surrounding countryside and who, upon reaching the boat, would be saddled up with two one-hundred-pound barrels of smuggled brandy. The line of men trudged back up the beach between two long flanks of batmen armed with clubs, flails and pistols, before pushing on into the dark and desolate marshes beyond.

Next, it was the turn of Samuel Banister. He moved closer to the boat and looked up at the blackened face of their leader, Cephas Quested, but the darkness retained his features.

'Ready?' Cephas barked, his breath heavy with liquor. Without waiting for a response, he passed the rope straps, which held two half-anker barrels, over Samuel's head. The barrels thumped hard onto his chest and back, thrusting the air from his lungs. 'Off!'

Samuel side-stepped away from the boat, struggling to catch his breath. He moved as quickly as he could up the beach, but the waterlogged shingle sucked his boots down with each stride. This, his third night of smuggling—if the other two were to be equalled—was going to be long, arduous and punishing. But he had little choice; he was twenty-two years old with a pregnant wife and young boy at home. One evening of running contraband earnt him eight shillings—almost one week's labour on old Banks's farm.

'Move on, will ya!' the tubman behind him snarled, elbowing sharply past.

Samuel's grunted, breathy response was lost to the sound of a pistol firing noisily into the air above them. Then, chaos. Every man on that beach knew the implication of the gunfire: it was a beckoning call from the blockade officers for help. The tubmen in front of Samuel suddenly quickened their pace up the beach, whilst the batmen protecting them readied their blunderbusses and muskets with guttural, opprobrious roars.

'Hold! In the name of the King; hold, I say!' a voice shouted from nearby.

Samuel paused for the briefest of moments and turned to await Quested's orders. His muscles tightened as he glimpsed movement in the sea behind the galley; a boat full of blockade men was already sailing towards the shore.

An indistinguishable command was bellowed from the galley and the batmen on either side of Samuel began angling their weapons in the general direction from which the pistol had been fired. Seconds later, a sharp volley of muskets and shot cracked open the air, firing onto the position of the blockade men.

A cacophony of shouting from all around him competed with the resonance of gunfire.

Ducking down as much as the barrels strapped to him would allow, Samuel pushed harder up the sloping beach, cursing the shifting, enveloping stones under his feet. Behind him, the two lines of batmen began to fold into one rear-guard, the torrent from their weapons continuing to pound the blockade men's position.

Finally, the shingle levelled out and Samuel stopped to take breath. He turned to see that the blockade ship had landed on the beach and a group of a good dozen officers had poured forth onto the stones. The rear-guard of batmen desisted firing and began to run towards Samuel and the rest of the fleeing tubmen.

'Move, you buffle-headed dunty,' one of them bawled at Samuel.

Walland Marsh that lay before him had absorbed the rest of the tubmen into its bleak desolation. He needed to move fast, but the barrels of brandy were holding him back. If he ditched them now, he could certainly outrun the blockade officers, but without deliverance of the brandy he would receive no pay. With a renewed determination, Samuel pressed on. At last, the ground beneath him, firmed by sand, mud and sparse vegetation, resisted the heavy footfall of his boots and his progress increased.

The gunfire behind him had at last abated, but now he could not see which way to go. Searching the darkness for direction, Samuel caught sight of movement up ahead—another of the smugglers—and moved towards him. He ignored the deep aching in his chest and pushed on faster, drawing alongside the two men. One was Quested, his left arm around the waist of a limping tubman. Samuel could see from the man's blood-drenched breeches that he had sustained an injury to his leg.

Quested glanced at Samuel. 'We just need to be a-getting to Lydd. I got carts a-waiting at Scotney Court Farm.'

Samuel nodded. 'How far?'

'Four mile-odd,' Quested answered breathlessly.

He couldn't; there was no way Samuel could maintain this pace for a further four miles. Then he thought of Hester anxiously awaiting him at home, having pleaded with him not to get involved in the wicked trade, after losing two brothers to the gallows for the same crime. It was with every conscious effort that Samuel fought the desire to drop the barrels and run directly home.

Placing himself on the other side of the injured tubman, Samuel hoisted the man's left arm over his shoulder.

'The blockade will give up soonest,' Quested said, as if intuiting Samuel's doubts. He guided them to the edge of the field and paused, squinting into the darkness.

'Please—be a-leaving me here,' the man between Samuel and Quested begged.

'Don't be blethering on, man. Stay quiet.'

Samuel noticed Quested turn to look behind them and followed his gaze, wishing that there were even a hint of moonlight by which to see. Behind them, hulking shadows danced and shouted. Evidently, they were still being pursued. The flashing of a blunderbuss briefly illuminated the scene following them: not fifty yards away the batmen were beating a retreat towards them. Pursuing the batmen closely were now upwards of twenty blockade officers.

'Dump the barrels,' Quested instructed.

'But...' Samuel began.

'Don't be a-worrying, you be getting your dues. Sling them in the sewer and happen we'll find them tomorrow.'

Samuel obeyed his leader and heaved the half-ankers over his head. Seeking one last look of assurance from Quested, he tossed them down into one of the many ditches which dissected the great Marsh, receiving a loud splash in response.

The commotion from behind them was drawing ever closer.

'Let's be a-getting out of here,' Quested ordered.

Without turning, Samuel became aware that something was happening behind them; the men's footfall had ceased. Seconds later, the muskets and blunderbusses were opening up once more; the batmen were stopping to provide cover for their withdrawal.

Two pistol shots fired in succession, immediately succeeded by two wolf-like cries piercing through the night sky, as two of the batmen were slaughtered.

The blockade men were close now.

Another shot rang out and Samuel felt the man beside him suddenly weaken. He slumped noiselessly to the ground, instantly devoid of life.

'Run!' Quested shouted.

Samuel, trying to ignore the fact that he was running dangerously close to the edge of the water-filled ditch, pushed his body until every muscle in his legs was screaming.

'Over there!' Quested yelled, pointing into the darkness.

Evidently, he could see something which Samuel could not.

They continued running, with the mêlée of conflict between batmen and blockade officers just yards away, until Quested suddenly thrust out his arm.

Samuel drew to a stop just in time; they had reached the terminus of the field, their escape route blocked by Pig's Creek Sewer—another of the marsh's notorious dykes.

Their game was up.

Samuel bent double, his body aching and his mind in chaos. Swamping his thoughts were images of Hester and his little boy, John. She had been right in her vehement opposition to his smuggling; now he would pay the price.

The retreating batmen were almost upon them.

'Are you a-coming?' a voice called from the pitch darkness of the opposite bank, just as a thin wooden plank fell propitiously over the watery divide.

'Come on—whip-sticks,' Quested said, pushing Samuel towards the makeshift bridge.

Fearful of the freezing water below, Samuel tottered carefully onto the wood, trying to ignore the groaning bounce that occurred as he made his way across. Just three more steps and he would be on the other side.

Then, more gunfire. Musket balls passed overhead.

'Hurry!' someone shouted. The voice did not belong to Quested; Samuel guessed that the batmen had caught up to them, which meant that the blockade officers were almost upon *them*, too.

With one final spring, Samuel pushed off the plank to the relative safety of the dark field beyond. There, he could just make out several silhouetted figures: tubmen, by their lumbering appearance.

One by one, the batmen crossed Pig's Creek Sewer. Cephas Quested was the last man to cross and the plank of wood was hastily retracted through the swampy water, out of reach of the blockade men.

'Come on—there be no time to—' Quested began, but his sentence became lost to a barrage of angry pistol fire from across the water.

Something with the force of a stampeding ox smashed into Samuel's right shoulder, sending him crashing to the floor in agony. Reaching across with his left hand, he touched what felt like a pulpy sponge; his arm was full of shot and was bleeding profusely into his smock-frock. The pain, like a dozen tiny daggers piercing his flesh, was unbearable.

'Be keeping low,' someone behind him yelled.

Despite the agonising pain in his shoulder, Samuel lay still. Around him were other men—he could not see them but he could hear their heavy breathing, hear their bodies shuffling on the cold, damp field beneath.

Samuel lay still, gripping his shoulder, for what felt like hours, praying that time would speed up.

After a while, the gunfire ceased.

Fragments of broken discussion reached Samuel's ear from the other side of the embankment. Mumbled snatches of blockade men's conversation. But what he heard was enough; they had been ordered to cross the dyke by any means.

He had to escape.

He stood awkwardly, a rush of fresh pain firing out from the wound. 'They bain't giving up,' Samuel whispered, 'we need to be a-running.'

Men rose from the ground around him with grunts and moans. Evidently, he had not been the only one to sustain an injury.

'This way,' Quested's voice said definitively from the dark.

The group—numbering half a dozen—crossed the field at a fast pace, before passing through a low hedge and entering another field.

'What way you be a-bringing us, Quested?' one of the men barked when they reached the edge of the field to be confronted by yet another water-filled ditch. 'Wainway Petty Sewer? If we cross this one we bain't got no choice but to cross Lower Agney Sewer, then

Horsehead Petty Sewer. This weren't the plan, Quested. There be nobody waiting to help us cross.'

'Then be going your own tarnal way,' Quested shouted. 'Go on!'

'I just be asking because why,' the man responded.

'Stand whist and you be hearing why,' Quested said.

The group fell silent, as instructed.

Samuel heard it: the unmistakable sound of the blockade men, still in pursuit.

'They bain't letting go this night,' Quested said. 'We be tarnal fortunate to make the night alive or untook. Now, I be going across here—you be a-pleasing yourselves.' He turned his back on the men, sank down onto the bank and began to slide down into the water.

For Samuel, no decision existed. He moved to the edge of the dyke, sat and used his heels to pull himself down the bank. He retched at the foul smell rising from the disturbed water, as it clawed its way painfully up his legs and around his abdomen. The coldness—for the water was near to freezing—quickly penetrated inside him, causing an acute shaking in his limbs. Samuel continued to wade across the ditch, always checking the depth of his next step with an extended foot. The water was just a couple of inches from his injured shoulder and he knew that if its filth touched it, he would be finished.

At last, his foot met the sloping edge of the opposite bank. Quested offered his left hand and heaved Samuel to the top. He collapsed to the ground, shivering.

'We be warm, soonest,' Quested said, 'when we be a-moving again.'

They waited for the other four men to join them, then followed Quested's lead across another field.

Samuel didn't know if the pace had been slowed for him in particular, or if the whole group was suffering as was he, but he was grateful nonetheless. Somehow, the freezing water had dulled the pain in his shoulder—perhaps masking it with the addition of an overall discomfort throughout his body.

When they reached Lower Agney Sewer, they stopped again to listen. Sure enough, the blockade officers were still in pursuit. They had no choice but to cross it.

The ditch was shallower than the previous one and only reached just above their waists. Yet, despite this, the temperature of the fetid water seemed to syphon more of the men's energy, and once they had crossed it, progress for the next two miles was hampered by a waning, sluggish pace.

The six men reached Beacon Lane, on the outskirts of the village of Brookland, some three hours after their retreat had commenced.

'You made it,' a voice called from the darkness.

'We beleft you dead or captured,' another added.

'Merciful Lord!' Quested blurted at the sight of five batmen, perched at the side of the road with their blunderbusses fixed on Quested's position. 'There be a whole bunch of blockade officers just yards behind us. Be a-readying yourselves!'

Exhaustion consumed Samuel; his muscles were taut and his resolve weak. He spotted a low stone wall and slouched down behind it, beginning to shake all over. He touched his shoulder and held blood-wetted fingers up to his face. He knew that if medical help were not forthcoming quickly, he had seen his last sunrise. 'I be a-needing a doctor,' he mumbled.

'Soonest—we only be a few mile from home, now,' Quested answered, dropping down beside him. 'Amputation, I don't wonder.'

A cold realisation washed over Samuel. 'I don't be a-wanting no amputation,' he said, as insistently as he could.

'That be for the surgeon to decide.'

'The heart-grief this be giving my Hester...' Samuel uttered, his voice quivering.

'The same from my Martha—I be set for such a bannocking in the morning.'

A short moment of silence that descended over the men was sharply snapped away by the firing of many guns.

Without warning, the body of a tubman fell backwards over the wall, landing lifelessly beside Quested.

'I be thinking it's over,' Quested mumbled, prising the musket from the dead man's hand. 'Sit whist—there be more pistol shooting from the blockade men than what we got to fire back.'

Samuel tried to steady his shaking limbs and listen. Though his mind was listless, he counted the pistol cracks, estimating there to be at least twenty men from the blockade—possibly more.

'If I get took tonight or be killed, be making sure this gang bain't done with—you hear?' Quested said.

Samuel, not liking his own chances of surviving the night, couldn't entertain the idea of another smuggling run. 'Happen it bain't in my blood...' he responded quietly.

'Contrariwise—be thinking of your Hester and what you can be a-giving her. Tidy money this trade be a-bringing.'

'But the boat?' Samuel said. 'There be no way she be sitting on the shore a-waiting us tomorrow.'

Quested laughed, as he fiddled with the dead man's musket. 'Buy another boat—heavens, buy two boats.'

The volley of gunfire continued, punctuated by the odd cry or yelp of an injured man.

'I bain't got a shilling to my name,' Samuel countered, clasping his hands together to stop the acute shaking.

Quested fell quiet, then faced Samuel: 'I can be a-telling you of the place of two barrels *full* of gold guineas if you be pledging to see my Martha right.'

'Gold guineas?'

'Aye—hundreds of them. What say you?'

'Alright...' Samuel found himself answering.

'Right. In the woods on me old aunt, Widow Stewart's farm be a pigpen—under the floor be a cellar—a tub-hole—that be where you find the barrels. She don't be causing no fuss—she be hockatty-hick and don't be a-leaving her house.'

'From where have they appeared?' Samuel asked.

'Gold speculation during the French Wars,' Quested replied haughtily.

'And what be that, justly?'

'A-buying gold in London for price and a-selling it in Paris for price and a quarter.'

'You be once being a gold speculator?' Samuel questioned. He knew little of Cephas Quested, but his reputation was as an uneducated labourer who was always concerned in liquor and never to be found in church save for weddings and funerals.

'Well, no. One night a-fishing off Folkestone my uncle happened upon one of the galleys on its way out to France and, well, he nabbed the lot. He be telling me of it on his deathbed last winter. Then I gets into smuggling and here we be.'

Samuel realised then that the guns had, at some point whilst they had been talking, fallen silent. There were the sounds of men moving, some shouting.

Quested turned and peered up over the wall. 'Here!' he called, leaping over.

Samuel watched as Quested approached the man, offering him the dead smuggler's musket. 'Take this and blow some bloody officer's brains out.'

The man, dressed like his fellow smugglers in a dark gabardine, took the musket, flipped it around and held it to Quested's head. 'In the name of the King, I am apprehending you under the Smuggling Act. My name is Charles Newton and I am a deputed Officer of Customs. You are to come with me.'

Despite the darkness of the night, Samuel could see from Quested's posture that he had given up the fight.

'What is your name?' Newton demanded.

'Quested—Cephas Quested.'

'Treader!' the blockade man called. 'Take this wretch to the watch-house and see that he makes no trouble.'

Samuel watched as another blockade officer—this time dressed in the uniform of his station—arrived and grabbed Quested by the collar.

Quested flicked a final glance in Samuel's direction before being led off into obscurity.

Samuel was alone.

His thoughts were swathed in a thick, mulish fog, interwoven with the distancing echo of ricocheting pistol shots and muffled shouts. The torturous pain had returned to his shoulder. He knew that he needed to move on from here, but his shuddering legs refused to bear his weight.

Samuel slumped down onto his side then began to crawl through the damp grass on his knees towards some kind of building which he had spotted in the distance.

He made it a good many yards—how many, he could not tell—before collapsing back onto his front.

He closed his eyes, welcoming the numbing distraction that delirium offered. He was at home with Hester. She was sitting beside the fire smiling. John was there, too. Then, the welcome pull of anaesthetising darkness.

He was floating—in the air or in water—he didn't know which. Something was moving underneath him—something constant like a millstone. Scratching, hurting his legs and lower back. And the pain in his shoulder! Even through the mask of hallucination, he felt the excruciation of the open flesh.

He opened his eyes to discover the sky full of shooting stars—each and every one was racing through the blackness above him. Then they vanished. Not one single star remained in the sky. And the millstone had stopped grinding beneath him. And a vice under his armpits, of which he had been unaware previously, released.

Light! Terrible, terrible bright light. Samuel threw his left arm over his face to shield his eyes.

'Hello,' someone said. A girl or woman. Hester? It did not sound like her. 'What be your name?'

'Sam,' he answered, drawing the words from within. He slowly pulled his arm from his face and saw an upside-down young woman staring back at him holding a candle. Not Hester.

'You be in a bit of bother, Sam,' she said. Her voice was soft, gentle.

Samuel tried to sit up. 'I need to be a-getting the guineas,' he muttered, before falling back down onto what he realised was a pile of straw. He looked around him, lucidity touching the edge of his addled thoughts. He was in a barn.

'Oh. And what guineas do they be, then?' the woman asked.

'The barrelful beneath Widow Stewart's pigpen,' he managed to say.

The woman laughed. 'I don't be thinking you're going anyway soonest,' she said.

His eyelids began to close, sleep pulling him back in.

'My name's Ann, since you ain't be asking—Ann Fothergill.'

Chapter Two

Morton Farrier was intrigued. On the table in front of him was a collection of documents pertaining to the life of one Ann Fothergill—the great-grandmother of the elderly man sitting opposite him. Morton glanced over the final record, then met the old man's enquiring eyes which had lit up his pallid face in anticipation. Arthur Fothergill was, as he had declared proudly upon opening the front door to Morton, ninety-five years of age. Sitting beside him, in the protective role of mildly mistrusting family member, were his nephew and niece, neither of whom had contributed anything during the half-hour that Morton had been there, and who clearly held no interest in what was being discussed.

'What do you make of it all, then?' Arthur asked.

'She certainly sounds as though she lived a colourful life,' Morton answered. He glanced to the nephew—sour-faced and staring at the wall clock—then to the niece, who vaguely returned his smile.

'I'm not sure if it's *colourful* or jolly strange,' Arthur disputed, seemingly critical of Morton's choice of adjective to describe his great-grandmother. He began riffling through the paperwork, his jittery hands scattering the documents across the table. In his left hand, he held aloft a newspaper report printed from the internet. He clearly knew the report well, for he quoted from it without hesitation: '*1820. Ann Fothergill…an illiterate vagrant… sent to prison no less than 36 times…*' Arthur said, speaking more forcibly, but without letting his gaze fall from Morton's eyes. '*His Worship expressed his regret that the Court could not dispose of her permanently, for she appeared to be a perfect pest to society… committed once again to prison for two months.*' Without pause, he reached for another piece of paper, this time reading it verbatim: '*22nd July 1827. The Bell Inn, Hythe. Dear Sam, I do hope that you are well and that you have settled out there. I must again refuse your offer. My life, with this inn and the boy, is here and after all the difficult years in this area, things have returned to the quietness of the old ways. It is an opportunity to leave behind the wicked deeds of the past. In answer to your question, and with the imposed distance between us I may now tell you that the barrels of gold guineas were hidden below ground in an outhouse close by, and that is the way they shall remain, being of little use to anyone now. I beg that you will settle your mind on the matter and look instead to your new future.*

Your ever-loving friend, Ann Fothergill.' Arthur cleared his throat and asked quietly, 'From perennially drunk, illiterate vagrant to an articulate businesswoman in seven years. A bit more than *colourful*, wouldn't you say?'

All three sets of eyes on the opposite side of the table came to settle firmly on Morton, awaiting his response to the nonagenarian's diatribe.

Morton considered the question carefully before answering, much to the chagrin of Arthur's nephew who emitted a large sigh at the unnecessary hole in the conversation. 'Yes, she certainly does sound enigmatic,' he admitted.

'And worthy of your investigation?' Arthur pressed.

'That depends on what you want to know about her,' Morton replied.

Arthur shifted around in his chair, as if he had not considered the question before now. 'Just a picture—as detailed as possible—of her life during those intervening seven years to understand that shift in her character... Where she lived, who she was associated with and, if it's possible, to know the identity of my grandfather's father.'

'The period that you're talking about isn't exactly brimming with archives,' Morton warned, 'there might literally be *nothing* to find in the 1820s about Ann.'

'Will you at least give it a go?' Arthur pushed.

The case intrigued him, he had to admit it. Before he could answer, the nephew, whose name Morton had already forgotten, waded in with another question: 'And what about these golden guineas, then? Any truth in that?'

'Truth?' Morton questioned, unsure of what was being asked of him.

The nephew picked up the envelope—clearly *not* the original, Morton noted—which had contained Ann's letter and tipped the contents out onto the table: one golden guinea. The coin performed a short pirouette before settling in front of Morton.

'How much do you reckon that's going for on eBay?' the nephew asked. 'Go on, take a guess.'

'Well, a guinea, I suppose,' Morton said with a wry smile. 'So, one pound five pence?' His humour fell flat.

'Nope,' the nephew said. 'Try again—my sister's husband looked it up, didn't he, Clara?'

The niece nodded her agreement.

94

'Two hundred pounds?' Morton guessed, hoping that this game would be a short one.

'Nope. *Average*—,' he said, stretching the word out. '*Average*—six hundred quid, though if they're in good nick like this one, about a *thousand* quid.'

'Right,' Morton said flatly.

'For *one*,' the nephew clarified needlessly.

Arthur smiled and patted his nephew on the back. 'I think what he's trying to understand is whether these barrels of coins mentioned in Ann's letter might still be hidden?'

Morton laughed, presuming it to be a joke. When their expressions told him otherwise, he tightened his face into seriousness and said, 'After a hundred and ninety-odd years? I've no idea, but I doubt it.'

'But if you knew where she'd been living in the 1820s..?' the nephew pushed.

Morton looked at the three faces vaguely, not understanding. 'And you think I could just walk up to the house with a metal detector and ask if I can pop into their back garden, start digging, then waltz off with a few carrier bags of guineas?' he stammered incredulously. He had been asked to do some strange things in his past cases, but this could take the prize for the most bizarre.

'Not exactly like that, no,' Arthur said.

'They *might* still be there,' the niece added.

'I've no idea…' Morton said, happily displaying his bewilderment to the three people sitting opposite him.

'I can see you're confused,' Arthur said. 'Let me put Ann into context for you with a little recent family history. You've heard of Fothergill's—the big London stockbrokers? They got into a bit of trouble during the credit crisis but seem to have pulled out of it okay…'

Morton nodded, awaiting the inevitable link to Arthur's family tree.

'That was set up—initially as a bank—by Ann's son, William, after she died, using the money that he had inherited from her: a substantial amount, I might add. The business prospered and he passed it to his two sons, Frederick and my father, Harry. Now, not to want to cast aspersions on the deceased, my father was a bit of a gambler. He gambled his marriages, gambled his money and tried to gamble the business, before his brother stepped in and bought him out of the company. Fothergill's flourished. Frederick died a multi-millionaire; my father died penniless.'

95

It suddenly dawned on Morton, sitting in this small, neglected bungalow, what was being asked of him. He held his hands aloft, as if surrendering, and gathered up his belongings. 'Listen, I'm a forensic genealogist, not a gold hunter—you need to employ somebody else—a private detective or… somebody; I don't know.' He pushed his chair back and stood to leave.

Arthur held up his hand. 'Wait, wait, please,' he said. 'You've got it all wrong. Yes, there's an interest—' he flicked a quick sideways glance to his nephew, '—in the guineas, *if* they still exist, but what I really want to understand is that chasm in Ann's life between 1820 and 1827, because it clearly had a deep-reaching impact on several generations of the Fothergill family—one, yes, being financial. I don't want to hire a private investigator—I want to hire *you*. We've read up on some of your past cases and think you're the right man for the job. What do you say?'

Morton didn't know what to say. The case did hold an odd appeal for him, he had to admit. He sat back down, hearing himself saying, 'I'll see what I can find, so long as you understand that my research will be directed at Ann Fothergill's life, with particular reference to the 1820s. What I'm *not* offering are treasure-hunting services.'

Arthur smiled. 'Wonderful. And how will you go about it, exactly, may I ask?'

Morton suppressed a sigh, not liking the implication that his methods were being questioned before he had even begun working on the case. 'I use a mixture of methods: traditional, like visiting archives, libraries and churchyards; and modern, like DNA testing, the internet and photo analysis. I've got subscriptions to all the major genealogy companies and I go to local, regional and national archive centres to find whatever I can—that might be letters, photographs, wills, certificates, newspaper reports… I pull it all together on a wall in my study at home. Basically, I do whatever it takes to complete the case.'

Arthur nodded. 'I see.'

'And how long will this take?' the nephew asked.

Morton shrugged. 'If, like your uncle says, you want the job doing thoroughly, then it takes as long as it takes. Some cases I wrap up in a couple of weeks, others take more time.'

'Take as long as you need,' Arthur reassured.

'Okay. With regard to identifying the father of Ann's baby, one avenue, which can help corroborate anything else I might find out, is if you take a DNA test,' Morton said.

The corners of Arthur's lips turned down as he nodded in consideration. 'Yes, if you think it would help.'

'Excellent,' Morton said, pulling his bag up to the table.

'You've got one here already?' Arthur said.

'I buy a stock of them whenever Ancestry drops the price,' he said. 'If we do it now, then I can get it sent off today.'

'Okay,' Arthur agreed.

Morton unwrapped the test kit, instructed Arthur to spit into the small test tube, then sealed it and placed it in his bag. A brief smile, then he stood and indicated to the pile of documents on the table. 'Can I keep hold of these while I work on the case?'

'By all means,' Arthur said.

'Not this,' the nephew said, snatching up the gold guinea.

'Can I photograph it, then?' Morton asked, trying to contain his annoyance.

The nephew slid the coin back across the table and Morton pulled out his mobile and took several photos of it.

'Thank you. I'll be in touch,' Morton said, shaking their hands, and then making his way to the front door, with Arthur following closely behind.

'Cheerio,' Arthur said.

Morton said goodbye, stepping out into a cold, windy afternoon and hurried to his Mini. He started the ignition and pulled away—homeward-bound. As he took a fleeting glance back at Arthur Fothergill's bungalow, an uneasy feeling about this case murmured inside of him. It intrigued him, yes, but it also slightly troubled him.

Morton arrived back at his home in Rye, East Sussex twenty minutes later. His main reason for taking this ominous case in the first place had been due to its proximity to home. He did not like being away from his wife, Juliette, and their eleven-month-old daughter, Grace, for longer than was absolutely necessary. He bounded up the stairs to his home—*The House with Two Front Doors*—with an inane grin on his face. In truth, the recent genealogical cases, which he had undertaken, had paled in comparison with his new role as a father, which he loved.

'Hi,' Morton called out. 'Hungry and thirsty forensic genealogist here.'

'Shh!' Juliette whispered, rushing from the kitchen.

But it was too late. From upstairs came Grace's startled scream.

Juliette rolled her eyes: 'Thanks.'

97

'Sorry,' Morton apologised. 'I'll go.' He took the stairs two at a time and entered Grace's darkened bedroom. 'Hey, hey,' he soothed, bending over her cot and lifting her out. 'Did I wake you up?' He held her to his shoulder and gently jiggled her against him. Her sobbing began to subside, and Morton sank down into the chair beside her cot. Holding her small hands in his, he stood her up on his thighs, and her brown eyes widened as she blinked away her final tears. She looked a comic sight, bouncing up and down with glee, as her dark brown hair—too short to be styled or tied back—shot about in its own dogmatic direction.

Morton's eyes began to adjust to the low light. The room was painted in soft pink and white, complemented by drawings of rabbits and flowers in the same colour scheme—a far cry from the room to which they had brought her home eleven months ago. Owing to a slight blunder at the twenty-week scan, they had decorated the room in various shades of blue, believing that they would be having a boy. Morton grinned now at the mix-up. It was their own stupid fault—they had been warned by the nurse conducting the scan that she had not been completely certain of the baby's gender.

'She can come downstairs now and I'll feed her,' Juliette called up.

'Shall we go and have some dinner?' Morton said to Grace, in a strange, childlike voice which he reserved for dogs and infants. 'Shall we? Go and see Mummy?' He carried her down the stairs to the kitchen. 'What's on the menu, then?' he asked.

Juliette lifted up a small blue pot containing some home-made concoction of hers. 'Dover sole, butternut squash, apple and kale.'

'Delicious,' Morton enthused to Grace, as he sat her in the highchair. 'Think I'll give that one a miss, though. I meant what are *we* having?'

'Whatever *you're* making, darling,' she said, pointedly.

'Fish and chips?' he suggested.

'Perfect,' Juliette answered, heating up the baby food on the hob.

'Hello, by the way,' Morton said, kissing her. 'Did you have a productive day?'

She stared at him as though he had just asked the most ludicrous question in the world. 'I haven't even got around to getting dressed; that says it all.'

'You'll miss it when you go back to work on Wednesday, though.'

'Of course I will, I'm absolutely dreading it,' she answered. 'The only good thing being—' she placed her hands over Grace's ears, '—

that I'll have adults to talk to.' She removed her hands from Grace's head, kissed her on the forehead and began to spoon some of the indistinguishable mush into her mouth.

'Do I not count as an adult, then?'

Juliette's look of incredulity answered the question for her.

'Right, on that note,' Morton began, 'I'm heading out for a take-away. Any fish preference?'

'Skate wing or plaice, if they've got it, thanks.'

'See you in a few minutes,' Morton called, heading back out the front door.

Pulling his coat tight, he sauntered up the cobbles of Mermaid Street, then down The Mint to Marino's fish and chip shop. Come rain or shine, there was always a queue to be found here and today was no exception. But it was always worth the wait; they did the best fish and chips in Rye. Morton stood in line, scrolling through the camera roll on his mobile. Hundreds—thousands—of pictures of Grace over the last few months gave way to the images which he had just taken of Arthur Fothergill's gold guinea. When he thought of this latest case, an edgy sensation rose in his stomach. What was it about it that bothered him so much? He still could not put his finger on the problem. Maybe it was just the anxiety of starting up another complex case. The ones, which he had taken on since Grace's birth, had been standard, simple ones which had been completed with little fuss and little travel from home; this one felt as though—given his circumstances—he might have bitten off rather more than he could chew. How many records did he think existed between 1820 and 1827, anyway? He guessed he would find out tomorrow when he commenced work on the case.

The queue shifted, and Morton shuffled forwards, closer to the tantalising waft of hot batter. He slowly swiped through the images of Grace with a wide grin on his face. Time had implausibly vaulted since her birth and that helpless thing which they had brought home from the William Harvey Hospital now had her own discrete personality. The most recent photographs and videos of Grace were of her standing unaided. Incredible.

'Hello?' a voice said, not for the first time, Morton realised, pocketing his mobile.

'Sorry,' he said to the grinning man behind the counter. 'Two portions of plaice and chips, please.'

'Coming right up.'

After a short wait, Morton was presented with two open packets of food, which he doused in salt and vinegar, then began the short trek back home, all the while trying to resist the tormenting smell floating up from the take-away bag.

Arriving home, he didn't want to make the same mistake as earlier, so he crept inside and noiselessly closed the front door behind him. Silence.

He popped his head around the lounge door and smiled. Juliette, mouth gaping wide, was fast asleep on the sofa and in her hand, she was clutching the baby video monitor, which meant that Grace was back in her cot asleep. Despite the fish and chips being ready to eat, he decided to let Juliette sleep, so he slowly snuck up the stairs to his study and quietly pushed the door closed.

Sitting down, he unravelled one of the packets and began to devour the food, as though he had not eaten in several weeks. As he ate, he looked at the four framed photographs which were perched on the edge of his desk; individual pictures that formed the portrait of his fragmented family. On the left was the first ever photo of Grace, taken just minutes after she had been born. She was in his arms wrapped tightly in a white knitted blanket, quietly staring at him, as tears streamed down his tired face.

Morton shoved a piece of fish into his mouth as his eyes moved on to the next photograph on his desk—his adoptive parents and adoptive brother, Jeremy. He sighed as he stared at them, recalling the day when, at sixteen years of age, the man whom he had called Dad, Peter, blurted out the truth: that he had been adopted. It had taken another twenty-three years for him to reveal finally the identity of his biological mother: Peter's sister, Margaret, the person he had spent his entire life calling 'Aunty'.

The adjacent photograph was the sole known image of Morton's biological mother and father together. It had been taken on the 5th January 1974—the last day that the two of them would ever spend with one another. It was a photo which often drew his attention whilst he would sit here at the desk. Sometimes, he fantasised about a different life—one where his biological parents had raised him together. The reverie often played out like a choose-your-own-adventure story, where sometimes his father, Jack—an American—would return to England upon discovering that he was going to be a father and the three of them would live happily ever after in a Kentish seaside cottage. Other times, his pregnant Aunty Margaret would defy the will of those

100

encouraging her to give up the child and instead take herself off to the East Coast of America, where the three of them would live in a house on the shores of Cape Cod.

He smiled at his indulgent sentimentality and looked at the final photograph on his desk: his and Juliette's wedding day eighteen months ago. The photographer had done his best in trying to Photoshop out the black eye that Morton had received when the genealogical case upon which he had been working had turned violent. The case had made the headlines of the local newspapers after Morton had inadvertently unearthed a seventy-year child-selling racket. The two perpetrators, Shaohao Chen and Tamara Forsdyke were now both serving five-year prison sentences for their parts in the case. The wall in front of Morton, upon which he collated evidence from his genealogical investigations, had been rammed with information pertaining to this difficult case. Now, it was entirely empty.

He threw a handful of chips into his mouth, wiped his greasy fingers onto his jeans, then took a piece of plain paper and wrote 'Ann Fothergill' in large letters and stuck it in the centre of the wall.

The Fothergill Case had begun.

Almost an hour later, Morton's initial investigations ended when a bedraggled Juliette stumbled into the room. 'I feel like death,' she said, slumping down dramatically onto the floor.

'You look like death,' Morton agreed.

'Thanks. Is my dinner cold?'

Morton placed his hand on the remaining packet of fish and chips. 'Yep. Time of death…about an hour ago.'

Juliette groaned. 'You should have woken me up.'

'Yeah, that would have gone down well. I'll go and warm them up for you,' Morton said, sliding out from behind his desk. 'Come downstairs with me and I'll tell you about the case I've just started.' He pointed at the wall. Colourful string now threaded out from Ann Fothergill's name to a small collection of papers which related to her life.

'Oh God, please don't,' Juliette replied, following him down the stairs. 'I think it'd more than I can take. Just heat up the food, stick the television on and let me snuggle up next to you.'

'Okay,' Morton said with a laugh.

They entered the kitchen and Juliette slumped down at the table, using her arm as a pillow.

With precision timing, Grace began to wail. Morton looked at Juliette and grinned.

Chapter Three

The day was miserable. The whole of the town of Rye—so heavily reliant on tourism—seemed to sit glumly under the despair of the dismal clouds that lingered overhead. Morton had cranked the central heating right up and had even resorted to pulling on his thick winter cardigan to try and counteract the dreariness of the day. He stared out of his study window through the incessant rain to the wet cobbles below. He hadn't clapped eyes on a single soul for several minutes.

'Come on, get back to it,' he told himself. He needed to make good use of the next three days; Juliette had taken Grace to visit her mum, Margot, leaving a strangely quiet house behind. He strolled over to the investigation wall. Below Ann Fothergill's name, Morton had added the key dates for his research: 1820-1827. A *very* small window of time. Pre-census and pre-civil registration, it was a period not exactly renowned for its abundance of genealogical records. However, in order to understand those seven years of Ann's life, he needed to have as complete a picture as possible of the years which had preceded and succeeded them. Arthur had furnished Morton with copies of the 1841, 1851 and 1861 censuses. In each of them, Ann was described as a publican and living at the same property: Honey Pot House, Castle Avenue, Dover, Kent. Other residents, including an impressive array of domestic servants and her son, William Fothergill, came and went across the three decades.

The last official document of Ann's life was her death certificate. She had died 2nd December 1869, aged sixty-six years at Honey Pot House. Her cause of death was listed as 'paralysis and age'. The informant of the death was her son, William, who had been 'in attendance'. According to the scant reference details of Ann's will, which Morton had accessed last night on the Ancestry website, William had inherited a substantial sum from his mother: '...effects under £12,000'. Morton had then placed an order for a full copy of her will.

About Ann's early life prior to the period in question, Arthur had given him very little information. Morton logged on to the FindmyPast website and typed 'Ann Fothergill' into the search box of their newspaper collection. The top result, dated 10th December 1820, was the report from which Arthur had yesterday quoted significant excerpts: '*Maidstone Petty Sessions. Saturday—Before the Mayor (R.Haynes, Esq.) and J.L. Lowry, Esq—thirty-sixth appearance of Ann Fothergill, a woman charged with being drunk and disorderly in Strond Street, Dover, on the night of 26th November; also charged with assaulting Police Constable Pennells; also charged with having wilfully, and against the peace of His Majesty the King, very much alarmed the inmates of the Compass Inn, Strond Street, and broken one of the windows of that establishment, to the value of 5s. Mr William Driver, landlord of the Compass Inn, said that on the previous evening the lady, who had so frequently honoured the bench with her presence, came to his house in a happy state of inebriation, and evidently labouring under the effects of some 'slight sensations', which rendered her conduct highly reprehensible. On seeing her in this state he politely told her to leave the house, when without the slightest cause she placed herself in an attitude to fight, and ultimately threw a pot at his head which fortunately missed it. She then with the 'pride and dignity of a queen', walked towards the door as though she was disgusted and intended to leave the house, but upon opening the door, was confronted by Police Constable Pennells. Prisoner then picked up a chair and threw it with malicious intent at the officer, striking the side of his head. The prisoner, an illiterate vagrant, was according to Superintendent Blundell, only liberated from prison on the previous morning. His Worship expressed his regret that the Court could not dispose of her permanently, for she appeared to be a perfect pest to society. She was then committed to prison for two months.'*

Morton finished reading the article with a slight smile on his face. She certainly was an interesting character, he thought, as he printed the report and fixed it to the investigation wall. He returned to the newspaper search results and worked through the remaining stories. The bulk of Ann's thirty-six crimes had been recorded in the papers. The vast majority were for being drunk and disorderly. According to the various articles dealing with her criminal propensities, they had begun in 1817 when Ann was just fourteen years old; the final mention of a criminal act—at least for which she had been charged—had occurred in 1821. Morton concentrated on this particular report, wondering what had changed after this moment: *'18th October 1821, Maidstone Petty Sessions. Ann Fothergill, a well-known visitor to the bench, was charged with stealing a pair of shoes, the property of Mr R. Cousins, of Dover. The prisoner pleaded guilty and was sentenced to two months hard labour.'*

Morton wondered what had taken place following her release. Judging by the lack of reports, her criminality had ceased. Perhaps she had seen the error of her ways, he wondered, or perhaps she had simply become better at not being caught.

He read Ann's letter of 1827, making salient notes as he went: *Sam—departure. Settled 'out there'—Ann worried for him. Difficult years in the local area—quiet now (July 1827). Wicked deeds of the past (her crimes / his crimes?). Gold guineas hidden nearby.*

Sitting back in his chair, Morton re-read the letter several times, on each occasion possible scenarios springing into his mind, but with nothing quite fitting. He stuck the letter to the wall and moved on to the photos of the gold guineas. Having zoomed in to the photograph of the coin and establishing that it was dated 1810, Morton ran exhaustive searches online. Described as 'The Third Guinea,' they had been issued between 1797 and 1813, owing to a shortage of gold in Britain caused by the Napoleonic Wars. Morton thought back to Ann's letter. Could they be the 'difficult years' to which she had referred? It seemed a bit of a stretch, given that it was all over by 1815, some twelve years before the letter had been written. Just as Arthur's nephew had suggested, a coin of this period and in this condition, was worth around a thousand pounds. It was little wonder that the nephew was practically salivating over the frankly ridiculous prospect of discovering long-lost barrel-loads of them.

Morton opened a packet of blank postcards and began to transcribe the key events of Ann's life onto separate cards, attaching each to the bottom of the wall. Stepping back to take in the complete timeline, he could clearly see the gap between Ann's final court appearance on the 18th October 1821 and writing the letter to Sam on the 22nd July 1827. He needed some records to help fill in that gap—but what?

An odd drain-like gurgle erupted from Morton's stomach. He was hungry. He looked at the time: it was only just gone eleven in the morning—coffee time, he reasoned, strolling downstairs to the kitchen.

Switching on the kettle, he smiled as his eyes came to rest on the adornment hanging just above it: a piece of snow-fence wood, upon which had been painted a northern cardinal—a beautiful and striking red bird from North America. It had been painted by his Aunt Alice and given to him and Juliette as a present last summer, when they had visited Cape Cod to try to track down Morton's elusive biological father. The sight of it made him smile every time, epitomising, as it did for him, their incredible honeymoon.

He selected the largest mug upon which he could lay his hands; one concealed at the back of the cupboard and one so large that it would surely have been confiscated by Juliette, had she known of its existence. He lifted up the coffee jar and, with absolute horror, opened the lid to find it empty. Not a single coffee granule. Just a note: '*I needed it more. You need to cut down xx*'

Morton couldn't help but chuckle and slightly agree; his already-high coffee consumption had skyrocketed since Grace's birth. Rummaging in the cupboard for anything resembling caffeine, all he could find were attractive boxes whose labels looked as though they were describing the undergrowth in his back garden. Nettle. Echinacea. Rosehip. Hibiscus. Elderflower.

Delicious. Time to brave the delightful English weather, then, he decided, heading into the hallway and pulling on his thick winter coat and boots.

Outside was every bit as ghastly as it had appeared from his study window. With a grimace, he hurried down the steps of his house onto Mermaid Street, pulling his coat tight and keeping his head down, as he marched up the road. He was not in the mood to sit in a café today—he just wanted to get a drink and get back to his work and, since he was supposed to be cutting down on coffee, knew just the place.

Morton made it most of the way along the High Street before he passed a single other person, the town having yet to wake from its winter slumber. He continued along to where the High Street seamlessly gave onto East Cliff. His destination, a modest building situated beside the ancient Landgate Arch, drew into sight: Knoops. Stepping under the white canopy bearing the shop name, Morton was relieved to enter the warm building.

'Ah, good morning,' the proprietor, Jens Knoop, greeted with a smile from behind the counter.

'Morning,' Morton replied, shaking the water from himself like a dog, small puddles forming on the stone floor around him.

'Lovely day,' Jens said.

'Isn't it just,' Morton agreed.

'What can I get you?' Jens asked, glimpses of an almost-indiscernible Germanic accent coming through.

Morton reached for a napkin and wiped his rain-soaked face. Behind the counter were hanging fifteen clipboards, each of them—headed with numbers ranging from 28% to 100%—indicating a different type of hot chocolate. The best hot chocolate in the world in Morton's opinion. 'I'll go for the 67% today, please,' he chose. *Dark chocolate. Single origin (Madagascar). Notes of liquorice, blueberry and coffee.* Even Juliette couldn't complain about a 'note of coffee.'

'Okay,' Jens replied. 'And how is your little daughter?'

'She's great, thank you. She'll be a year old in a couple of weeks. God only knows where that time's gone,' Morton said, gazing through the misty window panes to the adjoining Landgate Arch, one of his favourite buildings in the town. He often tried to imagine it when it had been built in 1340, giving Rye—then an island—the only connection with land at high tide, its history quietly stowed away behind its thick stone façade, which still served as the main vehicular entrance to the High Street.

Jens smiled as he made the drink. 'Such a lovely age.'

'Yes,' he answered, his thoughts drifting back to Grace's birth.

Then it struck him that there was one thing which he had failed to add to the gap in the timeline: the birth of Ann's son, William. Owing to the year, obtaining a birth certificate for him was impossible, but locating his baptism should not be. Morton struggled to recall where the census had said that William had been born.

'Here you go,' Jens said, presenting him with a take-away cup. 'Enjoy.'

'Thanks very much, Jens.' Morton paid for the drink, said goodbye and, with a renewed burst of energy, hurried out into the wet morning.

He arrived home, kicked off his boots and hung his soaked coat out to dry, then bounded up the stairs to his study. Standing in front of the investigation wall, he took his first sip of the drink, relishing the hot chocolate's glow slowly pervading through him, gradually warming his insides. Perfection.

Morton removed the 1851 census from the wall, running his finger down to the residents of Honey Pot House: Ann Fothergill, her son and five domestic staff. He traced along the line of William's details. He was unmarried, aged twenty-six, and his occupation was stated as being 'assistant publican'. His place of birth was given as Aldington in Kent.

Morton did a quick mental calculation. William had been born around 1825. He had heard of Aldington, but didn't know much about it. A quick Google search later and he had learned that it was a rural village eight miles outside of Ashford in Kent, situated on a steep escarpment overlooking Romney Marsh, with a population of just over one thousand people. Hoping that Aldington was one of the 127 Kent parishes covered by the FindmyPast record collection, Morton typed in William's details. He was in luck.

Name: William Fothergill

Baptism date: 2nd July 1825
Relationship: son
Parents: Ann Fothergill, a single woman
Residence: Aldington

Morton noted the new details onto a postcard and added it to the chasm in the timeline. Without a precise date of birth, it was impossible to gauge accurately when William had been conceived. Given that most baptisms occurred at some point within the first three months of a baby's life, it was likely that William had been conceived in the summer months of 1824. It was reasonable to suppose that he had been conceived in the village of his baptism, Aldington. Morton wrote the village name on his notepad of next steps to pursue.

As he looked at the entirety of the investigation wall, it was hard to imagine Ann's seismic shift from an illiterate vagrant criminal to a literate wealthy property-owning businesswoman.

The bubble of his thoughts was lanced by the ringing of the home phone. 'Hello?'

'Hi there,' came the cheerful greeting. It was Jack, his biological father.

'Hi, Jack—how are you?' Morton asked, glancing at the clock. 'You're up very early.'

'Best part of the day. Yeah, we're all good here, thanks. How's my little granddaughter?'

Morton brought Jack up to date with Grace's latest exploits, despite the fact that it had only been a handful of days since their most recent video call.

'So, I got your email,' Jack started, 'and just wanted to quickly say that the three of us would like it—if it's okay with you—to come over for little Grace's birthday? I mean, she's my only grandchild, I don't want to miss it.'

Morton paused, a little too long.

'Not if it's a trouble, though,' Jack added.

'No, no trouble,' Morton stammered. 'Erm... It's just that... My Aunty Margaret is also planning on coming...'

'Oh. I see.'

There was another pause in the conversation as the two men weighed up the situation.

'Well,' Jack began, 'I for one would love to see her again, unless you think she wouldn't like it?'

Morton drew in a long breath. He had no idea whether she would like it, or not. The last time that they had spoken about it, on Christmas Day in 2014, she had made him promise that he wouldn't tell her *anything* about his search for his biological father. But he desperately would love Jack, his wife, Laura and their son—Morton's half-brother, George—to be at Grace's first birthday. Now what? Now, he took a monstrously *huge* gamble. 'I'm sure she'll be fine, too,' Morton said coolly. 'That would be amazing to have you all there. Fantastic.'

'Listen, I'm going to give you a couple of days to speak with Margaret before I go ahead and book the flights. We can come another time when it's less... awkward for you.'

'No,' Morton insisted. 'Book the flights.'

'You're sure?'

'Totally. You can stay here with us. I think Aunty Margaret was planning on treating herself to a few nights in the Mermaid, so we'll have the space.'

'Okay,' Jack replied. 'I'll get right onto it.'

'See you soon, then,' Morton said with a wide smile.

'See you, then, son. Goodbye.'

Morton put the phone down and stared at it for an inordinate amount of time, as he replayed their conversation in his head. 'Oh. My. God,' he said to himself, with a nervous chuckle. An odd tenseness tightened in his stomach. What on earth was he going to say to Aunty Margaret? What should be the epitome of normality—his mother and father together to celebrate their granddaughter's first birthday—felt to him like the unfolding of a very large train wreck.

Morton pulled out his mobile phone and selected his Aunty Margaret from the contact list.

Phil was bored. He was sitting in the lounge of his council flat, flipping the gold guinea up in the air, playing *heads or tails*. Pointless, really; there was just him home, sitting here in front of his laptop watching the time slowly counting down on his eBay auction listing. *Heads it sells. Tails it doesn't.* He flipped the coin, just as the time turned red, indicating that the listing had less than one minute to run. *Tails.*

'Damn it,' he said, as if the outcome of the sale really was in the hands of the flipping of a coin.

The bid changed. £650.

Forty-seven seconds to go.

'Come on,' he grumbled.

Thirty-two seconds.

New bid. £890.

'Yes!' he enthused, slamming his fist onto the desk, making the coin leap.

Twenty-two seconds.

£950.

'Come on, new bidder!'

Sixteen seconds.

£1,020.

He clenched his fists and leapt up, unable to contain his excitement.

Five seconds.

£1,120.

Listing Closed.

Phil yelped with delight, picked up the gold guinea and kissed it.

Chapter Four

4th March 1821, Aldington, Kent

An unusual sound stirred Ann Fothergill from fitful sleep. With a grimace, she turned onto her side, plucking at an aberrant piece of straw which protruded through the palliasse on which she lay. The sound—if there had even been one, which she now doubted—had stopped. She pulled the woollen blanket up to her chin and drew her knees to her chest to ease the shivering. As with most mornings, her first thoughts turned to drink, specifically rum and water. Just one or maybe two glasses usually saw her straight.

She rocked onto her back and turned towards the fire grate. Nothing but soot. Now that she was awake, she really ought to get up and remake it. If not for her sake, then for his.

Reluctantly she stood up, tugging the blanket around her shoulders, and approached his bed. His eyes were shut and his mouth slightly agape. Same as she found him most mornings. Most of the time, in fact.

Ann pressed her hand gently to his forehead. Her fingers met with a light dampness and she peeled back one of the several layers of blanket which covered him from chin to toe.

A short, grating groan emanated from his throat as his head rolled to face towards the shuttered window.

She heard the sound again—raised voices from downstairs, she realised. One voice was undoubtedly that of the mistress, Hester, but the other belonged to a man. Deep and hoarse. Most irregular-sounding in a house which, for the past three weeks, had contained just two women and the young boy, John. The man's voice both intrigued and perturbed her. Who was he and what was he doing here?

She padded lightly over to the door. It was open—as it always had to be, one of the many strict conditions imposed upon her by the mistress. With her neck craned towards the direction of the conversation, she raised a hand to cup her ear. She sniffed in annoyance, hearing nothing but low murmurings. Deliberate, no doubt to stop her from hearing.

Ann sniffed again as she heard the stairs moaning under the weight of two sets of feet. She was half-minded not to move. After all, she wasn't doing anything wrong. The mistress had said nothing about standing by the door. But what about the man? He could be anyone. She quickly stole from her position and just managed to flop down onto her palliasse before Hester waltzed into the room with a deliberate touch of the dramatic. She clutched at the tips of her shawl, as though it might fly away of its own volition, were she to let go.

The gentleman behind her—and from his fine blue coat and high black polished boots, Ann knew that he certainly was a gentleman—stooped down to get under the low door frame. He was in his mid-thirties and a fine figure of a man.

'This be a surgeon—a *real* surgeon,' Hester blurted, nodding in Ann's direction as she laboured the word 'real'.

'Doctor Papworth-Hougham,' he introduced, the front curls of his long black hair dipping over his eyes with the nonchalant tip of his head. He pushed back against the fallen locks with the thin fingers of his left hand, placed his red leather case down beside the bed, and then turned to the patient.

'Nice to be a-meeting a man in your profession,' Ann said, tucking her lank hair behind her ears. For his benefit, she plumped out her chest.

The doctor ignored her, placing his hand on Samuel's fevered brow.

Hester scowled in Ann's direction and then addressed the doctor. 'This be my Sam. He be a-bearing this fever for twenty days now.'

'He was one of the Battle of Brookland men?' the doctor enquired.

'That be right—terrible business,' Hester confirmed. 'Almost left me a widow.' She began to run her hands over her protruding belly, as though trying to elicit the future from a crystal ball.

'From the mess that I saw the following morning, he's lucky to still hold his life. Many men on both sides fell that night.'

Hester eyed Ann. 'I be so sorry, Doctor, for not a-bringing you in sooner, only I were led to believe that this *woman* had dealings in medicine and could be helping him. Not to say that I bain't been well meself of late.'

'A doctor, are you?' he asked, throwing a glare in Ann's direction.

'No, I-'

'No, of course you're not,' he retorted.

'Be a-waiting downstairs,' Hester yapped at Ann.

Ann was inclined to stay and argue but what was the point? She didn't care a jot for the bruff opinions of the mistress, or the doctor for that matter. She nodded and flounced from the room, mimicking the theatrics of Hester's arrival. As she descended the stairs, she heard Hester muttering, 'She be on her way, soonest.'

Downstairs, Ann knelt in front of the fire, raising her chilled hands to within inches of the flames. The pleasure of the heat stinging her skin quickly turned to pain and she dropped her hands into her lap, accepting the news that she was headed back to vagrancy with numb indifference. It was the only life which she had ever known. Truth be told, she would be glad to leave and get back to the uncontrolled and scabrous backstreets of town life. Country dwelling was not the life for Ann Fothergill.

Movement outside drew her attention. It was the boy, John, playing some made-up game or other with another boy of a similar age. It had surprised her how fond she had grown of the lad, believing there not to have existed a single maternal bone in her body.

'Ann!' It was the mistress calling. 'Be a-coming up here, dreckly-minute.'

Ann heaved the blanket tight around her shoulders and began to climb the stairs, all the while readying herself for a berating.

Hester, hands on hips, met her at the door. 'The doctor be wanting to know what you be doing to my Sam. Three-week of fever like he got, he be a-needing his blood-letting.'

Ann glanced past Hester's dark eyes to the doctor, who was leaning over the bed in the process of removing the dressing from Samuel's shoulder.

'I be doing what I thought best,' Ann replied airily.

'His wound—it's almost healed,' the doctor said, unable to contain his astonishment. His eyes narrowed suspiciously as he gazed at Ann, holding up the dressing. 'Where did you learn to do this?'

Hester gasped and ran a hand to her chest. 'Witchcraft! Lord, what have I brung upon this house?'

The doctor placed a placating hand on her shoulder. 'Please, let her speak. Her answer rather intrigues me.'

'My father—well, he bain't my father, he be just the man what helped raise me—he were a travelling apothecary.'

The doctor touched his neat beard, as if deliberating the truth of her explanation. 'I see. *My* father was a surgeon-apothecary. Tell me your procedure.'

Ann looked uneasily at the doctor, and then at Hester whose contorted face continued to express her disbelief. 'I pulled out the shot, washed the wound with water then made him a poultice.'

'From what was the poultice made?' the doctor probed.

'Some herbs. Few other bits and pieces.' Ann shrugged indifferently.

'Specifically?'

'Comfrey root to slow infection. Sage for antiseptic. Bit of willow bark, which got traces of opium for the fever and pain relief.'

'Very good,' he praised.

She noticed for the first time that the doctor's face had softened. She gave him a soft smile, which he returned.

'What of that foul-stenching tea you be a-making night and day?' Hester snarled.

'Willow bark tea with mutton broth.'

'I think you have saved this man's life,' the doctor acknowledged.

Hester turned resentfully. 'If he be a-living, then it be God's own wishes, not some *travelling apothecary*.'

'Whether it be God's work, witchcraft or this woman's affinity for natural cures and medicines, the outcome will be that your husband lives.'

'But the blood-letting for his fever?' Hester demanded.

'His fever is almost gone. I do not think blood-letting would advance his recovery. My advice would be to allow this woman to continue with her work,' he said, picking up his case and making for the door. 'See to it that she has all that she needs. Good day, Mrs Banister.' He paused as he neared Ann and offered her his hand. 'A pleasure to meet you, Miss..?'

'Fothergill—Ann Fothergill,' she beamed.

The doctor nodded, ducked his head under the doorframe and ventured downstairs, closely followed by the mistress.

Ann tossed her head back and grinned. She sat on Samuel's bed— breaking one of the mistress's rules—and waited. She heard more mumbled conversation, then the street door opening and closing. Then, the mistress appeared at the doorway.

'So, what do you be a-needing?' she asked.

'A mug or two of rum,' she began. 'A nice bath—I ain't got me numbers enough to know how many days be passing since the last one. And some new clothes.'

'No,' Hester snapped. 'That bain't happening. The doctor was a-meaning things to help my husband get better.'

114

Ann gazed dreamily towards the shuttered window, as if she had all the time in the world. 'Maybe my witchcraft be stopping to work, then, and your husband be dying.' Ann shrugged her shoulders.

With a dramatic huff, Hester turned from the room and stormed down the stairs.

Ann grinned once more.

'You be a-knowing this,' Hester called, as she marched back up the stairs, 'Dreckly-minute my Sam wakes from his fever, you be back out on them streets.' Hester had reached the top of the stairs and stood with her hands on her hips.

'I be welcoming it, Mistress, I really do.'

'Back to *prison*. Oh, yes, I be a-knowing all about you. *Thirty* times in gaol.'

'Thirty-six by my reckoning,' Ann corrected with a half-smile.

'Thievings, beatings, drunkenness, lewdness—God forgive me what I brung under my own roof. You just be a-keeping your distance from my boy,' Hester bawled, with a glance upwards, before thrusting an open palm towards Ann. 'Here.'

'What be this?' Ann asked suspiciously, seeing three guineas in her outstretched hand.

'It be all I got. Be a-taking your bath and rum someplace else—not here.'

Ann snatched at the money, barged past Hester and strutted down the stairs and out of the street door.

Knowing that Hester was certain to be peering out through the cracks in the shutters, Ann did a fancy twirl, holding her skirt and circling round and round, just as she had once seen the Parisian dancing troupe doing at the Royal Theatre in Dover. She laughed gaily as she pirouetted from the cottage, clutching the guineas tightly in her fist.

The cold cloaked and wrapped itself around her body just as assuredly as if it had been a layer of imperceptible clothing. Her fingers, having turned a peculiar hue of light mauve, were burning from where the blood had retreated, as she pushed down the iron latch to enter the Walnut Tree Inn.

She walked haughtily inside, as though she were royalty, and marched towards the bar, where she propped herself up on one elbow on the wooden bar top. This being her first visit here, she took stock of the room. For such a rural tavern it was fair lively, the tables filled with the usual agricultural labourers cotchering over an ale or two. She inhaled blissfully, the hot smoky air thrusting out the last vestiges of the wintry outside from her lungs.

'What do you be wanting?' a short, bearded man asked from behind the bar. His hair was ragged and straw-like and he wore a smock stained to such a degree that it was impossible to identify its original colour.

'Three pints of rum and water, thank you, landlord,' Ann ordered, stretching out her throbbing fingers, as the blood began painfully to restore them to life.

'Three, you say?' the man repeated, taking an exaggerated look around her. 'You got two friends tucked somewhere I can't see 'em?' he asked, cocking one eyebrow.

Ann studied him for a moment. He was making no effort to get even one of the drinks, never mind the three which she had ordered. She had met men like him before now. He would most certainly be the landlord of this establishment. 'Listen, I ain't no lushington, I just be needing a drink, is all.'

'That right?' the man said, running his tongue over his decaying front teeth. 'What be your business in Aldington?'

Ann's gaze shifted from the red brick floor to the beamed ceiling, taking her time to respond. She thought on giving any one of several answers that tumbled into her head, none of them true. Her propensity for lying stemmed from the triviality and tedium which often came attached to the truth. She doubted any story—true or made up—would sway this landlord from his decision; he was either going to serve her or he wasn't. For no reason, other than it was the simplest answer in this case, she chose to relate the truth. 'I been up at Braemar Cottage— Samuel Banister's dwelling-house after he were shot smuggling at the Battle of Brookland.'

The landlord scowled, turning his head this way and that. 'Don't be blethering so loud, Miss,' he told her. 'What do you be knowing about smuggling?'

Ann raised her eyebrows. 'Nigh-on all there to know, I shouldn't wonder. The loose tongue of a delirious man don't be having no boundaries. I be knowing all about Cephas Quested and the Aldington Gang. The landing spots all along the Marsh. The lookout places from *certain* public houses perched high on the Aldington knoll. The *landlords* what be selling the contraband.'

'Whist your tongue,' the landlord hissed across the bar. 'Three pints of rum and water and I want no more talk of smuggling—do you hear? You be having no business talking this way.'

Ann nodded indifferently, passing a guinea coin across the bar, and waited for her drinks.

'How does he fare?' the landlord asked eventually, seizing the money and placing one glass of rum on the bar in front of her, before then placing down her change.

'Who?' Ann asked, knowing full well about whom his enquiry was directed.

'Sam Banister,' he said quietly.

'He be doing well. Some fancy surgeon—Doctor Popham-Hopworth or some such—visited today and said he'd be out of bed soonest.'

'Papworth-Hougham,' the landlord corrected. 'He said that, did he?'

'That he did,' Ann confirmed, sinking the first rum in one go and pushing the empty glass back across the bar.

'Then you be moving on your way, I shouldn't wonder,' he said, holding a sneer, which exhibited his two black upper teeth.

It was not a question, but rather a boorish statement, so she didn't answer. 'Don't suppose you be having a bath here, landlord?'

He looked at her silently as he poured the second pint. 'You think this to be a public wash-house?'

Ann placed another guinea down onto the bar and, using one finger, slid it across to him.

'Rose!' the landlord yelled through an open door behind him, placing the second pint of rum and water before her.

A young girl, who Ann thought to be around seventeen and slightly younger than she, sauntered out and glowered at the landlord.

'Run this lady an 'ot bath, will you,' he instructed, setting down the next drink.

The young girl sighed, spoke no words and disappeared through the door.

'Three rum and waters,' the landlord said, placing the last one down.

'One for each hand,' Ann said, picking up the two remaining drinks and taking a gentle sip from each.

'Hey, Miss!' the voice repeated.

117

The words barely filtered into her languid, soporific mind, as though they were trapped behind a net, just out of her reach. She turned listlessly. The room was angled incorrectly and her eyes refused to pull focus onto the origin of the speech.

'You be brown-deep in thought, Miss. I runned you an 'ot bath, like what you asked.'

Ann's mind assembled enough disparate pieces of information for her to understand. She was in the public house. Drinking rum and water. The girl had run her a bath.

She squinted and saw her muddled outline. 'I be wanting your clothes,' she said.

'Pardon me, Miss?'

'Your clothes. One guinea for them,' Ann said, attempting to stand from the bar. She picked up her one remaining drink and carried it towards the girl. She tried to ignore the liquid running over her fingers, intending to rebuke the landlord for daring to serve her drink in a glass pitted with holes. That tarnal rotten-toothed nabbler, she thought.

'Here,' the young girl said, taking Ann by the elbow and leading her into the room behind the bar. The windowless room was dark and lit by just one dancing tallow candle and a sedate fire grumbling in the grate.

Ann's vision was in perfect unison with her thoughts—both swimming in the abstract haze of inebriation. Feelings, worries and ideas all whirled together as insignificant as the items of furniture around the room, which her eyes recognised but which her brain failed to identify.

Ann turned to face the girl. She was standing beside her bathed in soft amber light, entirely naked with her clothes pooled around her ankles.

'A guinea,' the girl said, unfurling her hand.

Ann remembered and placed the remainder of her money there, looking the unabashed girl up and down. 'Ever been with a man?'

The girl shook her head. 'You?'

Ann sniggered. 'One or two. None of them be worthy of a place in my memory.' She smiled. 'Now I got myself a *surgeon*. Doctor Popham-Hopham. *Ralph*. A real gentleman,' Ann boasted, beginning to strip off her clothes.

The girl said nothing more. She turned her back to Ann and disappeared through another door, which she locked with a clatter behind her.

118

Ann stepped heavily down into the bath, wincing at the high temperature, giving her equal jabs of gratification and discomfort. She stood still for a moment, watching as the flesh on her legs that fell below the waterline turned bright pink, whilst the rest of her body erupted in tiny goose bumps.

After several seconds, she sat down in the bath and shuddered as the water nibbled at her bare skin. Wrapping her arms around her knees, she laid her head to one side, allowing her hair to trail in the hot water, and her mind to begin to reverse its current state of disarray.

Sufficient time had passed for the water to become intolerably cold. Ann stood from the bath and dried herself with a towel which the girl had left. The effects of the rum and water still blighted her thoughts but she was once again aware of herself. Aware, as she dressed in the girl's clothes, that she was a slightly different person to the one who had arrived here. A cleansing, of sorts.

She took her time in dressing, enjoying the discovery of the new clothes. Hems, seams and buttons in places not found on her own clothing. She looked at the discarded pile of her garments, carried them over to the fire and tossed them into the flames. The clothes writhed as though containing their own life source, then blackened, before fiery spikes rose and ravaged the material. It took just seconds for the apparel to be unidentifiable. It would have been easy to have simply bundled them up for cleaning, but that was not Ann's way of life. She possessed nothing other than that which she wore.

She ran her fingers through her damp hair, tugging as her nails caught on a knot. Then, she stopped. The low-level rumblings of talking, drinking and laughter, which had unified in providing the background noise to her bath, had altered, as though a maestro had entered the bar and suddenly changed the tempo.

Ann hurried to the door which led to the bar and pressed an ear to the oak frame. Yes, something had changed. There was a kind of excitement. Discussions had heightened. People were speaking over one another, throwing questions to one individual in particular. Ann failed to catch fully what he was saying, his answers being splintered and muffled by the intervening partition.

Ann blew out the candle, pitching the room into near-darkness, then slowly lifted the latch and inched the door ajar. The conversations suddenly came alive, words crystallised. She arranged the sounds in her mind until she found the voice of the man who seemed to have drawn the attention of the inn.

'He didn't give none of you up,' the man imparted. 'He were a true Aldington smuggler to the end.'

She heard murmurs of gratitude before he was questioned again.

'So, do that be that, then?' one asked.

'Aye,' he confirmed. 'That be that; no more smuggling.'

A general groan of discontent erupted from the men around the pub. From the sounds of their unified chorus, everyone had gathered around this news-bearing visitor and they were not happy with what he had come to say.

'I ain't told the worst of it, yet,' the man relayed. The men fell silent to hear the news. 'They tooked the poor bugger to the gallows, now they be wanting to hang his body in chains in the middle of Brookland to steer folk off following his path.'

The news was met with gasps and tirades of incredulity.

'Gracious heart alive!' one shouted.

'I bain't standing to see old Quested's body hanging in the middle of the village—bain't right,' another ranted.

'Disgusting.'

'He not be there long before folk cuts him down and buries him proper, don't you worry.'

'I best make this me last pint if I bain't got no more tub-running duties,' one jested, to the murmured agreement of numerous others.

Ann continued to listen for several minutes more until the questioning of the visitor bearing the news of Cephas Quested's death had ceased. She closed her eyes, fighting against the fog in her mind, trying to retain all that she had heard.

She opened the door and strode confidently through the bar, glancing sideways to the landlord. 'Thank you kindly,' she called, marching out of the street door and into the freezing air. She looked up at the ominously grey sky, certain that snow was imminent.

Thirty-three minutes later, Ann re-entered Braemar Cottage, shivering. She found John in the parlour in front of the burning fire, building a tower from small rectangles of wood.

'Where be your mum, John?' Ann asked, trying to stop her teeth from chattering.

'Upstairs,' he replied, without taking his eyes from the stack in front of him.

Ann touched his mousey hair with a smile.

'Ann! Ann! Do that be you?' Hester shouted from upstairs, her voice nettled and upset-sounding.

Ann rushed up the stairs and into the main bedroom.

'He be back to life!' Hester declared. Her cheeks were lined with tears that plopped from her chin into her lap.

Samuel was sitting up in the bed looking brittle and frail, like a man twice his age, shrinking back from the boundary between life and death. For the first time, he smiled. It was a thin smile which appeared to be effortful. 'Hester be telling me you be saving my life,' he wheezed. He feebly offered his left hand. 'Nice to meet you.'

Ann shook his hand and could not contain her gratification at his recuperation. 'How do you be feeling?'

'Like I been struck by a cart,' he answered. 'You be freezing cold.'

Ann shrugged. 'I be needing to sit by the fire and you be needing rest,' she advised sagely. 'Now be getting some sleep.' She patted his leg and made for the door, followed by Hester.

'The Lord be looking favourable on you today,' Ann said, upon reaching the parlour. Standing with her back to the fire, she folded her arms and held a posture of knowing self-importance.

'What do that little comment supposed to be a-meaning?' Hester snapped.

'He granted your wish—the Aldington Gang be no more.'

'Because why?'

'Because they hanged Cephas Quested,' Ann revealed. 'He went to the gallows at Newgate this morning.'

John looked up, interestedly. 'Hanged him?'

'What?' Hester shrieked. 'Oh, my good merciful Lord! And where did you be a-hearing such blessed news?' Hester begged, doubt quickly abrading her initial elation.

'It be all the talk at the Walnut Tree. Quested be dead and the gang be disbanded.'

'The Aldington Gang be no more,' Hester exhaled, in an almost dreamlike fashion. She moved over to the window and gazed out at the light dusting of snow falling from the sky, repeating to herself in a whisper, 'The Aldington Gang be no more. Thank you, Lord. Thank you.'

'They be hanging his body in chains in the village of Brookland—a warning to others,' Ann added, delighting in her role as news-bearer.

Hester turned. Her eyes locked with Ann's but her thoughts were elsewhere. ''Tis time you be on your way.'

121

'Pardon, Mistress?' Ann said.

'It be time you be a-leaving.'

'Right this moment?' Ann demanded. 'In the snow? It be pretty nigh dark out there.'

Hester raised her shoulders. 'I don't be a-wanting you in my dwelling-house no longer. Good day to you.'

'Do she be going?' John questioned.

'Aye, that be right,' Hester said.

'But I be liking her,' he complained.

Ann crouched down so that she was level with the boy. 'Goodbye, John. I be seeing you around, certain-sure of that.'

Without another word, she raised herself up, opened the street door and stepped out into the dusky late afternoon. The door closed behind her and she stood, barefoot in the white ground with her back to Braemar Cottage.

It was time to move on.

Chapter Five

6th March 1821, Aldington, Kent

'What do you mean, she be gone?' Sam asked. He was sitting up in his bed, cocooned in blankets, watching the snow softly tumbling outside his window, a small pile mounting against the glass pane.

'I be a-meaning that she be gone—went on her way two day ago,' Hester informed him. 'She be a dirty street-vagrant. I don't be a-knowing why it causes you such bother.'

Sam didn't quite know why it bothered him, either; but it did. He touched the ugly scarring on his right shoulder—all but completely healed, now. All because of Ann Fothergill, a stranger who had tended to his wounds for three weeks, but of whom his fever had clouded any lucid recollection. He knew, by the way that Hester spoke of Ann, that she likely had not been treated well in his house, despite her apparent altruism.

'Did she be saying where she were headed?' Sam asked, wincing in pain as he tried to lift his right arm higher than his chest.

Hester shook her head. 'To the godless back streets of Dover, I shouldn't be a-wondering. A black-tan such as she be back in prison before the week be done.'

'Were she treated good here?' Sam asked.

''Course she were,' Hester retorted defensively. 'Now you be a-getting some rest, Samuel.'

Sam slowly swung his legs out of the bed.

'What do you think you be a-doing?' Hester demanded.

'Getting meself some work,' he answered, reaching down to the bed frame for support, as he slowly shifted his weight onto his weak legs and stood up.

'What? I been doing laundry work—we been a-coping fine.'

Sam ignored his wife's pleas and began to walk towards the door, his leg muscles tightening with each new step.

'Sam!' she protested.

'Be looking at *yourself*, Hester—you be giving birth be Lady Day. Then what be happening?'

'Then we be asking the overseers to be a-helping,' Hester said.

'The overseers?' Sam begged. 'Tell me you ain't gone begging to them?'

Hester shook her head. 'Bain't me what went a-begging—it were Ann. It were when I were unwell; we were a-given some mutton, barley and flour.'

'Happen she be saving *all* our lives,' he muttered, continuing to the stairs.

'You be thinking Mister Banks be having you back out on them fields like this?' Hester scorned.

'I bain't going to see Banks—I be going to see Quested to be getting me dues,' Sam snapped, stopping at the top of the stairs to confront his wife.

Hester reached out for his hand. 'Quested be dead, Sam—he were hanged at Newgate.'

Sam felt his calf muscles recoil at the news and he reached out to the wall to steady himself. The events of that last night smuggling spooled through his mind at high speed, before slowing down at the moment when he and Quested had reached the village of Brookland. They had been hidden behind a wall, he remembered that clear as day. Then Quested had got up, handing a pistol to a man who had turned coat and then captured him. And there his memory stopped. Whole days had been irretrievably removed from him, when he had been under Ann Fothergill's spell. He searched the murky blackness of his mind, trying to force himself to remember what had happened next, but his request was rebutted by darkness.

'What were he hanged for?' he asked, already knowing the answer.

'Smuggling—for what do you be thinking?' Hester answered.

With a renewed determination, Sam carefully made his way downstairs. His legs were cramping but he was becoming used to the pain. He hauled on his hat, coat and old boots, then pulled open the street door.

'Sam—don't be so dead-alive! It be a hell of a night out there—at least be a-waiting until mornin',' Hester remonstrated.

Without another glance back, he closed the door, his boots crunching down into the fresh white powder. Through the fissured grey clouds, a strewing of subdued stars and a thin-sliver moon gave him just enough light by which to make his way from Braemar Cottage.

The oppressiveness of the stark skeletal branches of the hedgerow, which lined the narrow lane, was softened by the pristine carpet of white upon which Sam walked. He lumbered along, without hurry, partly due to the resistance from his legs and partly to savour the return of his freedom. Breathing in long gulps of the chill air, he thought

124

again on the fact that he seemed to owe his life to the benevolence of a stranger. A prickly qualm burrowed into his heart at the abruptness with which she had departed. He felt strongly that he owed her something, but then, what could he offer her in exchange for a renewal of his life?

He chewed on the thoughts as he continued towards the village, unable to reach an answer which satisfied him. He came upon his destination with gratitude, hoping that he would be afforded a few moments' rest. Rapping the iron knocker, he stepped back, removing his sodden hat from his head and tapping off the fresh snow.

The door was pulled open by Quested's widow, Martha, a small creature in her early thirties, whose efforts to conceal the grief from her puffy eyes had failed. 'Hello,' she greeted meekly. She took a step back and widened the yawn of the door. 'Come on in.'

Sam entered the cottage, clutching his hat to his chest. The parlour, which he had entered, was tiny and lit by the orange glow of two reed candles on the side dresser. 'I be terrible sorry to hear about your husband,' he said.

Martha nodded but kept her eyes looking to the ground. She mumbled an answer which Sam failed to comprehend.

'And…' he began, but his words caught in his throat. '…with what they be doing with him—you know.'

Martha looked up, perplexed.

'With his body,' he explained.

Understanding pressed through the veneer of sorrow, enlightening her dark eyes and raising her frown. 'His body be here,' she said, tilting her head to the side.

Sam looked in the direction which she had indicated and saw the edge of a coffin.

'It were old Knatchbull, the Ashford magistrate what saved him. Got him brought back to Aldington for a decent Christian burial.'

'It be only right,' Sam agreed, shifting his weight from one leg to the other.

'He weren't a God-fearing man, like. Church weren't ever somewhere he liked to be, but still,' she said. 'Do you be wanting to see him? I be having a raft of folk wanting to pay their respects to him. Go on through.'

Sam baulked at the idea. Although it was normal practice to display the dead at home until burial, he felt his acquaintance with Quested to have been minimal. But now that he was here and now that she was staring at him, encouraging him through, he needed to view the body and pay his respects. Despite himself, he found that he was moving into the adjoining room, which was shrouded in darkness. A single rush light in the corner of the room painted ugly, harrowing shadows on Quested's face.

Sam bowed his head and tried to search his mind for an image of Quested crouching behind the wall in Brookland. He failed. All that he could now see was the darkened soulless face in front of him, which looked to Sam as though it could never have been alive. His skin was grey and his eyes sunken against the rigid contours of his nose.

'How do you be managing, with money I be meaning?' Sam asked, turning his back on Quested's body.

Martha shrugged. 'I bain't managing,' she muttered.

'Before he died, he were talking of having some gold guineas hidden away at his aunt's place,' Sam ventured.

Martha emitted a low laugh of derision. 'That what he been telling you?'

'You never be knowing my husband well. He were full of fanciful tales, full of promises,' she derided. 'Now be looking at him.' Her eyes glistened, as she shot them to the coffin. She folded her arms and met Sam's gaze. 'He died with nothing. Not a shilling. That what you here for? What he be owing from smuggling runs? I bain't got nothing to give you.'

Sam shook his head. 'No, that weren't it. I be wanting to see that you be alright.'

'Thank you,' she replied, although Sam couldn't determine whether she was being genuine or not.

'I best be going,' he said, moving towards the street door. 'Again, I be truly sorry. If there be any help I can be giving…'

'Thank you,' Martha said, following him to the door. 'Goodbye.'

Sam found himself back out in the freezing night, having not had opportunity to rest his tired legs. He was desperate to return home but his work for the night was unfinished.

The aching in his legs determined the slow trudge through the snowy lane. At a fork in the road, he turned away from the village and began to climb a dirt track that wound its way through an unmanaged woodland. Here, his pace further dwindled as the trees obscured what little light there had been and the incline of the hill was nigh-on unbearable. As he ploughed on, thoughts of despair began to creep into his mind. What if he couldn't make it back home? What if he

126

collapsed here? What would happen to Hester, John and the baby? Peculiarly, he thought again of Ann Fothergill, envisioning that she would return heroically to Braemar Cottage to help his family once again. Absurd, he told himself, nudging the thought to one side.

Sam paused as a squat wooden house came into view, cowering under a fleece of white. The combination of the surrounding snow and the flickering amber light from within gave the property a pleasing romantic feel that belied its dilapidated condition. He watched the slow silhouetted movement from inside, whilst giving each leg in turn a brief respite by standing flamingo-like on the other.

Snow had obliterated the path which ran past the house. Sam had been a few times before, casual-labouring for Widow Stewart's now-deceased husband. He had fitted fences here and repaired a stone wall on her boundary, and so knew from memory that the path would bring him perilously close to the house; so, he opted instead to stick to the dark treeline.

He slogged on, putting one foot in front of the other, stumbling and falling at regular intervals over snow-cloaked hazards. By the time he reached the top, Sam had become convinced that the wickedness of his deeds bestowed upon him the misfortune of finding each and every rabbit-hole, boulder or fallen branch.

In every way imaginable, the pigpen was unremarkable and the most unlikely storage facility for a barrelful of gold guineas.

Sam felt a sudden rush of foolishness. His cheeks flushed with anger and, even though nobody knew of his being here, embarrassment. Slumping down on the low wall, Sam finally gave in to the pain in his legs. As he exhaled noisily, the relief from his muscles gripped him.

Several minutes passed and the cold began to permeate through his clothing. He stood again and looked at the pigpen. Now that he was here, he might as well take a look in the cellar. Clambering over the wall, he headed towards the stone enclosure. He poked his head inside the unilluminated room, startling the swine into a panicked squeal. 'Sshh!' he urged, brushing his left foot around the excrement-covered wooden floor, trying to feel for an indentation or perhaps a handle to gain access to the floor below.

His foot caught on something and he reached down, touching with something sticky and wet. He traced the cold surface, realising that it was a pull ring. Exerting some degree of force, he pulled until the heavy door creaked open, falling backwards in a giant stretch.

Sam crouched down and stared below. For all that the blackness revealed, the cellar might have been just a foot deep or the county's deepest cave. Having no method of lighting the space, he had no choice but to try and get inside it. He sat down over the hole and began to dangle his legs into the void. He couldn't feel the bottom. 'Tarnal place be damned!' he yelled.

As far as he could see, he had two choices: he could leave now without the knowledge of what was down there, or he could drop down into the abyss and risk breaking his legs with little possibility of ever getting back out again.

He thought no longer and pushed himself off the edge. He landed with a jolt just a few feet below. He sighed as he glanced up and saw the black outline of an inquisitive pig.

With his hands outstretched in front of him like a blind man, Sam began to search the cellar. It took little time, bouncing off the four walls, to realise that the room was empty. Completely empty. He even shuffled his boots around the stone floor to check that nothing had spilled out.

Sam made one final sweep of the cellar before hoisting himself up into the foul mess of the pigpen floor. Slamming the door shut, he stormed back out, over the wall and down the path beside the house, not caring whether he was seen or not. What was Widow Stewart going to do if she caught him? The woman crawled around her house on all fours, so was hardly likely to rush out brandishing a weapon.

His sense of his own foolishness swelled inside him, mutating into a burning anger towards Quested's departed soul. He cursed the day that he had ever met him. But now, his options were few. With his injured arm, there was no way that he could continue his former work as a labourer. If he couldn't work, then he would be thrown out of the tied cottage. In his heart, he knew the future; could see it like a little galley on the distant horizon, bringing him and his family ever closer to their destiny, to the poorhouse.

Five days later, with no coal, candles or food and down to his last shillings, Sam Banister trudged through the gates of Ruffians Hill Farm, the humiliation of walking through them more injurious than the musket shot to his arm. In front of an open barn were some other men from the village: Thomas Chittenden, James Fry, Thomas Ashdown, Robert Butcher and George Horn. Men whose apparel—tattered and threadbare—revealed the desperateness of their situation. They looked up expectantly but their sudden switch to sullenness made explicit that it was not he for whom they were waiting. Most nodded or made vague murmurings of greeting, before settling their gaze elsewhere. Ruffians Hill Farm, run by the parish to provide provisional work for its unemployed men, was akin to a purgatory for the poorhouse. That the men and their families were just one step away from its doors was a fact implicit in their unsettled behaviour.

Sam moved closer to them but nobody engaged with him. He dug the heel of his right boot into the ground. The fact that it was still frozen from the night's frost and, but for a few muddy crumbs, refused to budge, gave Sam a knotting sense of foreboding.

He, with his practically useless right arm, had much more to fear than the other men. If he could not work here, then he was finished.

'Right!' someone called, striding out from behind the barn. It was Mr Pilcher, tossing down the half a dozen shovels which he had been cradling in his arms. 'Follow me.'

The men bent down, picked up a shovel each and followed him across a muddy yard. They passed other outbuildings and arrogant farmhands tending to the livestock, who turned their backs to the pitiable procession of the parish poor.

They silently crossed another field before reaching their destination: a large dug-out quarry. To one side were four carts with their tailgates open.

'Them four carts need to be filled by the end of the day with good quality flint. It be going down to the new turnpike road, so we don't want no rubbish, clay or mud,' he bawled, 'just good Kentish flint. Anyone not be understanding that?'

The men remained still.

'Get cracking, then,' he instructed.

Sam positioned his hands on the shovel and thrust it downwards, but the hard ground refused the lacklustre effort of his right arm. 'Tarnal hell,' he muttered, trying again. Back and forth he smashed the shovel into the ground, cracking only an inch or so of the icy topsoil open. Changing the positions of his hands, making his left dominant, made little difference.

After several minutes of futile attempts at digging, Sam stood up to take a breath. He took a quick glance over at the other men. They were struggling to break the ground, too but they were at least pulling out rocks and tossing them into the backs of the carts. As he returned his gaze to the ground beneath him, he caught Mr Pilcher's curious stare.

129

With a redoubled effort, Sam plunged the shovel into the earth, managing to reveal a small nugget of flint. He dug the clay loose from beneath the stone then prised it free with his hands. Feeling a minor sense of triumph, he flung it into the nearest cart.

He poised the shovel, ready to strike again when an odd sound caused him to look up. It was Mr Pilcher, clapping his hands in Sam's direction. Sam paused to blink the sweat from his eyes.

'You be thinking we got four hundred years to finish the turnpike road?'

'No,' Sam answered.

'So, you be thinking that the overseers be full of money, then?'

'No,' Sam repeated, about to explain about the weakness in his right arm but then thought better of it. Every man had a story, a reason for being here.

'Then you best get digging, you little black-tan, or I be telling the overseers that you be owed nothing.'

Sam funnelled his anger into the shovel and plunged it hard into the ground. His endeavours, however, produced little effect against the mocking earth.

In a roar of frustration, Sam launched the shovel in Mr Pilcher's direction. 'Damn the overseers, damn the turnpike road and damn you, Mr Pilcher.'

Sam staggered into the Walnut Tree Inn, exhaustion having consumed every part of him. 'Pint of ale,' he stammered breathlessly.

'Merciful Lord, Sam Banister—you be a-looking pretty nigh-ready for the grave,' the landlord remarked.

Sam could not find the words to answer. He sat at the bar and slumped down into the crook of his elbow. Against the wooden bar top, he sensed the reverberation of his drink being placed down close to his head.

'Six pence,' the landlord said.

'I be getting this,' someone said from beside him.

Sam sat up and met with the inky eyes of George Ransley. 'Thank you,' he said, quiet suspicion rising inside him. He stared at Ransley. He had very dark hair and eyes, the ruddy complexion typical of a carter, and a grubby gabardine. The feature which most drew attention, and of which he was self-conscious, was his projecting upper teeth.

Ransley twitched, seemingly anxious. He glanced around him, catching the inquisitive gaze of the landlord. He leant in closer to Sam and spoke softly: 'What do you be thinking about the Aldington Gang?'

Sam shrugged, uncertain of the meaning behind Ransley's question. 'A good thing for some it be done and a bad thing for others,' he said, gesturing to the working folk around the room, who had relied on the extra income which they had derived from smuggling.

'And what if we don't be letting it be over?' Ransley whispered, taking a glug from his beer.

'Same answer,' Sam said. 'Good for some, not so good for some. And, it be needing someone with money to be leader.'

Ransley drank more beer and grinned. He drew his mouth close to Sam's ear. 'I got the means but I be needing a deputy. What say you, Sam Banister?'

Sam was taken aback. 'Me?' Whatever the fortunes of others, *his* days smuggling were over. As a demonstration, he attempted to lift his right arm past chest height, but it was impossible. 'My last tub were dumped in the Pig's Creek Sewer a few week ago and I don't be wanting no more of it.'

He tapped Sam on the head. 'That still be working alright?'

Sam nodded his head. 'Yes.' He thought of Hester, John and the new baby and the fact that he had almost died in the last smuggling run. It was too dangerous and Hester, having lost two brothers to the trade, would never forgive him.

'I be needing a right-hand man. Someone to help organise.'

'That right?' Sam responded doubtfully. 'Why me?'

'You be almost family... I be needing a fellow what can be trusted and I be thinking Sam Banister be that fellow.' Ransley sank the last of his beer, belched loudly and drew in a long breath. 'What say you?'

'No, that be what I say,' Sam said. 'Hester—you know what she be like.'

'Aye—not keen on me—but I be offering three guinea a week, no matter what runs be happening,' Ransley offered, folding his arms. 'Another two after each successful run. Even my dear Hester not be minding that.'

Sam ran his fingers through his hair. The offer of so much money suddenly flipped the firmness of his decision into the void where thoughts of what he could do for his family and the possibility of keeping them out of the poorhouse vied with thoughts of remaining alive for them. 'And no tub-running?' he clarified.

131

Ransley shook his head. 'No tub-running.'

'I be offering you this,' he found himself saying, 'one month, then we see what be happening. I be walking away, if that be what I choose.'

Ransley smiled a big toothy grin and thrust his thick hand at Sam. 'Good man. The Aldington Gang be back in business.'

Sam shook the extended hand, uncertain if he was doing the right thing.

Time alone would tell.

Chapter Six

Morton's satnav announced that he had arrived at his destination: Aldington Church. He slowed his red Mini to a crawl, then pulled over onto a stretch of gravel which ran beside a none-too-high boundary wall topped with ivy. Switching off the engine, he climbed out of the car and stretched, enjoying the warmth of the sun on his face as he took in the peaceful surroundings.

Opposite the church was a well-trimmed hawthorn hedgerow, over which Morton could see a vast tract of open grassy farmland. Adjacent to the church was a miscellaneous assortment of farm buildings and small cottages, whence came the only sound to be heard: the low rumble of a piece of farming machinery.

Morton pushed open the lych-gate and ventured into the churchyard. It was typical of a rural Kentish parish church: a twelfth-century stone building with later additions, set amongst a turfed graveyard, with headstones of varying conditions and legibility dating from the 1600s.

He meandered slowly towards the church, taking in the unobtrusive setting of the place. As he walked, he pictured Ann Fothergill on this very path in 1825, holding her baby, ready to present him at the font for baptism. He saw her as tough, hardened by life on the streets with an unkempt physical appearance to match, an opinion formed following his limited research into her early life. As he had expected, he had found very little. According to the later census records, she had been born in 1803 in Ramsgate. The entry, for St Mary the Virgin Church, Ramsgate, which he had located in the FindmyPast Kent parish record collection, had been brief and not particularly illuminating: *19th July 1803, Ann, baseborn daughter of Sophia Fothergill.* By digging still a little further into the records for St Mary's, Morton had then discovered that her mother, Sophia Fothergill, had married an Isaac Bull there in 1816, she dying just two years later and being interred there in June 1817. This he had noticed, when he had added the information to Ann's timeline, was just one month prior to her first conviction for theft. Little wonder, he mused, imagining that any sense of a childhood had come crashing to an end with the death of her mother.

Whilst conducting his research this morning, Morton had received a link to download Ann's will. It was short and to the point: her ownership of three public houses—the Packet Boat Inn, the Palm Tree and the Bell Inn—along with all of her household goods and chattels were bestowed upon her son, William.

Morton reached the church door and was disappointed to find that it was locked. He touched the very wooden door, imagining Ann's splayed fingers as she would have pushed the same door open and stepped inside the cool building. Would anyone else have attended the baptism? he wondered. Presumably, the father had not been present, given that his name had been omitted from William's baptism entry.

Letting his imagined fantasy fade, Morton slowly ambled around the grounds of the churchyard, catching glimpses of the names of villagers who had resided here at a similar time to Ann.

Having taken some photographs of the church and its surroundings, Morton opened Google Maps. It appeared that the village, although small, was sprawled out over a large area, constituting, as it had done during Ann's time here, a patchwork of agricultural fields. What looked like the centre of the village—including the majority of the houses, the school, pub and village hall—were all a good twenty-minute walk away. As he stood in a coin of sunshine, he contemplated leaving the car and enjoying a walk along the country lanes, but time was short, and he convinced himself that the forty-minutes roundtrip could be put to better use elsewhere.

He unhurriedly returned to his car, then drove along the Roman Road, taking stock of the buildings that he passed as he went. An assortment of properties, from crude post-war social housing to grand fourteenth-century homes, clustered around the village centre.

Morton parked up beside a children's playpark. A young man was in the throes of pushing a toddler on a swing and two older children were climbing the steps to the top of a slide. Morton smiled, beginning to walk the main street of the village, thinking about Grace and how much he was missing Juliette and her, despite their having only been gone for one day. Then he remembered Grace's upcoming birthday and he felt a pang of anxiety. He still had not spoken to his Aunty Margaret. Every time that he had dialled her number, he had immediately ended the call in cold fear of the discussion which would have ensued. Last night, spurred on by the uninhibited courage which had emanated from having polished off a bottle of red wine by himself, he had rehearsed what he was going to say to her. Then, he had phoned her, listening to the ringing tone for what felt like an age. He had been about to hang up when she had answered with a gruff

'Hello?' Her voice had shredded through his prepared speech, leaving his mind wiped and his mouth empty of words. He had hit the red button and ended the call without uttering so much as a single syllable. Now, he felt foolish. A foolish coward. What was the worst that could have happened? That her reaction would have been frosty and that she might have changed her mind about attending the party?

Morton walked the main stretch of the village absentmindedly, unable to shake a muddy and uncomfortable question that had entered his mind: if it came to a choice, which one of his biological parents would he prefer to have at the party? His sugar-coated memories of Aunty Margaret held the more deeply seated longevity of close family, beginning at some stage in his hazy formative years, the specific date or occasion now indiscernible. Of his biological father, Jack, memories had begun to form with a jolt just nineteen months ago. By comparison, the latter were shorter and fewer in number, yet had taken on a profound and unexpected intensity which were absent from those of his Aunty Margaret.

It was not a choice which he could make, he realised. Nor one which he should have to make. It was his daughter's first birthday and both grandparents were openly welcome to attend; the multifarious threads of their emotions and feelings could not be his to unravel.

He breathed in at length, working the pernicious thought from his mind, noticing then that he was standing beside a bed of bright yellow daffodils, out of which rose the Aldington village sign. It was in black metal cut in the shape of a shield. At the top was the village name, at the bottom was depicted a range of farming tools and sheep, indicating a rich heritage of agriculture. Above the sheep were three wavy lines, on top of which stood three men with large barrels upon their backs. Smugglers, Morton supposed. He photographed the sign, then continued through the village.

He reached his car, opened the door, then glanced to the other side of the road at the Walnut Tree Inn. He looked at his watch: almost twelve. Lunchtime, sort of. He crossed the road and entered the pub, finding himself in a deserted room with a short bar.

'Afternoon. Are you after food or...?' a barmaid greeted. She was young—late teens, Morton guessed—with olive skin and incongruously bright red hair.

'Food *and* drink, please,' Morton answered.

'Take your pick of tables,' the barmaid said, handing him a menu. 'Specials are on the board.' She pointed at a blackboard behind him. 'See what you fancy and I'll be over to take your order.'

'Thank you,' Morton replied, distracted from the specials board by the surrounding decorations. Tankards, barrels and old pistols were displayed on almost every wall and shelf around the bar. On one wall, written on the light wood in large black letters was a poem:

Smuggler's Song by Rudyard Kipling.
If you wake at midnight, and hear a horse's feet,
Don't go drawing back the blind, or looking in the street,
Them that ask no questions isn't told a lie.
Watch the wall my darling while the Gentlemen go by.

'Ready?' the barmaid asked.

'Oh…' Morton said, not yet having moved from the bar. He quickly glanced at the blackboard and plucked the first thing upon which his eyes settled. 'Chicken and mushroom pie with new potatoes and veg, please. And a small glass of house red. Thanks.'

The barmaid tapped his order into the till. 'Fourteen pounds fifty, please.'

Morton handed over his credit card. 'Was this a smugglers' pub?' he asked, gesturing to all the apparel dotted around the room.

The barmaid handed over the credit card machine. 'I don't know to be honest, I've not been here long. It might just be decoration. I can ask the landlord if you like.'

'If they're around, thank you,' Morton replied, typing his PIN number into the machine and handing it back across the bar.

The barmaid turned behind her and yelled, 'Dave!'

A middle-aged man with a receding hairline and potbellied stomach appeared with a tea-towel, wet wine glass and a slightly disgruntled look on his face. 'What's up?'

'This gentleman wanted to know if the pub was used for smuggling.'

The landlord smiled at Morton. 'The wicked trade—yes, it went on here. It was a kind of headquarters for the Aldington Gang—have you heard of them?'

Morton shook his head. 'Do you know when that would have been?'

136

'Around the 1820s,' he answered. 'They were quite a big deal at the time, so I gather. They used to meet here before and after landing their contraband on the Marsh.'

'Interesting,' Morton said. 'Do you know any of the names of those involved?'

The landlord thought for a moment. 'I think the leader was a man called Ransley. Other than him, no, I don't.'

'Thank you.'

'You're welcome,' the landlord said, turning back towards the rear of the bar.

'Where are you going to sit?' the barmaid asked, pouring his wine.

Morton turned and pointed to a round table. 'Over there by the window.'

'Lovely,' she said, handing him his drink.

Morton carried the wine over to the table and took a sip, as he mulled over what the landlord had just told him. If what he had said was correct, then smuggling was going on in this very village at the time when Ann had resided here. It raised a possible question: Was Ann somehow involved? He re-read the Kipling poem above him: *Watch the wall my darling while the Gentlemen go by.* Then, he tried to recall the contents of Ann's 1827 letter. Something about life returning to the old quiet ways and the chance to leave behind the wicked deeds of the past. The landlord had just described smuggling as 'the wicked trade'. Had Ann been referring to smuggling in her letter? For a woman so linked to the combination of trouble and alcohol, it was certainly a possibility to be taken very seriously.

Shattering the stillness of the room and Morton's train of thoughts came the sound of his mobile ringing. He pulled it out and looked at the caller identity: Juliette. 'Hiya,' he greeted warmly. 'How are my girls?'

'We're very good, thanks. Just been to the park with my mum and fed the ducks. Played on the swings and had an ice-cream. What about you?' she asked.

'Just doing some research for the latest case,' he answered.

'Here we go,' the barmaid said, placing his plate down in front of him. 'Any more wine?'

Morton shook his head vigorously. 'Thanks.'

'Wine?' Juliette quizzed. 'Where are you?'

'A pub in Aldington—it's with my lunch,' he defended.

'Lunch? It's not even midday yet.'

'It's all in the name of work.'

'Hm… I'm sure it is. What did your Aunty Margaret say about Jack coming to the birthday party?'

'I haven't managed to get hold of her yet,' he lied.

'Morton,' Juliette scolded. 'That's ridiculous—stop dithering and get on with it.'

'I've been too busy,' he mumbled.

'Well, find the time—it's not fair on her. The party's in six days, for goodness' sake.'

'I'll do it,' he promised.

'Right, I'd better go, Grace's eating stones. Love you.'

'Love you, too. See you in a couple of days.'

'Phone her,' Juliette said, swiftly ending the call before he could speak again. He stared at his phone, thinking that he could do it now. He took a swig from his wine, still focused on his mobile. What was stopping him from phoning her? Fear of losing what little relationship they had? Another mother-figure gone from his life?

'Everything alright?' the barmaid called over.

The imbalance of his quandary polarised and he pocketed his phone. 'Yes, fine, thank you.'

He picked up his knife and fork and began to tuck into his food.

Phil stood in the queue at the Post Office, fidgeting nervously. He rolled the small package over in his hands several times checking that the address was clear and the edges taped down sufficiently. When it was his turn at the counter, he sent the package Royal Mail Special Delivery Guaranteed and with a grand's insurance, even though it cost him all the cash that he had on him. But there was more money coming. £1,120, to be precise. And hopefully that would just be the start of it. It needed to be, he was up to his eyes in serious debt.

He slung his hands into his grey tracksuit bottoms and walked out of the Post Office. He strode for a short distance before arriving at the bungalow. He pressed the bell several times repeatedly. The old man hardly ever heard the first two or three rings. He was probably asleep.

'Oh, it's you,' Arthur Fothergill said emotionlessly. 'You coming in?'

Phil shrugged. 'Ain't really got the time. Has he been in touch yet?'

'Who?' Arthur quizzed.

'That genealogist bloke. Farrier.'

'No, but it's only been a few days. I'm just making a cup of tea. Would you like one?' Arthur asked, pulling the door wider open.

Phil shook his head. 'Let me know as soon as he phones.' He turned back down the path towards the road.

'You haven't seen that guinea anywhere, have you? I can't seem to find it,' Arthur called after him.

Without turning back, Phil shook his head again and continued walking.

Morton wrote SMUGGLING in large letters on a piece of blank paper, looping a circle around the word for good measure. He stared at it, then added a question mark to the end. It was still just a possibility that Ann had somehow been involved in smuggling; the link was tenuous to say the least.

He slid his chair out from under his desk and stood up with a yawn. He carried the piece of paper to the investigation wall and fixed it up in prime position.

He looked over his afternoon's findings, having researched the three pubs of which Ann had ended up as the proprietor. According to the internet, all three—the Packet Boat Inn, the Palm Tree and the Bell Inn—had links to smuggling at some point in the 1820s. Most had been used as a muster point for the hundreds of men pulled from the surrounding countryside, a place to converge before heading to the beaches and retrieving the illicit goods. The problem was trying to link the three pubs with Ann; he had no idea when she had taken ownership of them. His research had confirmed, though, what the landlord had said: that a smuggling group by the name of the Aldington Gang had been active in the area in the 1820s under the leadership of a man named George Ransley; a man whose two cousins had been hanged in 1800 for the same crime. Even if Ann herself had not been involved in smuggling, she had certainly surrounded herself by the people embroiled in it.

He yawned again. It was time to stop for the day.

He turned to collect his mobile from the desk and, as he did so, caught sight of the photograph of his Aunty Margaret and his father, Jack, together. He had to ring her. Now.

Taking a deep breath, he pulled up her name in his contact list and hit the call button.

It was answered almost instantly. 'Hello?' It was her voice.

'Hi, Aunty Margaret, it's Morton,' he said.

'Oh, hello, love. How are you?' she asked.

'Good thanks. Erm… I've got something that I need to talk to you about.'

'Go on,' she said.

Chapter Seven

Morton felt like he couldn't suck enough air into his lungs to get the next sentence out of his mouth. 'Do you remember what we spoke about on Christmas Day in 2014 when Juliette and I came down to stay?'

'About your roots, do you mean?' she asked.

'Yes. You made me promise that I wouldn't tell you anything about it,' Morton said. 'I'm afraid I am going to need to break that promise.'

The line went quiet and all that Morton could hear was her soft exhalation at the other end. It was her turn to speak, to say something. To grant him permission to break his promise or to refuse it and put down the phone. Not to stay silent.

'I've met him. Jack, I mean,' Morton blurted.

'I know,' Margaret finally said.

'You know? How?' he begged, his brain presenting and rejecting various connections which could have led such a crucial piece of information to wind its way down to his Aunty Margaret in Cornwall. 'Jeremy,' he spat. It had to be him.

'Does it matter that I know already?' she asked with a light chuckle. 'I was just about to find out, anyway.'

It didn't matter, he supposed. It had just caught him off-guard.

'I take it there's a reason behind you telling me now?' she probed.

'He's planning on coming to Grace's birthday party. I did try and explain that...'

'And do you need me not to come up?' she interjected.

'Yes,' he replied. 'I mean no, not at all—I *do* want you there—that's why I'm phoning.'

There was another short pause in the conversation before she spoke again. 'Well, I don't *think* it's a problem but it's something I haven't given any thought to. Given that more than forty years have passed since I last clapped eyes on him, I didn't think the day would ever come when I'd have to consider how I'd feel if I were to see him again.'

'I understand,' Morton said.

'I'd love to be at Grace's party, Morton, really I would. I just don't know...'

'You don't have to decide now. Have a think about it. We'd love to have you there, obviously, but I understand that it could be a little awkward.'

Margaret sighed. 'I'll have a chat with Jim and...we'll see. Anyway, how is my little great-niece getting on?'

'She's good, thank you. She and Juliette have gone to stay at Juliette's mum's for a couple of days.'

Morton shared some recent anecdotes of what Grace had been up to, before winding up the phone call. She said goodbye, telling him that she would be in touch with her decision.

Morton blew out a puff of air as he strode down the stairs from his study. He was relieved that the conversation was over, but the relief was tarnished by a sense of aggravation that had washed over him. He was irked that Jeremy had told her about having found Jack and questioned his motivations in doing so, imagining Jeremy's gleeful face as he spilled the beans down the phone.

Morton poured himself a large glass of red wine, sensing that his glumness did not just stem from Jeremy's gossiping; something else about the conversation had bothered him. He sat at the kitchen table with his head propped in his hands, gazing at his wine as he replayed their discussion. His spooling thoughts settled on the problem: she had asked him how her great-niece was getting on. Great-niece. Why didn't she just prefix it with the word 'adoptive' to demonstrate clearly her steadfastness to their established relationship? Could she really not bring herself to say *granddaughter*? Since Margaret's own two daughters had yet to produce any offspring, Grace was her first grandchild. Christ, but his family was complicated. When the truth that his Aunty Margaret was actually his biological mother had first been revealed to him, he hadn't expected any shift in their relationship, largely out of respect to his adoptive father. But, following his death three years ago, Morton had hoped for some subtle change, particularly since Grace had been born. But no, she was the same Aunty Margaret as she had always been. It saddened him immensely to think of the physical and emotional distance that might always be manifested between Grace and her biological grandparents.

He downed his wine and stood up, wanting to shake off his morose mood. It was time for bed.

Morton dropped his empty take-away coffee cup into a bin outside the Dover Discovery Centre and strode through the automatic doors. He recalled from previous visits the layout of the building and marched confidently through the Adult Lending Library to the Local Studies section tucked, as they often were, at the rear of the building. The area, comprised of several tables and two microfilm readers, was deserted. Morton paused to take in the various sections of shelving which lined the walls of the open-plan room. *Family Research. Local Studies. Dover Collection. Oversize.* He spotted that for which he was searching: *Directories of Kent.* He headed over to the shelving and scanned across the various titles until he found a run of several volumes of *Pigot's Directory of Kent.* He needed to be methodical, to check every year of the period in question, until he had identified exactly when Ann Fothergill had taken ownership of the three pubs. Selecting the chunky red book, dated 1820, Morton sat at the nearest table and carefully pulled it open. It was arranged alphabetically, featuring the county's larger towns and cities. Skipping through several pages, he settled on Dover, then ran his finger down the various services offered in the town at that time. *Academies. Agents. Attorneys. Bakers. Bankers. Basket-makers. Baths. Book-binders. Braziers. Brewers. Bricklayers.* He turned the page and continued checking until his finger came to rest on *Inns. Packet Boat, Josh. Hoad, Strond Street. Palm Tree, Robert Griggs, Elham.* Moving on to Hythe, the town in which the Bell Inn was situated, he found its proprietor to be one Henry Marshall. As Morton had expected, Ann had owned none of the pubs in 1820. Having made a note on his pad, he placed the tome back onto the shelf and selected the edition for 1827. The Packet Boat Inn had changed ownership to a John Finnis, while the Palm Tree had remained in the care of Robert Griggs. The Bell Inn, however, was now owned by Ann Fothergill. Morton smiled as he photographed the entry and scribbled the information onto his pad.

'The Bell,' someone said beside him with a Southern American voice.

He looked up, seeing the inquisitive face of a young lady with a staff lanyard around her neck, which read Amber Henderson. 'They do a scrumptious bacon and onion suet pudding—making me hungry just thinking about it.'

Morton smiled politely.

'Ever been there?' she asked, squinting at him.

'No,' he answered. Time was ticking and he had wanted to make some progress on this case before Juliette and Grace returned home.

'What's your interest in it—if I may ask?' Amber said. Keeping the page with one finger, she flipped the book shut and looked at the title: 'Pigot's. 1827.'

'Yes,' Morton confirmed, starting to lose patience.

She flicked the book open again and folded her arms, oblivious to Morton's growing exasperation. 'You know all about the *bodies*, don't you?' Amber asked cryptically.

'Bodies?' he repeated.

Amber's eyes opened with delight and she hurried off to the bookshelves in the *Local Studies* cabinet. She plucked out a book with an inaudible mumble and brought it to Morton's desk, laying it on top of the Pigot's directory.

'*Kent Smugglers' Pubs*,' Morton read, watching as Amber turned back and forth between several pages.

'Here we are,' she began. '*In 1963, a builder made a gruesome discovery of two skeletons when he uncovered the back of the old inglenook fireplace. They were identified as being Revenue Officers because their boots, belts, hats and badges had survived. All were taken to the local coroners.*'

'Oh, right,' Morton said, his demeanour towards her softening. 'Does it say what happened to the bodies? Or when they were put in there?'

Amber turned up her nose. 'No, that's all. I'm not an expert on smuggling, but I guess that puts it to around the early nineteenth century.'

'Smuggling?' Morton questioned.

'Revenue Officers,' Amber clarified. 'They were employed by the Admiralty to prevent smuggling.'

'Of course,' Morton said, feeling a little foolish for not having made that connection for himself. 'Do you have any more information on the discovery of the bodies?'

'*The Folkestone, Hythe and District Herald* would be your best bet—see if it made the local paper.'

'Do you have them here?' Morton asked.

Amber shook her head. 'No, we've got a few old local papers, like *The Cinque Ports Herald*, but not for this period—you'll need to visit Folkestone Library for that. Do you know where it is?'

'Yes, I've been there a few times,' he answered, wondering how an American came to know so much about Kent local history. He knew Folkestone Library well. Among several visits for genealogical cases, on which he had worked in the past, it had also been the place in which he had made his first big strides in locating his biological father, when Morton had learned of his stay in Folkestone in January 1974.

'Good luck with it,' Amber said, sliding off into the lending library.

'Thanks,' Morton muttered, as he returned the directory to the shelf and selected the previous year, 1826. He found Ann there, proprietor of the Bell Inn, the place in which, he had just learned, the bodies of two Revenue Officers had been discovered in 1963. He photographed the page, then swapped the volume for the previous year. Ann was there again. He then checked the years 1821-1824, but the pub had still been in the ownership of Henry Marshall, meaning that Ann had taken it on in the year of her son's birth, 1825.

One thing, he realised, which might help him to ascertain a more precise timing of her tenure of the Bell Inn, was the date upon which the Pigot's guide had been written. He took down the 1825 edition again, and began to thumb through the opening pages until he found the month of publication: August.

Amber had left the copy of *Kent Smugglers' Pubs* on the desk, so Morton copied down the text that she had just read to him, wondering if a link could be made to Ann and her ownership of the pub. He looked at the time; just approaching midday. He still had plenty of time to finish his research here before heading over to Folkestone Library.

He spent some time checking the directories for the subsequent years, discovering that Ann's ownership of the Packet Boat Inn had occurred in 1831 and the Palm Tree Inn around 1836.

Shortly after two o'clock, Morton headed back to his car, satisfied with the day's progress so far. As he started his Mini, ready to leave the car park and drive to Folkestone, he remembered that Ann had lived for the last thirty-plus years of her life in a house close to the town centre, and decided to pay it a quick visit. He flipped the pages in his notebook, struggling to remember the name of the property. He found the address: *Honey Pot House, Castle Avenue.*

It took him three minutes to reach Castle Avenue and a further two minutes of crawling along the kerbside to locate the house. The road was lined with a motley collection of practically every type of house: handsome Edwardian dwellings sat beside ugly 1980s bungalows. As far as he had seen, there were no pre-Victorian properties on the road apart from Honey Pot House.

'Impressive,' he said to himself, taking several shots on his mobile.

The three-storeyed brick house, set behind wrought iron gates and fencing, was situated in a sprawling plot that now boasted tennis courts and what looked from the road to be an outdoor swimming pool. Ann Fothergill had undergone a Dickensian transformation from illiterate street vagrant in 1820 to the owner of a pub in 1825, followed years later by a large house and two further pubs. Impressive.

Morton rubbed his chin as he looked at the house, deliberating his research so far, before climbing back into his Mini and driving along the coast to Folkestone.

The dull beige, hardback binding that held together every edition of *The Folkestone, Hythe & District Herald* for 1963 flopped onto the desk with a thump. Morton turned the first large page over with a smile. When so many newspapers had been transferred to microfilm or fiche, or digitalised to computer, it was always a pleasure to handle original ones such as these. Having no idea when the two bodies had been discovered that year, he knew it was necessary to search each and every edition until he had found it. As he needed it to be, his search was thorough and methodical; he checked every story on every page, despite suspecting that the unearthing of two Revenue Officers' corpses would actually be headline news for this quiet seaside town. Sure enough, it was. On the 10th July 1963, the story had made the front page. *MURDER?* the headline shouted above a grainy black and white image of an inglenook fireplace, at the base of which, surrounded by piles of bricks, were two skulls protruding from dark clothing. The picture looked almost comical to Morton, like a bad pub Halloween display. Yet, the story confirmed what Amber Henderson at Dover Library had said to him: '*Whilst knocking down a dividing wall in the central fireplace of the Bell Inn on Wednesday, a builder unearthed two human skeletons fully dressed in the outfits of Coastguard Officers. Local man, Paul Major, was the person who made the gruesome discovery, thinking at first that the bodies were a pile of old rags. The remains were conveyed to the Coroner's Office by Mr F.W. Smith, who told reporters that the skeletons dated from the early nineteenth century, therefore an inquest into the deaths was unnecessary. Although the two bodies showed no visible signs of how they met with their deaths, owing to the mere fact of their concealment, the circumstances are highly suspicious. 'Looks like they were murdered,' Ian Austen, the forty-seven-year-old owner of the pub said yesterday. 'Why else would they have been bricked up in a fireplace?' One local historian and maritime expert, Clive Baintree, who saw the skeletons shortly after their discovery believes that the two men would have been part of the Coastal Blockade set up to prevent smuggling in Kent and Sussex. Having remained closed while the police concluded their investigations, the Bell Inn is once again open to the public.'*

Morton photographed the report, made a note of it on his pad, then continued searching through the newspaper for further mention of the two bodies. Despite the likelihood dwindling with each passing edition of the paper, he persevered but reached the end of the year finding nothing more. Evidently, whatever discoveries had been made by the Coroner had not warranted the column inches.

He handed the volume back and returned to his desk, removing his laptop from his bag.

Opening a web browser, he found the details for the Central and South-East Kent Coroner's Office and sent them an email requesting any information which they might have had on the two skeletons. Next, he emailed various local cemeteries and churches, spelling out the case and requesting a search be made in their registers for the burial of the two men. Finally, he ran various searches for Clive Baintree, figuring that being both an expert in maritime history, and having seen the two bodies, he would be a good person to whom to talk. Having found an address and phone number for him in Hythe in an online electoral register, Morton was able to identify him correctly on Facebook. Without revealing the finer details of the case, he sent Clive a message regarding the discovery of the skeletons.

Morton closed his laptop lid and packed away his things before walking back to his car and driving home.

Juliette and Grace would be home at any minute. Having added his latest research to the investigation wall, Morton was rushing around the house doing what he considered to be tidying up. There was no time left to clean the kitchen, which resembled a student hovel. He grabbed the necks of three empty bottles of wine, wondering how he had managed to work his way through them all by himself, and dumped them in the recycling bin outside.

He was standing by the front door considering where to tidy next, when he heard a key in the door. He turned to see Juliette stepping inside, carrying Grace in one arm.

'Welcome back!' Morton greeted, throwing his arms around the pair of them. 'I've missed you,' he said, planting a kiss on each of their mouths.

Juliette sighed and passed Grace over to him.

'Dadda!' Grace said, with a smile.

Morton, mouth agape, stared at Juliette. 'She just called me Dadda!'

Juliette grinned. 'Typical that's her first word. I've spent most of the last two days trying to get her to say Mummy.' She leant in to Grace and spoke softly: 'Mummy. Mummy.'

Grace stared at Juliette. 'Dadda.'

Morton laughed.

'Looks like she's going to be a daddy's girl. Right, well, you stay with *Dadda*, then,' Juliette said, going back outside for her suitcase.

Morton squeezed his daughter tightly. It was a strange thing to think, but Morton felt that Grace had grown in the few days since he had last seen her and her new ability to speak only compounded that feeling. He carried her into the lounge and sat her down on the carpet, watching as she sped off on all fours in the direction of the telephone.

'So, what have you been up to, then?' Juliette asked, dropping her bag at the door. 'Judging from the mess in the kitchen sink, just drinking and eating.'

'Work, mainly,' he countered.

'Oh, God, don't say the 'W' word,' she groaned, sinking into the sofa. 'Two days of freedom left.'

'You'll be fine,' Morton reassured her, watching Grace as she picked up the house phone and held it to her ear, babbling a lot of nonsense. 'Sounds like you when you're talking to your friends.'

'Very funny,' Juliette said. 'Look, she's going to try and walk.'

They watched as Grace used the edge of the sofa to haul herself up onto her feet. Still gibbering into the phone, she took one step then fell backwards onto her bottom, unperturbed.

'You'll get there,' Morton said.

'Have you eaten?' Juliette asked.

'Not yet—I was waiting for you two,' he answered, sitting down beside her and placing his hand on her leg. He turned to face her. 'Is it just me, or is all we talk about food, drink and Grace?'

Juliette looked up at the ceiling for a moment. 'I think that pretty well sums it up.' She placed her hand on his and tapped it lightly. 'You get the wine and I'll watch Grace then make dinner.'

Morton smiled, placed a kiss on the top of her head and stood up.

Just then, his mobile began to ring with an unidentified caller. 'Hello?' he said, moving into the kitchen and plucking a bottle of red from the wine rack.

'Good evening, is this Morton Farrier?' a male voice asked.

'Yes, speaking,' he said, pulling the last two clean glasses from the cupboard.

'This is Clive—Clive Baintree—you sent me a message earlier today about the skeletons in the Bell pub?'

'Ah, yes—thanks for getting back to me,' Morton said. 'I'm just doing some research into one of the pub's former owners and happened upon the story of the two bodies. I was wondering if you could tell me anything you can remember?'

'Of course,' Clive began, 'The landlord at the time was a friend of mine and, knowing my interest in maritime history, he called me in when they found them. Living in the street opposite the pub, I actually got there before the police arrived. What was it you wanted to know, exactly?'

'Anything at all that you can remember about the bodies.'

'Erm, they were in pretty good condition. Their uniforms, despite the long passage of time, were in pretty good order, too. It caused quite a stir in the area, I can tell you.'

'I bet. Do you know if a time period was ever established when they were put in there?' Morton asked, as he poured the wine. 'Because this could actually be totally irrelevant to the person I'm researching.'

'Well, what kind of time period are you looking at?' Clive asked.

'The 1820s,' Morton replied. 'The person I'm looking into, Ann Fothergill, took ownership of it in 1825. It was hers until her death in 1869.'

Clive snorted, but Morton wasn't sure at what.

'Those two skeletons,' Clive said with a theatrical revelation, 'were buried in that fireplace at some point *after* 1822.'

'Right,' Morton said. 'How can you be so certain?'

'Their uniforms. These men were wearing coastguard uniforms, which was only formed in 1822 with the amalgamation of the three smuggling prevention services—Revenue Cruisers, Riding Officers and the preventative Water Guard,' Clive explained. 'The pub was used by smugglers at this time, so I shouldn't wonder that these two chaps from the preventative service got clobbered then bricked up in the fireplace.'

'Okay,' Morton said, carrying the two glasses from the kitchen. He thrust one at Juliette, who was pulling an inquisitive face regarding who was on the phone, then strode upstairs to his study and stood before the investigation wall. 'So, it could have happened before Ann Fothergill took over the pub...or after.'

'Well, yes. My money—for what it's worth—would be on it having happened *after* 1825,' Clive said.

'Really? Why's that?'

'Smuggling of one kind or another has been occurring in Kent and Sussex since the 1700s and it's still going on to this very day, but instead of rum and brandy coming over, now its immigrants or drugs,' Clive said with a mild titter. 'The mid-1820s marked a turning point where local gangs had, to all intents and purposes, industrialised smuggling. We're talking hundreds of men a night bringing tons of contraband across the Channel. Three groups in particular: the North Kent Gang, the Hawkhurst Gang and the Aldington Gang. They had the market covered in the South-East of England. Because of this the government, via the Admiralty, stepped up their efforts to end smuggling… These two factions clashed and the period from the mid-1820s was the worst for murders and revenge-killing. Dozens were killed every month on both sides… The two skeletons in the pub are really only worthy of comment because of how long they had lain undisturbed… put them back into a contemporaneous setting and they're just two men among hundreds who died because of smuggling.'

'Thank you very much—that's really helpful,' Morton said, scribbling notes onto his pad. 'Was it ever established how they died?'

Clive was quiet for a moment. 'I don't think so, no. I had a good look at the skeletons—morbid, I know. My wife wouldn't let me go near her for a few days afterwards, thinking I could have picked up some germs from them! Ha! I remember that there were no physical signs of injury. I'm certainly no doctor but the bones were pretty intact. I would have expected a gunshot wound or a knife wound, but there was nothing.'

'Right,' Morton said. 'And then they were taken to the coroners then buried—do you know where?'

'Sorry, no, I don't.'

Morton thanked him again and ended the call.

Leaning on his desk, with the investigation wall before him, Morton gazed at the timeline. Something was bothering him. He moved closer to the wall and re-read his copy of Ann's letter, written 22nd July 1827: '…*after all the difficult years in this area, things have returned to the quietness of the old ways…*' If, as Clive Baintree had just suggested, the smuggling gangs, along with the concomitant violence, were at their peak in the mid-1820s, then how had life suddenly become quiet once again by 1827? It made no sense.

One thing about which he was now becoming almost certain was that the 'wicked deeds of the past', to which Ann had referred in her

150

letter, had been smuggling. He did not yet know for certain of her involvement and, at this stage most of his links were unsubstantiated, but he was determined to find out.

Chapter Eight

10th November 1821, Sandgate, Kent

They had chosen a spot to the west of Sandgate Castle, some half a mile from the nearest blockade men stationed at Martello Tower number four. Still, Sam was nervous at the thought of being seen by the Riding Officers who patrolled the coast on horseback throughout the night. So far, the crescent moon had not betrayed them; a passing patrol would see nothing on this stony beach but the breaking of the stormy November seas. Even he, from his crouched position on the shingle, doubted the presence of the three hundred men who he knew surrounded him, all with their eyes fixed on the breaking waters. Somewhere to his immediate right was George Ransley, holding a small lamp which only projected light in one direction—out to sea—to guide in the boat.

'Where do they be?' Sam whispered impatiently.

'Darned if I be knowing,' Ransley answered. 'But I don't be doubting the storm to be the cause of the delay.'

Sam mumbled his agreement as he watched the undulating and lurching waves rise up threateningly, just yards before them. He was thankful not to be out there on the boat this night, as he had been on several previous runs, when Ransley had requested that he oversee operations from launch in Folkestone to the loading up of the cargo in France, to the return journey to the shores of Kent. Ransley, for his part, had always been true to his word, handing him three guineas at the end of each week, regardless of the illicit cargo which they had managed to smuggle in. Some weeks he had done nothing whatsoever to earn his money, which had gone some way to appeasing Hester, who had begged and pleaded with him not to become embroiled with the gang. But he had had little choice, as the few shillings, which she had previously earned from her laundry work, had ceased since the birth of their daughter, Ellen. It was for Ellen, John and Hester that he was out here—exhausted and ice-cold before any goods had even been landed.

'There!' a voice exclaimed from the darkness. 'I be seeing a boat.'

Shingle shifted under the men's boots, as they shuffled to gaze more closely at the rolling horizon.

'I see it!' another voice said, pointlessly adding, 'over there!'

'Do you see it?' Ransley called to him.

'Not yet,' Sam answered, scouring the almost imperceptible black seam which zipped together sky and sea.

'There!' another voice called.

'Whist your tongues!' Ransley erupted. 'It mayn't be ours.'

The sounds from the men lulled below the noise of the rancorous waves and southerly wind.

'She's ours!' Ransley confirmed. 'She's ours! Be readying yourselves!'

The news cascaded quickly through the group of men, each one poised to get into position the very moment that they knew of the boat's precise landing point.

Now that they knew for certain that the boat was theirs, Ransley aimed the lamp definitively towards them, guiding them in to shore.

The boat drew closer, becoming less of an abstract silhouette. Sam could now see the oars, then the low grunts and curses of the men fighting against the heavy water reached his ears.

Finally, on the crest of a large wave, the galley's bow hit the beach with a crash.

Without a word from Ransley, the tubmen poured towards the boat, whilst the batmen formed two opposing lines through which the laden tubmen would soon flee with the contraband.

Sam took a long breath and, on Ransley's heels, rushed towards the vessel.

'Merciful Lord!' said a man, whose voice Sam recognised to be Evan May, one of the Folkestone fishermen who led many of the voyages. 'That were a grabby storm—I nearly be a-turning back.'

'Let's be getting her unloaded, then,' Ransley ordered.

Seconds later, the first in a long line of barrels was being heaved over the side of the galley into Ransley's open hands. He took the barrel, then tossed it over to the first tubman in the line, who set it down and waited for the next, before taking the two barrels to one side and strapping them to his chest and back.

With his right arm all but useless, Sam always felt inadequate at this crucial, pinnacle moment in the smuggling run. He had proven himself to be a good deputy to Ransley, yet still he knew that, the moment in which the boat hit the shore, he ceased to be of any great use to the gang. He had absolutely no bearing on the success or failure of the run at this point in time.

The first tubman was ready to go.

Sam ran ahead of him through the line of batmen to make one final check that there were no signs of any of the blockade. 'Go!' he instructed to the two men waiting behind him. They hurried up the beach, soon lost to the darkness. Sam spun around to the next three tubmen, who were ascending the beach incline towards him, 'Be hurrying yourselves!' he called out needlessly.

The men snorted as they pushed past him.

Despite the inclement night, the run was going smoothly so far. From his position at the top of the beach he could just make out vague black shapes moving in the gloom of the night. A constant line of tubmen were now trudging past him on their way to the meeting point at the Bell in Hythe.

Sam jiggled his pistol nervously at his side. The worst part of not being able to take an active role was that it worsened his apprehension.

Just then came the loud crack from a pistol shot.

Sam whirled around to see that it was one of his batmen who had fired the shot. But why? He couldn't tell. The men began to shout, but their cries were snatched on the wind.

'Hurry!' Sam shouted to the tubmen heading towards him, as he ran back down the beach towards the galley.

More gunfire. This time half a dozen of his men had opened up. Now there was return fire and shouting.

'Ransley—it be the blockade men!' Sam called. 'We need to be getting out of here!'

'I'll not get the boat back out of here in these conditions,' Evan May yelled down.

'Leave the tarnal thing—move to the meeting place,' Ransley bawled at the men around him.

The waiting tubmen ran up the beach without any cargo, followed by Sam, then Ransley. In the midst of battling gunfire, the line of batmen then folded into the gap, making their own slow retreat up the beach.

The cries and screams of injured men provided a melancholic punctuation to the sounds of intermittent musket fire. Sam had no idea from which side the men were falling, just that he needed to get as many of them to the meeting point as possible.

As the beach levelled out, Sam and Ransley met with the last in the line of tubmen laden with barrels.

'Dump 'em,' Sam encouraged, knowing that they stood a much better chance of survival without the extra weight hanging around their necks.

The men obeyed and threw down their loads.

Sam stood still for a moment to catch his breath and turned to look behind him. The gunfire had stopped for several seconds, allowing the batmen to progress away from the beach. He squinted into the darkness, trying to make out if they were being pursued, but it was impossible to tell what or who the shifting dark shapes were.

'Come on!' Ransley called back. 'Only another mile or so and we be there.'

The group continued apace, only pausing for the briefest of moments. By the time the Bell came into view, Sam was certain that they had left the blockade officers behind. As Sam had organised, there were four horses and carts awaiting them, hidden in the shadows of the yard to the rear of the inn. They were there ready to take the bulk of the goods onwards to Aldington, the knowledge of which location was kept from most present, thereby protecting their final destination from any potential discoveries through bribery.

'Brenbutter, landlord!' Ransley barked, kicking open the street door.

Sam followed him inside, the heat from the spluttering fire instantly smacking against his cold skin. He glanced around him. Every table, every nook and space available was taken with the Aldington Gang. Then he noticed a man writhing on his back, clasping at his stomach. His gabardine was hoisted up and Sam could see a large, blood-filled hole in his navel.

Sam thrust an elbow at Ransley, indicating the injured man. Then he saw another—James Carter—collapsed at the foot of the bar holding a cloth to his leg, a small piece of white bone jutting from the crimson pulp around it. How he had managed to get here, Sam had no idea.

Ransley strode into the bar and looked around him. 'You,' he said, pointing to Thomas Denard, 'Take one of the horses and go fetch Doctor Papworth-Hougham from Brookland.'

'We be needing someone else, Ransley,' Sam muttered. 'Be looking around you.'

'He be all we got,' Ransley snapped. 'Now be doing your job—pay these men and get Marshall to be hastening with the brenbutter.'

155

'It be coming,' Henry Marshall, the landlord said breathlessly when Sam approached the bar. He was lining up pints of beer as two women scurried about the place with plates of bread, butter and cheese—part of the men's payment for their night's work.

Sam crouched down beside the man with the injured leg. 'Help be coming,' he said.

The man nodded, wincing.

'What about the rest of us?' a man next to him asked, holding up his left hand, where only two swollen fingers remained, jutting from a spongy mass of torn skin and ligaments.

Sam stood and surveyed the rest of the men, noticing even more injured among their number. There was no way Doctor Papworth-Hougham could attend to all of them. He hurried over to Ransley. 'I be knowing of someone—an apothecary who can be helping.'

'She the one what brung you back to life?' Ransley asked, downing his beer.

'That be her, yeah.'

Ransley belched in Sam's face. 'Take one of the horses and be bringing her back here.'

Sam nodded and hurried for the door.

In the yard behind the pub, Sam approached one of the three draught horses. He chose a black shire, seventeen hands in height, and unchained it. Hoisting himself up into the saddle, Sam trotted out onto the track by which they had all just arrived.

Holding the reins in his left hand, he pushed the horse into a canter. It would not take him too long to reach Dover, but once he got there he had no idea how he would track her down. A good starting point, he thought, would be the town's many inns, taverns and public houses.

'She been barred from here,' the landlord of the Castle told him when he arrived. 'Try the City of Antwerp.'

'Not here,' he was told in the City of Antwerp. 'You been to the Plume of Feathers? That sometimes be where she hangs about.'

At the Plume of Feathers his request was met with blank faces. 'Try the Three Mackerel—by St James's Church.'

The landlord of the Three Mackerel sneered that he had thankfully not laid eyes on her for several days. 'I seen her,' a drunk old-timer propped at the bar drawled, as Sam was leaving. He was standing in ragged clothes with one boot missing. 'Not long out of prison, she ain't.'

'Where does she be now?' Sam asked.

The old timer jangled his empty beer glass on the bar top.

Sam tossed some coins down in front of him.

'The Packet Boat,' the old-timer slurred. 'Not forty minute ago.'

Sam tipped his head in gratitude, hoping that he had not just wasted his money on the advice of a man too drunk to realise that he was only wearing one boot.

The ride to the Packet Boat Inn on Strond Street took Sam barely two minutes. Inside was noisy, smoky and crammed with inebriated fishermen. Sam barely received a second glance as he pushed through the crowds, searching for her, but there was no sign.

'You seen a lady here this night?' Sam shouted at the barmaid. 'Ann Fothergill be her name.'

The barmaid laughed raucously, revealing the gummy inside of her mouth. 'Ann Fothergill a lady!' She laughed again as she poured a pint of beer. She handed the drink to a man at the bar, then pointed at the plump rear end of a woman bending in towards a seated crowd of fishermen. 'How's about Eliza, over there?'

'No, I don't be looking for... for that... I be looking for Ann—she be a friend,' Sam clarified.

'Do that be right?' the barmaid said. 'Happen you ain't seen what be a-lying in your shadow.'

Sam turned quizzically. She was standing directly behind him, beaming from ear to ear, as she tried to balance a pint of rum and water on her head. 'Ann.'

Ann lowered her drink, took a swig from the glass, then prodded Sam's right shoulder. 'All better?'

Sam nodded.

'What do you be wanting with Lady Fothergill, then?' she asked, placing one hand on her hip.

'I be needing your help,' he said, lowering his voice and leaning in closer to her. 'I got friends who be hurt.'

Ann pursed her lips and frowned. 'Friends what got hurt the same way you got hurt?'

'That be right, yes.'

'And your fancy doctor—he don't want to be helping?'

'He be asking for your assistance personally,' Sam lied.

At this revelation Ann seemed to drop her act. Her face became serious. 'If that be right, then I best not refuse a man of such high qualification.'

Sam watched as she tilted her head back, held the glass up to her mouth and sank the drink, as much liquid pouring down her chin and onto her dress as went down her gullet.

Ann positioned her hand in a regal fashion, pushing it towards Sam's face. 'Sir?'

Sam took her hand and led her from the tavern back out to the waiting horse.

'Where do they be—these friends of yours?' she asked.

'Hythe,' Sam answered, 'Jump on.'

Sam hauled himself into the saddle, then offered his hand to Ann.

'What pleasure be mine!' she exclaimed as she pulled herself in behind him and wrapped her arms around his midriff.

Sam kicked the horse into a gentle trot, and they slowly picked their way down Strond Street, weaving around the oblivious drunks and itinerants slumped at the roadside until they reached the quieter streets on the outskirts of the port.

Pushing the horse to go as fast as it could, he felt Ann's grip tighten around his waist, pleasure at the touch of her fingers stirring in his mind.

The coastal road was mercifully deserted and Sam's worry that he might draw the attention of a Riding Officer, out in search of the smuggling party, was unfounded. They reached the yard of the Bell just as Thomas Denard arrived with Dr Papworth-Hougham.

'Miss Fothergill,' he said, bowing and nodding his head. 'An unexpected pleasure.'

Ann bobbed her dress comically, clearly not used to such deference. Then, she glowered at Sam. 'I were told my help be requested.'

'They will certainly be of use to me,' he enthused, leading the way inside.

Sam found the pub a much calmer one than that which he had left. The men were in the process of devouring their bread, cheese and beer and some of the more seriously injured had passed out, though whether from pain or intoxication, Sam could not tell. Dr Papworth-Hougham led Ann over to the first injured man.

Sam found George Ransley, sitting alone at a table, drinking ale.

'Reckon we lost two tonight,' Ransley informed him.

'Unless they be out there somewhere—making their own way?' Sam suggested.

Ransley sniffed and spat a globule of phlegm onto the floor beside him. 'Not from what the men be saying. John Hart took a musket to his chest and Richard Hill to the head. I don't be a-reckoning they be making their own way anywhere.'

'I be seeing their widows right,' Sam mumbled.

Ransley nodded his agreement and drank some ale. 'Be giving the men their dues then we best move on.'

Sam did as he had been instructed and moved around the pub, paying each man according to his role.

'Let's be getting these carts loaded,' Ransley called and the men began to shuffle from their seats to the back door.

In the yard, the men formed four lines which ran from the rear of the carts, converging at the stack of barrels. With meaty grunts, the men heaved the contraband along the line into the awaiting carts, but only two were completely filled—half the expected quantity.

'That tarnal lot,' Ransley complained. 'Be putting the men what be hurt in there.'

On his instruction, the injured men were heaved into the back of the two empty carts.

Sam spotted someone in apparent good health among their number. 'You, out,' he ordered. He had the arm of James Carter—the man with the bone protruding from his leg—slung around his shoulder. Sam did not recognise the other man, and the knowledge of from where their smuggling gang operated was strictly withheld from strangers.

'I'm helping him—he can't walk for himself,' the man answered.

'He be alright—my life be owed to him,' James Carter defended. 'Weren't for him I'd've taken another musket.'

'What be your name?' Sam demanded.

'Jonas—Jonas Blackwood.'

'Which parish do you be hailing from, Jonas Blackwood?'

'Folkestone of the last seven months, Stockwell before that.'

Sam stared at him suspiciously, saying nothing.

Doctor Papworth-Hougham leant over and whispered in Sam's ear. 'That leg will likely have to be removed tomorrow. I need someone to watch him overnight.'

'Alright,' Sam conceded to Jonas. 'But this doctor needs to be finding him alive in the morning.'

Jonas nodded.

'Right!' Sam called up to George Ransley, who was one of the four horse riders. 'You be ready to go.'

Ransley dug his ankles into his horse's sides and proceeded from the yard, followed by the second and third cart. Sam clambered into the back of the fourth and nodded for the rider to follow on.

'Where do that be leaving me?' a voice demanded.

Sam turned to see Ann with her arms folded and her eyes reeling with rage. 'Hold!'

The horse was pulled to an abrupt halt.

'Here,' Sam said, offering her his left hand.

She stood motionless, holding his gaze, saying nothing.

Sam motioned for her to take his hand.

'Ready?' the rider barked down.

Ann reached out and climbed inside the cart, squeezing into a tiny space beside Sam.

'Go!' he called out and the horse trotted from the yard.

As they progressed in silence through the back roads and dirt tracks towards Aldington on this starkly cold night, Sam took some ignoble gratification from the warm closeness of Ann's body pressed to his.

'Why don't you be coming back?' Sam whispered to her.

Ann grinned and placed her hand on his leg.

Chapter Nine

18th November 1821, Aldington Frith, Kent

Ann delighted in the way that the room danced in time with the music. Richard Wire, a local smuggler was playing *Robin Hood* on his violin. Three topless women from the village were parading around, their breasts heaving to the beat of the music. By some clever trick Richard Wire had made the walls move to the rhythm of the song. Even the floor was undulating beneath her feet. Men from the village were sitting at small tables, gambling with cards and dice, their feet tap-tapping a unified beat into her head. In stark opposition to the bitter temperatures outside, in here the air was clammy and sticky, permeated with the heady stench of male sweat, smoke and spilled beer.

Ann closed her eyes and took another sip of her rum, savouring its warmth at the back of her throat, then she began to sing, '*The sheriff attempts to take bold Robin Hood. Bold Robin disdains to fly: Let him come when he will. We'll make merry in Sherwood, vanquish boys or die.*'

Someone spoke inside her head: 'Interesting place,' he said.

Ann opened her eyes and turned from side to side. A man was staring at her. A handsome man, by all accounts. Tall muscular and tidy-looking. 'What be?'

The man held an open hand to the room. 'Here—this place.'

'The Bourne Tap?' Ann said. 'Ransley's new home don't make for a bad place, no.'

The man picked at the tips of his dark moustache as he considered her words. 'And with its own unlicensed beer house attached. Middle of nowhere, surrounded by acres of woodland, serving his own smuggled rum and beer at low prices…'

'You'll not see many, save the bruff landlord of the Walnut, complaining at the price of liquor here!' Ann stated.

'I don't suppose so,' the man agreed. 'And yet no sign of the man himself.'

'Ransley be too shrewd for that.'

'So it seems,' he said, sinking the last mouthful of his beer. He licked the froth from around his mouth, then thumped the glass down onto the table.

Ann tried to tighten her focus on the man and to force her brain to understand his questioning. But he hadn't actually asked any questions, she realised, just blethered some open statements which had elicited a response from her.

'Goodnight,' he said, placing his hat upon his head and strolling towards the door.

'Goodnight,' Ann answered, trying to recall knowledge of him from previous smuggling runs. He was one of the tubmen, she thought. Or was he one of the batmen? Her befuddled brain refused to supply her with any further information and his attractive face quickly slipped away as the music thudded back into her head.

'Rum, Miss Fothergill?' one of the men said, passing her a pint of rum and water. It was Alexander Spence, a man whose superficial injuries she had tended after the last smuggling run four nights ago. Although the cargo had been landed without detection, Alexander had suffered minor rope burns to the palms of his hands.

'Thank you, kind sir,' Ann beamed, taking the drink with delight. Such rewards from the grateful men, whom she had helped to heal, had come forth in plentiful supply since she had been given a permanent role within the Aldington Gang.

'And a dance?' he asked with a lopsided grin, offering her his hand.

Holding his hand in hers, Ann examined his injured palms. 'They be healing nice,' she commented.

'That be your medicine what did it—all that slime.'

Ann smirked at his obsequious comment, recalling how her remedy had first been received with scorn. Even Doctor Papworth-Hougham had doubted the merits of having an escargatoire of snails trailing over his burns, prior to the application of an aloe and honey poultice; but it had worked and healed the wounds. She sloshed some drink into her mouth, then set the glass down, before gently taking Alexander's hand and joining him in a rollicking clumsy jig around the room. He spun her around in tight circles, weaving gracelessly between other dancing couples. Ann laughed as they stepped on each other's feet. She flipped her head backwards, her hair trailing behind her. Upside-down glances of heaving bosoms and black-toothed merriment darted across her vision.

'I be hearing you be on the lookout for lodgings,' Alexander said.

Ann pulled her head up in line with his. 'That be right—the mistress be wanting me out of Braemar Cottage in the morning... for the second time.'

'Happen I be knowing somewhere,' Alexander said with a coy grin.

'Don't be holding whist,' she said, playfully slapping his chest.

'My house,' he revealed.

Ann rolled her eyes. Thankfully, the song had come to an end, met with a minor round of applause and a somewhat coy bow from Richard Wire. Ann shook herself free.

Alexander released his arms from around Ann's midriff, one hand casually settling on her right breast. 'Do you be fancying a little walk in the woods?' he asked.

Ann picked off his hand and glowered at him. 'Great grief, I bain't no lushington and I certain-sure bain't not going walking in the woods with *you*, Alexander Spence.'

Alexander muttered some expletives under his breath, storming his way across the room to his friends in the far corner.

He was generally a decent man, and, under other circumstances, she might well have considered him suitable for her. But not now, not after what Ralph had said a few days ago whilst they were treating the injured smugglers at the Bell Inn. He had taken her to one side— deliberately out of everyone's earshot—and had said, 'Listen, I'm terribly sorry for my shortness with you a few months ago, you see my wife had just died and, well…'

'It be of no bother, Doctor—really it don't,' Ann had insisted, feeling an unexpected muddle of sympathy at his loss and a guilty sense of pleasure that he was no longer married.

Then he had said, 'Please—call me Ralph,' and he had touched her on the arm.

The warmth of the memory faded, leaving Ann with a fresh awareness of her surroundings. The air in the place had suddenly lost its allure and the stench of sweat began to make her feel nauseous. Striding back to her table, she picked up her rum and held it to her mouth without drinking. She gripped the glass there, pressed cold to her lips for some time. She was drunk, but not too drunk to see herself in a detached way—the way that others clearly saw her. Her skills as an apothecary and being in receipt of good regular wages had seen her rise from her vagrancy days in Dover and yet still she was perceived as a drunk no-good streetwalker.

For the first time, at least as far as her memory would permit, Ann left the barely touched pint of rum on the table and walked away.

She ambled slowly back to Braemar Cottage, craving the sobering sensation brought on by the freezing temperatures. Her whole body was quivering when, finally, she reached the front of the house. The effects of the alcohol had numbed the edges of her pain and stripped her errant thoughts back to a simple monotony of placing one foot in front of the other; nothing else was given space in her mind.

Ann looked through the un-shuttered parlour window at the dim room. The silhouettes of two figures flickered from the flames of the fire. Sam, with his back to the window, appeared to be talking to Hester. Ann watched them, mesmerised. They were a curious couple whom, despite having lived with them again for the past eight days, she had failed to understand. When she had tended to Sam during his largely unconscious period of fever, she had suffered daily under the oppressive temperament of his wife, Hester. Ann had fabricated a limp hollow personality for Sam, subservient to the demands of his imperious wife. The man whom she had resurrected, however, had been entirely different to her imagined version of him. He was a strong-willed, defiant man with a fortitude easily matching that of his wife.

Ann continued watching their exchange, assuming from the way which Hester's exaggerated hands moved from flapping animatedly in the air to being thrust onto her jutting hip, that the conversation which she was now witnessing was actually an argument.

The perfect time to make an entrance, she mused, with a wry smile.

With a confident stride, Ann marched towards the house. Just yards from the door she stopped dead. It was not Sam at all. He—whoever *he* was—took something from Hester. Money, perhaps, then moved towards the street door. In a panic, Ann wondered what she should do or where she should go, but she had no time to go anywhere or do anything.

The door opened and the man saw her. He hurriedly pulled his hat down over his eyes, but she had seen him. It was the man from the Bourne Tap. The handsome man who had played with his moustache whilst making oblique statements about the place. Without a word, he strode past her and was absorbed into the darkness.

'Who be that?' Ann demanded of Hester on entering the house.

'It bain't be none of your business,' Hester answered, slamming the street door.

Ann felt the devil rise inside her. 'Happen I be asking Sam what a man be doing here at night giving his wife money.'

Hester looked visibly shaken. 'He be a friend and not what you be a-thinking.'

'What do he be called, this friend what gives money to folks at night time?' Ann asked.

'Jonas Blackwood.'

Ann nodded. 'What say—quitter for quatter, like—that I *not* be moving on tomorrow and be lodging here a while longer? Happen, then, I be forgetting all about men what pay you in the night time.'

Hester's narrowed eyes displayed such bilious anger. Short snorts of air fumed from her nostrils, as, with hands on her hips, she contemplated Ann's threat.

Ann stretched exaggeratedly, as though she had all the time in the world to wait for Hester's decision. In her peripheral vision she spotted movement outside. Sam was walking the path to the house. Ann danced her way to the door and pulled it open. 'Sam, what a delight. We be just talking about you.'

'What grabby weather,' Sam complained, removing his boots, shooting curious looks between the two women. 'What you be saying?'

Ann looked to Hester.

'Ann be a-staying on here a little longer, if that be alright by you, Sam,' Hester said softly.

Sam smiled. 'She can be staying here as long as she be liking.'

'Most gracious,' Ann said, flouncing from the room.

Chapter Ten

Phil was sitting in his battered Volvo looking at his cheap watch. Counting down. Forty-five seconds to go. He glanced up at the bungalow and back down to his watch. Forty seconds. He looked up again and saw that the door was now open.

'You're thirty-three seconds early!' he said with a laugh, banging the steering wheel.

He watched the old man shuffle out, shut the door, then check that it was locked three more times.

'Jesus, will you just hurry up. IT'S LOCKED!' Phil yelled, unheard from the confines of his car.

Arthur Fothergill, with a hessian jute bag in one hand and a walking stick in the other, ambled down his garden path and out onto the main road, where he paused and took a lengthy look up and down the street.

Phil flopped his head onto the steering wheel with exasperation at the time he was taking.

Finally, the old man wandered down the road towards the bus stop. It was the same routine, week in week out. Every Tuesday he would take the 10.16am 101 bus from New Romney to Folkestone, where he would spend the day shuffling around shops into which he didn't need to go, spending money which he didn't have, on stuff which he didn't need.

Once he was completely out of sight, Phil clambered from his car, crossed the street and walked up the path to the bungalow. Taking out his key, he opened the door and went inside.

Phil switched on the light, but it did little to drag the dark and dingy hallway from the shadows. He entered the dining room and headed straight for the bureau where he knew Arthur kept his official documentation. Opening the drawbridge-style door, Phil could instantly see from the chaotic mess of paperwork that his task was not going to be as quick and easy as he had first thought. Still, he had all day.

He pulled out the first stack of papers—bills from British Gas and EDF. As he sorted through the pile, he paused, thinking that he had heard something. He quickly stuffed the papers back inside and closed the bureau door. Without moving, he listened. Yes, someone was standing at the front door, struggling to get their key into the lock.

Now what? The front door opened, meaning that he was now prevented from escaping via the back entrance. He was trapped in the dining room and had no alternative but to hide in the first place that a child might check in a game of hide-and-seek: behind the door.

'I actually feel sick about it,' Juliette whined, standing from the table and rubbing her stomach under her nightshirt, preparing to scoop Grace up as she crawled around the kitchen floor.

'But that's just because you've had a year off—it's normal,' Morton said, taking a bite of his toast. 'Once you're back out there you'll be fine.'

Juliette sighed. 'Even though it's only three days a week, it feels different now we've got Grace. It's not exactly the safest job in the world. Mind you, with the stupid things you end up doing, your job's just as bad.'

'I promise I'll be more careful,' Morton tried to reassure her.

Juliette crouched down, lifted Grace and spun her around one hundred and eighty degrees away from the oven. 'I mean, look at her—she's so vulnerable.'

Grace scuttled across to Morton's chair and clambered herself up. 'Dadda,' she said, offering him a clump of fluff from the floor.

'Thank you, Grace,' he said with a grin.

'Yes, thank you, Grace,' Juliette said sarcastically. 'That's the other problem: I just don't know how I'm going to get anything done. It's the party in four days' time and we've barely done hardly anything for it, except to invite loads of people here. And Jack, Laura and George will be arriving on her birthday—in two days' time. Look at the state of the place.'

'Stop worrying. I'll have a clean-up later and do some shopping for the party. It's all fine,' he said, reaching out for her hand. 'Really.' Morton shoved the last piece of toast into his mouth and bent down to pick up his daughter. 'Come here, Miss Farrier,' he said, sitting her on his lap. 'What do you want to do today? How about helping me find out about the Aldington Gang of smugglers?'

'How about a trip to the playpark with your daughter and darling wife on her last full day of freedom?' Juliette suggested. 'Maybe take them out for a meal?'

'Sounds good to me,' Morton replied.

It was Arthur. He had inexplicably returned and was now fussing in the hallway, wondering how he could have forgotten to switch the light off. 'I'm sure I did,' he muttered. 'Is anyone here? Steve? Clara?' When no reply was forthcoming he said, 'Nope, just you, Arthur, you silly old fool.'

Phil stood rigidly behind the dining room door, holding his breath as Arthur trundled down the hallway to the lounge, all the while narrating as he went. Apparently, he had forgotten a faulty alarm clock, which he was going to return to the shop in Folkestone.

'Right,' Arthur mumbled. 'Keys. Where did I put those?'

Phil took an incredulous long breath in.

'Now, remember to switch the light off,' Arthur reminded himself.

Seconds later, Phil heard the *dink* of the light switch. Once Arthur was out of the door, he was half tempted to switch it back on again, just to confuse him. He remained still until he heard the door slam shut, then he allowed himself to breathe normally again. He still dared not move, though, not until Arthur had completed his double- and triple-checking of the door.

Silence.

Phil moved slowly towards the front window and just caught sight of Arthur turning back in the direction of the bus stop.

Returning to the bureau, Phil began to sift through the muddle of paperwork. Letters. Bills. Receipts. Take-away menus. Insurances. Notes. Scrap paper.

He let out an infuriated groan.

Then, he reached a bundle of papers bound together with an elastic band. Arthur's birth certificate was on the top. This is more like it, Phil thought, thumbing through the pile. He caught glimpses of Arthur's marriage certificate along with the birth and death certificates of his wife. Then he found it: the last will and testament of Arthur Fothergill.

Phil withdrew the document and, skipping over the legal niceties and funeral and burial details, he came to the important information: the distribution of the assets which, he read, were to be divided equally between Arthur's nephew and niece.

With a triumphant smile, Phil placed the will back in the bundle, returning everything to the bureau as he had found it.

The old man hadn't been stringing them along, after all. No cats' homes or sympathetic neighbours or distant cousins. Equal shares between nephew and niece. He was happy with that.

168

It had been a surprisingly tiring day for Morton. The three of them had taken a Knoops hot chocolate down to the playpark, where Morton had divided his time between pushing an ecstatic Grace on the swings and consoling a miserable Juliette on the bench, who had sat for the most part with her head in her hands. Then, they had sauntered through Rye, popping into various shops before having dinner at *The Globe* restaurant. Now, Grace was tucked up in bed and Juliette was throwing an iron over her police uniform, which was making its debut outing for the first time in twelve months.

Morton carried a large glass of red wine up to his study and switched on his laptop. It was the first time all day that he had had a chance to look at his emails or do anything resembling work. He guessed that this was how life would be now, for a while at least.

From the twenty-two emails which downloaded into his inbox, he chose to read those associated with the case first. One of them was from the Coroner's Office: *'Dear Morton, Thank you for your email and interest in this case. I have spoken with our archiving team and unfortunately, they cannot find any files or information that we have stored regarding this. They did suggest that it may be worthwhile looking in Folkestone Library as they will hold copies of local newspapers from the time of the discovery, or possibly even speaking with the pub where the skeletons were discovered, but we have no information that we can offer on this case I'm afraid. Best wishes, Sandy.'*

Visiting the Bell was not a bad suggestion. It was highly unlikely, though, that the owners were the same people from 1963, or that any better recollection of the discovery could be provided than that which he had already heard from Clive Baintree.

The next email was from the Burial Officer at Shepway District Council, who informed him that, upon checking all the municipal cemeteries in Hythe and Folkestone for 1963, she had found no 'unknown males' in the registers or anything which might have been the two bodies. The same negative response came from St Leonard's, the main parish church of Hythe.

On his investigation wall, Morton placed a small cross beside the meticulous list of local churches and cemeteries, which he had drawn up regarding the burial of the two skeletons. Then, returning to his laptop, he opened an email from Hawkinge Cemetery & Crematorium with a smile. *'Good afternoon, Morton. I always like to think that there is no such thing as a strange request, but I think this may qualify! I have indeed located the men's burial, although the information is rather vague, I'm afraid. It is identical for both: Unknown male, estimated 30-40 years of age, found dead 7th July 1963 in the Bell Inn, Hythe. The two men were buried in communal graves in Plot G at Hawkinge Cemetery. There is no further information in the registers. I hope this helps, Irene.'*

Morton printed the email and fastened it to the investigation wall. He had found the burial place of the two bodies but, as he had expected, there was little information which would develop the case. And he still did not actually know if the two men had been interred in the fireplace during Ann's tenure of the pub.

Sitting back at his desk, he took a swig of wine. There were no other emails which warranted his precious time this evening, so he switched his focus to finding out about the Aldington smuggling gang.

Google kindly offered him 79,600 results for his search enquiry. He drank some wine and clicked the first link: a Wikipedia page for the group. Making notes as he went, Morton completed the page and selected the next link.

After some time of reading, the study door was pushed open and there stood a grumpy-looking Juliette in her police uniform.

'What's the matter?' Morton asked.

'Look at me,' she answered, lifting her arms up by her side. 'It's far too tight.'

'Is it?' Morton said, pretending not to have noticed the obvious. 'I think it looks okay.'

Juliette huffed. 'Don't be ridiculous. I look like a whale in a bikini.'

A discussion of her weight was as easy to negotiate as a freshly laid minefield. If he said that she looked fine—which he thought she did, just about—she would become annoyed at him for lying. If he said that the few extra understandable pounds of baby weight would shift in no time once she was back patrolling the streets, it meant a tacit agreement with her idea of being overweight, which would only make matters worse. Instead, he stupidly said, 'Maybe your uniform's shrunk?'

'Oh, for God's sake, Morton,' she said, turning on her heels and mumbling that she was going to bed.

'I'll be there in a minute,' he whispered after her.

That minute mushroomed into several hours reading on the Aldington Gang. He was several pages into Google's suggested list of links but was now adding little to his notes. The websites were tending to repeat the same basic information about the gang: active from late 1820 under the leadership of Cephas Quested, a man who was captured at the Battle of Brookland in 1821. He was hanged, after which time a new leader, George Ransley took over. Various websites were in agreement in their assertion that Ransley had somehow acquired the means to continue the group and build a new home for himself called the Bourne Tap in the village of Aldington, from where he orchestrated the gang's many large-scale runs. In 1826, however, Quartermaster Richard Morgan had been murdered by one of the gang and several of their number had stood trial before being transported to Van Dieman's Land in 1827, bringing the last major Kent smuggling group to a definitive end.

The gang's transportation in April 1827 tied in perfectly with Ann's letter of July of that year, in which she spoke of the renewed quietness of the area.

Morton's suspicions that Ann's letter had been written to one of the convicted smugglers had not been borne out in the published lists of those convicted. And yet, he was more certain than ever of Ann's involvement with the gang.

Pondering where an agricultural labourer had gained the means to build his own house and maintain a smuggling racket, Morton wrote 'The Bourne Tap, Aldington – gold guineas found by George Ransley???' on a piece of paper and stuck it to the wall.

Finishing the last dregs of his wine, he stared at the timeline on his investigation wall, thinking. His gut instinct told him that the common link between all of the evidence, which he had so far uncovered for the 1820-1827 period, was smuggling. He now needed to uncover firm documentary evidence to substantiate that link. He knew what his next steps needed to be, but right now, having just gone midnight, it was time to sleep. The morning would be a competition between Juliette and Grace as to which one would wake Morton first. He had a busy day ahead of him, trying to juggle the case, looking after Grace and preparing for the party. In just two days—one, technically, now that it had passed midnight—his biological father would be arriving with his family from America. He had yet to hear from his Aunty Margaret about whether or not she would be attending.

As he pushed his laptop lid down to a close, a tangled sensation began to form inside him at the thought of Jack and Margaret meeting for the first time since 1974.

Chapter Eleven

Morton's day was not going well. He had been woken several times during the night by Grace screaming, then had been duly summoned by her shouting 'Dadda' at the top of her voice at some ungodly moment before five o'clock that morning, refusing to go back to sleep. Then Juliette had risen in a satanic mood on this, her first day back at work in over a year. Morton's attempt to pacify the situation, by pointing out that she didn't actually start work until three pm, was met with a derisive rolling of her eyes. It was only when he had shown her the online menu for the Bell Inn, suggesting it as a late-breakfast destination, that she began to calm.

Hungry and rattled, they reached the pub mid-morning. Grace had inexplicably cried for the entirety of the twenty-one-mile journey. Carrot sticks, Peppa Pig videos, nursery rhymes and a variety of toys had done little to subdue her.

'Great. I hope she's not sickening for something just before the party,' Juliette commented, as Morton parked the car beside the pub. She exhaled, climbed out and proceeded to unfold the pushchair, before removing Grace from her car seat. Finally, she stopped crying.

Morton looked up at the old two-storey building. It was painted brilliant white, the lower half plastered and the upper half cladded in weather-boarding. Sandwiched between the two storeys was the name of the pub in large golden lettering. With the roof in terracotta tiles, it was the quintessential Kentish pub.

'Brilliant,' Morton mumbled, as he approached the front door. The website had expounded its range of wonderful menu options, yet had failed to mention anywhere the crucial fact that the pub was shut. Closed down. Empty. They had just driven all this way with a screaming child for nothing. Excellent.

'Oh, you're joking,' Juliette sighed, when she too realised that they had wasted their journey here.

'No lemon sole goujons for us, then,' Morton lamented, pressing his nose to the grimy window. Inside was completely devoid of furniture. At the back of the room he could just make out the open fireplace where the bodies had been discovered in 1963. Zooming in on his mobile, he took a picture of the fireplace for the case file.

'I was just thinking,' he said.

'Dangerous,' Juliette quipped.

'Do you fancy popping to Maidstone for lunch?'

Juliette shot him a dubious look. 'No, I don't. I'm guessing you don't, either. You actually want to visit the Kent History and Library Centre. Right?'

'Er...'

'Look, if you need to go there then just drop us home and go—as long as you're back before half past two when I need to leave for work.'

'Sure?'

'Very—I just want to go home now and sulk,' she answered, putting Grace back into her car seat.

Morton smiled and collapsed the pushchair, appreciating his normal little family unit. Over the next few days, if his Aunty Margaret did arrive, all that normality might well go flying into the wind with the conjoining of his biological and adoptive families. It was something that he absolutely craved and dreaded in equal measure.

He slowly pulled away from the pub and Grace began to wail.

The glass doors to the Kent History and Library Centre parted in an automatic welcome; Morton stepped inside and headed to the main reception desk, where he received an access card on a lanyard from the smiling young librarian. Walking with a purposeful gait, Morton headed into the far-left corner of the building and swiped his access card to gain entry to the archive reading room. Aside from the man single-finger typing at a computer keyboard behind the helpdesk, there were just two other researchers occupying spaces at one of the three large tables in the centre of the room. Morton placed his laptop, notepad and pencil on one of the spaces and headed over to a bank of colourful folders, which provided indexes to all of the archive holdings. From a run of blue files, Morton selected *Parish Records Addington-Bearsted* and carried it over to his desk, where he flipped through until he reached the parochial records pertaining to Aldington. Hopefully somewhere in here he would find documents which might shed some light on Ann Fothergill's time in the village.

The records covered a range of topics and a range of dates. He slowly ran his finger down the lists, past the baptisms, marriages and burials to the other documents relating to the organisation of the village. *Workhouse registers. Rates. Minutes of the Parochial Church Council. Bastardy Bonds. Settlement & Removal Orders.*

173

Under the heading of '*Overseers—Miscellaneous*' his finger stopped on a particular record dated 1824. *Survey of the Parish by William Stiles giving name of occupiers, acreages and land use. Probably compiled for tithe and rating purposes. This paper is complete.*

Morton filled in the white document request slip and carried it over to the man who was still single-finger typing behind the desk. 'Hi. I'd like to order this, please,' he said, handing over the slip of paper.

The man took it with a near-smile. 'It's on microfilm. Is that okay?'

'I might need to get copies. Is it alright to photograph the screen?'

The man grimaced. 'Afraid not—the Church of the Latter-Day Saints owns the copyright—you'll need to print out any copies you need.'

Morton held back from his desire to argue the absurdities of the Mormons begrudging his photographing a document on-screen compared to printing it out. Clearly this couldn't be the case. 'Right.'

'It'll be a few minutes,' the man said, carrying the slip out through a door behind him.

Returning to his seat, Morton continued scanning the list of parish records, identifying several more documents for the relevant period which might be of interest. Some, he realised, would be contained on the microfilm that he had just ordered. He reached the end of the parish of Aldington. Only a few further documents were to be found in the small window of time in which he was searching. He completed two further request slips and walked them over to the helpdesk, just as the single-finger typist reappeared carrying the small black box of microfilm.

'Here you go.'

Morton thanked him and carried it over to the reader, where he loaded the film and buzzed through to the correct section—*Aldington P4/18/1*. The records had a preamble, handwritten by the compiler in 1824. *An account of the admeasurement of the Parish of Aldington in the County of Kent, giving an account of the quantity of land in the occupation of each person whose names are hereafter inserted where the plough and scythe goes, including woodland and orchard, taken in the respective months of March, April and May in the year of our Lord One Thousand Eight Hundred and Twenty-Four by me, William Styles.*

The first section of the document was arranged according to the land and building holdings of each owner. Morton wound his way through the property owners of the village, thankful that Aldington was a relatively small parish. *Mr Thomas Carpenter. Mr Edward Epps. Mr Foord.*

Mr Mills. Mr Rogers. Mr Edward Marshall. Mr Bridger. Mr Thomas Pilcher. Widow Sealy. Mr Robert Scott. The valuations spanned several pages, but there was no mention of either Ann Fothergill or anyone by the name of Sam. Although Morton was not surprised that Ann—a street vagrant just three years prior—was not among the land-owning villagers, she had already confounded his expectations by owning the Bell Inn just a year later, in 1825, so he was keeping an open mind as he searched.

Morton wound through a long trail of black film, which was sandwiched between the ending of one record set and the commencement of the next. A stirring of optimism rose inside him when he saw what appeared on-screen before him: a complete breakdown of each owner's holdings and a valuation for each. Crucially, house names were stated, as were the names of the main occupier. If Ann hadn't owned a property in Aldington, perhaps she had been listed in one as a tenant.

His methodical search took him just over half an hour. Ann had not been listed, but Morton did find mention of one Samuel Banister on a record of '*Cottages belonging to Court Lodge Farm*'. He was stated to be the tenant of Braemar Cottage and garden, valued at £1 and 10 shillings.

Morton studied the printout. At this stage, there was no evidence that Samuel Banister had anything to do with Ann, other than the fact that he shared the same Christian name as a man to whom she had written in 1827.

Wary of the fact that time was slipping from him, Morton fast-forwarded the roll of film through several records, which pertained to a much later period of time, stopping at *Overseers Accounts – Assessments & Disbursements*, which spanned much of the nineteenth century. Not knowing when Ann had arrived in the village, Morton began searching the accounts from 1820. Among the initial records were two which gave an indication of why and when the Aldington Gang had been created.

15 April 1820
Two bushels of barley for Cephas Quested. 9 shillings
Paid Mrs Fagg for attendance on Cephas Quested's wife. 5 shillings 6 pence

Then, later that month:

Paid Cephas Quested in need. 5 shillings

It was clear to Morton that Cephas Quested had started the smuggling gang owing to his apparent poverty. Tellingly, there were no further mentions of the Quested family in the file. He hit the print button, then continued his trawl.

Just a few minutes later, he found something.

28ᵗʰ February 1821
Paid doctor's attendance to Hester Banister. 6 shillings
2ⁿᵈ March 1821
Paid for coal and candles for Braemar Cottage, requested by Ann Fothergill, lodging there. 8 shillings 4 pence

Morton now had documentary evidence that Ann had been residing with the Banister family at Braemar Cottage from at least the end of February 1821, implying that the 'Sam', to whom she had written in 1827, was indeed Samuel Banister.

'Here's your other film,' the single-finger typist said, placing another black box beside the microfilm reader.

'Thank you,' Morton said, briefly taking his eyes from the screen. He printed the entry, not quite satisfied to move on, and yet unable to give himself a reason as to why. He zoomed in to isolate the entry and read it several times more. Hester had obviously been sick enough to require a doctor and for Ann to have been the person to make an appeal for coal and candles. Why had Sam not been the one to have made the claim? Or to be providing for Hester, whom Morton presumed to be his sick wife? Knowing the parsimonious reputation shared by Parish Overseers throughout the land, they would not have paid out a single penny had Sam been sitting idle; he would have to have been either absent from his home or himself incapacitated.

With just over one hour until he had to leave, Morton persisted with the Overseers' records until he reached the end of the roll of film. There were no further mentions of Ann, Hester or Samuel.

Morton rewound the film and then loaded the next one, which began with parish registers for the village. Knowing that they were already online, Morton buzzed past them, intent on finding more about Hester and Samuel Banister when he would have time at home. He slowed the film down, pausing at intervals to check which records were currently on screen. Following a band of black film, P4/12/3, a ledger

176

recording work and wages of unemployed labourers on the parish farm appeared. At the top of the page was written *Ruffians Hill Farm*. Running down the left in a long column was a list of men's names, beside which were the number of days worked in the week, followed by pay received. The volume commenced in 1820 and Morton began to scan down the list of names. The year ended without mention of a single Banister. In the first quarter of 1821, however, Morton discovered a baffling entry.

Week commencing Monday 5th March
Sam¹ Banister ½ day £0.0s.0d

His was the only name which had zero financial reward. Morton hurriedly printed the page then carried on through the ledger, deliberately checking both names and pay. The register ended in December 1825. In that period there were no further mentions of Samuel Banister, nor did anyone else not receive pay for their efforts on Ruffians Hill Farm.

He had no time left in which to ponder—he had to leave.

Having rewound the film and handed the two boxes back to the single-finger typist, Morton gathered up his belongings and carried the printouts to the main reception desk then left.

'Jesus, Morton,' Juliette greeted him when he arrived back home. 'I've literally got to leave in thirty seconds.'

Morton looked at his watch and shrugged: 'You said be home by 2.30. It's 2.29.'

'Heaven forbid you'd want to sit down and have a drink with me before I go,' she snapped, pulling her work shoes from the cupboard beside the front door.

'Sorry, I didn't think…'

'Hmm,' she responded, bending down to tie her laces.

'Where's Grace?' he asked.

'Afternoon sleep. You've got a good hour to get the house cleaned and tidied before she wakes up.' Juliette stood up and tugged at various parts of her tight uniform, which had gathered up in unsightly places. 'Right, bye.'

Morton kissed her on the lips, then pulled her tight to him. 'It will all be fine,' he whispered.

He felt her body relax in his grip, as she began to breathe more deeply. 'I hope so.' She broke away, pecked him on the lips again and said, 'See you in the morning.'

With a moody sigh, she turned, opened the front door and was gone.

Morton plodded into the kitchen, made himself a coffee, then carried it, along with his bag, up to his study. He sipped at the drink and studied the investigation wall. His eyes roamed from one record to another, whilst his brain tried to join the dots together. From his bag, he pulled out the printouts and his notebook and began to add the new information to the wall and timeline. Ann Fothergill, lodging at Braemar Cottage, had, at the end of February 1821, applied to the parish for a doctor to see Hester. Days later, she had received coal and candles. Shortly after that, Samuel Banister had undertaken half a day's work on the parish farm, for which he had received no payment. Morton's current assumption was that Samuel was himself ill at the time when Ann had sought help from the overseers and had then attempted half a day's labouring. The implication for receiving no pay was that his work was unsatisfactory or uncompleted: perhaps he had been too ill to work, Morton mused. And then, the family had needed no further financial support from the parish—ever again. Why? The answer—smuggling—was obvious; the documentary evidence to substantiate this, however, was paper-thin. As Morton re-read his notes on the Aldington Gang, he was drawn to the transition period between the two leaders. The pivotal moment had been the Battle of Brookland on the 11th February 1821. Was it too much to consider that perhaps Samuel Banister had been injured in the battle, thus unable to provide for his family?

One thing was certain to Morton: Samuel Banister's connection to Ann Fothergill was proving to be a crucial one and he needed much more detailed research.

Just as he opened his laptop to begin searching the Aldington parish registers online, Grace announced that she was awake with a glass-shattering cry.

For a day which had started out so badly, it was ending in a much more constructive way, Morton ruminated, as he sipped from a mercifully large glass of wine. He was back up in his study, having fed Grace, played with her, bathed her, then put her to bed. He had run a series of searches in the Aldington parish registers and had found, in 1795,

Samuel Banister's baptism record, meaning that he had been around six years older than Ann. Morton had been unable to locate a marriage, but did find the baptism of two children: John and Ellen. The burial register had revealed only Hester's death in 1852. There having been no sign of Samuel, Morton ran a search in the civil death registers from 1837 onwards, but to no avail. He had not been unduly surprised. He believed that Ann's letter of 1827 had been written to Samuel and that he was not living in England at that point, a fact confirmed by both the 1841 and 1851 censuses, which stated Hester to have been married, yet with no sign of her husband.

Morton's phone beeped an announcement of a text message. It was from Juliette: '*Hi. How's it going? Did Grace go down okay? You did remember to give her dinner?! Grim here. Sent out alone to pull a suicide attempter off a bridge. Told off for not letting the station know I was okay. Want to come home xx*'

He stared at the message for sufficiently long enough for the screen to go black. He did not know how to respond. Sarcasm and suicide attempts were not exactly great bedfellows. And she never took well to being pandered to. Simple and neutral was best, he decided. '*Hi. All good here. Grace ate her dinner and went to bed nicely. Sorry the first shift isn't great. See you later. Love you. Xxx*' He re-read the message and found it to be sufficiently simple and neutral, then clicked send.

His gaze seemed to gravitate of its own volition towards their wedding photograph on his desk. People often spoke about their wedding day as having been the happiest of their lives, which Morton had always found an odd thing to say; the implication being that nothing thereafter could ever match up to those precious few hours. The truth, for him, was that the wedding had been a pinnacle moment—he could see that now. It was the closing of a chapter of his life. The years, which had followed his being told that he had been adopted, had been marred by anger, frustration and an insatiable search for the truth, and which, until Juliette had entered his life, had left him restless, with the desire to marry or have children repressed. The day that he had married Juliette would certainly be *among* the best of his life, but its significance went way beyond a handful of hazy fleeting moments in the company of friends and family.

He drank some more wine, sighed thoughtfully, then turned back to his laptop.

Logging in to The Genealogist website, Morton ran a search in the Tithe & Land Owner record collection for Braemar Cottage,

Aldington. Receiving just one result, he clicked it and a large-scale map of the village loaded before him. Dated 1842, the map carved the village up into its composite parcels of land, with houses and buildings marked and annotated with the owner and occupiers' names. Braemar Cottage was, by 1842, occupied by one Thomas Tutt.

Zooming in closely, Morton could see that Braemar Cottage was one of several tied to the estate of Court Lodge Farm. Directly beside the farm was the parish church, and it dawned on Morton then, that he had seen the farm and some of the small tied cottages when he had made the trip to the village three days ago. From what he could remember, they were small and modest affairs.

Before printing the map, Morton spent some time moving his cursor around the village, zooming in to various areas of interests. He found Hester Banister living in what appeared to be sizable cottage close to the Walnut Tree Inn. Crucial to his theory that her husband, Samuel was no longer in the country was the fact that Hester was among only a handful of women without the prefix of 'widow'; those other women being the wives of transported smugglers.

Morton was startled by the house phone ringing beside him. The area code—01326—told him exactly who was calling him. He paused, staring at the phone. He might not have answered it but for the fear of the continual ringing waking Grace making his decision for him. 'Hello?' he said, in way which suggested he had no knowledge of the caller's identity.

'Hello, Morton, it's your Aunty Margaret, here,' she said brightly.

'Oh, hi,' he answered casually. 'How are you?'

'Muddling along as usual,' she said. 'What about at your end?'

'Great, thank you. Grace is tucked up in bed and Juliette went back to work today.'

'Oh, dear. I don't imagine she liked that,' Margaret sympathised. 'I was *more* than happy to give up work when I had the girls.' She chuckled.

'I think she went back with mixed feelings—it was her choice to go back,' he said, feeling an odd sense of defensiveness, as though he had been the one forcing her back to work against her will.

'It's the way these days,' she said.

'Yes,' Morton found himself agreeing, although to what, he wasn't quite sure.

A pause in the conversation began to swell as they both circumvented what she needed to say, and what he was waiting to hear.

180

He decided to plough straight in. 'So, have you—' but his words collided with her saying, 'So, I've made a decision...' Another awkward pause. 'Sorry, go on,' he said.

'I've made a decision about coming down,' she repeated, before adding an unnecessary moment of suspense akin to a television talent show host on the verge of announcing a winner's name.

'Right,' Morton said coolly, as though he had forgotten all about it.

'Jim and I *will* be coming to Grace's party.'

The curdling mixture of anxiety and elation instantly returned to Morton's stomach. 'Brilliant,' he replied. 'I'm so pleased you'll be there.'

'So, we'll be arriving at the hotel across the road from you just after lunchtime tomorrow.'

Morton felt a cold lurch inside him as the reality of the situation dawned on him. Jack, Laura and George were arriving just after lunchtime tomorrow. He glanced at the clock in the top corner of his laptop: 8.56pm. In fact, if their flight had been on time, they would be in the air right now.

'Excellent,' Morton muttered, wondering if he should go to the hotel to greet them, or have them come to the house. Since they would be meeting at the party, he opted to plummet straight into the abyss. 'Jack, Laura and George will be here around that time; would you like to come for dinner, as it's Grace's actual birthday tomorrow?'

Margaret cleared her throat. 'Yes, that would be lovely if it's not too much trouble?'

'No trouble,' Morton answered.

'Smashing. We'll see you tomorrow afternoon, then.'

'Great—have a good journey.'

'Bye.'

He said goodbye, ended the call and looked with bewilderment at the photograph of Jack and Margaret together in 1974, wondering what an earth kind of awkward mess dinner tomorrow night was going to be.

'What have I done?' he said to himself.

Chapter Twelve

26th March 1822, outside the town boundary of Dover, Kent

The cold night sky seemed endless to Sam, as he stared up in awe at the tiny white dots littered against the pale grey backdrop. His neck stiffened, and he gently rolled his head around, grimacing at the clicking of his bones. He glanced sideways, in the direction of where Alexander Spence and Thomas Brazier had disappeared some minutes before. On this part of the coastline, just outside of Dover, nothing moved or stirred but the gentle roll of the tide. He gazed out at the erupting, cream-tipped waves, breaking a short distance from him, seemingly conjured from a dark hem sewn between earth and sea.

He turned to stroke the horse which was tethered beside him, after it had snorted and impatiently pawed one of its hoofs on the ground.

'They not be long,' Sam said, giving a firm slap to its shoulder.

He looked again into the darkness, but there was no sign of the two men.

In a drunken agreement last night, Spence and Brazier had accepted Ransley's request for two volunteers to earn extra money. Sam had brought them down to Dover in one of Ransley's horse and carts in order to purloin as many compasses and telescopes as the two men could plunder. Sam hoped, as he searched the horizon in the direction of the moored vessels, that the fact that no ruckus or disturbances had so far occurred meant that the two men were being successful in their task. He wondered now, in chilled sobriety, how the men measured their decisions. It had been another night of liquor and debauchery at the Bourne Tap. A night which had seen several barrels of rum, ale and brandy run dry, as was becoming the custom there. At the margin of the gaiety, Sam had studied Ann closely, as she had danced merrily and without inhibition. His scrutiny of her had been laden with an unhealthy amalgam of admiration for her free spirit, an appreciation of her curative talents and, increasingly of late, growing desire. Her coquettish behaviour towards him was, like her entire demeanour, capricious and seemingly governed by whim. One moment she was pulling him into a flirtatious dance, pressing her breasts against him knowingly, while the next moment she was aloof, apathetic. It was all part of her wild existence, he reasoned, her way of resisting the normality of a staid life. Yet he could see that she was becoming restless with this way of life, too, and he wondered where her impulsive internal compass would take her next.

His reveries were interrupted by the unmistakable sound of a pistol firing.

Sam's heart kicked into a higher rhythm as he scanned the coastline for the location of the gunfire. He couldn't be completely certain, but it had come from the approximate direction in which the two men had headed.

'Damn it,' he cursed, withdrawing his own pistol and beginning to load it. He held the weapon unsteadily in his weak right hand and began to jog towards the gunfire.

Another shot resounded loudly.

He was getting close now and so slowed his pace to steady his breathing. A dragging sense of inadequacy diminished his valiant dash towards the confrontation, as violent shaking in his right hand forced him to switch the pistol to his left.

Muffled grunts and the sound of tussling were emanating from the shingle just up ahead. Silhouetted figures—at least four of them—were brawling and shouting at one another.

Sam crouched down and took a moment to allow his eyes to discern any detail from the darkened scuffle. He flinched as another musket pierced the air. Then he saw what looked like a gun tumbling to the ground, then another.

The behaviour of two of the men, whom Sam could now identify as Spence and Brazier, suddenly slackened into compliance, becoming submissive to their captors.

Sam needed to act now to save them or it would be too late.

Something—whether pure cowardice, an unfavourable appraisal of the potential outcome, or the flashing into his mind of images of his family—entrenched him, making his breathing heavy and his hands tremble.

The striding crunch of the men's boots away from him chimed perfectly with the weakening of Sam's resolve to act to save them.

He watched as their shadows melded, shrank and then vanished.

An overpowering shudder coursed across his flesh and he dropped his pistol to the ground.

Sam stood quietly staring into the impenetrable oblivion of where the men had disappeared, as if he could somehow will them to return. But they did not and another shudder, this time streaked with the cold night air, ran down his body.

Stooping to pick up his pistol, Sam turned and slowly trod back to the horse and cart.

The revelries at the Bourne Tap were continuing when Sam descended from the horse and strode into the warm room. Richard Wire was playing on his violin and several dancers—their faces glazed with sweat—were making merry under the gapes of the ale-swigging men and women stood at the edges of the room. Various games of dice and dominoes were taking place on candlelit tables.

'Oh, look what be here!' Ann shouted, tossing her head this way and that.

Sam nodded embarrassedly, not liking the eyes of the place upon him.

Ann twirled over to him clumsily, lifted her hand to his face and ran the backs of her hot fingers down his cheek. 'What be the matter with your cruppish face, Samuel?' she asked.

'They be captured,' he answered quietly. 'Brazier and Spence.'

Ann's gaiety dissipated instantly, and he could tell by the change in atmosphere around him that others had heard it too and were now affected in their movements and conversations.

'What plaguesome news be this, Sam?' It was Ransley, stomping in from outside.

Sam forced himself to meet Ransley's glowering face. 'Preventative Officers tooked Spence and Brazier.'

'Starf take those tarnal men!' Ransley bellowed. He blew his cheeks out, sending a mist of fine spittle over Sam. He turned his face and yelled into the corner, 'Wire! That be enough of that damned infernal racket. All of you—' he gestured wildly to the room, '—be getting on your way.'

The unspoken truth that had existed since the very first days of the Aldington Gang was that the death of a smuggler was infinitely more preferable to capture. A dead tubman or batman could be replaced by any one of a number of eager farm hands; a captured tubman or batman, however, who might be strong-armed into turning King's evidence could bring down the entire enterprise.

Ransley was breathing noisily, impatiently, whilst he waited for the room to clear. When it was, he spoke quietly to Sam. 'We be needing to get them out.'

'From Dover Gaol?' Sam questioned.

'That be right. Be thinking on it,' he said, patting Sam on the shoulder.

Sam said goodbye and strolled back out into the night, his conscience all the heavier for not having offered or received any blame in the night's unhappy conclusion. As he walked home, he replayed the events in his mind, wondering if he might have been up to the job of shooting the Preventative Officers. Perhaps, he considered, merely stepping forward and outnumbering them might have been enough to have saved the two men.

When he reached Braemar Cottage, he found Hester and Ann in the parlour, obviously waiting for what news he brought.

'What be a-happening?' Hester demanded.

'Two men be captured down Dover,' he answered.

'The two what you carted down there?' she asked, her voice faltering with something Sam guessed to be somewhere between anger and incredulity. He nodded his agreement and her face knotted in utter exasperation. 'You buffle-headed fool, Sam Banister! When do you be a-learning?'

'What would you be having me do?' he shouted back. 'I bain't even able to lift a shovel on the parish farm.'

'We be a-managing,' she replied, a hint of understanding finally creeping into her voice. 'We a-done it before, Sam...'

'That were different,' he countered, 'that were an 'andful of days without labour; I can't be working, Hester, in no other job. It be this or the poorhouse.'

Hester rolled her eyes and he could see her on the verge of daring to say that the workhouse might be preferable. He stiffened himself to rebuke her, but she did not speak; Ann did.

'What be happening to Spence?' she asked, quickly adding, 'And Brazier?'

Sam knew that Ann had become friendly with Spence since she had helped to heal the rope burns on his hands. He gave a churlish shrug, borne out of his jealousy for their friendship.

'Happen you should rescue them, case they be getting jawsy,' Ann said pointedly.

'Happen we might be,' Sam replied, on his way to the stairs. 'I be going to bed.'

Chapter Thirteen

9th August 1822, Dover, Kent

The horse-drawn coach arrived at Dover Quay, pulling up beside the Gun Inn—an untidy amalgamation of one small squat building and one very thin narrow one, sandwiched between a long run of warehouses.

Ann Fothergill stepped down from the coach wearing a straw bonnet over her curled hair, which she wore from a central parting. Without asking, she had borrowed Hester's best outfit: a striped open gown with fitted bodice and elbow-length sleeves.

She breathed deeply, drawing the warm blended smells of the bustling quay to her nose. She savoured the sour mixture, separating them into their individual scents of tar, rope, fish and sea salt. She inhaled deeply, as she took in the humming quay: merchants were busy trading; cargo was being loaded onto the abundance of moored vessels; sweaty fishermen were heaving great crates of mackerel, plaice and cod into stacks on the wharf; ragged women and children were running handcarts of wares from a Dutch lugger into waiting wagons.

A hint of a smile crept onto Ann's face at being back in the town and remembering her time here—so very different from her existence in Aldington village. Then she recalled the purpose of her visit here and her smile faded and the melancholic veil, which had been present for these last weeks, returned to her shoulders.

With a briskness which she hoped might restore her doughy heart, Ann marched into town. The notion of unusual business which she had detected on the outlying streets became undeniable when she reached the Charlton High Road in the centre of town. Great swathes of people from the lower echelons of society jostled at the edges of the road; ostlers, brewers and labourers stood elbow-to-elbow with prostitutes, vagabonds and thieves.

Ann pushed unapologetically through the crowds, receiving the curses and devil-looks from those into whom she ran.

The crowds on Black Horse Lane were an astonishing seven or eight deep; she had no hope of getting anywhere near to the front.

Turning sideways, Ann attempted to edge her way between the two men in front of her. They turned simultaneously and scowled at her. 'Watch it, lady,' one of them growled.

'He be my brother,' Ann lied, with a sniff. 'Please be letting me through.'

One of the men remained resolute, the other huffed, then stepped aside to allow her to squeeze into the gap. 'Hey, be letting this lady through—she be his sister,' the man said, tapping the shoulder of the person in front of him.

The news that the condemned man's sister was in the crowd rippled through, magically opening a narrow gap through which Ann could push to the front. Though this was far from the first time that she had witnessed a hanging, she gasped when she saw the wooden gallows just opposite her. From the large windows of the Black Horse Inn, directly behind and facing them, Ann ruefully spotted the better-classed spectators—seated men in fancy coats and breeches, who had paid more than one pound for the privilege of a front row seat. In the main central window four seats had been left vacant. She scanned across the faces of the other men and saw someone whom she thought that she recognised. She pushed herself forward, squinting hard. He was standing behind one of the chairs, chatting to the Preventative Officer seated before him. The man was tall and handsome with a neat dark moustache and dressed in an expensive-looking coat. She was staring hard at him, trying to pull information from her mind as to from where she knew him. Perhaps it was here, at a previous hanging where she had seen him. He certainly was distinguished-looking and someone whom she might have noticed. The man suddenly shifted his attention and began to glance down at the crowd. Ann went to look away but it was too late; their eyes locked and certain familiarity dawned on the pair of them simultaneously.

The seated Officer in front of him pointed down the street and the rest of the men beside him suddenly became agitated. The crowd, too, erupted in heightened, excited conversation and Ann heard a chorus of shouts to the effect of 'There he is!'

Ann caught the first glimpses of the horse and cart making its way up the street to the taunts and jeers of the crowd. Looking back up to the window, there was no sign of the man, with whom, Ann now knew with certainty, she had chatted at the Bourne Tap, despite his almost complete alteration in appearance. It was the same man whom she had witnessed handing money to Hester in the parlour of Braemar Cottage, and whom Hester had named as Jonas Blackwood. He had recognised her, too, and had now vanished.

By now the people around Ann had worked themselves into a near-frenzy at the sight of the approaching horse and cart.

Ann's breath caught in her throat when she took the sight in fully. Sitting beside the driver was the fat heavy-faced executioner, the rope coiled portentously in his lap. At the rear of the cart, sitting upon what would be his own coffin, was Alexander Spence. He was sitting, legs apart with his head facing downwards and hands tied behind his back. Next to him stood a vicar, eyes closed, muttering a prayer.

The driver brought the cart to a standstill, before expertly manoeuvring the open rear so that it slid precisely underneath the gallows.

A lavish carriage drew to a halt beside the cart and out stepped the town mayor, Henshaw Latham, and several other dignitaries whom Ann had seen at previous executions. They all wore fine top hats, lavish long coats, high collars and the regalia of their respective offices. The crowd greeted them with a muddled chorus of cheering and heckling, as the line of four illustrious gentlemen entered the Black Horse to take the prime seats in the upstairs window.

The executioner loafed over to Alexander and hoisted him up under the armpits, so that he was directly below the end of the horizontal beam.

Ann called out his name but her words were lost in the excited commotion of the mob around her.

Alexander nodded respectfully to the uniformed man who had risen onto the gallows beside him: the Preventative Officer whom Alexander had repeatedly attempted to shoot dead.

'Be saving him!' Ann shouted at the officer, knowing full well that even if he had heard her, and even if he had been so minded, the decision to execute Alexander was sealed. Appeals for clemency at sparing this twenty-two-year-old man were rebutted and Sam's attempt back in April to break him out of Dover Gaol had failed when Alexander had been captured attempting to flee across the Channel to France. This was it. She was witnessing the last moments of his life.

The din from the thronging mass around her crescendoed to a new height, as the hangman raised a grubby hessian hood to Alexander's head. He took one final fleeting glance at the crowd, his eyes momentarily locking on to Ann's. 'Goodbye, Alexander,' she whispered hopelessly, the acute stab of guilt that had brought her here lancing at her heart. Naively believing that she had stood a chance with the widowed doctor, she now regretted the way that she had dealt with

Alexander at the Bourne Tap back in November, having barely acknowledged him since. But now, with the news having reached her that Ralph Papworth-Hougham had married a girl from Folkestone, she could see her foolishness set out clearly before her.

She watched as the hood was pulled down over his face and the executioner slung the looped rope over the beam, tightened it, then pulled it down over Alexander's head.

The vicar gently touched his fingers to Alexander's elbow, then opened a small black bible, from which, above the riotous clamour of the crowd, he conveyed the last perceptible words that Alexander would hear.

As the hangman strode to the front of the cart, about to drive the horse forward and remove the footing from beneath Alexander, the crowd began to clap and cheer. But, to Ann's horror, Alexander did not wait and kicked himself off the back of the cart, much to the hangman's disgust.

She watched as the rope snapped tight and his legs began to kick wildly.

As usual, the hundreds who had gathered to witness his death screamed and shouted with delight—even the injudicious number in her immediate vicinity who believed Alexander to have been her brother.

Inexplicably, as she continued to watch him die, she thought of the moment when he had accepted her advocated remedy for his rope burn injuries and his hands were covered in viscous bubbling snail trails.

Ann looked over at the windows of the Black Horse Inn. The seated men were smiling, nodding and talking animatedly to each other, but without taking their gaze from Alexander's writhing body. There was still no sign of Jonas Blackwood and doubt began to skulk into Ann's mind that she had been correct in her identification. What on earth would a smuggler be doing dressed up like that and in the company of the upper classes? It surely hadn't been him, she began to tell herself.

A disappointed groan and an instant disbanding of the crowd told Ann that Alexander had finally died. She remained still while the masses bustled around her. Quickly, she was left almost alone.

The body stopped twitching and swaying; the driver pushed the cart back below him once again. Taking Alexander by the hips, the hangman tossed him onto his shoulder before expertly loosening the noose and, freeing Alexander from the gallows, dropped him roughly into the coffin. She watched the vicar utter another prayer, the words 'forgive', 'wretched' and 'soul' reaching her ears.

The hangman placed the lid on the coffin and shouted for the driver to move on.

Within a minute the cart was out of sight and the street had returned to normality.

Ann held her attention on the door of the public house opposite, watching as the line of dignitaries streamed out. Even if she had been incorrect in her identification of Jonas Blackwood, the man whose gaze she had met from the upstairs window had not appeared by the time the last of the men from upstairs had left the inn.

Crossing the street, Ann entered the inn, desperate for a pint of rum. In a morbid parallel to the execution, the bar was several deep with an influx of dry-throated people, whom the two perspiring barmaids were struggling to serve. Standing back, she searched the room in vain for Jonas Blackwood. He had clearly scarpered moments after she had spotted him.

Ann turned around and caught a glimpse of the gallows through the window and suddenly the idea of drinking here became an uncomfortable one. Taking one final glance around the room, she walked out of the door and onto the street. She knew the town and its multitude of inns and public houses intimately, yet she began to wander aimlessly, her desire for rum having abated.

To her surprise, she found herself avoiding the familiar backstreets of Dover; evading the tiny filthy houses rife with poverty, larceny and prostitution, which had been a part of her life for as long as she could recall. Something had changed which meant that she was viewing life here with an odd sense of detachment, but she didn't know what had changed exactly. Standing outside St James's Church, she found herself staring up at the old castle perched high on the hill, as she pondered the thought.

'Soberness,' she said, her lips hanging onto the word unduly, as she mused its significance and implications.

'Wine is a mocker and beer a brawler; whoever is led astray by them is not wise,' someone said from behind her.

Ann twirled around to see a pretty young lady in a handsome yellow silk dress and matching bonnet, holding open a door to the building behind her. 'What be that?'

'Proverbs twenty, verse one,' the lady answered, stepping aside as a young girl entered the building saying, 'Good morning, Miss.' The lady looked at Ann with a fixed stare. 'You mentioned sobriety.'

Ann studied the building a little more carefully. It was a fine three-storey place, painted white; the type lived in by wealthy merchants.

Another well-turned-out young girl went inside with a gentle bob of her head and saying, 'Good morning, Miss Bowler.'

'Do this be some kind of a church?' Ann asked with a sneer. 'There bain't no bible verse what I ever be hearing what ain't condemning me to the fires of hell.'

The woman laughed heartily and pointed at the small plaque beside the door.

Ann took a fleeting glance at the sign, then rolled her eyes with indifference.

'It says *Miss Bowler's Academy*,' the lady said.

Ann shrugged and began to walk away.

'I teach girls to read and write,' she called after her, before adding, '*and women!*'

Stopping in her tracks, Ann turned her head back towards the lady, eyeing her with a detached inquisitiveness. 'And what good do that be doing someone like me?'

The lady smiled. 'Perhaps if you could read the bible, you would see that forgiveness commonly follows condemnation.'

Uncertainty prevented Ann from wandering off indifferently. Something curious about the lady and her fancy words made her stay a little longer.

'Four shillings per lesson,' the lady said. 'For girls and ladies who need to learn to read and write.'

'Don't know what I be needing,' Ann commented. 'A pub, a church or an *academy*.'

The lady laughed, as another proper girl who could have been no older than thirteen entered the building.

Ann joined in the laughter, seeing the absurdity of herself with a lurid flash of clarity: a drunk criminal sitting in a classroom among the young daughters of the town's bankers, solicitors, officials and surgeons. Without another word, she continued down the road towards the quay, all the while laughing.

The Strond Street clock tower had just struck midday. Three hours until the carriage departed.

Ann stood at the edge of the quay, watching life humming around her. Finally, she surrendered to herself and entered the Gun Inn, the air filled with the smells of the sea, as it bristled with mariners, sailors and fishermen.

Approaching the bar, she ordered two pints of rum and water and found herself a dim corner, where she could sit alone and release the distressing morning into a stupor. The first glass she drank quickly, spilling some down Hester's dress in her haste to speed up intoxication and soften the edges of her feelings.

Having finished the second drink and ordered a third, Ann's thoughts began to detach from themselves and trail off into a void before she had fully explored and understood them. Then another idea or worry would present itself, before following the same course into obscurity. The last thought—barbed with the hooks of regret—which she managed to maintain, before insensibility took full hold of her, was walking away from Miss Bowler's Academy and entering this God-forsaken place.

Chapter Fourteen

Morton carefully entered the dark bedroom. In one hand he held the baby monitor and in the other a fresh cup of coffee, which he placed down on Juliette's bedside table. Planting a kiss on her forehead, he threw open the curtains, sending a stretched rectangle of warm spring light across the bed.

'Oh, God…' Juliette slurred, withdrawing herself under the duvet.

'Morning,' he said with a forced attempt at breeziness. His short sleep had been intruded upon by an obscure fusion of the many jobs which needed doing this morning before everybody arrived, and utterly bizarre dreams, which even Freud would have had trouble decrypting. The final dream, which had been so shocking as to actually wake him up at the end, had been about this afternoon's dinner. Everyone seated at the table had been drinking copious amounts of champagne and, one after the other, had stood up and given a speech. Through alcohol-laden tears, Juliette had used her platform to decry the current state of the police force and to reveal that she was pregnant again; his Uncle Jim had then risen and had spoken in such a strong Cornish accent that nobody had understood him, yet they had pretended that they had by raising their glasses encouragingly at moments where they felt it to have been appropriate; his half-brother, George, whom he had yet to meet, was played in the dream by a television actor whom Morton could now not name, and he had spent some time declaring to the table how wondrous his upbringing had been as an only child before taking his seat; Laura, Morton's biological father's wife, chose to speak about a moment in her career as an obstetrician when she had delivered a multiple-pregnancy of eighteen healthy babies; his Aunty Margaret and his father, Jack had then risen together and spoken jointly, telling the guests that they had always loved each other and were going to spend the rest of their lives together, before fleeing the room; finally, Morton had stood and begun to sing 'Auld Lang Syne' until the horror of the situation forced his eyes open, leaving him with absolutely no desire to return to sleep whatsoever.

He had been up for over two hours now, yet still elements of the dream plagued him. As he had cleaned the kitchen, he had given serious consideration to the possibility of his biological parents' rekindling their love after more than forty years of having been estranged. He instantly castigated himself, remembering that it hadn't been love at all. It had been a week-long holiday fling between two teenagers from two different continents that had resulted in—facing facts—an unwanted pregnancy.

Juliette's cocooned voice asked, 'What time is it?'

'9.27,' he said in a tone nuanced with the suggestion that her stretch in bed ought now to be over.

Her face poked out from the duvet, tortoise-like, her eyes tightly shut. 'What time's everyone getting here?'

'Lunchtime.'

How she took that information, it was hard for Morton to know, for her head retracted sharply back under the duvet. 'Right,' he said, leaving the room.

Downstairs in the lounge he began to tidy away the abundance of Grace's toys, which were strewn liberally all over the floor.

A low nonsensical babble began to erupt from the baby monitor, informing Morton that his time preparing the house was over; a swell of mild panic quickened his heart-rate as his mind flicked through the catalogue of jobs which still needed to be done before anybody arrived. Grace's gibberish became suddenly clearer: 'Dadda! Dadda! Dadda!'

Switching off the monitor, he bounded up the stairs to her bedroom, where he found Juliette picking her out from her cot bed. 'Happy birthday, darling! Now say *Mummy*!' Juliette said, a little exasperatedly. 'Mummy!'

'Dadda,' Grace replied, opening her arms towards Morton.

'Here you go,' she said, handing Grace over to him. 'I'm going to shower and try and wake up a bit, then we'll give her her presents.'

'I'll make you some breakfast,' Morton called after her. 'Happy birthday, Grace!'

He carried Grace downstairs, sat her on the kitchen floor and watched with exasperation as she crawled over to her box of wooden blocks and promptly tipped them all over the floor. She began to select individual blocks, setting them on top of each other until the tower collapsed.

Morton watched her proudly and felt the tight anxiety from worry about the state of the house slowly dissipating. And with more new toys about to be added to the mix, the visitors would have to accept the house the way they found it.

'See,' Juliette said, two hours later. She was sitting beside Grace on the lounge floor, setting up a zoo with Grace's new plastic animals. 'You needn't have worried. The house is tidy, the bathroom's clean and the beds are made. We're ready.'

'Hmm,' Morton agreed, slightly absentmindedly, as he gazed out of the window onto Mermaid Street. All he saw, however, were the first vestiges of the year's many tourists, taking advantage of the unusually warm March day.

From his pocket, his phone beeped with the arrival of a text message. He quickly pulled his phone out and read it aloud. '*Hi. Traffic awful – be a couple of hours late – sorry.*'

'Which parent is that from?' Juliette asked with a wry smile.

'Aunty Margaret,' he answered, pocketing his mobile and checking outside once more.

'They're not going to get here any sooner because you're constantly curtain-twitching,' Juliette said, holding a small Dalmatian in front of Grace. 'Doggy. Doggy.'

Grace glanced briefly to Morton, as if to check that what Juliette had said was correct, then said in a crystal-clear voice, 'Dadda—doggy.'

'Good girl!' Morton exclaimed, bending down to kiss her.

'Great—she says 'doggy' before 'mummy,' Juliette complained. 'That's just brilliant.'

Morton returned to the window, his chuckle swiftly morphing into a minor gasp. 'Oh, God, they're here!'

Juliette jumped to her feet just as the doorbell rang. 'Go and open it, then.'

'How do I look?' he asked, his breathing suddenly becoming shallow.

'What are you? A teenage girl? Go and open the door.'

Morton moved into the hallway and took a deep breath, wishing that his heart would slow down. Then, with Juliette at his side and Grace at his feet, he opened the front door.

Five animated, excitedly spoken greetings tangled in the air, before Jack, who was standing directly in front of the door, pulled Morton into an embrace. 'How you doing, son?' he asked, slapping him on the back, before bending down and planting a kiss on the top of Grace's head. 'Hi! How are you?'

'Doggy,' Grace said, removing the Dalmatian's front paws from her mouth and offering it to him.

'Yeah, that's right—doggy!' Jack said. 'Happy birthday!' He kissed her again, then stood back and moved to hug Juliette. 'Lovely to see you again. Okay, introductions…' he stood to one side. 'This is my wife, Laura and this is our son, George.'

Morton embraced Laura as though she were an old friend, yet this was their first meeting. 'It's lovely to meet you,' he said with a wide smile.

'You too,' she beamed. 'It's such a great story you guys have!'

'Isn't it just,' Morton agreed, taking her in more fully. Like Jack, her face, hair and the way in which she dressed removed a good decade from her sixty-two years. Her dark eyes were enhanced by subtle make-up and her hair was trimmed into a neat blonde bob. She wore tight blue jeans and a small black leather jacket.

Laura took a step up towards Grace and Juliette, leaving Morton standing before his half-brother, George. He had seen plenty of photographs of George, yet to actually see him in the flesh was somewhat startling. He, just like Morton, had inherited many of Jack's physical features. The three of them shared the chestnut-brown eyes, the dark hair and the handsome boyish facial detail. The main difference with George was that he was taller than Morton and heavier set.

'Christ, look at you two,' Juliette exclaimed, evidently having seen the same thing.

'Wow—there's no mistaking your paternity,' Laura quipped.

'Hi,' Morton finally said, shaking his brother's hand.

'Nice to meet you,' George said, with a deferential shyness.

'How are you?' Morton asked.

'Exhausted,' George answered with a thin smile.

'Why don't you have a sleep? Your bed's made up. I'm afraid you're in Grace's room; not with her in there, I hasten to add.'

Juliette scooped Grace into her arms and directed everyone inside, asking them if they were hungry or thirsty.

'I might just do that,' George said. 'Leave you guys to catch up.'

Morton returned his smile, moving up the steps into the house, all the while wondering at George's comment, which obliquely placed him on the periphery of the reunion. He hadn't considered before now that George would be anything other than delighted to have a ready-made older brother thrust upon him.

Morton closed the front door, observing his half-brother carefully as he joined the others in the kitchen. Jack and Laura were seated comfortably at the table, discussing the house with Juliette. George slid in beside his father and Morton was sure that he exhaled in a way which suggested irritation. George ran the nail of his index finger down a grain line in the table, then looked up and caught Morton staring at him. Rather than smile, as Morton might have expected him to, he just stared back.

The short uncomfortable stalemate was broken when Morton smiled and glanced away, trying to latch on to whatever it was that Juliette had been saying.

'I wasn't very keen on this house at first, was I, Morton?' she said.

'No, I think you were after horizontal floors and vertical walls,' Morton recalled with a laugh.

Juliette rolled her eyes. 'And I still don't know why we have two front doors…but that's another question.'

'How old *is* this beautiful place?' Laura asked.

'Built in the early 1500s,' Juliette replied, leaving Laura's mouth agape in awe.

Morton looked at the time, then said, 'What do you feel like doing? It's going to be a good three or four hours until dinner. We can stay here, you can go for a lie-down or, since it's a nice day, we could go for a walk—show you a bit of Rye and get a cup of tea somewhere?'

'That sounds a great idea!' Jack said, turning to Laura. 'What do you think?'

'Perfect. I've heard so much about this little town; I can't wait to see it.'

'I'm going to stay here, if that's okay,' George said. 'I'll get the bags in and then have a sleep.'

Jack tapped him lightly on the back. 'Sure thing, Son.'

Morton watched their interaction with interest. He noticed that Jack had called both him and George *son* and wondered if he was being literal or if it was a term of endearment that any younger man received. He could hear him using it as an appellation for the young man who had fixed his car, or the student at the university where he lectured, who had held the door open for him, or the postman who had delivered a package.

'Morton, show them their rooms while I get Grace ready,' Juliette instructed.

'Follow me up the wonky, creaky stairs,' Morton said with a grin.

Jack, followed by Laura, followed by a seemingly reluctant George, trooped up the stairs to the first floor.

'That's your room,' Morton said, pushing open Grace's bedroom door. 'As you can see, we've decorated it especially for a thirty-seven-year-old American.'

Jack and Laura laughed as they stuck their heads into the room, casually taking in the pink and white walls adorned with rabbits and flowers. In the centre of the room was a single put-up bed with vaguely feminine bedding. 'It's cool,' George said. 'I've slept in much stranger places.'

'And you two are on the top floor,' Morton said, continuing upstairs with them behind him. He showed them into the guestroom, situated directly opposite his study.

'Perfect,' Jack said.

Downstairs, they found Juliette strapping Grace into the buggy. 'Look, here comes Grandpa and Grandma,' she said heartily.

'Gandpa,' Grace said, pointing at Jack.

'Yeah!' Jack cried. 'Good girl! Grandpa!'

'Gandpa,' Grace repeated.

Juliette flicked her head around, bemused. 'I wonder at what point in your fast-growing vocabulary you might like to say MUMMY?'

'She's doing it to annoy you,' Jack said with a smile.

Morton grinned, handing Jack and Laura their coats and pulling open the front door. 'Let's go *down* the hill,' Morton said. 'The cobbles are a nightmare with the buggy.'

They all stepped out into the warm afternoon and began to head away from the house. Morton took a cursory glance up the hill at the real reason for their heading this way—the Mermaid Inn, where his Aunty Margaret and Uncle Jim would be arriving at any moment—as a thorny coil of anxiety thrashed through his intestines at the thought of the impending dinner.

Phil had been about to give up and go home. Patience had never been his strong point. That was why he was here, now, standing outside the Mermaid Inn watching the house. He had arrived with no plan whatsoever, but now that he had seen all but one of the house's occupants leaving, one began to loosely form in his head. The remaining person—a man—was busy pulling suitcases from the boot of a car. Now was as good an opportunity as he was likely to get.

Slinging his hands into his pockets, he sauntered down the road and up the steps to Morton's house. The door was wide open and the man had his head in the boot of the car. He waited, on the verge of stepping inside until the man hauled another suitcase out onto the pavement. 'Hiya, I work with Morton Farrier on his genealogical investigations—I'm just dropping something off,' he said, holding up a supermarket carrier bag which was wrapped tightly around a block of cheese which he had just purchased from Jempson's for his tea.

The man shrugged disinterestedly. 'He's just popped out, but sure, go ahead.'

'Cheers, mate,' Phil replied, hurrying inside. He had no idea where he was going and quickly looked into the room on his left—the lounge. A nice television, pair of two-seater sofas, coffee table and some bookcases. The room to the right was the kitchen-diner. He headed up the stairs and found the bathroom, a child's room and what looked like the master bedroom. Continuing up to the top floor, he found another bedroom and then, typically being the last room that he searched, he found Morton's study. He entered the room and laughed scornfully when he spotted the wall covered entirely in a web of paperwork linked by string and coloured pins. It was totally melodramatic and ridiculous given his occupation, but exactly what Phil had come for. He didn't have long and began scanning his eyes around the wall. There. He lunged forwards and pulled the piece of paper from its tape, tearing the corner.

Taking out his mobile phone, he took a close-up photo of the paper.

'You alright up there?' the man called up to him. An American, by the sound of his accent.

'Yep—be right down,' Phil replied, swiftly reattaching the paper to the wall. 'Cheers for that!' he said, meeting the American on the first floor. 'Don't worry about telling him I came round—I'll see him later in the week. See ya.'

'Bye.'

Phil descended the stairs two at time and headed outside, closing the front door behind him.

With a wide grin on his face, he headed to the bus stop, thinking about the cheese on toast which he was going to have when he got home.

Having taken Jack and Laura for a cream tea and shown them some of the historic and ancient properties in Church Square, Morton found himself at the top of Mermaid Street—his own road and the one most renowned in the town—in a quandary. To get to the house and to show the visitors this notable street meant walking past the Mermaid Inn, something his legs seemed unwilling to do.

'What are you dithering for, now?' Juliette asked.

'Just thinking it's easier—with the buggy and all—to go down West Street, then around The Mint and up to the house.'

Juliette looked at him, wholly baffled. 'Good idea… Or—and an equally good idea—we could order a helicopter down to the harbour, catch a boat then get a taxi to our house, which I can see from here?' She shared her mystification with Jack and Laura, frowning in their direction, then saying, 'We've pushed the buggy down there a thousand times before. Come on.' She moved in front of the buggy and began down the road.

And that was it, they were heading down the cobbles of Mermaid Street, utterly in the hands of fate.

Morton's pulse quickened and something inside him recoiled as they approached the Mermaid Inn. His efforts to accelerate the pace of the group failed when Jack brought everyone to a standstill to admire the pub.

'I'm sure I had my photo taken outside here!' Jack declared, squinting hard, as he seemed to pull the memory forward in his mind.

Morton wanted to say, 'You did. I took a copy of it from your sister's photo album. I can find it easily.' He could even tell him the exact spot upon which he had stood in the photo but he wasn't sure that, if he opened his mouth, any words would come out right now. Through the archway that led to the rear of the pub, he had spotted his Aunty Margaret and Uncle Jim's green Land Rover. They were here.

He tried to get Juliette's attention to tell her but she was engrossed in conversation with Laura.

'Wow—did you hear that, Jack?' Laura said, tugging his arm. 'The pub dates back to 1420, but the cellars date from 1156. That is just mind-blowing. And you live so close to it!'

'Come on, let's get a group photo,' Jack suggested, accosting a young woman passing by. 'Hey—would you mind taking our photo, please?'

Morton found himself smiling inattentively at the stranger, sandwiched between Juliette and his biological father, all the while wondering if perhaps his biological mother was peering out of one of the windows behind them. 'Come on, then, let's get back,' Morton said, taking the buggy back from Juliette's grip and bumping Grace down the cobbles to the house.

Inside, they found George in front of the television watching a Pearl Harbour documentary.

'Oh, George—it's such a pretty town,' Laura said, sitting beside him and patting his thigh like a dog. 'You really must take a look around.'

'Did you get any sleep, Son?' Jack asked.

George shook his head. 'I tried…'

'Right, drinks,' Juliette murmured to herself.

'Oh, Morton,' George said, briefly glancing in his direction, before looking back at the television. Morton smiled inquisitively, wondering what his half-brother was about to say to him. 'Some guy called for you. He works with you—wanted to drop something off.'

'Works with me? What did he drop off?'

George shrugged. 'I don't think he said—he went up and left it in your office.'

'Okay,' Morton answered, not having the faintest of clues to whom George was referring, trying not to be aggravated that he had allowed a stranger into the house. He bounded up the stairs, casually glancing in his bedroom on the way up. In the study he found nothing. Everything seemed to be how he had left it. He wiggled the laptop mouse and the password-protected screen came to life, showing no signs of having been tampered with. He scanned across the bookshelves but could not see anything different. He looked around the floor and in the bin. He thumbed through the stack of paperwork on his desk pertaining to the Fothergill Case. When he found nothing, paranoia pushed him to check *under* his desk. Check the lampshade. Check the plug sockets. Nothing. He stood in front of the investigation wall and methodically ran his eyes across it, looking for signs of change or anything having been removed or added. Only one thing looked amiss, but he couldn't be certain that it hadn't happened before today. One piece of paper had a ripped corner and the tape had been reattached slightly lower down, as though someone had torn it hastily from the wall, then reaffixed it. But why? The paper, in his scribbled handwriting read: *'The Bourne Tap, Aldington – gold guineas found by George Ransley???'*

Morton stared at the paper for some time, mulling over his thoughts. *He* could very well have ripped the paper—he just had no recollection of it. Juliette could have ripped it, though why, when she rarely stepped foot inside his study, he couldn't fathom. George could have done it but this, too, seemed highly implausible. Or, it was this man who had visited the house?

201

Carefully removing the piece of paper from the wall, Morton carried it downstairs to the kitchen, where he found Juliette preparing the dinner. 'You didn't tear this, did you?' he asked.

'What is it?' Juliette asked, scrunching her eyes to read his scribbled handwriting.

'Probably nothing. It was on my investigation wall.'

'Does it matter that it's ripped? You can rewrite it, can't you?'

'That doesn't matter at all—I just can't recall having ripped it.'

Juliette said dismissively, 'Well, I can safely say it wasn't me. Can you see if they want anything to drink, please?'

Morton ventured into the lounge, finding Jack and Laura playing on the floor with Grace. George was watching them from the sofa, his head resting on a cushion and his legs tucked up beside him, appearing very much on the verge of sleep. 'Anyone want a drink?' Morton asked, then, when nobody said that they did, he asked, 'George—that man that arrived earlier—did he give his name?'

'No, he didn't. I assumed from the way he was talking that you were kind of expecting him. Should I not have let him in?'

Morton wanted to respond with, 'No, you *definitely* shouldn't have let him in' but said, 'Well, I have no idea who he was. What did he look like?'

George sighed and sat up. 'I only really saw him for a minute. Erm…about forty to fifty, very thin, grey tracksuit, bald or shaved head. Stubble. I think he might have had a mole here–' he pointed to beside his right eye, '—white sneakers… That's about all I can remember.'

Jack looked up. 'So, you don't know this guy?'

Morton shook his head. A niggling worry caused by what was written on the paper that the man might have been Arthur Fothergill's greedy nephew was rejected. The nephew was overweight, had a full head of hair and certainly no facial moles.

'George—you really shouldn't have let him in,' Jack castigated.

'He could have been anyone,' Laura added.

George flushed red with embarrassment, mumbling a quiet apology.

'How long was he upstairs for?' Morton pushed, now not choosing his tone or words with eggshell consideration.

'Erm…no more than like…five minutes. Probably two or three.'

'And he definitely went to my study—on the top floor?'

George nodded. 'I heard the floorboards creaking up there and I was coming out of my room when he came down the stairs.'

'And did you go into the study at all?' Morton asked. 'It doesn't matter—I just need to know.'

'No, I haven't been up to the top floor at all. I'm sorry—I guess tiredness and the way he seemed to know you…I'm sure he said your *full* name, too.'

'Not to worry,' Morton said, trying to sound as though he meant it. He left the room and began to walk back up to his study, perplexed by who the man could have been. He reasoned that there must be something else in his study that he had somehow missed that might reveal his identity. He got a third of the way up the stairs when the doorbell rang.

His blood suddenly ran cold.

This was it.

He turned back on himself, descended to the front door and took a deep breath.

He pulled it open and there stood his Aunty Margaret and Uncle Jim.

Chapter Fifteen

'Come in,' Morton said, nervously.

Margaret stepped inside with a broad smile. Morton could tell that she had made a special effort; her white, curly hair had been recently cut and, for the first time that he could recall, she was even wearing some subtle lipstick and eyeshadow. She reached out and grabbed him, throwing her arms around him. He wasn't completely sure, but he thought that he felt a light tremble in her hands behind him. 'Oh, it is lovely to see you, Morton,' she beamed. 'Where's that lovely wife of yours?' Then she spotted Juliette over his shoulder. 'There she is!' Margaret pulled back from Morton, planted a wet kiss on his cheek then moved towards Juliette.

'Nephew!' Jim hollered in his usual greeting, thrusting a brawny hand for Morton to shake. Where Margaret had made an extra effort for the occasion, Jim appeared as he always had; as though he had just stepped from his fishing boat. He was a big man, tall and wide with a flushed sea-beaten complexion and wild hair which looked as though it had not been brushed in a very long time.

Morton was aware, in his peripheral vision, of movement around the lounge doorway. He turned around to see Jack, smiling, holding Grace. Behind him, with her hand placed territorially on her husband's shoulder, was Laura.

Before the awkwardness was able to take a firm shape in the small hallway, Morton moved back, allowing Margaret and Jack to see one another for the first time in forty-four years. 'I don't need to introduce you two, do I?' Morton asked, with a chuckle which sounded odd even to him.

Jack and Margaret met awkwardly, him leaning in to kiss her left cheek, as she presented her hand to shake. Simultaneously realising the other's intentions, he faltered in his attempts to kiss her, while she retracted her hand, the result being a blundering mash, where she kissed his ear and his hand squashed into her right breast.

'Good to see you again, Margaret,' Jack said, treading backwards from the muddle, his face flushing in the way that Morton's did through embarrassment.

'It's been a very long time,' Margaret answered with a discomfited smile.

Ignoring the cringing spectacle of Margaret and Jack's meeting, Morton introduced Laura to Margaret and Jim, who, having been witness to the spectacle of their spouses' reunion, went for the safe hand-shaking option. Laura squeezed herself into the hallway, allowing George to be part of the introductions.

'Where's that birthday girl, then?' Margaret asked.

'Playing with her new toys in the lounge,' Juliette answered. 'I'll go and get her.'

'Let me take your coats,' Morton said to Margaret and Jim. 'Then go and take a seat in the kitchen for dinner.'

Morton used the time hanging the two coats to try and settle his breathing. He closed his eyes for a moment, leaning his forehead onto Jim's wax jacket, trying to will the surging adrenalin to subside. He took a long breath, counted to ten, then entered the kitchen cheerfully.

He could not help but smile at what was unfolding before him, as conversations had sprung ablaze which bridged family boundaries and divided the sexes: Laura, Juliette and Margaret were discussing the weather; Jack, Jim and George were comparing travel anecdotes about flights and about traffic jams. His family had, in those potentially awkward few moments, unitedly placed a seal over the single precise reason which had brought them together. Whether that seal was temporary, or whether the past would return during the meal, time alone would tell.

'So,' Juliette announced, ferrying the final dishes to the table, 'I've made a couple of salads, some garlic bread, a creamy courgette lasagne and a beef lasagne—so, please, help yourselves.'

Whilst everyone offered their gratitude to Juliette, who plopped herself down between Grace and Laura, Morton stood back in horror, taking stock of the seating arrangements, which a psychologist would have been elated to have analysed. The men had seated themselves on one side, with the women, including Grace, on the other. Just one seat remained—that at the head of the table—positioned appallingly as arbiter between both of his biological parents. It was a surreal moment for him and one that he had thought would never happen; so normal, and yet, so very *not* normal.

The plates and dishes of food were passed with polite exchanges, crossing the table until everybody had sufficient on their plates to begin eating.

Juliette deftly broke a short moment of silence by saying, 'So, Morton said that you've visited England before. Did you manage to get down to Cornwall?'

Morton was impressed at how her astute question had pulled Laura, George and Jim into one conversation. Now it was his turn to do the same with Jack and Margaret. Except, he did not know what to say. As he forked a heap of lasagne into his mouth, he deliberated over what they could talk about. If he asked either of them about their lives back home, then it was directly excluding the other, or presuming a mutual interest. The only common intersection between their lives, of which he could think, was the very thing about which nobody wanted to speak. He chewed slowly, taking a quick glance to each side. Both of them were eating, listening in with detached smiles to the conversation at the other end of the table. They were speaking about Cadgwith, the picturesque fishing village where Jim and Margaret lived. Morton tried to think of something which latched on to their conversation thread, but which he could pull back and make just between the three of them. But the moment passed.

It was Jack who filled the void. 'So, tell me about your life, Margaret,' he said, with a smile which suggested he was fully aware of the vastness of his question.

Margaret laughed. 'Well, Jim and I are retired now, although he can't quite stop messing about with fishing boats and giving advice to the younger ones in the village. We've got a nice little place overlooking the sea. I say I'm retired, but actually I seem to do more now than I did when I was working. I'm involved in lots of village activities, we go walking. I bake...' She shrugged. 'That's probably my life at the moment!'

'Sounds idyllic. How long have you lived in Cornwall?' Jack asked. 'Your accent sounds pretty Cornish now.'

'Does it really? I don't hear it, myself.' Margaret said. 'Gosh... When did I move down there? December 1976. I just had to get away from Folkestone. Stayed there ever since.'

'And what did you do down there—before you retired?' Jack enquired.

'What didn't I do?' Margaret answered. 'When I first moved down there I had visions of starting up my own little tearoom. My granny, Nellie,' she said with a nod to Morton, 'taught me to bake and it was all I thought I was good at.' She paused to bite from a chunk of garlic bread, then laughed: 'Of course, I didn't take into account all the finances and what-have-you of running a business and ended up working in someone else's tearoom. Two months into the job and that lump over there—' she aimed her fork at Jim, '—walks in declaring his love, we get married and I stop working to raise two little girls.'

Jack grinned. 'So, you deprived the good folk of Cornwall of *Farrier's Tearoom*, then, huh?'

'Probably not a bad thing,' Margaret responded. 'When the girls were growing up I did some volunteering in school, which led to a temporary job as a teaching assistant that lasted nigh-on twenty years.'

'Wow. What about starting up that tearoom now?' Jack asked.

'Oh, my goodness gracious, no. I make enough scones, jam, and cakes as it is for various fetes and charity sales.' She cut a portion of her lasagne, then suddenly seemed to notice that by comparison with the rest of the table, she had barely touched her food. 'I *must* stop talking. It looks like I've hardly eaten a thing. What about you, Jack? What line of work did you get into? Was I right in thinking you were into archaeology or some such thing?'

Morton's pulse quickened as he looked to Jack in anticipation. This was the first time that any hint of their previous relationship had been alluded to; up until now they might as well have been strangers forced into conversation at the dinner party of a mutual acquaintance.

'Yeah, that's right,' Jack confirmed. 'Well, kinda. I flunked out of Boston University and moved to San Francisco where I studied forensic archaeology. Laura and I moved to Alberta, Canada, where I now lecture in the subject, undertaking the odd investigation here and there.'

'Sounds like you've done alright. And you've got a nice boy, too,' Margaret said, nodding towards George at the other end of the table.

'Two, actually,' Jack corrected.

'Oh,' Margaret said, 'you've got another one at home. He didn't fancy a holiday, then?'

'Not at home,' Jack said. 'Right here.' He turned and patted Morton on his shoulder.

It was a moment so unexpectedly touching for Morton that he was forced to tip his head down, as if inspecting something in his dinner, to avoid anybody seeing the moisture rising in his lower eyelids. Margaret's facial expressions suggested that his words had somehow embarrassed her.

Jack, seeming not to have noticed either reaction, held forth, 'Yeah, George is into computer programming. Something to do with software creation.'

'Oh, I know just what you mean,' Margaret joked. 'And is he with anyone?'

'There's a question, jeez,' Jack said, lowering his voice conspiratorially. 'He got married young—in his early twenties—but that didn't work out. After that he had a string of girlfriends. The ones Laura and I approved of he dumped, the ones we didn't approve of he moved in with or got engaged to.' Jack smiled and raised his hands dismissively. 'Now he's doing the dating online thing.'

Morton listened to the pair of them intently as they continued to speak about their lives. He was like an unseen observer, hungrily snatching at new titbits of information which added to that which he knew of his biological parents. It was interesting to scrutinise their conversation, both of them having relayed some key events from their lives, without once referring back to their meeting in Folkestone in January 1974. The hiatus created by Margaret and Jack's being mid-mouthful gave Morton a window to broach the subject. 'It's funny,' he began, looking at Jack, 'that you packed up and left home in December 1976 and went to the other side of the country—' then he faced Margaret, '—and *you* left home in December 1976 and went to the other side of *this* country.'

'Oh my God,' Jack said, while Margaret just raised her eyebrows.

Morton knew that she was uncomfortable but he had one more thing to say. 'Which was when you, Jack, wrote your last letter to Aunty Margaret.'

Jack nodded in agreement. 'That's right.'

'I only received one letter from you,' Margaret said, 'a couple of weeks after you left Folkestone. I can't recall exactly what it said now, but I think it was full of teenage gushing. I thought I must have put you off.'

'No, not at all. I thought *you'd* lost interest.'

Morton stood up and went to the chest of drawers behind him, where he had put the three letters in the eventuality that the subject might be discussed. He sat back down with the letters stacked on the table in front of him. 'I don't know what to do with them. You wrote them,' he said to Jack. 'But you posted them and someone intervened before they got to you, Aunty Margaret. So, I don't know who they belong to now.'

Jack picked them up decisively. 'They're mine.' Then he passed them over to Margaret. 'And I give them—forty-four years late—to you, Margaret. Don't worry, I'm not expecting a reply.' He laughed.

She blushed, set down her cutlery, and took the proffered letters, holding them uncertainly, as though they might contain an incendiary device. 'Thank you,' she murmured, staring for some time at the name and address: *Margaret Farrier, 163 Canterbury Road, Folkestone, Kent.* 'I presume my father got to them first...' Her words petered out and her eyes glazed slightly.

In that moment Morton would have given anything to know what was going on inside her mind, as she stared at the envelope on top; her face gave nothing at all away.

Finally, she lowered the letters to the table. 'Shall I read them?' she said quietly.

Jack shrugged. 'They're yours.'

Margaret pinched her lips together and nodded her head, seemingly having made up her mind. 'I'll read them later, in private, with a glass of sherry by that lovely big fire in the lounge at the Mermaid.'

'More wine, down that end?' Juliette called, as though they were seated at some grand banqueting table.

'Yes, please,' Morton answered, receiving a welcome flashback of his dream last night. Thankfully—so far at least—it had just been a nightmarish vision and not a premonition. Nobody had stood up to give a speech and the chances of his biological parents eloping together seemed reasonably far-fetched, now. One thing, though, which he did notice: Juliette was only drinking orange juice.

'Are you having some?' he said to her, as she passed him the wine bottle. She shook her head and screwed up her face, leaving Morton wondering if she might actually be pregnant.

He topped up Jack and Margaret's drinks and watched again, as Juliette expertly stitched together the two halves of the table by bringing the focus to mutual ground: Grace's birthday. She brought to the table a lion's head cake with a lit candle in the shape of a number 1 and began to sing 'Happy Birthday.'

Morton joined in the song, then sat back with his glass of wine and allowed himself to indulge in holding on to this very moment. A moment without a past, with his mother, father, wife and daughter and the hope of many more occasions such as this.

He remembered his dream and smiled inwardly at the idea of standing up now and singing 'Auld Lang Syne'. The balance of stark inappropriateness would be weighted equally, he felt, against the pertinence of bringing to mind the rest of his family—his adoptive family—who had raised him and helped shape him into the man which he was today.

He didn't stand up and sing, but he did raise a silent toast to the two people who, despite their deaths, he still called Mum and Dad.

Chapter Sixteen

8th May 1823, Boulogne, France

The tide was low and there were several hours still left until the waters would return to raise the fishing boat, *Nancy,* from her sandy grounding. The crew—experienced fishermen from Folkestone—had scarpered into the ancient city's backstreets, spending their wages before they had been earned on whores, liquor and gambling. At the top of the beach, safely positioned above the highest of tides, was a small network of ramshackle huts which, Sam noticed, had grown exponentially in number since his first visit here. Outside of most of the huts were an assortment of men: a motley jumble of local French carpenters and Englishmen lured from their home parishes on the coast of Kent by the handsome profits to be reaped from the building of smugglers' boats.

'When the sea be a-coming for her, she be ready to go,' the carpenter—Rummy was his nickname—declared with a snort. He had been their usual boat-builder for a while in Deal, but, as with many others of his occupation, he had shifted his home and business to Boulogne in response to the English customs laws, which prevented the building of boats greater than twenty-eight feet in length. Rummy was a gaunt wiry man with no perceptible teeth and suspicious over-blinking black eyes.

This newly crafted boat, which Sam now carefully examined, was thirty-eight feet in length, capable of holding two hundred barrels of contraband.

Rummy waited patiently, scratching feverishly into his tangled ginger beard. When Sam had finished the inspection, Rummy opened his right hand: 'Forty pound.'

Sam raised his smock, revealing a leather purse hanging from around his neck. He took out the money and handed it over.

'Happen this one be a-lasting you longer,' Rummy said with a chuckle. 'Not that I be a-caring, course!'

'Hm,' Sam answered, turning his back on the carpenter and walking towards the *Capécure,* the old harbour area. Despite knowing from experience that he had plenty of time before the tide would reach the boats, he marched purposefully to his destination: one of the many warehouses situated just behind the busy harbour.

The buildings—mostly grey and starchily disinclined to reveal the nature of their wares—grew larger as Sam neared the harbour district. He entered a narrow cobbled lane, devoid of sunlight, owing to the tall repositories on either side, all the time walking with a lurching step in order to avoid the unforgiving merchants in their horses and carts, and the generous dollops of fresh manure which rose up indiscriminately in small hillocks. The last building on the street was demarked only by the name, *Delacroix* painted in large white letters above the gaping doors. This was the *entrepôt*, a microcosm of the city itself, an intermediary place which united producer and exporter.

Inside the vast warehouse Sam briefly took in the scene, now much less impressive than on his first visit. At one end of the building were dozens of carts containing goods of every conceivable kind: wine from Nantes; gin from Schiedam; genever from Brussels; lace from Bruges; brandy from Andalusia; rum from the West Indies; tobacco from Virginia—all of it stored in barrels and crates now being worked by dozens of men with the ferocity of a colony of ants. They carried the goods to the other side of the warehouse, where they were stored temporarily—often for just a few minutes—before another group of workers at the opposing end of the warehouse loaded them onto empty carts ready for export.

The process was almost mechanical in its methodicalness and was overseen by the watchful eye of Madame Delacroix from her office situated high above the main depot.

Sam looked up and, with a quick nod of her head, she acknowledged him, before turning to speak with someone unseen behind her. On his first visit here, Sam had been shown to the office and introduced to her. She was a formidable widow with a harsh face and, if the translator were to have been believed, a harsh tongue to match. At that meeting, Sam had negotiated the terms of business and since then he had been dealt with by one of her English-speaking underlings, Monsieur Comtois, who arrived now wearing a midnight-blue coat, buckskin breeches, tall black boots and carrying his top hat. As he approached, he twitched his giant black moustache, as he was accustomed to doing, then said, '*Bonjour, Monsieur.* Welcome back.' He quickly consulted the piece of paper in his hands. 'Monsieur Ransley would like the same, yes?'

Sam nodded. 'That be right, yes.'

'*Très bien.* Your cart is ready. *S'il vous plaît,*' he said, indicating that Sam should follow him. Close to the large exit doors, he was shown a cart laden with half-anker barrels, each containing three and three-quarter gallons of various types of liquor. Heaving himself up inside the cart, Sam quickly counted them: two hundred.

'*Bon*,' Monsieur Comtois said, slapping his hands together in a way which suggested that his time was precious and that he wanted the payment to wrap up the deal. 'One hundred and thirty pounds.'

Sam pulled the purse from around his neck and counted the money into the outstretched hand of Monsieur Comtois, who promptly spirited it away into an inside pocket of his jacket. 'Good day, Monsieur,' Comtois said, shaking Sam's hand, then, he called something in French to one of the workers and disappeared up the stairs.

Behind Sam, the workers were hitching the laden cart to a packhorse ready for the short journey to the beach.

The routine today was the same as it always had been: two French men incapable in English took the cart, with Sam in the back, to the boat where they would unload the contraband onto the sand before venturing wordlessly back to the warehouse. The men worked efficiently and had the cart emptied in minutes. Sam always felt the need to try and explain why he stood back, dumbly watching and not helping. The men rarely understood him until he showed the unsightly scars on his right shoulder with an accompanied mime of trying to lift his arm. Most gave an apathetic nod of the head so as to say that they had understood and did not really care.

With the cargo unloaded beside him, all Sam could do now was to wait for the return of the fishermen. He stood quietly, taking in long slow breaths of air, as he watched the sea edging slowly and reluctantly forwards. A dozen or more herring gulls swept overhead then came to a rowdy landing on the wet sand a short distance away, instantly tapping their yellow beaks on the surface at unseen creatures.

As time drew on, and his frequent glances at the city behind him continued in their failure to offer sight of the fishermen, so grew Sam's agitation. The calmness of the water sluggishly creeping inward had been supplanted by a worsening anxiety at the sea growing greedily close towards the contraband and the new boat. He had half a mind to enter the city in search of the useless fishermen, but it would be an exhaustive search among the myriad brothels, inns and public houses. Besides which, the last thing that he could do was leave the cargo unattended, just minutes away from the foamy reaches of the high tide.

'Looks like you be a-loading the boat single-handed,' Rummy called, then heard the joke hidden within his own words: 'Single-handed!'

Sam outwardly ignored him but inwardly he was thinking the same thing, that he would somehow have to load the boat by himself with only one fully functioning arm. He was certain that Rummy, standing facing him with a pipe hanging loosely from his mouth, would assist...for a price. But he only had the fishermen's wages left. He looked grimly at Rummy, who had already determined what he was about to ask.

Rummy screwed his shrockled face into a sort-of-smile and smacked his hands to his hips.

'Oh! Those tarnal French!'

Sam turned to see the unruly group of fishermen tramping towards him. Noticing that Rummy had scarpered back inside his hut, Sam said nothing but glowered at the men, who, clearly intoxicated, were struggling to keep the pace of Tom Swain. *Nancy* belonged to him and, as such, he had assumed the unofficial role of their leader. They arrived with a fear of Sam, all breathless and reeking of a displeasing mixture of ale, old sweat and tobacco. One of the men, William, was standing embarrassedly in only his drawers and under-stockings, hopelessly trying to use Tom as a shield.

'Those tarnal French,' Tom repeated. 'Moved and seduced by the devil hisself.'

'What be the worry?' Sam asked impatiently.

'We been robbed blind, that be what,' Tom answered. 'Tooked everything—including young William's trousers.'

'What you be meaning is some artful folk tooked your money—' with a look of contempt at William, '—and *your* trousers when you be in the brothel cavorting and ravishing with whores.'

The sheepish silence confirmed the accusation.

'If the tide be taking a single of these barrels, not one of you buffle-headed dunties be getting his wages!' Sam shouted.

Immediately the fishermen set to work, throwing the half-anker barrels down a line, from one man to the next, until they reached the boat.

The tide, Sam judged, would grant them no more than fifteen minutes' working time. The *Nancy*, slightly further out, was already beginning to awaken, her hull shifting like a sleepy whale in shallow waters.

'Be moving whip-sticks,' Sam ordered, wishing that they worked with the same diligence as the Frenchmen who had loaded and unloaded the cart.

Finally, the fishermen sank down onto the cleared sand, grateful that the task was over.

Sam approached Tom and issued the same warning which he did every time that he was not to accompany the contraband back across the Channel: two hundred barrels, untouched by the pilfering fingers of drunk fishermen, must be landed tonight at Romney Marsh. Then, with half of the crew on-board, Sam climbed into the *Nancy* and set sail for Folkestone, leaving the rest of the men waiting until darkness to land the goods.

Sam trekked the three-mile journey from Ransley's house to his own cottage in just under an hour. Having disembarked the *Nancy* at Folkestone, he had ridden one of Ransley's horses to the Bourne Tap, confirming that the smuggling run was all set for the night. He now had over three hours until he needed to make his way to the Royal Oak in Newchurch, the meeting place for the two hundred strong men, pulled from the surrounding countryside for tonight's smuggling run.

'Daddy!' John and Ellen yelled, jumping up from their game of spinning tops and hugging his legs.

'Be a-leaving him, for goodness' sake,' Hester said, appearing in the parlour.

'Did you be going to France, Daddy?' John asked.

Sam nodded.

'When I can, can I be coming with you?' John asked.

'And me!' Ellen joined in.

Sam smiled. 'When you be a bit older.'

'Not on your life!' Hester interjected. 'You be a-getting yourself out on them fields and earning yourself a living blessed by the good Lord.' John turned his nose up at the idea and returned to spinning the wooden top on the floor. 'You be back out again tonight?' Hester asked, a sourness to her question.

'Aye,' Sam answered. 'That be right.'

'Will you be shooting the preventative men?' John asked, making his fingers into a pistol and pretending to fire at his mother.

'Let's be hoping not.'

'Be a-stopping that,' Hester snapped, angrily slapping John's hands. Her furious eyes met with Sam's in a look which perfectly conveyed her unspoken thoughts. 'Ann not be with you?'

'I bain't seen her all day. Expect she be having herself a nice time some place,' he said.

Hester took a step closer to Sam and, with narrowed eyes, spoke to him quietly. 'What does she be *a-doing* with all her wages?'

Sam thought for a moment. 'She be giving us her lodgings—' he smiled at something that occurred to him, '—she be paying *my* wages.'

'How in the Lord's good name do you be a-reckoning a godless black-tan like Ann Fothergill be paying your wages?'

'She be spending most of her money up at the Bourne Tap, putting money in old Ransley's purse that he be passing back to me.'

Hester seemed to mull for some time on what he had said. 'Bain't you not noticed that she be less... lost in liquor these past months?'

'I don't be knowing such things,' Sam said with a disinterested shrug. In truth, though, now that he thought about it, he was aware that he had seen much less of Ann either at home or at her other favourite haunts, the Walnut Tree Inn and the Bourne Tap. Where she was going and what she was doing with her money, however, he had no idea.

Chapter Seventeen

27th June 1823, Dover, Kent

Ann entered the building on St James's Street without a trace of the self-consciousness which had been manifest in her first few visits there. She crept into the rear of the grand hall and gave an apologetic nod to Miss Bowler for her seemingly inadvertent premature arrival. It was the same routine every week: she would arrive early, standing at the back with a fixed smile and a look of near boredom, as though she were critical of what went on here, when in fact she was hungrily absorbing whatever lesson Miss Bowler was delivering to the previous class.

'And so, to the end of the lesson,' Miss Bowler said in a mock-dramatic tone, holding a book aloft in one hand, as she twirled around at the front of the room to the soft amusement of the dozen or so girls. She drew in a lengthy breath and raised the book. *'The Universal Epitaph.'* She paused and glanced theatrically around the room before beginning:

> *'No flattering praises daub my stone,*
> *My frailties and my faults to hide;*
> *My faults and failings are all known—I liv'd in sin—in sin I died.*
> *And oh! condemn me not, I pray,*
> *You who my sad confession view;*
> *But ask your soul, if it can say, That I'm a viler man than you.'*

Miss Bowler snapped the book shut. 'Good day to you, girls.'

The class murmured their goodbyes and began to file from the room.

Miss Bowler strolled energetically towards Ann, offering her a delightful smile. 'Ann—welcome.'

'That were a nice poem, Miss Bowler. I be knowing a fair few folk what could be having that on their graves.'

Miss Bowler grinned. 'John Clare. A lovely collection entitled *Poems Descriptive of Rural Life and Scenery.* Come and sit down,' Miss Bowler encouraged, pulling out a chair in front of her desk and setting down a clean slate and a fresh piece of white chalk.

Ann sat and marvelled at them, remembering Miss Bowler's bewildering prattle on her first visit here: 'Simple geology harnessed for

217

the betterment of humankind,' she had enthused. 'What happens when you combine a piece of metamorphic rock—' here she had picked up the slate, '—with a piece of sedimentary rock?' Then she had picked up the chalk, leaving Ann utterly baffled and wishing that she had not bothered to go there at all. Miss Bowler had smiled at her confusion, which had drawn an irritated flushing to Ann's cheeks. 'Literacy. You have the ability to read and write!' She had then put the chalk to the slate and had drawn a large shape. 'One letter like this letter, *A*—' Miss Bowler then added two more shapes with a flourish, '—becomes a word: Ann. One word becomes a sentence, which in turn becomes a paragraph and then into a story, or a letter, or a recount, or a biography! From these two humble pieces of rock come poetry, newspapers and books; wonderful books on every subject imaginable!'

Ann had sat quite still, listening to Miss Bowler's enthusiastic speech, her initial impatience having been quelled. Still, though, she had questioned herself about being there, again wondering what good an ability to read and write would do for someone like her.

Miss Bowler had then rubbed a piece of damp cloth over the slate. 'We're going to start with the first two letters in Greek, *alpha* and *beta*— alphabet.'

Ann pulled herself free from the memory of that first visit, startled by the progress which she had made to this point. She picked up the chalk and held it, as Miss Bowler had shown her, poised above the slate.

'Are you ready?' Miss Bowler asked with a kindly smile.

'I be ready, Miss,' Ann replied.

'I *am* ready,' Miss Bowler corrected.

'I *am* ready,' Ann parroted.

'Good.' Miss Bowler straightened her back and lowered her shoulders. 'My friend's dog sat at the gate.' She enunciated slowly and clearly, then she repeated the phrase twice more whilst Ann wrote down the words.

Ann handed the slate over to Miss Bowler and watched as she read.

'Very good, Ann! Just one mistake: you've spelt it *f-r-e-n-d*, the way that it sounds, but it needs an *i* before the *e*.'

'Because why?' Ann questioned.

Miss Bowler laughed. 'A very perceptive question. The rather convoluted reason is because three hundred years ago many of the first English book printers were Dutchmen, not used to our language. Sometimes they used Dutch spellings, adding an *h* after a *g*, like the word 'ghost' or 'ghastly' and sometimes they deliberately lengthened words like 'friend' or 'head', which suddenly acquired additional letters which served no purpose whatsoever.'

'Because why?' she said again.

'Because they were paid by the numbers of lines they printed; thus, the longer the word, the more money they earnt.'

'Why don't we be getting rid of them other letters now, then?' Ann asked.

'Another super question, Ann, but one which I fear is not in my capability to answer.'

Ann, finding herself strangely interested in this new peculiar world of words, was disappointed by Miss Bowler's answer. She wanted to press her further, but Miss Bowler said, 'Right, wipe the slate clean and I shall dictate another phrase.'

After one hour precisely, Ann paid Miss Bowler four shillings, and then left the building with the same sense of lament which she had felt after previous lessons had ended. Inside that hall Ann had keenly felt the sense of separation from her old life. Sitting opposite Miss Bowler, who had never sought to ask about her past or present, she was a different woman; a woman who could read and write with the possibility of a different future to that which destiny seemed to have prescribed her. Within the seclusion of that room, Ann was able to quarantine her past and view it as though it had belonged to somebody else, and she was merely observing those pitiful misfortunes from afar. But now that she was back out on the familiar streets of Dover, she struggled to hold on to the idea that she could be somebody else, somebody better. The notion was so terribly fragile in her mind, like a glass egg that might shatter at any given moment.

Ann walked quickly, crossing back and forth across the street in an erratic manner which she knew would make anyone watching her believe her to be drunk or quite mad. But she did it for a reason: to avoid the seductive beery plumes of tobacco which wafted out from the various public houses which she needed to pass in order to reach the quay.

On Strond Street she stopped. In front of her, from where she would need to catch the coach, was the Packet Boat Inn. She caught herself feeling the weight of the guineas in her purse and dropped her hand away. It was useless to deny that she craved a glass of rum. Again, she rebuked herself after glancing across to the clock tower, which told her that she had almost two hours yet until the 3pm coach departed for Ashford.

She stared at the inn for a long time, wishing that the coach stop was anywhere else but there. The more she looked at it, the more she knew that she had to go inside. Her thirst would be sated but her purse would be empty and that delicate glass egg, which promised a new future, would be cracked.

Ann forced her eyes away along the line of shops—drapers, tallow chandlers, watchmakers, notaries, bakers, auctioneers and warehouses—which edged the busy quay. Her gaze came to an unexpected halt at one of the businesses. *J. Minet, Fector & Co.* She strode quickly towards it, sweeping aside the doubts and questions that began to skulk out from that unspecified part of her which begged for alcohol, and marched confidently inside.

The outside of the building, tall and grand with long leaded windows, gave a very different impression to that which Ann now found inside: a small room, brightly painted, yet surprisingly dim. Three bookcases, laden with heavy leather-bound volumes, dominated one wall and at the very end of the room was a long wooden counter, which might well have originated from a public house. Behind it stood two gentlemen in matching grey morning coats and white cravats. They had long but neat hair and both had clipped dark moustaches and a fixed moue. Their shared look of curiosity rebounded off Ann to each other and then back to Ann.

'May we help you?' one of them said, stepping forwards and squaring his hands on the counter uncertainly.

'I be wanting…' Ann murmured, before correcting herself. 'I am wanting to open an account.'

The man passed a not-particularly-subtle look of wonderment to his colleague. 'And what, may I enquire, is the nature of your business?'

'A surgeon-apothecary,' she lied.

Both men struggled to contain a light snigger. 'How enthralling,' the other man said, now laughing out loud. 'A surgeon-apothecary.'

'Yes,' the first man chimed in, 'And yet he seems to be dressed as a woman!'

'A *poor* woman, at that,' the other added.

Time seemed to slow down for Ann and she saw the men mocking her, as if their movements were severely slackened by something cloying in their veins and muscles: sand, she imagined. She used the opportunity of extra time to think. She had choices. She did not have to succumb to the internal screams and pleas, which steered her out of this awful place into the Packet Boat Inn to sink a few glasses of rum, only then to return here with a deliverance of coarse invectives. She could return to St James's Street and politely ask Miss Bowler to accompany her to the bank and assist her in opening an account. She was certain that Miss Bowler would do it and that her station in life would satisfy the two bankers. Somehow, that seemed a worse option, as though the new Ann Fothergill was in some way weak and diffident and wholly reliant on other people, an unwelcome feeling which she had never felt in her entire life. She decided on simplicity and laughed with the men. 'I don't be too sure that Mr Henshaw Latham be happy about how long this be taking.'

The men stopped laughing and looked at each other.

'Mr Latham—the mayor?' said the one who had first spoken to her in a tone which suggested complete disbelief.

Ann shrugged. 'That be the man what sent me. He said—' here she drew on Miss Bowler's expressions and fancy words, '—to go and see the gentlemen at J. Minet and Fector bank and they will open an account for me.' She looked around her with exaggerated movements. 'Do this not be J. Minet and Fector bank?'

'Yes, Madam, it is,' the other man said flatly. He faced his colleague earnestly. 'If Mr Latham has recommended us, and if the lady is seeking to *deposit*, rather than seeking *credit*, perhaps we could assist.'

A nod of acquiescence from the first man and a false smile to Ann. 'If I could take some particulars…'

He pulled a large burgundy ledger from below the counter and opened it to a page with printed writing, which made Ann think of the Dutch printers randomly adding letters to make words longer. She wondered if any of those small upside-down words contained any pointless letters. Dipping a white quill into an inkwell beside him, the banker noted down Ann's name and address, and then asked, 'And how much will Miss Fothergill be *depositing* with us, today?'

Ann pulled out her purse and tipped the contents onto the counter.

The banker's bony index finger began greedily plucking at the coins, drawing them one at a time towards him.

Ann reached out, pulling sufficient money back to cover her coach fare, before grabbing a further six pence from the dwindling pile of cash.

'Two pounds and five shillings,' the banker confirmed, writing the amount in the ledger.

'Thank you,' Ann said, taking the proffered receipt.

The man placed the tome back under the counter and stood back level with his colleague, both with their hands tucked behind their backs.

Ann stared at them both mistrustfully. She had never handed money to anyone in her life and received nothing in return. She looked at the small piece of paper in her hand, trying to decipher what had been written. She smiled politely and tucked the piece of paper into her purse. 'Good day,' she said.

'Good day, Madam,' said the banker who had opened the account, with a wintry smile.

'Please pass our regards to Mayor Latham and tell him that we look forward to seeing him later in the week,' the other uttered.

Ann sighed as she stepped out into the warm afternoon. She was certain that her lies would find her out. But what was the worst that could happen? That they might close her account and hand back her money.

The clock tower struck one-thirty, just as she was looking at it. An hour and a half before the coach would depart; plenty of time for one glass of rum.

Inside the coolness of the Packet Boat Inn, Ann felt herself relax. Muscles, which she hadn't realised were tense, now slackened. The air in here—thick with the smoky exhalations of unwashed mariners and beer-infused belches of the labouring classes—was somehow easier to breathe than that in the bank. She stood impassively at the bar, awaiting her turn, among those of her kind: slop-sellers, cowmen, hawkers, vagrants and itinerants.

She always kept an eye out for any signs of Jonas Blackwood, but there had been none. She had mentioned the oddity of seeing him among the town's dignitaries at Alexander Spence's hanging to both Sam Banister and George Ransley, who both had not seemed especially interested, dismissing the likelihood of it having been him. Now, ten months distant, she too doubted the memory of that day. The figure that her recollection provided her with now was faceless, like a time-worn statue. And yet, as she had pointed out, Jonas had not returned to smuggling since that day.

She heard a coarse laugh and turned with a grin to see the unholy tripartite alliance sitting at the table nearest her: Jacob Reuben, the rope-maker, John Pittock the undertaker and the Dover hangman. 'You be but awaiting the Grim Reaper?' Ann asked with a laugh.

The three men looked up, but seemed not to understand, and returned to their beer and—judging by the words which Ann caught—their morbid discussion.

The landlord, Joshua Hoad, served Ann her pint of rum and water, which she carried hurriedly away from the macabre conversation to the other quiet end of the bar. She nodded to the straw-hat makers, Amelia Baxter and Sarah Cramp, then took her first sip of drink. She savoured the liquid in her mouth, then sighed with pleasure as it trickled slowly down the back of her throat, seconds later somehow percolating throughout her entire body.

Ann took another long gulp of her drink, then slowly turned to take in those around her. She viewed them with a disconcerting and unfathomable combination of pity, disgust and shame. She understood the pity: most present could not be anything other than that which they had been born to become. The feelings of disgust and shame at those vagrants, thieves and whores, took her by surprise, for she saw in them her own reflection.

Her complex sombre thoughts were pierced by a nearby conversation. The word 'smuggler' was said in an unfavourable tone. Ann drank more and cocked her head subtly to one side. Four men, blockade officers, were sitting behind her drinking and smoking. Without turning to face them, she tried to follow their exchange.

By the time their discussion had shifted to something else, Ann knew that what she had heard had been important: a third-rater ship, called the *Ramillies,* was being deployed off the coast of Deal to aid in the prevention of smuggling. The officers had spoken confidently that this new 170-foot-long boat, with its crew of more than six hundred, would bring about the end of smuggling in Kent and Sussex.

Ann left a good half-pint of rum and water in her glass and strode from the inn. She wanted to retain what she had just heard and, trying to counter the glossing effects of the alcohol, she rehearsed the information over and over, certain that it was of great import.

Chapter Eighteen

Darkness cloaked the old Volvo. It was parked, lights switched off, in the layby on Priory Road, on the outskirts of Aldington.

The dual yellow beams from a car—the first to pass in several minutes—flashed through the Volvo's interior, illuminating its emptiness. Then, Phil sat up and switched off the internal lights which would otherwise burst into life as soon as he opened the door. He paused, before reaching into the back seat for the metal detector and climbing from the car. He waited a moment for his eyes to adjust, but after a few seconds of impatient waiting there seemed little difference, so he began to walk the lane. The hedgerow along the layby was edged by some kind of tight tall shrub with unforgiving spikes, so Phil reluctantly continued along the road, hoping that no cars would appear.

In the distance, he heard the low rumble of an engine and broke into a jog. Just twenty feet ahead he spotted a fissure in the solid line of shrubbery and began to run towards it, as the engine—a motorbike by the sound of it—grew louder and a flicker of its headlight glimmered on the trees ahead.

Phil jumped sideways through the hole, just as the motorbike rounded the corner, its headlight fanning out over where he had been standing just a second before.

Now that he was off the road, he pulled out his mobile phone. The time, appearing in large white numbers read 2:56am. Perfect, he thought, switching on the phone's torch. The woodland around him was dense and without any sign of a footpath. Long tendrils of bramble had already reached out and snagged onto his grey tracksuit bottoms. His clothes would be ruined by the end of the night, but if he got what he had come for, then it would all have been worth it.

He began to push through the insidious undergrowth, swearing and cursing loudly every time that a strand of bramble refused to release his legs. The aerial view shown by Google Maps was of a vast oak woodland, not the veritable jungle that Phil was now struggling to traverse.

An unnoticed fallen sapling sent him crashing headfirst into a thicket of obnoxious bramble. 'Shit,' he cried, as pain shot through his hand from multiple locations. He picked himself up and pulled the spikes free from his hands, then continued through the woodland.

It took over thirty minutes for him to reach the low wire fencing which demarked the boundary to the Bourne Tap. Phil switched off the torch and peered down a steep tree-covered bank which ran down to the main house. He strained his eyes but he could see nothing. The house and the grounds were in complete darkness; exactly how he wished them to stay.

Slowly, he descended the bank until he reached the tennis courts. He paused there for several seconds. In front of him was a wide open lawn with no trees and no protection from being seen from the rear of the house. He studied the back of the property carefully, checking for movement. When he was sure that there was none, he ran across the wet grass.

His movement must have tripped a security light, for suddenly the whole back of the house and garden were illuminated by powerful floodlights. He had no choice but to keep on running. He made it to the small outbuilding and flattened himself against the brickwork. His pulse rate quickened as he heard a fierce-sounding dog barking from inside the house.

'Shit, shit, shit,' he muttered, sliding along the side of the building to the door. Luck was on his side—the door was unlocked. He opened it and slipped into the darkness, just as the barking of the dog became magnified in a way which could only mean that it had been let out.

He had no time. He switched on the phone torch and quickly scanned around the room. It was mercifully small. He could not work out what it might once have been, but now it was the repository for two broken bikes, a rotary washing-line, a stack of bricks and an assortment of children's outdoor toys.

Judging from the sound of its bark, the dog had torn over to the tennis courts.

Phil remembered the content of the letter, which had referred to the gold guineas. *Below the ground in an outhouse.* The torchlight fell to the floor. Concrete. He banged his heel into the ground at various points but found it to be completely solid. If there was anything buried below ground here, then it was well and truly encased in cement.

Quickly, he switched on the metal detector which he had purchased with most of the money from the sale of the gold guinea and began to arc it above the floor in long clumsy sweeps. Nothing. Nothing at all.

From what he had seen on Google Maps, there were no other outbuildings here. He switched off the machine and crept back towards the door, aware that the barking had stopped.

He stood still. The dog, he surmised, had returned to the house. He quietly pushed open the door and stuck his head out. The security lights were off and there was no sign of the dog. It was time to leave.

Phil pocketed his phone and began to sprint across the lawn, tripping the security light as soon as he left the safety of the outbuilding.

'Get him!' a man's voice yelled, making Phil's blood run cold as he glanced over his shoulder to see the dog, an Alsatian, running at full pelt towards him, barking rabidly.

Phil ran hard towards the tennis courts, but knew that he could not outrun the dog, especially once he had reached the dark edges and wouldn't be able to see where he was going. He ran faster than he was sure that he had ever run in his entire life, unable to pull enough oxygen into his lungs to satisfy the demands of his calf muscles.

He got to the tennis courts, certain from the bark that the dog was almost upon him.

The boundary fence was seconds away. He tossed the metal detector over and prepared himself to jump.

Then, he felt the agonising sear of teeth sinking into the Achilles tendon on his left foot, sending him hurtling to the ground. His head struck something hard, but the pain was nothing compared to the torture emanating from his foot.

Phil tried to drag himself towards the fence but the dog maintained his grip, shaking his head from side to side, just as Phil had seen lions and tigers doing with their prey on the television. He felt something in his heel snap and the pain increased dramatically. He knew that his only chance of survival was getting over that fence. He stretched out, his fingertips grazing the base of a wooden stake. He managed to shuffle himself forwards slightly, then grab on to the stake and pull himself to the fence. He knew that he would get one shot at this. Using all of his remaining energy, Phil kicked out with his right foot, catching the dog on the side of its muzzle. The dog yelped and released his left foot, allowing Phil to pull himself up and dive over the fence.

Just as he was going over, the dog bit down again, this time on his left trainer, holding it in his mouth as Phil fell onto the ground.

He crawled up the bank, his hands and face being cut with every inch of progress made. From down in the garden behind him, Phil was aware of shouting which was rendered inaudible by the dog barking. Then a powerful beam of light arced up from the garden, scanning the woodland around him.

226

Phil tucked himself behind the thick trunk of an oak tree, wincing at the pain in his foot. He reached down and felt his sock, sodden with blood.

Minutes passed before the torchlight was extinguished and the dog desisted from barking, yet Phil had still not regained his breath. Adrenalin pumped furiously around his body. He had to move on. Without doubt, the police would now be on their way.

Unable to walk on his left foot, Phil took an hour and fifty-five minutes to cross the woodland.

He saw the blue flashing lights long before he reached the hole in the hedgerow.

The police had found his car.

Phil sank down onto the cold ground and closed his eyes. His clothes were shredded and his hands and face bleeding profusely from multiple cuts. He withdrew his mobile and dialled 101. 'Hi, yes, I'd like to report that my car's been stolen, please...'

Morton was sitting in his study, alone in the house. Jack, Laura and George had gone to London for a daytrip and Juliette had taken Grace to the playpark. He was trying to shift his thoughts from the meal last night back onto work. He opened his laptop for the first time in two days to the 1842 Tithe map for Braemar Cottage, Aldington. He remembered that he had just been about to print it out when his Aunty Margaret had phoned to say that she would be coming to Sussex. Those two days had felt more like two weeks. Yesterday had gone better than he could ever have hoped or imagined. Soon after the meal had been over, George had gone to bed with a headache, and Jim and Margaret had also left soon afterwards, she taking the three letters with her. Jack had read Grace a bedtime story, then the four of them had adjourned to the lounge with another bottle of wine. Their conversations—on a range of subjects—had been thankfully relaxed and enjoyable. Maybe the alcohol, which he had consumed, now obscured any trace of there having been an awkward silence throughout the evening, but he certainly was not aware of one.

Morton smiled as he recalled some of the anecdotes and stories shared by Jack and Laura. He wondered when—or even *if*—he would ever reach a point when he stopped learning about his family's past. He doubted it.

He printed the Tithe map, then took it to his investigation wall, where he attached it close to the piece of paper, which had been mysteriously torn, and ran a red string line from the words 'gold guineas' across to the map of Braemar Cottage, not really sure why he was bothering to even consider the absurdity of where barrels of gold guineas might have been buried almost two hundred years ago.

Morton crouched down and looked at the timeline of Ann Fothergill's life. She had been resident with the Banister family in February and March 1821 but had moved to the Bell Inn, Hythe by August 1825. Just one month prior to that, her son, William had been baptised in Aldington Church, although that did not necessarily mean that she had been living in the village at the time.

His eyes moved around the investigation wall, settling on the word '*Smuggling?*' He was certain of her connection to the Aldington Gang, but could not quite join the dots together. What need did the group have of her? In her role from mid-1825, as landlady of a pub on the Kent coast, it was easy to imagine her use. Morton had read several accounts of how pubs had been the meeting point for smuggling runs, as well as being a storage location and, obviously, an outlet for the smuggled goods. But Ann's usefulness to the group prior to 1825 was a mystery.

He returned to his desk and flicked through his notepad to his research into the Aldington Gang, re-reading them for any clue which he might have overlooked. One thing he soon spotted: '*Ashford Museum—exhibits & artefacts for Aldington Gang.*' Pushing the pad to one side, he ran a quick Google search for the museum and found, among their list of exhibits 'Smuggling and the lives and demise of the 'Aldington Gang.' And they were open right now. Perfect.

Within ten minutes he was on his way to Ashford.

Despite being just a stone's throw away from Ashford's busy main shopping thoroughfare, the museum was situated on a quiet square which bounded St Mary's Church. The building was red brick and appeared to Morton, as he entered it, like a Victorian former school.

'Good morning to you, sir,' a red-faced, elderly man greeted through an open internal window. 'Welcome to our humble museum.'

'Good morning,' Morton replied, taking a quick scan around the room. It was small and dominated by a model train track on the opposite wall to the counter behind which the man was sitting. Each wall was adorned with various pictures, paintings and plaques and a glass cabinet to one side appeared to contain war artefacts. Morton could not immediately see anything related to that for which he was searching and asked, 'I'm looking for information on the Aldington smuggling gang.'

'Upstairs. Right above where we are now,' the man explained. 'Go left along the corridor—' he pointed through the open door beside him, '—then up the stairs. Then it's the first door on the right.'

Morton thanked him, then followed the instructions. As he had suspected, the building was the former Ashford Grammar School and, as such, came with a veritable labyrinth of narrow corridors, winding staircases and many small interlinking rooms. Upstairs, he found the room, which might once have been a master's bedroom, its being much too small for a classroom. On one wall was a large display cabinet, beside which stood a mannequin, dressed as a smuggler, holding a wooden bat and an oil lamp. Opposite to the cabinet were three chairs and a series of watercolour paintings depicting smuggling runs. It was the display cabinet which most interested Morton and he took his time examining and photographing the exhibition. Sitting at the bottom of the display, on a bed of purple silk, were various objects pertaining to smuggling in general: a cutlass, a pistol, a barrel of rum, a model galley, an example of smuggled lace. On the back-left side of the cabinet was pinned the Ransley family tree. It appeared that, at some point after George Ransley's transportation, his wife and children had followed him out to Tasmania. On the right-hand side was the Quested family tree and below it, was a tiny wooden shoe, the caption reading: *'Made by Cephas Quested. He was hanged in 1821 following a battle. While he was in prison he made this little wooden shoe for one of his children.'*

Morton read the explanations on the gang, inexplicably typed in the hard-to-read Old English font. Much of it he had already learned from the internet, but then he read a list of *'Known Aldington Smugglers & Their Associates.'* The list was unsurprisingly headed by George Ransley. Below his name was Samuel Banister, suggesting to Morton that he might have held a senior role in the gang. The names of more than a dozen men were followed by a short gap under which appeared the names of the gang's associates: *'Langham and Platt, Solicitors. Doctor Ralph Papworth-Hougham, Surgeon. Ann Fothergril, Apothecary.'* Her name had been misspelled but it was undoubtedly her. Morton smiled. Here was the evidence which not only provided the link between Ann and the Aldington Gang, but also answered Morton's previous question about what function she had performed for the group.

He photographed the list, then read the final piece of information: the demise of the group, which, as he had read online, came as a direct result of the murder of *Ramillies'* Quartermaster, Richard Morgan in 1826.

Taking one final glace around the room, Morton made his way back downstairs.

'Did you enjoy our little display, sir?' the man behind the front desk asked.

'Yes. It was very helpful and interesting, thank you,' Morton answered, dropping some loose change into the donations box.

He left the museum, deep in thought. He rested his elbows on the black metal railings which separated the churchyard from the footpath which bounded it, thinking about what he should do next. Now that he knew for certain of Ann's involvement with the group, he needed to obtain as much information as possible on the gang's activities. A good starting point, he reasoned, would be the local newspapers for the time, which were not currently available online. He remembered then that the knowledgeable American lady in Dover Library had told him that they had copies of a contemporaneous newspaper on microfilm. He looked at the time. He still had a couple of hours before he needed to be home in order for Juliette to be able to go to work. Just enough time, he thought, marching with purpose back to his Mini.

'You're back!' the American declared from behind her desk, when he arrived at the family history section of Dover Library.

Morton smiled and looked at her lanyard to remind himself of her name: Amber Henderson. 'Yes, more research.'

'Into the *bodies*?' Amber asked with a grin.

'Well...sort of,' he answered, vaguely. 'Which newspaper did you say you held here for the 1820s?'

'That would be the *Cinque Ports Herald,*' she answered, standing from her desk. 'Any year in particular?'

'I'd like to say 1820 to 1827, but I don't have the time,' he answered. 'So, 1826, please.'

'I'll go get it right now. Take a seat at the reader and I'll be right over.'

In the time that it took Morton to switch on the film reader and get out his notepad and pencil, Amber had arrived with the little white box labelled *Cinque Ports Herald 1825-1827*. 'Here you go.'

'Thank you,' Morton said, removing the film and threading it into the machine.

As the first edition appeared in front of him, he realised how grossly he had underestimated the enormity of the task. As was the case in most newspapers from this period, it was densely packed with small print and very few headlines separating individual stories. To search every edition for the two years on the roll of film would take hours and he had one hour and forty-five minutes until he had to leave. He would have to return next week, if necessary, but for now Morton decided to prioritise with the death of Richard Morgan.

He fast-forwarded the film, pausing at several intervals to check the dates, until he reached the edition of Saturday 5th August 1826. Morton sat up, moving closer to the screen and began to draw the plate slowly down the page, before winding to the next. Three pages in, he found the story under the caption, *'Murder of Richard Morgan.'* He zoomed into the story and began to read: *'A sanguinary affair, which has excited a strong sensation in every circle, occurred here on Sunday morning, about one o'clock. A smuggling galley arrived off the Marine Parade, opposite the bathing machine stand; the precautionary signals being exchanged between the persons in the boat and the party on the beach who were there in readiness to work the goods, the boat bumped ashore, and was surrounded by a vast number of men, who immediately commenced carrying away the tubs. Morgan, who was a first-class quartermaster, at that moment doing his rounds, came up but he was threatened by the smugglers with instant death if he attempted to give any alarm; regardless of the threatening, he fired his pistol as a signal, and the smugglers immediately shot him—he uttered an ejaculatory "Lord, look down upon me!" but never spoke more. The report of the firing brought down the lieutenant and a party of the blockade men to the spot, who removed him to a boat-house near at hand, and procured a surgeon, but he expired about twenty minutes after receiving his death wound. The smugglers were pursued by a party, but on account of their number, and consequently being lightly loaded, they got clear off. Their number was estimated at about 200 men, and they are stated to have been remarked coming into town from the country at a late hour. An inquest was held on the body on Monday before J. Finnis, Esq. and the jury brought in a verdict of "Wilful murder, against some person or persons unknown." Five hundred pounds reward is offered for their apprehension.'*

Without bothering to ask if the Mormons, or anyone else for that matter, held the copyright for the newspapers, Morton pulled out his mobile phone and discreetly took some shots of the screen, then pushed the film on in search of the inevitable capture of Ransley's gang.

It had not taken long. The newspaper reported the end of the Aldington Gang in the edition of 17th October 1826: *'THE*

ALDINGTON GANG—The leader of the unfortunate group of men, who were rounded up from the village of Aldington, has been revealed as George Ransley. As stated by our correspondent, Ransley and his gang were conveyed in the first instant on board the Ramillies *guard ship, and yesterday morning they arrived in the* Antelope *tender at Deptford, where they were delivered over to the Officers of Police, in waiting for them, and immediately escorted to Bow Street. The greatest anxiety was evinced by the public to be present at their examination; but it was conducted in a strictly private manner, and the prisoners were afterwards conveyed to the prison in Cold Bath Fields; it may therefore be inferred that they are not as yet committed for trial. The apprehension of these men, will, it is to be hoped, put a stop to those sanguinary conflicts, which have taken place on the Kent and Sussex coasts for many dreadful months.'*

Morton took a photograph of the story, less subtly this time.

He wound the film on, searching for mention of the trial. Several weeks' editions passed with no further mention of the smuggling gang.

When a stream of black film passed across the screen, followed by '1827' in stark white, Morton looked at the time. He had a maximum of half an hour left.

He fidgeted in his seat, then sat up straight, trying to force himself to concentrate harder, but it was pointless; he had to do the job thoroughly.

When he found the trial in the 13th January 1827 issue, he had almost no time left to read the story. He quickly read the opening paragraph: *'TRIAL OF THE ALDINGTON SMUGGLERS. Yesterday, at Maidstone, came on the trial of the persons committed on the charges in the above affair. Immediately on the Court being opened, ten individuals, viz, George Ransley, Samuel Bailey, Thomas Denard, Thomas Gilham, James Hogben, James Smeed, Richard Wire, Thomas Wheeler, Richard Higgins, and William Wire, were placed at the bar, and arraigned for the murder of Quartermaster Richard Morgan, on the beach at Dover on the night of the 13th of July last—to which they severally pleaded Not Guilty...'* The article went on with several further indictments against the men for breaking revenue laws and unlawfully assembling with firearms on numerous occasions in 1826. Morton hurriedly photographed the story, then rewound and boxed the film.

He just had time for one final thing: he opened his laptop and ran a search for George Ransley on the National Archives website. Zero results. When he searched instead for the Kent Assizes, he received more than a thousand results. A trip to the National Archives seemed to be in order.

'Thank you,' Morton said to Amber, placing the microfilm box on the desk in front of her.

'Oh, you're very welcome. Hope to see you again soon.'

Morton walked up the steps to his house feeling a welcome sense of calm that everything was okay in the world; in his world, at least.

'Dadda!' Grace called, scuttling along the corridor at a somewhat bewildering pace for a crawl. 'Dadda!' She reached his feet and hauled herself up, grappling with the folds and ripples in his jeans.

He reached down and picked her up, planting a big kiss on her cheek. 'Hello, darling. Have you been a good girl for *Mummy*?' he asked and, seeing Juliette appearing from the kitchen, placed great emphasis on the final word.

'No!' Grace answered with a comical frown.

Morton's amused eyes and mild laughter met with Juliette's.

'Yes, we've learned another new word today,' she said through a fixed smile. 'Do you want some lunch? No. Shall we go home now and play? No. Let's go and change your nappy. No.' She held her smile, directing it towards Morton. 'So now we can say "Dadda", "doggy", "Gandpa" and now the word that we won't hear the end of until she leaves home, "no".'

Morton carried Grace towards Juliette and kissed her on the lips. 'You wait—her next words will be "yes, Mummy".'

Juliette rolled her eyes and headed back into the kitchen. 'Drink?'

'Coffee, please,' he replied.

'Are we ready for the party tomorrow?' Juliette asked, the severe doubt in her tone answering her own question. She took the mugs from the cupboard and looked at him for an answer.

'I think so. We've bought the food...the house is reasonably tidy...we've invited people...we've got a cake. She's going to be *one*; it isn't the time—*yet*—for fancy venues, magicians and entertainers.'

'I know,' Juliette agreed. 'But still, people have come a long way to stand around just eating sandwiches and crisps.'

'They're coming to see my little Grace,' he said, stroking her hair. Juliette was right, of course. A lot of people had travelled a long way for what would ostensibly amount to a simple get-together. Yet he knew, and was deeply grateful, that they were coming for a greater purpose: because they were family. 'It will be fine,' Morton assured her.

Juliette sighed and accepted his assurance. 'So, how's your day been? Did you manage to get much work done?' She carried the two mugs of steaming drinks to the table and sat down opposite him.

Grace began to wriggle and point at the floor, so Morton set her down, and then began to give a brief rundown of his day. She then relayed the highlights of *her* day, ending by downing the last mouthfuls of her drink and saying, 'And now I need to go and get ready for work. Joy.'

Morton watched her leave the room with a slight flounce. 'Shall we go and play with your animals, Grace?'

'No.'

Morton had just put Grace into her bed and was backing out of the darkened room when, simultaneously, his mobile began to ring in his pocket as someone was lightly tapping on the front door. He whipped his phone from his pocket and hurried downstairs so as not to disturb Grace. It was Juliette calling.

'Hello,' he whispered, almost at the front door. 'You okay?'

'Yeah, good as can be expected,' she said.

'Hang on a second, someone's at the door. I expect it's Dad—' he stopped himself short at his slip-up, '—Jack…and Laura, back from London.' He opened the door to see their contented-looking faces. 'Hi, come in. I'm just on the phone—won't be a minute.'

They entered the house making polite apologetic faces.

Morton closed the door behind them and then returned the phone to his ear. 'Sorry—back again. You should know better than to phone at bedtime,' he joked, hoping that his blunder had gone unnoticed.

'I know. I just wanted to ask something about this case you're working on. You know that bit of paper you showed me that got ripped… Am I right in remembering that it said something about the Bourne Tap?'

'Yes, that's right—why?'

'Just that there was an attempted burglary there last night and I thought I recognised the house name. Bit of a weird coincidence,' she laughed. 'Anyway, I'll let you get back to it.' She was making sounds as though she were about to end the call.

'Hang on. What happened?' Morton asked.

'Er…just that. Someone was on the premises—chased off by the family Alsatian.'

'Was he in the house?'

234

'No, I think he was seen running from a shed. He didn't take anything.'

'Any idea who it was?'

'Oh, we're fairly certain it's a man called Phillip Garrow,' Juliette revealed.

'How do you know that?'

'The officers sent to investigate found a car close to the scene. Five minutes later Phillip Garrow phones—from home, he claimed—to say that it had been stolen.'

'So…?'

'Mobile triangulation actually places him somewhere within three quarters of a mile of his car when he made the call… So, not at home at all. It doesn't need Poirot to work out that having been caught trying to break into the house, he reached his car on the other side of the woods, saw police there, then called it in as stolen.'

'Have you picked him up?' Morton asked.

'He's not been home since. I've got to go. See you in the morning.'

'Okay, bye,' Morton said, absentmindedly. He had forever been suspicious of coincidences and this was no exception. A stranger entered his study yesterday afternoon. The only evidence of anyone having been there was a ripped corner on a piece of paper, which mentioned the possibility of a bunch of coins being hidden at the Bourne Tap. Last night, a stranger was caught trying to break into an outbuilding at the Bourne Tap. A thought occurred to Morton and he pulled out his mobile and sent a text to Juliette. *Does Phillip Garrow have any previous convictions? Photo? Physical description? Xx*

Before he entered the kitchen to join Jack, Laura and George, Morton took a moment to try and think who this man might be. Phillip Garrow. The name meant absolutely nothing to him. Perhaps it was a coincidence, but if so, he could not force himself to believe it. Right now, he had no more time to give it. His mobile beeped with Juliette's response: *No previous. Xx*

'Hi, how was London?' Morton said, strolling casually into the kitchen.

'Oh, my God, it was just amazing,' Laura enthused. 'Wasn't it?'

George nodded. 'Yeah, really cool.'

'Where did you go?' Morton asked.

Laura blew out a puff of air, as if she were being asked to recall a long-forgotten excursion. 'Buckingham Palace,' she began, placing an American stress on *ham*, 'Downing Street—'

235

'What we could see of it,' George interjected.

'Yeah, I notice security's been ramped up,' Jack added.

'Big Ben, Houses of Parliament, Piccadilly Circus, Covent Garden…' Laura's list faded out, as she searched her mind for anything which she had missed.

'Don't forget Oxford Street,' Jack said, in his best attempt at an English accent.

'I need to go back,' Laura declared. 'For like, a week.'

'Well, now we've got family here,' Jack said, a hint of promise in his voice.

It was minuscule, almost imperceptible, but Morton noticed George roll his eyes at Jack's statement.

'Have you eaten?' Morton asked.

'Oh, my God,' Laura said, touching her stomach. 'We had a huge meal—with cocktails—in some place off Covent Garden. Maybe a sandwich later on?'

'No problem. Are you still okay to babysit, if I go up and see Aunty Margaret later?'

'No worries, son,' Jack said, giving Morton another shoulder slap.

There it was again—the word *son* looming large in the room with its myriad complexities and questions.

'Thanks. Oh, Juliette's dug out those old embarrassing photo albums from when I was growing up…if you'd still like to see them?'

'Sure we would, let's go sit down and take a look,' Jack said.

Morton slowly pulled the front door shut, waiting for the soft click as the latch bolt was swallowed by the strike plate. A heavy coldness had descended on the back of the night's darkness. He had not bothered with a coat—the Mermaid Inn was literally thirty seconds' walk away. He pulled his arms tightly around his chest and headed up the unlit cobbled street towards the alluring warm lights of the pub.

He paused on the threshold and took a deep breath of the chilly air, then entered the lounge bar. Just as she had said she would be, he found Margaret sitting alone at a table close to the open fire. He observed her for just a moment. She had obviously made an effort for the evening, wearing a smart green dress, and had done something to her hair. She was holding a small glass of something and gazing into the fire.

'Hello,' he said, approaching her.

It took a moment for her to register that she was being spoken to. She turned with a look of surprise, smiled and stood to give him a hug. 'Hello, darling.'

He kissed her cheek, fairly certain that she had never called him 'darling' before.

'No Jim?' Morton enquired.

'Only if you want to be responsible for what happens when you wake him up,' Margaret said.

'No,' he stated with a short laugh. 'I'll just go and get a drink—are you ready for another?' he asked.

'Oh, go on then. I'm on the sherry,' she said with a chuckle.

At the bar, Morton ordered her drink and a large glass of red wine for himself. As he waited for the drinks, he glanced over at her, noticing then that the three letters from 1976 were on the table in front of her. As he pondered her thoughts on their content, his eyes moved to her and saw that she had seen him looking at the letters. She smiled, briefly, then turned back to face the fire.

'Here we go, Aunty Margaret,' Morton said, placing her drink down beside the three letters.

'Thank you,' she said. 'What sort of a day have you had, then?' She sat back, sipped her drink and waited, seemingly genuinely interested.

'Well, I'm working on this peculiar case at the moment—' he began, before she interrupted.

'You do seem to get a lot of those!'

Morton nodded his agreement. 'I seem to attract cases which are more complicated and—'

'Dangerous?'

'Yes, exactly.'

'Sorry,' she said. 'I interrupted you telling me all about the case you're working on at the moment. I'll keep my big trap shut this time.'

And so, Morton spelt out the fundamentals of the Fothergill Case.

'My goodness!' Margaret declared when he had finished. 'I don't know how you do it. And you're thinking you'll be able to solve it?'

Morton shrugged. 'I can't always. Sometimes the records simply don't exist and I have to give the client my supposition based on what I've found. Most times, though, the answer is out there.'

'Golly.'

They spoke more about his past cases and Morton enjoyed the feeling that she was understanding more of his life, more of him. Sometimes, as he was speaking, the realisation that she was his biological mother would pulsate through him anew, causing his words to falter and reddening his cheeks. He knew, though, with a pang of sadness, that however close they might become, she would forever see herself first and foremost as his Aunty Margaret. Perhaps that was for the best; he could never himself foresee a day when he would address her as *Mum*. Maybe after this weekend, where his, Jack's and Margaret's interlocked pasts had been confronted, they could all move to a new different relationship; what that might look like, though, he could not imagine.

Their conversation segued into Margaret's speaking about her brother, Morton's adoptive father. He had been proud of Morton, she told him, using actual detail which rendered it more than a banal remark, which he considered that she might have felt obliged to make.

'He was very proud of *both* of you,' she repeated.

Morton picked up his wine, took a sip and then clutched it in one hand. His facial expressions must have betrayed his anger towards Jeremy for telling Margaret about Jack, for she said, 'You mustn't blame him. Jeremy, I mean.'

Morton wordlessly fixed a half-smile on his glass, which he hoped said the words which he felt unable—or unwilling—to express.

'I asked him,' Margaret revealed.

'Pardon?'

'On your wedding day. I was standing beside him on the steps of Rye Town Hall, waving you off on honeymoon, and I just asked him if you were going to Boston to look for Jack, and he said yes, you were.'

'Oh...' was all that Morton could say. His annoyance towards Jeremy lessened somewhat, but there remained a lingering indignation that they had shared this information for more than eighteen months. Somehow, it highlighted and underlined the fact that he was adopted.

'At first it made me quite uncomfortable—' she went on, '—and the next day I was relieved to scuttle off back to Cornwall and not to have to think about it anymore... But, of course, that's not how the brain works, is it? At least, not my brain! Then I thought, "Don't be so silly, Margaret. Why shouldn't he go and find him *and* tell you all about it?". I was the first one to suggest that my friend, Sue, search out her birth family when she found out she was adopted... A bit different when it's close to home, I suppose.'

'It doesn't change anything,' Morton said, not really sure what he meant by his own words. Of course, it changed things.

'No, I know,' she agreed. 'I must admit, I was nervous as all hell when I saw him again, but, actually, the past is in the past. Speaking to him at the dinner table made me realise; we've all got our own lives, homes, jobs, kids, spouses. It's okay. *But*—' she set down her drink and picked up the three letters, '—then there are *these*. When you arrived, you caught me wondering.'

She looked at him with a smile and expression that dared him to ask, 'Wondering what?'

'Wondering what would have happened if my father hadn't intercepted them.'

'And?'

Margaret drew in a breath and seemed to hold it for an age. 'And… I don't know. I was quite a flighty little thing in my youth. I could well imagine me hopping on a plane and heading over to Boston just to see what happened.'

'Do you think so?'

Another long breath and contemplation time. 'Possibly. I'm almost certain that if things had been different with you, I would have gone. Or if I'd known how he felt at the time…'

Morton assumed that she meant that if she had kept him as a baby, then she would have gladly taken him off for a new life in America.

She sipped from her glass, then passed the three letters towards him. 'I think—with everything taken into account—you should have these.'

Morton reached out uncertainly and took them. Even though, yes, it did make sense that he should have them, it still did not feel right.

He allowed the conversation to ebb into a thoughtful silence, certain that they were sharing in the same alternative fantasy realm, where their lives had been very different.

'A whole world of *what-ifs*,' she muttered after some time.

'Yes,' he agreed.

Chapter Nineteen

'Keep still, for God's sake,' Katie said, impatiently dropping her hands to her side.

'I'm trying!' Phil shouted through gritted teeth. He was lying face-down on the sofa of her small lounge, whilst she was attempting to sew up the holes in his ankle flesh.

'I'm not going to say it again. I don't have the right equipment: you need to go to hospital. This is the needle and thread I use to sew Kyle's name tags into his school uniform.'

'And I'm not going to say it again. You're supposed to be a nurse and you're supposed to be a friend. I can't go to hospital, so bloody well get on with it.'

Katie huffed noisily, then returned to sewing up the bite marks on the back of Phil's foot. 'When did you last have a tetanus injection?'

'Don't know, don't care.'

Another sigh from Katie.

'Ouch! Jesus, Katie!'

'Almost done. Keep still. There, you're done.'

Phil sat up on the sofa and carefully picked his left leg up, and balanced it on his right knee. 'What a bloody mess.'

Katie shrugged. 'How long are you planning on stopping here for, exactly?'

'A few days…' he answered, not actually having a clue.

'I'm going to work,' she said, strutting from the room.

'Try not to butcher any other poor sod, like you have me,' he called after her.

She slammed the front door, leaving him alone in her flat, wondering what to do next.

Morton was in the lounge holding a photo of Juliette in her police uniform in front of Grace's face. 'Mummy! Mummy!' he said, drawing out the word.

Grace, in her red and white striped Babygro, crawled away from him. 'No!'

Morton followed her on all fours, keeping the photo in front of her face, despite her obvious protestations. 'Mummy! Mummy!' he repeated.

'No!'

'Mummy! Mummy!'

'Er...morning,' came George's voice from the doorway. 'Sorry to interrupt.'

Morton spun around, his embarrassment amplified by George's making it apparent that he thought that what Morton had been doing was odd. Maybe it was. In fact, it certainly was. 'I was just—'

George raised his hands as if surrendering, and left the room, muttering something which included the word "whatever", which seemed to make the whole situation seem utterly worse.

Morton picked Grace up and followed him into the kitchen. 'Sleep well?' he said, trying to sound normal.

'Pretty good, thanks. I was just going to grab a coffee?' he said, turning his statement into a question which, because Morton had followed him into the kitchen, now seemed to require his permission.

'Of course, go ahead,' Morton urged, ready to say that he would have one, too, if he were asked. He didn't get asked: George made himself a drink and slunk from the room, back upstairs, leaving Morton with the certitude that his half-brother had some kind of a problem with him. What that problem was, however, he had no clue.

Morton made himself a coffee, which he left on the worktop, and Juliette a tea, which he carried in one hand and Grace in the other, up to their bedroom. 'Give Mummy a kiss,' Morton encouraged, placing her down on the bed.

'No, Gandpa kiss,' Grace replied.

Juliette groaned and rolled over.

'I've brought you a tea,' Morton quickly said, pretending that Grace had not actually just said another new word which was not 'Mummy'.

He sat on the bed, patiently playing with Grace, whilst he waited for Juliette to surface.

Eventually, she sat up and cuddled her cup of tea in both hands, as though she lived on the streets and this was her first warm drink in a week.

'So, did any more happen with this Phillip Garrow guy? Did they find him?'

'No, at least they hadn't by the time my shift ended at two am.'

'What are they doing about that? Are they trying to find him?' Morton asked.

'Oh, yeah,' Juliette said. 'We've pulled CCTV of the area, got analysts working on Automatic Number Plate Recognition from his home address through to where the offence took place.' Morton now

241

knew that she was mocking him. 'And we've set up strategic road blocks around Kent.'

'Very funny. Are you actually doing *anything* to find him?'

Juliette looked down at her tea. 'I'm not doing anything, no. You've been watching too much television if you think we've got the manpower to go searching for someone whose crime amounts to trespassing.'

'And reporting his car stolen when it wasn't...'

'And low-level fraud,' Juliette conceded. She sighed in a conciliatory way then said, 'We went to his house. His wife said she hasn't seen him. We'd no reason to think she was lying. That's pretty well it. We'll try the house again and hope he's shown up.'

'Right,' Morton said, disappointed, then an idea came into his mind. 'What car was it?'

'An old Volvo.'

'Watch Grace for a minute, while I make a phone call.' He headed from the bedroom and, on seeing that the door to Grace's bedroom—where George was staying—was open and thinking him likely to be downstairs again, decided to make the phone call upstairs in his study.

He pushed the study door shut and dialled the number on his mobile. After a few rings, a breathy voice answered.

'Hi, Arthur. It's Morton Farrier, here.'

Morton could hear Arthur breathing as he processed the information about who was calling. 'Oh, yes—hello.'

'It was just a bit of a courtesy call, really, to let you know how the case is going,' Morton lied. He always avoided giving clients an interim report of any kind.

'Any progress?' Arthur asked, a hint of interest in his voice.

'Oh, yes, plenty,' Morton began, before giving him some of the brief highlights of the case so far. He alluded to Ann Fothergill's connection to smuggling, but did not go into detail. Then he asked after Arthur himself.

'Not so bad. Mustn't grumble,' he answered.

'And how's your nephew—the one that I met at your house? I can't remember his name, now.'

'Oh, Steve. Yes, he's alright.'

'Oh, that's good,' Morton said. He asked his next question, rendered redundant by Arthur's previous answer, just to be entirely certain: 'What car does Steve drive?'

'He can't drive,' Arthur revealed. 'Why do you ask?'

242

'No reason. Right, I'll let you get on and I'll be in touch in due course.' He said goodbye and ended the call. There was something that he was just not getting, that he knew he should. The nephew whom he had met at Arthur's house, Steve, could not have been the man, Phillip Garrow, who had trespassed onto the Bourne Tap. He sat at his desk and closed his eyes, teasing out the threads of memory of his meeting with Arthur and his nephew and niece. Snatches of conversation rolled through his mind until he thought about the gold guineas; the very thing which linked the stranger in his house to the events at the Bourne Tap. He worked to slow down the replay: Steve had been the main person to talk about the gold guinea; it had been he who had guarded it so preciously; he who had refused to allow Morton to take it away with him. But then Morton remembered something: the value of the coin had been found not by him, but by his sister's husband.

Opening his laptop, Morton ran a search for the birth of all Stephen or Steven Fothergills. The resulting list he cross-referred— using the mother's maiden name—to find further siblings. When he saw the name Clara Fothergill among the results, Morton recalled her name being used at the meeting and knew that he had found the correct siblings, born to Arthur's brother. Next, he ran a search for the marriage of Clara Fothergill. Five results. Running his eyes down the spouses' names, he settled upon the very one for which he was looking: Phillip Garrow.

Morton sat back to try to understand what he had just discovered. Recent events quickly linked together in his mind to form a satisfying picture. What he was not sure of, however, were the implications of what might yet happen. Phillip Garrow was out there somewhere with what appeared to be a keen desperation to get his hands on some phantom gold guineas.

Morton slunk out from behind his desk and left the room with a sense of mingled pleasure and anxiety at this new information.

'Morning!' Jack greeted, opening the spare room door. He was dressed in a navy-blue dressing gown with matching slippers.

'Morning,' Morton replied. 'Sleep well?'

'Yeah, like a baby. All set for the party?'

Morton's thoughts lurched dramatically away from the Fothergill Case and onto the endless list of jobs which he needed to do today for the party. 'God, no.'

Jack chuckled. 'Well, obviously, we're here to help.'

'Thanks. Coffee?' Morton offered.

'I would *love* one. Big and strong, please.'

'Me too,' Morton grinned.

The next three hours passed for Morton in a haze of tidying, blowing up balloons, hanging banners and helping Juliette to fill the kitchen table with buffet food. The first guest to arrive, at one o'clock precisely, was Morton's deceased adoptive father's fiancée, Madge.

'Hello!' she said, hugging him tightly, as though they were best friends. In truth, he had not even been minded to invite her until Juliette had persuaded him that it would be a nice gesture. She was in her seventies and still took great care over her appearance. Her white hair had been freshly permed and she wore a cream blouse over a tartan skirt.

'Lovely to see you again, Madge,' Morton said. 'How are you?'

'Not so bad, thank you. How's little Grace? I can't wait to meet her!'

'She's in the lounge. Go on through,' he said, feeling a wash of guilt at not having invited her over before now. He thought quickly about when he had last seen her: had it been at his father's funeral three years ago? Surely not. No, he remembered. It had been a year after that, when she had been clearing out the last of his father's things and had discovered the three letters from 1976. As per his insistent request, she had brought them to the house and stayed for a slightly awkward cup of tea.

His Aunty Margaret and Uncle Jim were the next to arrive. They greeted him at the door, then made their way inside. Margaret overflowed with delight upon seeing Madge and the three of them immediately struck up a conversation, which surprised Morton; he had had no idea that they had even met.

Another guest arrived, Juliette's best friend, Lucy. Morton showed her inside, then headed to the kitchen to pick up the tray of champagne glasses, which Laura had just finished filling. 'Thanks,' he said to her. 'Take one for yourself.'

'I'm not going to argue with that,' she said with a laugh and took one of the fizzing flutes.

'Champagne,' Morton declared in the lounge, carefully holding the tray whilst various hands reached in for the thin glasses. He noticed that Juliette took a glass, then passed it to Lucy, but did not take one for herself. 'Do you not want any?'

'Just a water would be great,' she replied, turning back to her conversation with Lucy.

Morton nodded, as his odd dream of Juliette declaring her pregnancy returned to him. The doorbell sounded and he returned the tray to the kitchen, then answered the door to Juliette's mum. 'Hi, Margot.'

'Hello.' She kissed him on both cheeks and stepped inside.

'Champagne?'

'Lovely—thank you.'

'It's just here in the kitchen,' Morton said, quickly scurrying in to the tray. She waited in the hallway and he returned carrying two glasses. 'One for Juliette. She's in the lounge with Grace.'

'Super,' she said, taking the flutes and wandering into the lounge.

Morton followed as far as the door, then peered through the crack and watched as Juliette welcomed Margot, who handed her the glass, which, without even taking a sip, Juliette promptly set down with a frown. She clearly was not drinking.

The next guests to arrive were Jeremy and Guy.

'Hey, brother,' Jeremy greeted, pulling Morton into his usual bear-hug. Morton smiled, genuinely pleased to see his adoptive brother. He stepped back to take him in fully. Several years in the army had showed on his body; his muscular frame stretched at the tight jeans and check shirt which he was wearing.

'Hi, Guy,' Morton said, hugging his brother's Australian husband. 'Nice to see you.'

'You, too.'

Morton closed the front door behind them. 'So, how are things with you two?'

'Good, thanks,' Jeremy answered.

'And life in Her Majesty's Armed Forces?' Morton asked.

Jeremy's eyes widened, and he glanced at Guy. 'Well, I've got just over a month left, then I'm out. I'll have done my service.'

'Really?' Morton said. 'It doesn't seem long ago that you joined up.'

'Four years, three months,' Guy chipped in, as if he were counting the days.

'Wow. So, then what?'

'Well,' Guy answered, looking conspiratorially at Jeremy, 'we're looking at starting our own business.'

'Brilliant,' Morton said without knowing whether or not it was brilliant. 'What business?'

'A scone shop,' Guy answered with a touch of drama.

'Oh, right,' Morton said, thinking it quite possibly the last thing that he could have imagined them ever saying. 'Just scones?'

'Just scones and drinks,' Jeremy confirmed. 'You know there was that craze for cupcakes? We're hoping to start our own craze for scones.'

'Sounds great,' Morton said, trying his best to sound enthusiastic.

'And...' Guy started, 'we're thinking that our first shop might be somewhere around here.'

'Really?' Morton said, now genuinely pleased. Living and working a few streets away from each other, rather than one of them in a God-forsaken warzone, might actually be the thing which could bring them closer together. His relationship with his brother had developed, of that he was in no doubt, but with Jeremy having been posted to various war zones, which were blacklisted by the Foreign Office as potential holiday destinations, it still suffered from a certain stiltedness.

'Is that okay with you?' Jeremy asked.

'Okay? I think it would be amazing,' he replied. 'Not that you need my permission.'

'Morton,' Juliette called, appearing at the lounge door, 'can you do another round with the champagne...' she spotted Jeremy and Guy and rushed over to them. 'Hello, boys!' She threw her arms around both of them. 'I'm so pleased to see you!'

'Wait until you hear their news, though,' Morton said, doing his best attempt at solemnity.

Juliette's face fell. 'What?'

Morton left the three of them in an excited babble of conversation. He collected the tray of drinks once again and stood back, like some kind of butler, watching in awe at the peculiar conversation combinations occurring around the lounge: Margaret, Laura and Madge were huddled together in one corner; Jim and Margot were chatting and laughing in another; George was clearly flirting with Lucy; Grace and Jack were playing on the floor in the centre of the room.

Jeremy and Guy, taking a flute each, made a beeline for Margaret, Laura and Madge, where a raft of greetings and introductions took place.

Morton turned to see Juliette heading towards him.

'Where's my water?' she asked.

'Why are you not drinking?'

'Why are you insisting I drink?' she countered.

246

'I'm not, but I've noticed you've not been drinking. You're not...'

Juliette laughed. 'Pregnant? No, I can assure you that I'm not pregnant—this month at least—unless it's by some miracle conception.' She smiled, rolling her eyes, and went to move past him.

'Hang on. What's the problem, then?'

She sighed and said nothing for a moment, as if weighing up whether to say what was on her mind. 'There's no problem. I just want to lose the baby weight, that's all.' She lifted up her t-shirt and gripped a sausage of fat from her stomach. 'Look at this.' He went to speak, to say the obvious, but she cut him short. 'Don't say it. Anyway, would it matter if I was pregnant? You look horrified at the idea.'

'Oh, God, no. I'd be delighted,' he insisted. 'What about you? How would you feel?' It was something which they had never discussed. Lucy and she were always bemoaning the fact that they neither of them had siblings and, in the past, had both said how they had wished at various points in their childhoods that that had not been the case.

Juliette shrugged. 'Yeah. I'd like more, if it happens. I'm not in a mad rush, though. I'm enjoying us and Grace for now.'

'Me too,' he said. 'I'll get you that water.' He kissed her on the lips and returned to the kitchen to get her drink.

'Can I be cheeky and ask for a cup of tea?'

Morton turned to see Madge loitering tentatively in the doorway, almost as though she might not be welcome in the kitchen. 'Of course—come in.'

She took a seat at the table and smiled. 'I'm not a big alcohol-drinker, plus I've got to drive home later. This looks a lovely spread,' she said, nodding to the food in front of her. 'You have gone to a lot of trouble.' She looked up at him. 'Thank you for inviting me—it means a lot.'

'You're very welcome,' he answered, feeling another pang of guilt about how he had almost not invited her. 'You're part of the family,' he found himself saying cheerily, as he made the tea.

'A much bigger family, so I gather from talking to Laura and Margaret.'

Morton stopped what he was doing. 'What do you think my dad would have thought about it?' The moment that the question had passed his lips, he regretted having asked it.

Time hung the question in the air for several seconds, neither of them speaking. 'He found it difficult at first; I won't lie. Do you remember that awful meal where you and Juliette came over and I got you into researching that old painting of Eliza Lovekin?' Morton nodded at the memory. 'He was just terrible to live with for days after that.' Madge sighed. 'Initially, when I asked what the problem was, he'd snap at me that it wasn't right, what you were doing, but I kept telling him that it was perfectly right and inevitable that you should want to know your past. I felt like there was something more to it and, despite his fiery temper, I kept pushing. Eventually, after he'd returned from the club a little the worse for wear, he told me that it was guilt that he was feeling.'

'Guilt for what?' Morton said, ready to jump in and defend him against any self-imposed culpability.

'He and your mum moved into their own home when you were born, but he went back to visit his own father, Alfred, from time to time—because you remember he was a widower. Once when he was round there—I don't know how—but he found a letter from Jack to Margaret and it terrified him.'

'What do you mean?' Morton asked.

'He thought that if Jack found out that he had a son, then he and your mother would lose you.'

'God, really?' Morton muttered.

'So, he showed the letter to his father, who I gather was quite a strict, harsh man and together they agreed to intercept any further letters from America. I really think they thought that it was in everyone's best interests...'

'Wow...' Morton said, trying to process the range of emotions that rose and fell on hearing this new information. On one level, he could understand how the possibility of further letters might have caused massive disruption to the family, but on another, the interference and invasiveness into Jack and Margaret's privacy shocked him.

'They wanted you so desperately,' Madge added, 'and couldn't bear the idea of anyone taking you away. You're a father now. Can you imagine someone walking in and taking Grace from you?'

He shook his head, all the while not appreciating the clumsy comparison that she was trying to make.

'He was very proud of you, you know,' she said, the second person to tell him as much in as many days.

'He didn't show it,' Morton said glibly.

Madge shrugged. 'He wasn't that kind of a man, Morton—as you know.'

A small silence was invaded by a sudden procession of people, led by Juliette. 'Come on, tuck in; it's all got to go!'

Loud and diverse conversations came with the swelling number, who bustled around the table, loading up plates, with comments, questions and compliments about the spread. Shifting bodies obscured his view of Madge and he returned to making her a cup of tea.

'Shall I get my own water, then?' Juliette asked, playfully leaning up against him.

'Sorry. I was just chatting to Madge. I'll tell you all about it later.'

'Sounds intriguing.'

'Hmm,' Morton murmured. '*Revealing*, would be the word.'

'Isn't it funny, seeing who's talking to who?' Juliette said, observing people as they filled their plates with food, then stood back to continue their conversations.

'You've noticed it, too…' He thought that he heard his name rise from one lively discussion between Margot and Jack on the far side of the kitchen. Margot said, '…and she actually *hit* the Prime Minister!' Morton grinned. She was telling him about the research that Morton had conducted into her great-grandmother, Grace Emmerson, a formidable suffragette, after whom he and Juliette had named their daughter.

'Everyone's getting on well,' Juliette commented. '*Despite* having empty glasses.'

Morton took the hint and went around the group topping up their champagne.

The afternoon progressed with the coming and going of other friends and neighbours. Morton tried to move around the group, speaking to each person on at least one occasion, although he was certain that some people had come and gone—including the new couple from across the street—without his having uttered a single word to them.

When the buffet had stopped being eaten, Juliette produced yet another birthday cake and they sang 'Happy Birthday' to Grace, before they all squeezed into the lounge and watched her opening her birthday presents.

Morton took several photographs of the occasion, very keen to immortalise the day forever. He then handed the camera to Lucy and asked her to photograph the family group. Switching to playback, he zoomed in to the image. In the centre were he, Juliette and Grace, a scene of relative normality. Beside Juliette was her mother, Margot.

The further he pulled out of the picture, the more bonkers it became: his American biological father with his wife; his biological mother (who was also his adoptive aunt) with her husband; his half-brother, Jeremy (who was actually biologically his cousin, and yet more familial to him than his actual half-brother, George, who was at the edge of the image, frowning) and his Australian husband; and finally, his deceased adoptive father's fiancée, Madge.

A perfectly normal family.

Chapter Twenty

Yet another smuggling run had ended in chaos. Since the arrival of the imperious *Ramillies*, stationed haughtily off the coast of Kent, many more runs had been postponed, delayed or intercepted. The summer months, when the hours of darkness were already too brief, were proving this year to be especially disastrous. Tonight's run had cost them at least two men, and under half the barrels had made it back for safe storage in Aldington.

'Everybody out!' Sam roared, upon marching into the Walnut Tree Inn.

The landlord, Sam could tell, was about to raise a protest, whether owing to the removal of his few final customers or because he was about to close for the night, Sam didn't know, or care. The landlord huffed, but said nothing, simply watching as the half-dozen customers sloped past Sam and out into the cool summer evening.

'Pint,' Sam ordered. 'The men be coming, wanting their brenbutter and ale. You best get to work.'

The landlord pushed open the door behind the bar. 'Rose! Be a-getting here dreckly-minute!'

Mournfully, like a funeral procession, the smugglers trudged into the pub. They were bone-tired, their smocks sodden wet with sweat and, for some unfortunate few, stained with blood. Of their own volition, there was no talking as they filed in. Sighs of relief could be heard as the men found a place to sit down.

'Your allowances be coming,' Sam said not sufficiently loudly for any but those still traipsing through the door to hear. He watched as the landlord and his daughter scurried back and forth from the bar with glasses of beer and chunks of buttered bread and lumps of cheese. When the men had been fed and watered Sam would give them their dues. Tonight, he doubted there would be a single guinea of profit.

The last of the men—those who had been injured—staggered or, in the worst two cases, were dragged inside by their arms; their cries of agony made all the worse by the stillness of the bar.

'God be damned,' Ransley snarled, striding into the pub and drawing the attention of everyone. He snatched a pint from the landlord's hand and thrust it with a violent jerk to his mouth, slopping the beer down his front, as he gulped and gulped until the glass was empty. He too was quiet for a moment, then shouted at Sam, 'Where be that tarnal surgeon?'

'He be sent for,' Sam replied, unable to stop his gaze falling onto the worst of the injured men, John Brockman, biting down on a lump of wood, his thigh bone proudly protruding through his crimson galligaskins.

The door opened, and Sam smiled as Ann walked in breathlessly. She nodded at him briefly, then hurried to the wounded to put into practice that growing knowledge gained from working alongside Dr Papworth-Hougham on so many occasions. Sam observed her from behind as she crouched down, a lust rising inside him. He watched her with a yearning desire, wanting her more than ever. In the process of helping John Brockman, she turned, and the sight of her blood-soaked hands instantly curtailed his want.

The street door was pushed open with the gust of authority that preceded Doctor Papworth-Hougham. Wearing his customary blue coat and long black boots and carrying his red leather case, he bounded over to Ann, trusting her assessment of the priority of assistance for the injured men.

'Amputation,' Ann said, almost as an instruction.

Sam could see that she had already removed John's trousers and placed a tourniquet around his upper thigh. The wound continued to bleed and give the man great distress.

The doctor pulled open the case and withdrew a shiny blade, causing John to resist the shackling grip of the two brawny tubmen who were holding him down. His eyes widened in terror and his head flicked ferociously from side to side as the doctor began to slice into his meaty thigh, which he pulled around the leg in a neat circle.

John issued a stifled scream, then passed out. At that same moment, a great geyser of blood spurted out into Ann's face; she baulked but kept her position.

The doctor placed the bloodied knife to one side and Ann passed him a steel saw from his case. She parted the carved thigh flesh with two fingers, then he pushed the saw blade down into the gap until it met with the bone. Then, in a quick thrusting motion, he ran the saw back and forth until the leg detached and dropped to the floor. The whole procedure had taken no more than a minute, but to Sam, always morbidly fascinated by an amputation, it seemed to have taken much longer.

Sam turned from the macabre spectacle and moved over to talk to Ransley, who, in a quiet corner, seemed to have calmed somewhat. 'There barely be enough money,' he whispered. 'Whatsay we be paying the men less?'

Ransley spoke through a glower. 'Be paying what we owe,' he said.

'But what about money?' Sam asked.

'Happen the next few runs we be a-taking less men,' Ransley suggested.

Sam nodded and obediently began to go around the room, offering the men their wages. Some stayed on and drank more, others left directly for the walk back home.

Within an hour, the injured men had been loaded onto carts and taken to their homes, their fate likely to be decided by dawn. Doctor Papworth-Hougham had taken a large brandy and then left on horseback for his home in Brookland.

'G'night,' Ransley mumbled, staggering out of the pub.

'Night,' Sam answered, taking a look at who was left. Only a pair of smugglers from the village—having drunk themselves to sleep—and Ann, slouched at the bar beside her third empty glass, remained.

Sam walked towards her, carefully stepping over the severed leg, ignored by everyone as though it might get up and walk out of its own will and placed his hand on her shoulder. 'You be wanting another?' he asked her.

Ann sat up and nodded. Her face was disgustingly comical. Her blue eyes, showing the effects of the drink, stared out from a face smeared almost entirely in John Brockman's blood. It had matted her hair and stained her clothes, yet she seemed somehow oblivious to the gruesome fact.

'Two pints of rum and water,' Sam called across the bar. 'And run a hot bath for this girl.'

The landlord nodded and disappeared momentarily out the back. Sam heard him talking, before he returned to the bar and served the two pints.

'You be looking like the devil painted your face,' Sam quipped.

'Thank you, kind sir,' Ann said with a drunken laugh. 'It be meaning a great deal.' She took a great mouthful of the rum and water and sighed with pleasure. 'It be getting harder, don't it?' she said, a playful sparkle in her eyes.

'What be?'

Ann raised one eyebrow and took a lingering swallow of the drink. 'Smuggling,' she finally answered.

Sam nodded. 'I bain't certain how much life there be in it.' He heard himself saying the words that he had feared for some time but had not spoken. He worried for himself and for providing for his family. As he stared at Ann, though, he knew that part of his fear stemmed from the tacit question of what would happen to her. For a reason he could not explain to himself, he knew that she would not return to her previous life of criminal vagrancy.

'What you looking at?' Ann asked.

'Where do you be going, Ann, when you be taking the coach to Dover every week?'

'That be none of your business, Samuel Banister,' she said with a heavy wink.

He smiled, accepting her answer with reluctance, then they drank together in amiable silence until the landlord burst from the back room with a loud snort. 'The bath be a-ready,' he said to Ann, then turned to Sam. 'You be settling your bill tonight?'

Sam nodded and emptied his leather purse onto the bar.

'That bain't what we were agreed,' the landlord said, having counted the money.

'That be all I got,' Sam replied, watching as Ann tottered through to the back room.

The landlord grunted something as he scooped up the money. 'Be seeing yourselves out.' He walked around the bar over to the two sleeping smugglers and banged his fists on the table between them. 'Out!' he barked. He moved quickly around the room extinguishing the tallow candles between his fingers. Without saying another word, he ventured through a side door and was gone. The two remaining smugglers wobbled out, leaving Sam sitting alone at the bar in all-but-pitch darkness; the only light the soft flickering flames of the open fire on the far side of the bar and the enticing yellow glow emanating from the open door to where Ann was bathing.

He finished the final dregs of his rum and water, then stood on his skittish legs, not knowing what to do next. He tried to pull sense from his sluggish and broken thoughts; he could just wait here for her to finish bathing, then walk with her back home. Or, he could yield to his returning desire and go to her. A third option, the one that he could feel his clearheaded-self pushing him towards, was that he leave right now and walk home alone.

Sam bent down and, inconsistent with his feelings, picked up the severed leg, carried it over to the hearth and tossed it onto the fire. He watched, briefly, as the long black hairs instantly tightened into tiny black curls before evaporating into a fizz. Sam caught sight of the toenails, each edged in black filth, before turning away as the repellent smell of burning flesh began to reach his nostrils.

His previous deliberation had softened and a decisiveness about what to do next had arisen. He walked, as if not quite in control of himself, around the bar and into the back room.

Ann was there, in the dull and battered copper bath. Her face was clean now and her wet hair was trailing into the steaming water. She rolled her head in his direction but her face remained impassive; she simply stared at him, watching as his eyes ran down her body to below the waterline. Then, she stood up and turned to face him with a playful smile.

He watched, somewhat breathlessly, as the warm streaks of water trickled over the curves of her body. Her left hand reached out towards him.

Chapter Twenty-One

21st September 1824, Aldington, Kent

Ann was grinning proudly, mirroring the wide smile on Miss Bowler's face.

'Read it again,' Miss Bowler suggested, nodding enthusiastically at Ann's slate. It was a dictation, another of John Clare's poems.

Ann looked down at her handwriting. It was a peculiar leaning script, the letters all of a different size, but it was *legible*, as Miss Bowler had insisted. Ann cleared her throat and sat up straight, holding the slate as she had seen Miss Bowler's girls doing: '*My loves like a lily, my loves like a rose, My loves like a smile the spring mornings disclose. And sweet as the rose, on her cheek her love glows, when sweetly she smileth on me.*'

Miss Bowler clapped a tight neat little clap then took the slate from Ann. 'We've got some work to do on apostrophes, but that is for another day.'

Ann nodded absentmindedly. She was focused on her slate, wishing that she could take it away with her to show everyone how far she had come. Here was solid proof that Ann Fothergill could read and write. But soon—any moment now—Miss Bowler would tell her to wipe it away and the evidence would be gone forever. Not that it mattered, really. Whom would she show? Nobody in the entire world but Miss Bowler knew of Ann's lessons. She had almost told Sam and Hester at various points in the last year but at each time she had feared what would inevitably be their first question: why was she doing it? Ann did not have an answer and as much as she loved the lessons, she knew that the possibility of ridicule would be enough to draw them to an instant end.

'Since you are becoming such an expert in poetry, Ann,' Miss Bowler flattered her, 'perhaps it's time that you wrote your *own* poem.' Ann looked up with a look which must have expressed her abject horror at the prospect, for she added, 'There's no need to look so terrified!'

'I don't not even know where to be beginning.'

'I don't even know where to begin,' Miss Bowler corrected. 'What do you know of love, Ann?'

Ann laughed in a short mocking way before she had even had the time to consider the question. 'I don't not...I don't know nothing about love.' She spoke the words like an embarrassed confession. She thought, for the first time with a hint of indignity, of the male acquaintances whom she had known in the past. Some had been isolated, others had lingered, but none had remained.

Miss Bowler took this as a surprise. 'Well, what about your parents?'

And there, for the first time, Miss Bowler had shone a light on Ann's past, inadvertently forcing her to reveal her background, or to lie about it.

She chose neither option and said, 'You be wanting me to write a love poem about my mother?'

'Yes.' Miss Bowler handed her a piece of cloth.

Ann paused to take one final look at her words, then cleaned the slate and sat with the chalk poised, trying to force herself to think. Her memories of her mother were few and, in truth, all came tarnished with a suffering and sorrow which she preferred to forget.

Miss Bowler sensed Ann's reticence and wrongly attributed it to her inability to begin the poem. 'Allow me to re-read *My Love's like a Lily*; I shall clap out the syllables as I read, so you can hear the rhythm:

My love's like a lily, my love's like a rose,
My love's like a smile the spring mornings disclose;
And sweet as the rose, on her cheek her love glows,
When sweetly she smileth on me.

Do you hear it?' Miss Bowler asked. 'The rhythm of the poem?'

Ann nodded, dragging her mind out of the awfulness of childhood recollection.

'At the end of the first three lines in the stanza, you have a rhyming triplet: *rose, disclose, glows*…but of course, for a first attempt you needn't be so adventurous.'

For a long time, Ann sat and thought. Then she wrote isolated words. Then she scrubbed them out and wrote a line. The next line appeared, as if by itself. The third line she found difficult to relate to the previous two and it took several attempts to satisfy her. Finally, she had written her poem. She checked it, made a correction, then passed the slate to Miss Bowler, who cleared her throat and then read aloud:

'Sophia
Life for you were like a wave

257

So short and difficult to save
Another minute with you I do crave
But you be returning to the grave'

She placed the slate down and raised a hand to her mouth. 'Oh, Ann.'

'Do it be awful, Miss Bowler?'

Miss Bowler shook her head. 'I don't think I have ever read a first poem so beautiful.'

'Really?' Ann asked.

'Really, it's lovely.'

The sound of the street door opening, and the diffident entrance of two young girls to the back of the hall, signalled the end of the lesson, though Ann could tell that neither she nor Miss Bowler felt ready to stop. Ann sensed that there was more to be said; encouragement, perhaps, or a critique of her poem. For she knew that it lacked punctuation and, now that she had heard it read back to her, she disliked the word 'returning', thinking that it sounded as though her mother were some kind of a half-dead, coming and going freely to the grave.

'Sorry, Ann,' Miss Bowler said.

Ann half-smiled, quickly trying to commit the poem to memory before wiping it from the slate. 'See you next week,' Ann said, standing to leave.

'See you next week,' Miss Bowler answered. When Ann had reached the street door, she called out, 'Well done for today. You're doing brilliantly.'

Ann nodded, strolling out into the chilly late morning air. She walked briskly back towards Strond Street, her mind in a blur. Usually she left Miss Bowler's academy with her thoughts spilling over with what she had learned, and she would practise the new spellings or a poem that she had learned, happily chanting them over and over in her head, or writing the words with an imaginary piece of chalk on her palm. Today, the elation which she had felt at writing her very own poem was dwarfed by the shadow of recollection of her mother and her past.

Ann reached the street door to *J. Minet, Fector & Co.* bank and took a long breath in. 'Good morning,' she said pleasantly, as she entered.

Mr Claringbould—she now knew him to be called—welcomed her: 'Ah, Miss Fothergill.' He bent down behind the counter and hauled up the usual ledger. 'I trust we are well, today?'

'We are very well, thanking you kindly,' Ann replied grandiosely. Having raised questions with Miss Bowler over her interactions with the bankers, she had rehearsed answers and now followed the script perfectly on each visit. 'And your good self?'

Mr Claringbould nodded, seeming to take great pleasure in Ann's clumsy attempts at formality. 'Very good, thank you. How much would madam wish to deposit with us, this morning?'

'Two pounds, two shillings,' Ann said, placing the money onto the counter.

'You have been saving hard, Miss Fothergill,' Mr Claringbould said. 'Well done.'

'Thank you, sir,' Ann replied. She shifted on the spot, wondering how best to ask something which deviated from their set script. 'I were wondering...'

'Oh, yes?' Mr Claringbould said, looking up sharply from the ledger.

'What be the chance of me buying a public house or an inn?' she asked, quickly looking down in embarrassment from the snickering and derision which she knew was about to follow.

'Freehold or leasehold?' Mr Claringbould asked.

She met his serious eyes, uncertain of his question. 'Pardon? What do you be meaning?'

'Ah. Freehold you would be purchasing—with a mortgage, of course—the business in question. Leasehold you would be...well, leasing it.'

Ann continued to stare at him blankly.

'Of course, it all depends on the terms of sale for the business, but...' he looked down at the ledger for a moment, 'I would suggest, looking at your current financial position, that you consider a leasehold with a mortgage—from *us*, of course.'

'Right,' Ann muttered, taken aback at the positive response.

'Do you have a property in mind?' he asked.

'No, not yet.'

Mr Claringbould nodded. 'Well, speak with us when you do.'

Ann grinned. A well-respected banker had just told Miss Ann Fothergill that she could buy her own public house. She thanked Mr Claringbould with an off-script shake of his hand, took the receipt for her deposit and left the bank, beaming.

Although she walked slowly along Strond Street, her thoughts were moving fast. Thoughts about a possible future. It was high time that she moved on. Her current income was derived entirely from smuggling and, since the arrival of the *Ramillies*, the contraband runs had dwindled in both number and successes. At the Bourne Tap, previous circumspect murmurings and infrequent rumours that the gang might not be able to continue, were now—at least outside of Ransley's earshot—openly discussed as the most probable outcome. The catalyst, however, for Ann, had been the incident at the Walnut Tree Inn last week with Sam.

The perishable recollection—obscured and dimmed through the passing days and the dazing effects of the rum and water—was replaying in her mind, when something hard jolted into her right shoulder, knocking her sideways.

Ann looked up to see two gentlemen in long black coats with black top hats and shiny black boots striding past. 'Oi!' she yelled. 'Don't be minding me!'

The men's snappish pace faltered, and they turned around at the same time.

'Watch where...' Ann shouted, before taking in the men's faces. One of them she recognised as being Jonas Blackwood. 'Jonas?'

The other man laughed in the mocking, patronising way that gentlemen of his sort were inclined to do. '*Jonas*?' he repeated. 'Is this some kind of a trick?' He twirled around, then faced her again. 'Are you the distraction while someone picks our pockets?' He slapped his arms down by his side and checked over his shoulder. 'I should warn you that we're armed with pistols.'

Ann stared at Jonas, certain that she was now looking at the same man whom she had seen at the Bourne Tap, in Braemar Cottage and, dressed similarly to now in the Black Horse, watching Alexander Spence die. His eyes had widened slightly. Perhaps, she wondered, with a hint of conspiracy, he was asking—without asking—for her to pretend that she did not know him?

'Do you know her, William?' the other man asked Jonas.

He shook his head with disdain. 'Never met her before in my life.'

'What do you want?' the other man demanded.

'I be wanting nothing from the likes of you,' Ann returned, spinning on her heels and marching indignantly to the coach stop outside the Packet Boat Inn.

She reached the stop and looked down the quay. The two men were now barely visible in the distance. Again, Ann found herself questioning what she had just seen, wondering if her mind were playing tricks on her; but, no, she was certain that the man was Jonas Blackwood, or William, or whatever his name might be. She did not know why she had allowed the other man to speak to her in such a way but there had been something in Jonas's face—a pleading in his eyes—which asked her to keep quiet.

The clock tower said that she still had an hour until the coach would depart for Ashford. As always, she had retained an extra six pence for a pint of rum and water before she left. This morning, however, she had settled her mind to bank the six pence and forgo the drink. But now that she was here, that firm decision began to crack; the unpleasant encounter with the two men mingled uncomfortably in her mind with the earlier fatigue of having trawled up her past in Miss Bowler's lesson.

Pushing past a drunk fisherman, Ann entered the inn and ordered a drink. She stood at the bar sipping from the glass, taking in the surroundings which she knew so well, consciously ushering her thoughts to the possibility of purchasing a place of her own like this.

A woman in a grubby iris-blue gown with matching bonnet slunk in beside Ann. 'You be a-looking for work, Miss?' she asked, revealing her dark brown front teeth. 'I got gentlemen what be a-paying a lot for a girl like you.'

Ann smirked but said nothing.

'Missy—I be a-talking to you,' the woman persisted.

'She's with me,' a voice said. 'Move along.'

Standing on the other side of Ann was the tall muscular frame of Jonas Blackwood. She turned her head back towards the lady and said, 'I don't be wanting nothing from you and your *gentlemen* folk.' Then she turned to Jonas and said, 'And I certain-sure *ain't* with *you*.' Ann picked up her glass and walked to the other side of the bar, where she found herself an empty table.

The woman sloped off out of sight, but Jonas—or William—seemed to be less easily dissuaded. He paid for the drinks, saving Ann the need to evade paying later, and carried his pint of ale towards her and seated himself, uninvited, at her table.

'"William, do you be knowing *her*?",' Ann mimicked. '"No, never seen her before in my life".'

Jonas smiled weakly, his eyes mildly accepting the rebuke. 'I'm sorry. I think you know that my real name is Jonas, not William Fry.'

Ann shrugged apathetically.

'I wanted to thank you for not revealing my true identity. I expect you've questions for me?'

Ann turned up her nose. She *did* have questions for him: besides the obvious ones, she wanted to know why a supposed gentleman's expensive clothes did not quite fit him; why his nails were grubby and his hands more calloused than a labourer's; why, when he spoke, his voice revealed subtle notes of both the upper and lower classes. But she said nothing and concentrated instead on tracing a fingernail around the rim of the glass.

Undeterred by her indifference, he said in a quiet considered voice, 'I'll tell you my story and hope you might forgive me by the end of it. My name *is* Jonas Blackwood; I was an orphan before I can remember and was placed in a workhouse. The streets of London were where I grew up, labouring when I could, thieving when I couldn't.'

Ann softened somewhat at hearing how closely his early life had mirrored hers. However, she was not yet ready to show it; she continued to sit uninterestedly drinking her rum, wanting to hear more.

'But it's no life living on the streets, going for days without food…freezing in the winter…accepting any kind of miserable work. So, I travelled around, hoping that life would improve elsewhere…but a vagrant in Paris is the same as a vagrant in London—but with the added difficulty of not being able to beg in your own language.'

His eyes locked onto hers with a warm smile, hoping, she suspected, that she would smile back. She did not: she held his gaze and held her tongue.

'I used to look at the rich gentlemen strolling past with more money than they could ever hope to spend and realised then that all my efforts and actions had been focused on the present moment: I stole food because I was starving; I would break into buildings at night because I was freezing and needed somewhere to sleep. I realised that I needed to think more adroitly and act for the future, *not* for the present. So, I stole a gentleman's outfit and found that pocket-picking was much easier if dressed correctly and speaking correctly. Then, a rather strange thing occurred: I found that I made *friends* among the upper classes. I was *given* things and offered places—grand places, at that—to lodge…for *free*. It was really most incredible.'

Ann narrowed her eyes, her interest in his tale now beginning to show on her face. Most of her internal questions, though, remained unanswered.

'And, as with any set of friends, I was told things—secrets. I observed dubious business practices, witnessed marital indiscretions, saw political impropriety; all of it giving someone with a mind for self-gain a great advantage and a far greater and more far-reaching reward than stealing half a loaf of bread to satisfy a desperate hunger.'

'Extortion,' Ann summarised.

Jonas glanced over his shoulder, carefully taking in the room. 'That would be the legal definition; I prefer to call it gentlemanly *persuasion.*'

'I be assuming that gentleman what you was just with, and the folk around you at Alexander Spence's hanging, all be to do with your gentle persuasions?'

Jonas nodded in confirmation. 'The auspicious Henry Purdon. He's an agent to the Hanoverian Consulate at Latham, Rice & Co. and author of many dubious transnational dealings.'

Ann's own issues had still yet to be addressed. 'Because why, then, did I be seeing you at the Bourne Tap *and* my mistress's house?'

Jonas reached out and placed a hand on hers. She suppressed her initial reaction to withdraw it, finding odd pleasure in the contact. He leaned closer and lowered his voice. 'Mister Banks—the owner of Court Lodge Farm, to which Braemar Cottage, among many others, is tied—is a *friend* of mine.'

'So you be extorting him?' Ann asked.

Jonas laughed, squeezed her hand gently and smiled. 'I'm merely developing and nurturing an acquaintance into a more advantageous friendship, let's just say. The more I know about Mister Banks—from his friends, tenants and workers—the better our *friendship* could be.'

'Happen it be very profitable if you be paying people like Mistress Banister for information.'

Jonas appeared almost apologetic. 'Acting for the future, Ann. You should try it.'

'Happen I am,' she said, her tone a mixture of defensiveness and pride.

'Oh?'

'I be having lessons,' Ann revealed, surprised to hear herself blurting out her secret, and to him of all people.

He raised his eyebrows, took a sip of ale, but inexplicably kept his hand on hers. 'And what lessons might they be?'

She went to say something fancy such as 'Poetry,' but it felt more appropriate to be telling the truth to a man like Jonas Blackwood, who had come from the same bleak place as she. So she said, 'Reading and writing.'

'Brilliant.' He smiled, drank some more, touched his dark moustache, thinking. 'You know, we come from very similar circumstances, you and I; you've chosen one path and I've chosen another and yet, here we are, together. Moving away from our pasts.'

Ann sank the last of her drink.

'Let me get us another,' he said.

Without allowing her time to protest, he made for the bar. She watched with growing intrigue as he ordered the drinks. Maybe it was a false warmth given by the rum, but Ann was finding herself strangely attracted to Jonas. He returned, setting a glass down in front of her, then slid back onto the stool opposite. She flinched momentarily, as his leg brushed against hers, and thought that he had made a miscalculation of her position, but no, he held it there, pressing it more firmly to her.

'Happen you be back in Aldington to be seeing your old friends anytime soon?' Ann asked.

'Old friends—no. *New* friends—yes.'

Ann took a large swig of her rum, then unhurriedly lowered her hand beneath the table, placing it onto her own leg, but cautiously raising her index finger so that it touched Jonas's thigh. He displayed no reaction to her touch, but nor did he move his leg in subtle reproach. If she could not get herself a real gentleman like Ralph, then maybe a sham gentleman would do. Jonas Blackwood and Ann Fothergill: she thought they sounded a rather handsome couple.

'And what of life in the old parish? Does the wicked trade continue unabated?' he asked sardonically.

'I think there be trouble coming,' Ann answered, finding that the alcohol was liberating the final lingering shackles of her previous reserve.

'Trouble?'

Ann drank more, then relayed the recent catastrophes which had befallen the Aldington Gang since the arrival of the *Ramillies*. Jonas listened intently, asking questions as she spoke. When Ann had finished, both of their glasses were empty.

'Time for another!' Jonas declared, jumping up.

'Gracious-heart-alive!' Ann exclaimed, suddenly aware of how long she had been drinking and talking. 'What be the time?' She sprang up and hurried for the door. Outside, the sun was hanging low over the horizon, painting the quay in a light orange hue. Sunset was fast approaching, and she had missed the coach back to Ashford by more than an hour. 'It be gone,' she lamented as she rejoined Jonas, who passed her another glass of rum.

'I shall take you back,' he said with a grin. 'After this drink.'

Ann sat back down contentedly light of mind and spirit. The rum smoothed any apprehensions at her missing the coach and removed her original misgivings about Jonas Blackwood.

His small pleasing smile parted his lips as he stared at her.

She returned the smile, feeling an unfamiliar coyness.

The journey on horseback was passing in a haze of giddiness. Ann had clung tightly to Jonas's midriff, sometimes through the absolute terror of falling, sometimes—when the horse was at a steady canter—simply to feel the hammering of his heart beneath her exploring fingers.

Though the darkness was springing and dancing around her, Ann knew that, having reached the village of Aldington, they were now riding along the incorrect road. 'You be going the wrong way!' Ann shouted.

Jonas pulled the horse into a trot and arched back his head. 'Pardon?'

'You be going the wrong way,' she repeated. 'I be lodging at the Walnut, now.'

Jonas accepted the news, slowed the horse, then turned back on himself. A few minutes later, they had reached the front of the Walnut Tree Inn. Ann dismounted first, glancing across at the silhouetted figures passing behind the flickering candles in the windows.

Jonas jumped down skilfully and quickly tethered the horse. 'Why are you living here?' he asked, his words breathy and warm on her face.

'I were rather in the way at Braemar Cottage,' she mumbled, eschewing the truth, which probably would have sufficed as an explanation, but the darkness empowered her to reveal more. 'I also be having some attention from Mister Banister.'

'Oh,' Jonas said, though Ann could not tell from that single utterance how he had taken the news, until he added, 'I better be on my way.' Then, she knew that it had been accepted as a warning.

'No, I bain't meaning...' She moved in closer to him and kissed him lightly on the lips.

A few short seconds passed, their mouths close but not touching. She kissed him again, with reciprocal vigour and intensity.

Chapter Twenty-Two

Morton was standing in the centre of a stretched hoop of sunshine, which poured through the kitchen window, as he waited for the kettle to boil. A motley assortment of six mugs stood on the worktop beside him. He looked on them as direct representations of the people currently chatting in the lounge and grinned to himself, thinking that the last few days could not have passed off any better. The day after the party had been a relaxed one. He and Juliette had met up with Margaret and Jim for lunch, then had had dinner out with Jack, Laura and George. A pleasant excursion with them to Canterbury had followed the next day.

His meandering mind skipped with the click of the kettle. He made the drinks, then placed the mugs onto a tray and carried them into the lounge. In a peculiar rollcall of his family, Morton matched the mug with its recipient.

'How did you find staying at that hotel?' Laura asked, her eyes passing between Margaret and Jim. 'It looks kinda spooky to me.'

'*Absolutely* lovely,' Margaret answered, with a vague nod of agreement from Jim. 'In every nook and cranny, you can *feel* the past. It's like it's alive with history.'

'I think that's what Laura means,' Jack laughed.

'The only fright *I* had in the night,' Jim began, 'was Margaret in a nightdress and hair-rollers.'

Margaret rolled her eyes and blushed a light pink.

'You guys sure picked a good day to be travelling back home,' Jack said to Margaret and Jim.

'Yes, and we'll have missed rush hour by the time we've finished this drink,' Margaret agreed.

'When are you flying back to Canada?' Jim asked.

'Friday morning; so, we only have two more full days left,' Laura replied, curling her lower lip.

'It's been such a great trip,' Jack enthused. 'We really have to come over here more often.' He turned to Juliette. 'Don't worry—we wouldn't expect you to put up with us every time.'

'Don't be silly—you're welcome here anytime,' Juliette said. 'All of you.'

'Well, if this date goes well, we won't need to worry about convincing George to come again,' Laura said with a chuckle.

'I wonder how they're getting on...' Juliette said to nobody in particular.

The chat about George and Lucy going on a date continued with parental scepticism about the wisdom and perils of a very-long-distance relationship, but Morton's mind drifted elsewhere. He noticed that Laura had implied that George had needed convincing to come to England. Morton still had no idea if George was just a naturally distant person, or if he had some kind of a problem with him. They had still yet to hold anything resembling a conversation which moved beyond the perfunctory; the time for any such growth in their relationship was fast disappearing.

Morton zoned back into the discussion to hear Margaret shuffling forwards in her seat and placing her mug down onto the tray. 'Right,' she said, tapping Jim on the leg. 'Time we made a move.'

Jim obediently downed his drink and stood up, an action mimicked by Jack, Laura and Juliette.

Morton felt a twinge of rising awkwardness at the parting, fearing a repeat of their uncomfortable arrival. He watched as his Aunty Margaret moved to Laura, hugged her and said goodbye, then to Jack. She paused in front of him and smiled.

'It honestly has been lovely seeing you again, Jack,' she said. 'I won't deny I was quite nervous at the prospect and...well, I even considered not coming at all, but I'm glad that I did. You've got yourself a beautiful family.'

They embraced and Jack—indicating Morton—said, *'We've* got a beautiful family.'

A tinge of embarrassment mottled Margaret's neck and cheeks. She smiled, pulled her cardigan tight and moved over to hug Juliette. 'Give that little girl a nice big kiss from me when she wakes up.'

'Will do,' said Juliette.

'I'll see you out,' Morton said, following them into the hallway and passing them their coats.

'I'll go and get the car warmed up,' Jim said, giving Morton a bear-hug and thanking him for his hospitality.

Outside, Margaret said, 'It's been a wonderful trip, Morton. I've really loved spending time with you all—especially little Grace.' She gazed down at the Land Rover puffing grey fumes into the cold air, as she searched for the right words. 'You know, I'd like to be more like your... like Jack—in the way he is with you and Grace—but... it doesn't come easy, you know?'

'I know.' He reached out and touched her arm. 'It's the American in him,' he joked, with a conscious effort at easing her discomfort.

'Anyway—hope to see you down in Cornwall sometime soon.'

'We'd love to come back down.'

She hugged him, said goodbye, then walked down the steps to the car.

Morton stood waving until they had turned the corner and disappeared from view, then headed back indoors. 'Ready for your first trip to the National Archives?' he asked Jack.

'Give me two minutes and I'll be good to go,' he said, bounding up the stairs.

'Are you ladies sure you will be okay by yourselves?' he asked Juliette and Laura.

'Very much so,' Laura answered. 'I can't wait.'

'Glad to get rid of you,' Juliette added.

Phil opened the door to Katie's flat with dramatic caution. 'Get in,' he snapped, reaching out and grabbing her by the wrist.

'Nice to see you, too,' Clara said, shaking off his grip and, from her other hand, dropping a black sack on the floor.

He slammed the door shut, hobbled across the room to the sofa and muted the blaring sound of morning television.

Clara sat beside him, perched at the edge of the seat, as though she were not staying long. He looked at her nice clothes—tight blue jeans and black jacket—with a mixture of lust and envy. Here he was living in this hovel, wearing the same clothes which he had worn for God only knew how many days.

'Did you bring my stuff?' he asked.

'It's over there,' she replied, pointing to the bag.

'Cheers. Have they been round again?'

'Who?'

'The police! Who do you think?'

'Oh. Yeah, they came around yesterday to see if you'd turned up yet. They didn't really seem that bothered when I said I hadn't heard from you. Look, how long's this going to go on for? When *are* you coming home?'

'When I know for sure whether there are any more of those gold guineas buried somewhere.'

Clara shot him a derisive look. 'You do know how stupid you sound, don't you? It's like that genealogist man said—if they did exist, there's not much chance of them still being hidden after all these years.'

'We need the money, Clara. Unless you've got a better way of clearing our debts? Ain't it worth even trying?' he retorted. 'It was only a few weeks back that some amateur metal detector found millions of pounds of some Saxon burial or other. By *accident*. Why would you not at least have a go? Did you not see how much *one* bloody coin sold on eBay for? Yeah, I can see, actually, you're wearing some of the proceeds.'

Clara huffed in the way that she did when she knew that he had a point. 'I've made an appointment with the Citizen's Advice Bureau to see if they can help us with the debts…'

'Just give me a bit longer,' Phil interrupted.

Clara began to get upset. 'We've had another red demand this morning. They're threatening to send in the bailiffs if we don't pay within seven days.'

He placed a hand on her shoulder. 'I'll have it sorted by then—one way or another.'

'Not exactly the prettiest of London buildings,' Jack commented, as he strode beside Morton towards the entrance of the National Archives in Kew.

'No,' Morton agreed, as they passed beside a large expanse of still water; the lack of any type of organic matter accentuating the starkness of the building which loomed over it like a staid old judge.

'It looks like someone bolted a giant sunroom onto the front of a lump of concrete,' Jack observed, taking in the vast edifice.

'But it's what's on the inside that counts,' Morton replied, watching a small flock of geese glide down onto the water. 'Canada Geese…or just geese, to you, I suppose.'

Jack gave a wry smile, continuing to study the building as they walked towards the main doors.

Inside, they passed through the obligatory security search, deposited their coats and bags in the cloak room, then made their way up to the first floor, where Jack was issued with a reader's ticket. It meant something inexplicably profound to Morton, having Jack standing beside him in a place of such significance to his work, taking a genuine interest in what he did.

'Where now?' Jack asked.

'Second floor,' Morton said. 'Map and Large Document Reading Room.'

Jack nodded for Morton to lead the way and the two men went to the main staircase and up to the next floor, passing through a security entrance into a large search room filled with desks and busy researchers. Morton led them around to the far left, where a set of glass double-doors opened automatically, leading into a rectangular room bisected by a long wooden counter. 'Hi,' Morton greeted the young man standing behind it. 'I've got two documents reserved under seat number 10B. Is it possible to have both out? My dad can have one—he's just registered a new card but doesn't have a seat number, yet.'

'Yeah, sure,' the young man said, tapping something into a computer, then glancing up at Jack. 'I'll put you at 10A.'

'Great,' Jack said, with a look at Morton, which suggested that he had no idea what was happening.

Whilst he stood watching the man head over to the orange pine shelving behind him, Morton felt his cheeks redden when he realised that he had just said, 'My dad...' He took a surreptitious look at Jack, who seemed either not to have noticed, or not to have cared. Morton watched as the archivist ducked down and then tiptoed to examine the yellow labels jutting out from the various records contained on the shelves. He pored over one label longer than the rest, then pulled out the document from which it emanated: a large flat brown box which he carried over and placed on the counter. 'There's one—ASSI 31/25,' he said, returning to the shelves and retrieving what looked like a bundle of dirty washing. 'And here's the other—ASSI 94/1985.'

'Wow,' Jack commented, placing a hand on the string-bound document entitled *'Kent Lent Assizes 1827 Felony File.'*

Morton smiled at the thought of what he hoped would be contained within that file. He picked up the box and headed from the room, with Jack carrying the other bound document behind him. Stopping at the nearest free desk, Morton set down the box and removed the lid. Inside was a large book with a thick, hard binding that might have once been white or cream in colour but which was now dappled and streaked in various shades of brown. In black ink on the front was written, *'Fair Agenda Book Lent 1826-Lent 1829.'* He pulled out the book and carefully set it down between two foam cushions.

Jack watched Morton with a look of marvel or pride, as he carefully opened the tome: a summary account of the Home Circuit Assizes between 1826 and 1829.

'Do you want me to make a start on this?' Jack asked, pointing to the bundle.

'Yes, please,' Morton replied. He had spent most of the two-hour drive to Kew explaining the Fothergill Case to Jack, including some key names and dates, so he only felt the need to recap, 'so, you're looking for any mention of smugglers, Aldington, George Ransley, Samuel Banister, Ann Fothergill...'

'Got it,' Jack confirmed, gently teasing apart the string binding which held it together.

Having deduced that the volume had been arranged chronologically, Morton turned the pages until he reached one titled, '*Kent. 7th George 4th 1827*,' meaning the seventh year in the reign of George IV. Morton cast his eyes down the sepia mottled paper then turned to Jack and said, 'The trial began at Maidstone on the 12th January 1827.'

'Thanks,' Jack said, beginning to unravel great long sheets of curled paper. Morton watched for a moment as Jack began to pore over the document, then returned to reading his own. The summary of the case began with the usual legal opening for this '*special session of the Kent Winter Gaol Delivery*' before moving on to the cases being presided over. *Forgery. Highway Robbery. Murder.* Then he spotted the Aldington Gang: George Ransley, John Bailey, Samuel Bailey, Thomas Denard, Thomas Gillham, Richard Higgins, William Wire, James Smeed, James Wilson, Charles Giles, Richard Wire, James Hogben, Thomas Wheeler and James Quested.

Morton studied the names for some seconds. No sign of Samuel Banister.

The first indictment against the men was, '*For feloniously being assembled with firearms in order to be aiding and assisting in the illegal landing and carrying away of uncustomed goods*,' to which all had pleaded guilty. Beside their plea came the judgement against them: '*To be venerally hanged by the neck until they be dead on Monday the 5th day of February next.*' From his research, however, Morton knew that the men's sentences had been commuted to transportation for life. Next, the same men had been charged with the murder of Richard Morgan, to which they had pleaded not guilty. The judgement was listed as '*Acquitted.*'

'I don't think this is right,' Jack said, standing back to allow Morton to see the problem which he had found.

'What's up?' Morton asked, looking at where Jack was pointing.

'The Lent Assizes were held on the 19th March 1827—two months *after* your guys were tried.'

'But that doesn't make sense…'

'I've had a quick look through the cases and there's nothing that fits,' Jack reported.

'That's odd. Wait there,' Morton said, striding to the far side of the room, where he was confronted by a long bank of files and folders. He searched the shelves, quickly finding and selecting a thin black book and carrying it back over to Jack. Flipping through the pages of indexes to the various Home Circuit Assize Courts, his index finger came to rest on 1827. 'Lent, Summer, Special,' he read. 'Same for the other counties in the Home Circuit. Essex, Surrey, Sussex and Hertfordshire, they all follow that pattern.'

'So,' Jack began, 'if Lent is too late, then Summer also stands to be too late. Should we order the Special, then?'

Morton nodded, biting his lip. He suddenly felt the weight of Jack's presence and wished that he were more knowledgeable on the Assizes: 'I just want to go and speak to someone about it—just to be certain before I order it up.'

'Sure thing,' Jack said. 'I'll double-check this one, just to be absolutely sure.'

Morton ventured to the helpdesk, where a genial man with greying brown hair pulled into a ponytail on the back of his head, and thin glasses perched on his nose, sat typing at a computer. He looked up as Morton took the seat opposite him.

'Hello, what can I do for you?' the man asked, a strong Southern Irish accent pushing through his dry lips.

'Hi,' Morton said. 'I've got a question about the Home Circuit Assizes…' He explained his problem, probably with unnecessary detail about the trial of the Aldington Gang smugglers.

The man listened without interruption, then tapped into his computer. He nodded at something on-screen, then faced Morton. 'So, Lent comes first, then Summer, then Special. If the Lent Assizes took place in March 1827, then you're probably looking at the Special for *1826*—not 1827.'

'But the trial took place in January 1827,' Morton said.

'But the thing is, the Assizes didn't happen in one day. They might have gone on for five or six weeks, depending on the number of defendants. What you need to remember is that the Assizes were paid for by central government, so local magistrates would happily pass lots of cases to the Assizes to save local money.'

'Right, I see. So you think it will be late 1826 into early 1827?'

'That's right. Special in the case of the Assizes usually just meant Winter.'

'I'll give that a try, then,' Morton said, standing. 'Thank you.'

'You're very welcome.' Morton turned to leave when the man added, 'Have you tried looking for your smugglers in the letters which went between the Board of Customs and Excise and the various South-Eastern ports?'

'No, I haven't,' Morton answered, being not aware of such documents.

'It's possible they'll mention smuggling. One second,' the man said, looking up the details on his computer. 'Yes, there's a volume specifically for letters to and from the town of Dover. End of 1826, was it?'

'That's right,' Morton confirmed, watching as he scribbled the information onto a piece of scrap paper—CUST 54/56.

'There you go. Worth a shot,' the man said, handing him the paper.

Morton thanked him and returned to Jack. 'He thinks we should order the Special for 1826 because it was probably the winter session, which ran into early 1827. He's also given me something else which might have mentioned the smugglers.'

'Excellent,' Jack said. 'I've just been through this again and there's definitely no mention of the group.'

'Could you bind it back up again, then take it back for me, please? I'll get these items ordered.'

'Sure thing.'

While Jack warily rerolled and bound the file, Morton headed to one of the computer terminals designated for searching and ordering. He swiped his reader's ticket, then ordered the two documents. According to the reference number given to him by the Irishman, the file contained copies of letters between the Board of Customs and Excise and the Blockade Service, based at Dover.

Returning to the desk, Morton placed the *Fair Agenda Book* back inside the box and carried it through to the returns table.

'What now?' Jack asked.

'Now, we wait for the documents to be brought up,' Morton said. 'That can be a frustrating part about following a lead: the thirty-to-forty-minute wait.'

Thirty-two minutes later, when Morton scanned his reader's ticket at the computer terminal for the sixth time, the two documents were finally listed as delivered. He and Jack collected them together, hurrying keenly back to their table. Jack eagerly turned to the bundle of Assize records, titled '*Kent Winter Gaol Delivery 1826 Felony File*' and unravelled the packet.

'This is the one,' Jack said, excitement rising in his voice.

Morton craned his neck and read the typed text, '*Kent. Gaol Calendar for the Special Gaol Delivery to be holden on Saturday, the 6th Day of January, 1827, at Maidstone before The Honourable Sir James Allan Park, Knight.*' Morton smiled and side-stepped back to the book of letters on his desk, only for Jack to call his attention straight back again.

'Jeez, would you look at this!' he exclaimed, unfurling the next sheet in the bundle, which rolled all the way to the end of the table. It contained the names of all the defendants and the charges brought against them for the special Assizes. 'Seventy-two names!' Jack drew his finger down the list. 'And here are your guys: '*Brought by Habeas Corpus*—is that Latin for something?—*from His Majesty's Gaol of Newgate, charged with having been guilty of the wilful murder of Richard Morgan, on the 30th day of July last, at Dover.*'

'That's them,' Morton said, pulling his mobile from his pocket and switching on the camera. 'Could you take photos for me, please?'

'All of it?'

'All of it; you never know what you might need later. Thanks,' he said, opening the large book containing copies of letters from April to December 1826, the precise period of Richard Morgan's death and the group's eventual capture. Like the previous volume, it was large and worn, and arranged chronologically. If he had had the time, he would gladly have read each and every page, but, assessing that that would take many hours, which he did not have, he instead skipped through to the crucial period at the end of July. It took just a few seconds for him to locate the first entry: '*30th July 1826. Enclosed it is our painful duty to submit to you a report from Lt. Hellard Divisional Officer of the Blockade Force on this station of one of the foulest and most deliberate murders that ever was committed in this or any civilized country. We have the whole of this morning been endeavouring by enquiries to ascertain what Public Houses were open late last night, and the names of the parties who were drinking therein and we hope tomorrow in co-operation with the magistracy of Dover to review them. In the meantime, should you think it more probable that a discharge of the parties engaged in this disgraceful and brutal transaction tonight be more readily effected by the activity and address of two*' *intelligent Bow Street Officers, accustomed to deducing information from circumstantial points, we would appreciate that they should be directed to proceed without a moment's delay to Folkestone and communicate with Lt. Hellard, who occupies the battery – the murder having been committed close to the bathing machines and consequently within the precincts of the Town of Dover-'*

'Got it!' Jack declared, a little too loudly, drawing the attention of nearby researchers.

Morton grinned at his enthusiasm and stepped to the side to see what he had found. Pages and pages of handwritten text which, upon closer scrutiny, Morton found to be largely legal and repetitious. 'Excellent. Let me know if you see Samuel Banister or Ann Fothergill's name crop up.'

'Will do.'

Morton continued reading the letter, which led into a summary of the murder by Lieutenant Hellard: '*Casemates, Dover, 30th July. It is a most distressing part of my duty to report a smuggling transaction which took place this morning about 1am near the bathing machines, attended with the most deliberate act of murder ever before heard of on this part of the coast, the particulars of the case are as follows:- Richard Morgan, late Quartermaster, was sent by Lt. Thomas Hale with the coach dispatch to Townsend Battery at midnight on the 29th instance and on his return along the beach about 1am near the spot where he met his death he observed a boat in the surf, and addressing himself to the lookout man, Richard Pickett, ordinary seaman, who had charge of that station, asked what boat is that, and immediately ran forward with the lookout man, the latter pulling the trigger of his pistol for an alarm, which only flashed in the pan – Morgan then fired one of his pistols, when a party of smugglers armed with long duck guns stepped forwarded from the main body of their party, and fired in a volley at them, by which Morgan was shot in the left side near the heart, which caused almost instant death, there being three shots within three inches of each other, one of which appeared to be a musket ball – and I am of the opinion more wounds will be discovered when the body is examined before the coroner. Richard Pickett received several severe blows from the armed party, who after expending their ammunition assaulted him with the butt ends of their firearms and from his statement I fear a great part of the cargo must have been carried off, as only 33 half-ankers of foreign spirits were seized by our parties. S. Hellard.*'

Morton photographed the entry, then read through the letters of the following days, noting on his pad specific points of interest to be followed up at a later time. A substantial reward of five hundred pounds had been offered for the capture of the smuggling gang.

'Hey, listen to this,' Jack began, '...*not having the fear of God before their eyes but being moved and seduced by the instigation of the Devil on the day and year aforesaid with force and arms*...blah blah... *gun of the value of ten shillings then and there loaded and charged with gunpowder and with three leaden bullets*... blah blah... *did then and there feloniously wilfully and of his malice shoot and discharge to against and upon the said Richard Morgan*... *three other mortal wounds of the depth of twelve inches each and of the breadth of half an inch each of which last mentioned mortal wounds he the said Richard Morgan on the day and year aforesaid at the Parish aforesaid in the county aforesaid languished mortal and languishing did live for the space of one hour*... Then it lists the men charged with murder and then—' Jack glanced at Morton with a knowing glint in his eyes, then carefully lifted the page, '—Prosecution Witnesses... You need to see this, Morton.'

'Prosecution Witnesses?' Morton repeated.

Jack pointed to the page and Morton leant in to see a list of ten names—all of them unfamiliar, all except one.

Chapter Twenty-Three

'Samuel Banister was a witness...for the *prosecution?*'

Jack nodded. 'I've had a quick look through and after each indictment against the men, there is a list of witnesses called by the prosecution. Unlike all the other witnesses, Samuel appears on *every* list, *every* time—like he's the main guy.'

Morton frowned, not quite understanding. 'So that effectively means that he testified *against* his fellow smugglers...'

'That's the way it looks, yeah.'

'I wonder what on earth happened?' Morton said, his mind running through a variety of possibilities, none of them settling quite right with him. 'Nothing on Ann, yet?'

Jack shook his head. 'No, but there's a hell of a lot to read here.'

Morton was about to raise some of the potential scenarios which were playing out in his mind, when he recalled something that he had just read in the letters from the Board of Customs and Excise. He turned back a few pages, to the week after the murder of Richard Morgan and re-read part of one letter: '...*we are informed that the officer from Bow Street has been on the coast some days last week, endeavouring to get depositions to some of the material facts and that although he had not succeeded to the extent desired, <u>something</u> has been elicited which gave him hopes on the eventual discovery of the identity of the murderer...it is with regret we have seen for years the little effect of rewards offered for the discovery of offenders and we would like as a further inducement, a promise of protection for the informer, as he has no alternative but that of quitting the county when his name is known, or else he must fall as sacrifice to the vengeance of the smugglers generally on it being ascertained in what part of England he is.*'

Two things struck Morton about the letter. One, was that the writer of the letter seemed to suggest that the Bow Street officer had found a specific informant but was seeking a promise of his protection. Was it too much to wonder if that informer had been Samuel Banister and that, following the trial, he was offered protection and the help to disappear? But why would he turn on his fellow smugglers in the first place, and be prepared to leave his wife and children behind in the proposed anonymity? He recalled Ann's letter of 1827, where she had written something along the lines of 'tell me how you have settled *out there.*' It had not read as though she had been referring to another town or county, but rather a different country. At this stage, it was purely speculation, but very much worthy of further investigation. The second thought which struck Morton, was the involvement of an officer from Bow Street. Although he was no expert in this area, he knew that they had been the forerunners of the modern police force, operating out of the Bow Street Magistrate's Court in Westminster.

He glanced down to pick up his reader's ticket and saw that it was sitting beside Jack's. A warm proud feeling rested on him, as he stared at the two cards. The colour headshots, taking up a third of the right-hand side of each card, clearly showed that they were related. The same face shape and hairline; the same chestnut-brown eyes, with a hint at potential mischief; the same strong jawline. Evidence of their *dis*similarities were largely those unavoidable traces of aging, which featured more prominently on Jack's picture. The other difference—their names—seemed, now that he was looking at them more closely in large white letters, to dominate the cards. Perhaps a casual passer-by, upon seeing the cards sitting side by side would actually *not* think the two men related at all: 'Mr Morton Farrier' and 'Prof. Harley Jacklin.' His gaze switched dolefully between the two names, as he half-heartedly wished that they shared the same surname. Bizarrely, he had never really thought about the implications of that difference before now. 'Morton Jacklin,' he mouthed silently, the two words with one fewer syllable somehow sounding clunky together, unnatural.

'Pardon me?' Jack said.

'Oh...' Morton said, embarrassed, and hoping to goodness that Jack had not heard him. 'I was just talking to myself about what to do next.' He hastily reached down for his reader's ticket and hurried to the computer terminal, typing 'Bow Street' into the search engine. Four thousand, three hundred and twenty-two records were listed as having a reference to Bow Street. Morton filtered the results by date to the nineteenth century, quartering the number of suggestions. He quickly noticed that all of the relevant documents—correspondence, court registers, extradition ledgers, gaoler's records, applications for warrants, accounts—were held at the London Metropolitan Archives. He looked at the clock; there was no way that they would have the time—at least an hour—to travel across London to the LMA building in Clerkenwell. It would have to wait.

Morton typed a new search term into the box: *Ramillies*.

The search results—two hundred and fifty-nine for the nineteenth century—comprised mainly of ships' logs, muster rolls and letters from the captain. More irrelevant results appeared further down the list including, Morton noted, a convict register from the 1860s when the ship was used to transport prisoners out to Australia.

Having spent a few minutes filtering and fine-tuning the results, he placed an order for the ships' logs for the last quarter of 1826, the captain's log 1825-1830, and letters from the captain, 1826.

'Everything okay?' Jack asked, when Morton returned.

'Yep, I was just jumping ahead to the next step. Any new developments?'

Jack screwed up his nose, placed a finger on the document as a place-holder, then looked at Morton. 'Not really, no. It's just pages and pages of the indictments being read against all of those guys. Samuel Banister still seems to be the most important witness; but no mention of Ann, I'm afraid.'

'Let's finish with these records, then go and get some lunch. By that time the stuff I've just ordered will be up.'

'Great,' Jack replied, 'I sure could use a coffee right now.'

'Me too,' Morton agreed, settling back to reading the letters to and from the Board of Customs and Excise.

For the next thirty-five minutes, Morton silently worked through the book, occasionally scribbling a note on his pad and intermittently reaching for his mobile, which he and Jack were sharing to photograph their respective documents. There had been no mention of Ann, Samuel or the Aldington Gang specifically, although various smuggling incidents along the Kent and Sussex coasts had been reported. Jack completed the *Felony File* moments after Morton had finished with his book of letters. Having returned them, they gathered their belongings and descended to the ground floor.

'Café or restaurant?' Jack asked, his eyes flitting between the two possible outlets, both of which opened onto a spacious seating area.

'I think Juliette might be cooking something tonight, so we probably should just use the café.'

'Sure, let's not get into trouble.'

They strolled across the wide space, dotted with chairs and tables, to the small café across from the bookshop. Two elderly ladies, engrossed in conversation, were queuing in front of them.

'What are you having?' Jack asked, pulling a bulging black wallet from his back pocket, as he squinted up at the menu board.

'I'll get these,' Morton insisted. 'You're slaving for me, after all.'

Jack grinned, still holding his wallet uncertainly and gazing at the menu. 'I'm *loving* it.'

Morton turned to him with a frown, unsure if he was being sarcastic. 'Yeah, I bet.'

'No, really,' he insisted, meeting his eyes. 'I can see why you love this job. It's like you're a detective, lifting the slabs of history to dig down to the truth—it's very similar to my job… I think you might just have inherited my tenacity.'

If such a personality trait *were* hereditary, then he supposed Jack was correct; he certainly would never have described his Aunty Margaret as 'tenacious'.

'Can I help?' a pasty-faced young man asked, barely looking at them.

'Two large coffees, please,' Morton ordered. 'And I'd like the goat's cheese panini and—' he faced Jack, '—what did you want to eat?'

'I'll have the same, please,' he answered, freeing a twenty-pound note from his wallet and passing it over the counter to the pale man.

'Thanks,' Morton said.

'No problem, son,' Jack replied, placing his hand on Morton's shoulder.

His hand stayed there, although its initial weight quickly waned, and Morton took a surreptitious glance to the side to see if it still remained there. It did, leaving him wondering if Jack was consciously keeping it there, perhaps as a manifestation of his pride, or whether perhaps it had been a mechanical action of which he had not really been aware.

'Two large coffees,' the man said, drearily handing over two cardboard cups.

'Thanks,' Jack said, his hand sliding from Morton's shoulder as he reached out for the drinks.

'Grab a seat and I'll bring the food over,' Morton said.

Jack headed to a table with two large red chairs and sat facing in Morton's direction. A long low beep emanated from somewhere behind the counter, prompting the man to turn with a pair of metal tongs and withdraw the two paninis from the contraption which had just heated them up. Morton watched as he dropped them into two paper bags, then thrust them over the counter, addressing the next man in the queue with a dull parroting, 'Can I help?'

'So,' Jack began, as Morton sat down. 'How does what we've achieved this morning compare to your other cases? Are we at an expected point? Or…?'

Morton nodded, while he chomped through a mouthful of panini. 'It's okay, yeah. To be honest, most of the cases that I work on are difficult and involve following a scent and seeing what comes up. I couldn't have known, when I was sitting in Arthur Fothergill's lounge, that I would need to order letters from the captain of *HMS Ramillies*; one document leads to another and… here we are.'

'Yeah, I get that. So, you think you'll crack this one?'

'I think so, yes.' Morton tilted his head to one side as he considered the question. Arthur had ostensibly requested three things of him during the 1820-1827 period: where Ann had resided; the rather nebulous question of what Ann had been up to; and finally, the identity of her son's father. The first point Morton considered practically achieved. The second, was continuing in a satisfying manner. On the third he had made little progress and hoped that, with a little work, the results of the DNA test might verify this in the next few days.

'Excellent. Are you going to be working tomorrow?'

'Erm…' Morton looked at Jack, wondering at his question. Was Jack wanting him to be working more, perhaps so that he could help? Or was he hoping that Morton would take the day off, so that they could spend it together doing something more interesting or relaxing? 'Well, work can happen at any time. What do you want to do?' He hoped his diplomatic answer gave Jack the space in which to say what he actually wanted to do.

'Okay. I was wondering if maybe you wanted to take a trip over to Folkestone?' Jack asked.

'Yes, of course. What do you want to see there? It's not exactly the cultural capital of England.'

'I'd like to go back and take a look at the place we stayed when we came over in seventy-four—show it to Laura and George.'

Morton nodded, for some reason finding it odd that he should want to show his wife where he had fathered a child with another woman forty-four years ago. 'That'll be nice. Juliette's working all day, so I'll have Grace.'

'Shame she's working but great that I get to spend more 'Gandpa' time with little Grace.' Jack smiled and tucked into his panini.

Having finished their food and drink, Morton led the way to the first floor. They passed through the security search, swiped their cards and entered a lobby area, containing rows and rows of translucent orange lockers, each embossed with a large number and letter. Morton headed to 10B and opened the locker door to see three large cardboard boxes stacked neatly on top of each other. 'We can have one each,'

Morton said, taking the top box and passing it to Jack, then withdrawing the second for himself. 'Follow me.'

Opposite the bank of lockers was the Document Reading Room, set behind a wall of glass. Morton proceeded through the set of double-doors into the room, which was filled with desks and busy with researchers.

'That's you,' Morton said, indicating the seat, 10A, beside him on the octagonal table.

'So, what have I got here, then?' Jack asked, pulling out the yellow slip from the side of the box. 'ADM 37/7670.' He shrugged.

'The log book for *Ramillies*, first of September 1826 to thirty-first of October 1826. You're looking for any mention of the usual suspects.'

Jack removed a large bound volume and placed it down with genuine deference. 'Wow,' he said, opening the first page.

Morton checked his own yellow slip—ADM 51/3400—Captain's log, July 1825 to March 1830. The ledger was large with sepia pages, headed with the words, '*Remarks, HMS Ramillies in the Downs.*' Each day, divided by a neat ruled line, seemed to vary in length according to the events and incidents which had necessitated recording. It took Morton a few minutes to decipher the long sloping style of handwriting, as he read through the first day's account on the 1st July 1825: '*AM moderate and cloudy. At 2 same weather. At 4 fresh breeze. Washed clothes. At 7 cleaned decks. At 8.30 communicated with office. Carpenters employed repairing boats. Armourers at the forge cleaning arms. At 11 the Captain came on board and punished Thomas Marchant with 48 lashes for acknowledged bribery, William Coffee, 36 lashes for 5 sovereigns being found secreted in the soles of his shoes, James Clark, 36 lashes for absenting himself from the watch-house for two days, Sergt. O'Keefe, 12 lashes for drunkenness and insolent conduct. Noon fresh breezes and fine. PM moderate and fine. At 6 same weather. Sent a galley with Lt. Reed to look out for smuggling boats. At 11 fresh breeze and fine. Midnight same weather.*'

The account for the subsequent days followed the same pattern: citing deliveries of provisions, regular weather reports and punishments meted out to the men. Occasional irregular activity was noted, such as the capture of smugglers' galleys, but with scant detail. The size of the book forced Morton to skim read through the lines of text.

'You don't need a list of *Ramillies* staff or ship routines, do you?' Jack asked. In front of him was a large sheet of vellum, on which was written a long list of names.

'Check the names, but otherwise, no.'

Morton pushed into the crucial year of 1826, photographing the sporadic mentions of smuggling. So far, the logs had failed to name a single smuggler or give any specifics at all, and so he was unsurprised when he reached the entry for the 17th October 1826 and read, among the usual information, '...*Received 10 smugglers*...' The following day provided the brief additional information, '...*discharged 4 mariners with 10 smugglers to be turned over to civil power*...' So the smugglers had only been on board *Ramillies* for one night, Morton noted, taking a photo of the entry. He continued through to the end of the year, slightly perplexed at not having found mention of the capture of the remaining smugglers. He looked at the time—they only had just over two hours until the archive closed; this urgency forced Morton to stop reading the Captain's Logs once the trial was over in January 1827. He closed the volume and looked at Jack's ledger, feeling suddenly disappointed with their progress. Although the revelation that Samuel Banister had turned King's evidence against his fellow smugglers was significant, they had not found a single mention of Ann Fothergill. He rubbed his eyes and exhaled noisily.

'What's up?' Jack asked.

'Oh, nothing...' Morton half-smiled. 'I get like this when the record office is about to close and I don't feel satisfied with the results.'

'Oh, come on,' Jack said, 'you must have realised by now that for five paths in front of you, only one will get you were you wanna go, but you've still got to explore those other four paths. Go and get that other document from the locker. Go.'

Morton grinned, knowing, of course, that he was right. He re-boxed the Captain's Logs and carried it out through the glass double-doors, where he placed it on the counter of the Returns Desk. At his locker, Morton removed the yellow slip from the remaining cardboard box—ADM 1/2360.

He carried the box back to his desk, just as Jack was closing his ledger.

'Nothing—even around the time of Richard Morgan's murder or when the smugglers were captured,' Jack said, trying to sound positive about the fact.

Morton nodded. 'You can help me with these,' he said, opening the heavy box. Given that it only contained correspondence to the Admiralty from naval captains with a surname beginning with P, in the year 1826, the quantity of letters inside was astonishing. 'We've got under two hours to get through it.' Morton explained how the file was organised, then removed approximately half the correspondence, and placed it in on the desk in front of Jack. The letters were loosely assembled, vaguely but not entirely conforming to chronological order, which meant that Jack having the latter half of the year, would very likely be the one to discover anything connected to the murder of Richard Morgan or the capture of the Aldington Gang.

'Wow, this is real hard to read,' Jack said, picking up the first letter and holding it close to his face.

Morton leant over. 'It gets easier once you get used to it. Look—' he pointed at the first lines and began to read, his index finger tracing the words as he spoke, '—HM Ship Ramillies, January 2nd 1826. Sir, From the great distance between the present quarters of the Coast Blockade at Hougham Court and No.1 Tower Eastware Bay near Folkestone, where the most notorious smugglers reside, and from their repeated attempts to corrupt the men when on duty, I would respectfully request that you will do me the honour to move my Lords Commissioners of the Admiralty to direct a gun brig or some vessel of such description to be—' Jack began to join in, enunciating the words slowly, as though learning to read for the first time, '—sent to the place beforementioned for the purpose of being hauled on shore at high watermark, and that such vessel may be fitted to receive a midshipman and twelve men. I have the honour to be, Sir, your most obedient humble servant, Captain Hugh Pigot.'

'Got it?' Morton asked.

'Got it,' Jack replied.

The two of them began to wade through their stack of letters. The first mention of smuggling came quickly in Morton's pile, on 23rd February: 'Sir, I regret to be under the painful necessity of reporting to you for the consideration of my Lords Commissioners of the Admiralty, the neglect of duty of Lieutenant William H. Woodham, of His Majesty's ship under my command, who is stationed at the Grand Redoubt, Dungeness and I request you will be pleased to acquaint their Lordships that about 11 o'clock on the night of the 8th instant, a French tub boat fitted with two sails and rowing eight oars succeeded in landing a cargo of (it is believed) at least 200 casks of spirits on the western part of the officer's station...' The letter went on to describe the actions of the Coast Blockade officers in allowing the smuggling run to take place. Just five days later, Captain Pigot sent another letter to the Admiralty, requesting that a new Lieutenant be appointed to the Ramillies following the serious injuries inflicted on one of his men in a smuggling run on 6th September 1825. The account went on to describe how Lieutenant William Fabian had been bludgeoned, as he had attempted to stop the smugglers moving inland with their cargo, '...leaving him in a *state of insensibility – his head was swollen to a great size, and covered with blood which seemed to have issued from five wounds in the scalp, from one to four inches in length. Several bruises were observable on his body, particularly the neck, shoulders and arms. Since receiving the above injuries, Lieutenant Fabian has complained of loss of memory, dimness of vision, headache and giddiness…'*

As Morton continued to read the barbaric accounts, he realised that his perception of smugglers had been of a kind of romantic Robin-Hood-esque gang of poor labourers living on the breadline, forced to commit low-level crime which only affected the rich King and his government; a different perspective, however, was appearing from these official documents of increasingly desperate and vicious men.

'Do you want me to photograph this letter from June 1826, with the names of four arrested smugglers? They're not your guys—Thomas North, William Derrick, George Taylor and James Banks alias Drum.'

'Yes, please,' Morton confirmed. 'They were probably all part of the gang.'

The next two letters from Captain Pigot were similar to that which Jack had just found; confirmation of the capture of several smugglers. Clive Baintree had been correct in his assessment: the mid-1820s had been a prolific period of smuggling for the Aldington Gang.

Captain Pigot's next transmission to the Admiralty, in April 1826 contained an enclosure by Lieutenant Samuel Hellard, reporting two further smuggling runs that had taken place that month.

'This could be interesting,' Jack said, nudging his elbow towards Morton: *'3rd July 1826. Sir, In reply to your letter of the 29th June, I have the honour to acquaint you for the information of my Lords Commissioners of the Admiralty, that William Kelly, one of the men who received two sovereigns as a bribe for allowing certain contraband goods to be run on his station, made the confession of the same with reluctance, and not until a search was ordered and the seams of his bed, where the sovereigns were found, to be cut open. This man was punished for the offence with twenty-four lashes and is the only person who could identify the man giving the bribe, but from the manner in which he prevaricated, no credence could be given to what he asserted: that the man was named Sam, hailed from the parish of Aldington and had suffered some degree of injury to his right arm. Therefore, the case was not communicated to the Board of Customs for prosecution…'*

'Sam from Aldington with an injured arm…' Morton mumbled, remembering his own theory that perhaps Samuel Banister had been hurt at the Battle of Brookland in 1821.

'Could this be our guy?' Jack mused.

'Maybe, yeah,' Morton answered, liking the way that Jack was referring to 'our guy', assuming a central role in the case. 'But it really is circumstantial at this point; there was another Samuel—Bailey—also from Aldington who was part of the gang, and probably several others with that name, as well.'

'I'll keep going, then.' Jack smiled, taking a photograph of the page, before moving on.

A few pages later and Jack came to the inevitable report of the murder of Richard Morgan. He summoned Morton with a beckoning wave of his hand. Morton leant over and began to read the account: '*30 July 1826. Sir, It is with extreme regret that I have to report the melancholy death of Richard Morgan, first-rate quartermaster, of His Majesty's ship under my command, who was shot by an armed party of smugglers about 1.00am near the Bathing Machines at Dover, under the circumstances set forth in the accompanying letter from Lieutenant Samuel Hellard, superintending the Right Division of the Coast Blockade—*' Morton paused and looked at Jack. 'I've seen an exact copy of this letter already today in the Board of Customs and Excise book,' Morton said, continuing to read further through the letter in confirmation. 'Yes, definitely. What's next?'

Jack turned the page, and the two men silently read through the letter: '*30th July 1826. Sir, With reference to Captain Pigot's letter of this date transmitting copy of a letter with its enclosure addressed to Vice Admiral Sir Robert Moorsom, relative to the melancholy death of Richard Morgan first-rate quartermaster of the Ramillies, I do myself the honour to forward for the information of my Lords Commissioners of the Admiralty a letter which has just reached this place from Lieutenant Samuel Hellard superintending the Right Division of the Coast Blockade requesting that officers from Bow Street may be sent to assist in the apprehension of some of the parties concerned in this lawless outrage. I have the honour to be, Sir, Your Most Obedient Humble Servant, Senior Lieutenant Williams, HMS Ramillies.*'

'What's this about officers from Bow Street?' Jack asked.

Morton explained that they had been the first police officers. 'Is the letter from Samuel Hellard there?' he asked.

Jack carefully turned to the next page and read the short letter: '*30th July 1826. I respectfully submit to you, Sir, the propriety of one or two of the most active officers from Bow Street being immediately sent to this town, which I am firmly of opinion can secure the arrest of this lawless party…*'

'Well, they were successful…' Morton said, just as his mobile began to ring in his pocket. He grimaced, fished it free, and promptly silenced it. Arthur Fothergill's name was flashing up on screen. He deliberated momentarily whether to answer it but decided that he would call him back later; his time was better put to use here. 'Arthur,' Morton said to Jack.

Jack nodded, having turned to the next letter. He glanced up at Morton and asked, 'Does the name Jonas Blackwood mean anything?'

Morton shook his head. 'No, why?'

Chapter Twenty-Four

'Thank you, sir,' Ann said, unable to hide her wide grin.

'The pleasure is all mine, Miss Fothergill,' Mr Claringbould declared, clutching his top hat to his chest.

They were standing outside the Bell Inn, both of them looking up at the building, stark white against the belt of grey sky above, in a shared sense of unveiled astonishment at what someone of her station in life had managed to achieve.

'It really is marvellous,' Mr Claringbould said, shaking his head.

Ann forced herself to contain her giddiness and maintain her propriety, as Miss Bowler had shown her. With a gentle bow of her head, she held out her hand.

'Ah,' Mr Claringbould said, taken aback, then shaking her hand. 'On behalf of J. Minet, Fector & Co. bank, I should like to express our sincerest of wishes for the future success of this fine establishment.' With a nod, he placed his top hat back onto his head and strode off in the direction of Dover.

At last, Ann could relax. She exhaled at length, releasing her taut stomach muscles, and watching with dismay as her shawl protruded out in front of her. Had Mr Claringbould noticed her little secret? she wondered. Now four months gone, it was becoming almost impossible to hide. The only person in whom she had confided had been Miss Bowler, who had taken the news surprisingly well, with a blithe and diplomatic, 'You have lived a varied and vibrant life, Ann; you have seen, I am sure, the best and worst of our society and the manner in which it operates. Use that knowledge to strive to bring your child into a different world to that into which you were born.' Miss Bowler had tactfully skirted—as she always did—the issue of Ann's early life, at which she had only ever hinted during their weekly sessions.

The chill from a flurry of overnight snow pervaded the early morning air and began to leach the heat from Ann's blood. She looked at the closed door, then down at the key in her hand; a sharp feeling of disbelief that she actually owned the inn prevented her from moving.

'Come on, Ann,' she whispered to herself, her left foot stepping down into the untrodden snow with undue cautiousness, as though there might be something lurking unseen underfoot. She took another pace to the door, her breath reaching forwards as she raised the key to the lock.

A drift of snow, whipped and buffeted from the sea wind last night, gracefully arced upwards from the ground in a smooth curve, hugging tightly to the base of the door, as Ann turned the key and swung the door wide.

Inside was no warmer. In fact, there was a coldness to the air which carried with it a sense of permanence, despite the fact that it had been vacant for just a small handful of weeks. She glanced at the fire, catching a glimpse, through the open space, of the bar on the other side. The fire grate was unsurprisingly empty, containing just a small pile of ash and a stubborn chunk of blackened wood.

Ann stood still, twisting slowly around to soak up the place fully. It had been left furnished, but without any alcohol, something George Ransley had promised to rectify, as soon as she be ready.

Another smile erupted on her face; the cause of this one not being found in an amazement at what she had achieved, but rather in relief at the realisation that she was free once again. Free from the Aldington Gang, free from the Walnut Tree Inn and free from Braemar Cottage.

Small rippling echoes from Ann's boots on the stone floor predicted her steady progress through the building to the wooden staircase. She shivered as she began to climb the stairs, all the while feeling as though she were an intruder. Upstairs were three rooms of a comfortable size. The vendor's definition of furnished was stretched to the extreme up here: one room was entirely empty and with bare floorboards; another held a Windsor chair, a thin bedstead, dresser, wardrobe and an old threadbare rug; the third contained an empty wooden tea chest and what looked like a discarded mahogany table with three legs, which rested on the apex where the fourth leg had presumably once been. Somehow, the sparseness motivated and excited her all the more: anything she did to improve the place, any new furniture which she might purchase, would all be her own.

Ann returned to the room with the bedstead: her bedroom, she decided. It was a curious and strange feeling to have possessions, now. She had spent her entire life owning nothing at all but the clothes in which she had stood. Now she had an entire business and her own home. She stooped down to look through the leaded windows, but a layer of thick grime, compounded with the fresh falling snow, gave little view to the outside. She could just make out the indistinct movement of horses and carts as they rattled past on the busy Dover-to-Folkestone road.

Ann shivered as she left the room and made her way back downstairs. She stood, an elbow resting on the wooden bar top, thinking about her mother and what she would have made of Ann's success. Her thoughts roamed the maze of indefinable early childhood recollections to the point when her mother had met Isaac Bull, the itinerant apothecary who had taught Ann the rudiments of his trade.

A loud rapping at the door startled Ann, flinging her memories back into the past. She hurried to the door and pulled it open. There, almost as a dark lopsided silhouette against the fast-falling snow, stood James Carter, squinting against the blizzard.

'You be a-picking a beautiful day for this,' he said, his voice echoing in the room behind her.

'Shall we be doing it another time?' Ann said, quickly standing to one side and gesturing for him to come in.

James shrugged, but did not move. 'Now be as good a time as any...'

'Let's go, then,' Ann said, waiting, as his one remaining leg did an ungainly jig which struggled to keep time with the swivelling of his wooden crutch.

Ann locked the door and followed him to his horse and carriage. 'Do you need help?' she called, seeing him struggle to pull himself into his seat.

James shook his head, grunting as he manoeuvred himself up and on.

Ann climbed into the carriage and pulled her shawl tight; their journey started with a fierce jolt forwards.

The ride to Dover was rough and bumpier than she had ever experienced. A deluge of rain last week had been followed by a dense freezing fog, and now heavy snow, which had left the usual deep ruts and hoof indentations in the road as solid as stone. On several occasions, Ann had been thrown from her seat and was grateful when they finally reached the quay, where the horse was brought to a standstill. She stepped from the carriage to see James tethering the horse to a large iron ring.

'Ready?' he asked.

'I be...*I am* ready,' Ann confirmed.

The blizzard, driving hard across the Channel, seemed much heavier here, concealing the long run of businesses which lined the quay behind a veil of white and grey. Ann led them by recollection, rather than by sight, over the cobbles, maintaining the pace of her one-legged companion until they reached a smart red-brick-fronted building. Above the door was a neat painted sign which read, *Latham, Rice & Co.* Below the name, in a smaller font was written, *Agents for Hanover, Vice-Consuls for Russia, Prussia, Spain, Portugal, Sardinia, Sicily & Mecklenburg.*

Ann pushed down on the brass door handle and entered a small, yet surprisingly busy office. Their arrival was heralded by a jangling bell just above the door. Six smart men, sitting at individual desks around the room, looked over at the new arrivals, all of them holding a fixed and mechanical rictus that appeared to be the standard greeting for visitors. Ann hesitated, unsure of which desk she should approach; none of the men appeared any more welcoming than the next. A well-dressed gentleman with a white beard entered the room from a door at the rear, carrying two large ledgers, which he deposited on the desk furthest away from Ann and James. The man at the desk whispered something to the bearded gentlemen, which clearly involved the new visitors, for he shot a quick look in their direction, before fixing his own smile likewise and walking towards them.

'How can I be of assistance?' he asked, mildly pleasantly.

Ann took a moment to choose her words. 'I should like to speak with Mr Henry Purdon, agent to the Hanoverian Consulate,' she said, hoping that her memory of the conversation with Jonas was somewhere close to being correct.

The bearded man frowned and took a lingering look between Ann and James. 'I'm terribly sorry but Mr Purdon is currently not available. On what business are you enquiring?'

'It's about his friend, William Fry,' Ann said, with feigned confidence.

The man clearly held prior knowledge of the name William Fry, for he emitted a mild gasp, which he promptly tried to conceal. 'I see. Do bear with me for a moment.'

Ann watched as he hurried through the door at the back of the room, noticing then that their conversation had drawn the attention of all six men sitting at their desks. Some looked away sharply, others continued to stare.

James leant in close and whispered, 'You be stirring trouble, Ann.'

Ann smiled. 'I certainly be hoping so.'

Very quickly, the man reappeared at the door; another older man quickly barged past him. His plump face was flush but devoid of any visible emotion and, as he strode towards her, Ann could not tell how she was going to be received.

'Come with me,' he instructed, turning on his heel back towards the rear of the room. His voice betrayed no emotion, but it also left Ann with the distinct lack of choice in the matter.

The man held the door, waiting with an impatient look, as James hobbled his way through the office. With Ann and James inside, he slammed the door shut and said, 'Who the devil are you?'

'Miss Ann Fothergill,' she introduced, in her best mimic of Miss Bowler's voice and accent. 'This is James Carter. And you are?'

'Mr Rice, one of the partners here. And what do you know of William Fry?'

Ann guessed, from the manner in which they had been herded out of the earshot of the other men, that she held some unspecified advantage, and decided to try her luck. 'What do *you* know of William Fry?' Ann asked. 'That's what *I* should like to know.'

Mr Rice exhaled as he slumped down into the chair behind his desk. 'Only that that damned fellow vanished on the same day that half my bloody office were arrested.'

'Oh, I see,' Ann said, though she did not see at all. 'And when do this be... when would this have been?'

'Two months ago, or so. Do you know of his whereabouts? I'm certain he's at the root of all these arrests.'

'I'm afraid I don't,' Ann replied, enjoying the haughty sound of her contrived voice. 'I'm looking for him myself and I were hoping that Mr Purdon might be able to help me.'

'Well, you'll find him currently residing in Canterbury Gaol.'

'Oh. What were he arrested for?' Ann asked.

'Fraud—like the rest of them.'

Ann quickly tried to assemble the pieces of information at her disposal to form a picture of what might have taken place. She had last seen Jonas around two months ago, around the same time that men from this office had been arrested and, under his alias of William Fry, Jonas had vanished. It did not make sense to her.

She thought of the last time when she had seen him. It had been at the Packet Boat Inn on a pre-arranged meeting where they had drunk rum together and made plans for another meeting the following week, but he had not shown up. Ann had left a hastily written note with the

292

landlord and returned on several occasions to enquire if he had returned, but he had not. Her initial anxiety at his whereabouts slowly shifted to anger as the days since she had seen him became weeks. In the last days, however, the anger had softened again, allowing space for concern to grow inside her, as she began to fear that the worst had happened to him. Two days ago, she had contacted James Carter, the man who Jonas had helped to keep alive after being shot in the leg, to request his help in finding him.

'It doesn't sound much like we can assist each other,' Mr Rice said, 'so, if there is nothing else…'

Ann nodded in agreement. 'Thank you for your time. We be seeing ourselves out.'

Mr Rice grunted something of a goodbye, then turned to the open ledger on his desk.

They left his office and, under the curious gaze of the men in the outer office, made their way out through the door onto the street outside, where they found that the descending dusk had brought with it two competing winds, which whipped the snow from the ground in icy blasts.

'You be wanting a rum?' James shouted.

Ann thought for a moment, then gratefully accepted and they dashed inside the warm inn, where James ordered them a rum and water each.

'Well,' James said, once they were seated. 'That fellow be of no help in finding Jonas.'

'No,' Ann said, somewhat absentmindedly, still trying to assimilate the new information. The most obvious solution was one which she was reluctant to accept, that Jonas had swept into these men's lives, garnered enough information to blackmail them, then disappeared, but not before informing the officials of their offences. This theory, though, rendered Ann just another play-piece in Jonas Blackwood's game of self-betterment. She stroked her belly, as she took a long gulp of the drink.

'How do it be back in Aldington?' she asked, consciously shifting the subject.

'Much the same,' James answered.

'You still smuggling?'

'Bain't got no choice. Course, I be driving the carts now, not lugging the barrels. It be that or double-hard labour bricklaying for half the guineas.'

'What about Sam Banister?' Ann asked, trying to sound indifferent to whatever answer he gave.

James smiled, a knowing look lighting his eyes. 'Certain sure he be a-missing you.'

'Really?'

James nodded, sniffed and shifted in his seat, revealing to Ann that he had something to say. He drank more rum, then asked, 'You be with child, ain't you?'

Ann thought about denying it but what would the point of that be? Everyone would know soon enough. 'That be so, yes.'

'What I don't be a-knowing, though,' James began, 'is if you be *escaping* the father or *searching* for him...'

Ann met his eyes, perturbed at his perception. In one long swig, she downed her rum. 'It be time to leave.'

Chapter Twenty-Five

2nd July 1825, Aldington, Kent

Samuel ran his smock sleeve across his forehead and glanced down at the small darkened patch of sweat which it had collected. He was in the children's bedroom at the front of the house, staring out of the window. His gaze, almost unblinking, was fixed on a thin space offered between two large yew trees, where he could just make out the path which led from the road to the church. He sighed, partly from the intensity of standing in direct sunlight and partly through impatience, having waited here for what was fast approaching an hour.

'Certain-sure, you must be a-thinking me a fool,' Hester said, startling him. He glanced behind to see her standing in the doorway but quickly refocused his attention on the church.

'What do you be blethering about now?' Sam retorted, pleading ignorance.

Hester snorted. 'Rose be a-telling me a thing or two.'

'Rose?' he repeated with a false laugh. 'You be a-listening to a cotchering young barmaid?'

'You bain't not even able to take your eyes from the window.'

Sam spun around. 'There,' he said, folding his arms. 'Now what do it be what you want to be a-saying to me?'

'She be back, don't she,' Hester said, a matter-of-fact statement, rather than a question.

'Who be back?'

Hester cackled a ridiculous raucous laugh, which gave rise to an instant nettling anger within him. His fury towards her swiftly overpowered any suggestion of her having the right to be questioning him. 'Who be back?' she mocked, frowning in exaggerated deliberation. 'Who could it be what might be a-turning up at the church for the baptism of her *bastard* baby?'

Sam saw his own anger amplified and reflected in his wife's eyes. There was no point in pretending that he did not know to whom she was referring. He choked back his irritation and said, 'She be the one what saved my life.'

Hester rolled her eyes in contempt for this trite defence. 'That be four year ago!' she bellowed, then added softly but firmly, 'I ain't the only one what be a-noticing things…'

Sam looked at her with unambiguous disdain, as a crowd of virulent responses came to the forefront of his mind, vying to be spat from his mouth. He drew in a long breath and barged past her, knocking her backwards into the wall. He heard her gasp as he bounded down the stairs, through the parlour and out of the front door. She would be watching him, of that he was certain, as he marched towards the church.

A hollow sinking feeling instantly quelled his anger towards Hester, when he saw Ann appear through the church door with the baby in her arms. Sam stopped dead, the impetus and desperation to reach the church on time having abated: he was too late—somehow, he had missed her. Ann was standing in the stretched shadow of the church vestibule, staring down at the child. She casually glanced up, expecting not to see anybody, and so her eyes briefly returned to the baby, before snapping back up towards Sam.

They held each other's gaze for some time, neither of them speaking or moving. Then, with a nod of his head, Sam walked slowly towards her.

'That were a short service,' Sam muttered, as he approached her, noticing her smart dress. He stood close to her, framing every detail in his mind, trying to work out what was different about her. Her clothes, undoubtedly. But there was something more than that, which he could not quite place—perhaps something in her eyes? She certainly looked and smelled fresh, clean and more attractive because of it.

'I didn't want anything fancy,' she replied. 'The vicar was good enough to conduct it without questions.'

'About the baby's father, you mean?' Sam said.

Ann flushed with colour. 'No, I be meaning about where I'm living... no longer of this parish.'

'And what be the reason for that?' Sam asked. When Ann merely shrugged, he proposed two of his own competing theories. 'To be hiding the illegitimacy from your new parish? Do that be it? Or do it be in some way to do with the child's father?'

'Maybe it's not either of those reasons,' Ann said.

Sam knew from the look of resentment on her face that she was close to snapping. 'Can I see the little one?'

Ann thought for a moment, then turned the baby to face him. 'William Fothergill,' she stated.

Sam looked at the boy's tiny round head. He was sleeping, and his lower lip was protruding in a mildly comical way. 'Fine-looking lad,'

Sam said, stroking the boy's clenched fist. 'Like his mother,' he added, noticing the contours of the boy's pronounced cheekbones and closed eyes. His hopes that this might be a subtle way to get Ann to reveal the identity of the boy's father failed.

'We must be leaving,' Ann said, a curt tone to her voice. She pulled the boy more tightly to her and set off down the path. Sam observed then a new elegance to her gait, as he watched her go. Part of him just wanted to stand and watch her leave but another, more strongly willed part, urged him to settle the internal questions which had plagued him since their dalliance last year. 'Do you still be looking for Jonas Blackwood?'

Ann stopped abruptly and turned. 'What do you know about that?'

'Carter be telling me you be wanting to find him. Says you be desperate.' The words came out in a way which Sam instantly regretted, sounding critical and goading, not the curiosity that he was actually feeling.

'Have you seen him?' Ann asked.

Sam shook his head and walked hurriedly towards her. He reached out for her hand and she allowed him to take it, hold it. 'Come back.'

'No, Sam,' Ann said, a firmness to her voice that told him that it would be futile to persist. 'Let me go.'

Sam allowed her hand to drop. She turned and walked the remainder of the path to the road and was quickly gone. As he pulled in a long breath and took in his surroundings, he realised that he was standing in the sunlit space between the two tall yew trees. He looked to the side and there, in the upper window of the house, was Hester.

Chapter Twenty-Six

'Oh, for goodness' sake,' Morton said, as the display screen on his car dashboard revealed who was calling him. 'It's Arthur—*again.*'

'Maybe it's important?' Jack suggested from beside him on the passenger seat.

They were just pulling into Rye, having finished for the day at the National Archives. Perhaps Jack was right; Arthur Fothergill had tried calling multiple times on the journey home, quite what the urgency could be, however, Morton had no idea.

He hit the hands-free answer-button. 'Hello?' he said, trying to conceal his annoyance.

'Is that you, Morton Farrier?' Arthur's soft voice asked.

Morton flashed a quick look at Jack, then answered, 'Yes, that's me. What can I do for you?'

'It's Arthur Fothergill here. I don't mean to pester, but how is the work on my great-grandmother coming along?'

'Great,' Morton said, 'I think. I've been working on her today at the National Archives.'

'Oh, right. So, it's close to finishing, then?' Arthur said.

Morton wondered how Arthur had reached that conclusion based on what he had just told him. 'Well... there's still work to do—if you want it doing thoroughly.'

There was just enough suggestion hanging in Morton's words that the case could be ended prematurely at any moment for Arthur to quickly say, 'Yes, yes—I want it done thoroughly...' The line went quiet. Seconds passed and Morton glanced at the display to see if the signal had failed, leaving poor Arthur chatting in an unheard soliloquy. But, he spoke again. 'And, with regard to Ann's places of residence during this time, have you... identified anything?'

Morton looked again at Jack, both of them believing that Arthur's nephew had clearly pushed him into making the phone call. Given what had happened at the Bourne Tap the responsibility for what might happen if he told Arthur about Braemar Cottage momentarily skewed Morton's thinking. But he couldn't *not* tell him. As he turned the car onto Mermaid Street, an idea struck him. 'Just one place,' he lied. 'Somewhere called Braemar Cottage, next to Aldington Church.'

'Braemar Cottage,' Arthur said, taking his time to enunciate the words.

Jack mouthed the words, 'Writing it down.'

'Near Aldington Church, you say?' Arthur repeated.

'That's right,' Morton answered, a hollow sense of disappointment settling on him, as he realised that for Arthur and his family the main focus of the case was on a ludicrous treasure hunt, not anything which he might find out about Ann and her life. This was confirmed when Arthur said 'Right, I'll let you go,' without asking any further details of his research. Morton said goodbye somewhat curtly and ended the call.

'Wow. Do you think the nephew was there with him?' Jack asked.

'That would be my guess, yes,' Morton said, parking the car behind his house.

'Do you think that was the right thing to do, giving him the name of the cottage?' Jack asked, voicing Morton's own fears.

Morton nodded slowly and uncertainly. 'I hope so. I've got an idea,' he said, leading the way around the house to the front door.

'I hope it's a good one,' Jack said.

'We shall see,' Morton replied, as they reached the front door. 'Hello,' he called into the house, placing his bag down.

Laura responded with a greeting from upstairs, Juliette from the kitchen.

'Dadda!' Grace greeted the moment that Morton stepped inside. She crawled from the kitchen doorway towards him with remarkable speed, then grappled with his leg to hoist herself up.

Morton picked her up with a wide smile and kissed her. 'Hello, Grace. Have you had a nice day?'

'No,' Grace answered, looking over his shoulder. 'Gandpa!'

Jack held his hands apart as though he were holding an imaginary child, and Morton passed Grace over to him, then moved into the kitchen. Juliette, wearing slim jeans and a loose-fitting denim shirt, was busy chopping a slab of white fish into small chunks.

'Hi,' she said. 'Good day?'

'Very good, thanks,' Morton said, pushing himself to her side to kiss her. 'Yours?'

'Lovely—very relaxing. We went to Tenterden, did some shopping, had lunch, went on the old steam railway to Bodiam, then came back here and watched *Frozen*. Laura's just having a bath. Oh! Oh! And guess what?' she said, hurrying to the sink to wash her hands. 'Follow me!'

Morton trailed her into the lounge, where Grace was on the floor, playing cars with Jack.

'Grace,' Juliette said. 'Say *mummy*.'

Grace looked up and, for a brief moment, Morton thought that she was not going to oblige. 'Mumma,' she said.

'Good girl,' Juliette praised, bending down and kissing her on the forehead.

'Great stuff,' Jack said. 'You just wait, though, there'll be moments in the future when you'll be sick of hearing that word.'

'I'm sure,' Morton agreed.

Juliette laughed, then headed back into the kitchen, with Morton close behind her.

'Listen, before I forget—there's something you need to do workwise.'

'Well,' Juliette said, picking the knife and brandishing it in his direction, 'it might have escaped your attention, but I'm actually *not* at work; I'm at home, making dinner for *you* and your family.'

'It's kind of important...' he persisted.

'Isn't it always?'

'Basically,' he began, not giving her much choice but to listen, 'I think Phillip Garrow might try breaking into Braemar Cottage in Aldington tonight.'

'Why?'

'Because I've just told him about it—via his uncle.'

'Of course you have,' she said, her knife slicing through the fish with renewed ferocity. 'Start from the beginning.'

Leaning on the worktop beside Juliette, Morton relayed his conversation with Arthur, expecting a sarcastic response along the lines of bringing in armed response officers and putting the ports on high alert, but actually she said, 'I'll phone it in and we'll see what the boss thinks. They might send a car out if there's the manpower available.'

'Thanks,' he said, feeling a sense of release from the burden of his knowledge. 'Where's George?'

Juliette shrugged. 'Out somewhere—think he's sulking because Lucy dumped him.'

'Oh, did she? Why?'

Juliette looked at him, as though the answer should be obvious. She lowered her voice and said, 'There's something up with him, isn't there?'

Morton nodded. 'I'll speak to Jack about it tomorrow. He wants to go over to Folkestone and see the house he stayed at in 1974. He wants to show it to Laura.'

Juliette scrunched up her nose. 'Really?' she whispered.

'Apparently.'

'Fair enough.'

'I'm just going to sort my stuff out from today,' Morton said, leaving the kitchen, collecting his bag from the hallway, and bounding up the stairs to his study. His first job was to start up his laptop and transfer the hundreds of photographs, which they had taken today at the National Archives. Whilst the pictures were transferring, Morton opened his notepad, where he had written any special points of interest. The first was that Samuel Banister had been a key witness in the trial of the Aldington Gang, which he noted in red capital letters under Samuel's name on the investigation wall. Then, he wrote a new name on a fresh piece of paper: Jonas Blackwood. He stuck the paper to the wall and ran a string line from it to Samuel's name. Below Jonas's name, Morton wrote the words, '*Principal Officer, Bow Street.*'

The following morning, Morton drove to Folkestone. Jack sat beside him in the passenger seat, with Laura, George and Grace in the back. Morton took the scenic route through the villages on the Kent and Sussex border, arriving fifty minutes later at Canterbury Road in Folkestone. Morton drew the car up on the opposite side of the street from the house and switched off the engine.

'Is that it?' George said, making no effort whatsoever to disguise his lack of enthusiasm for the house.

'Yep, that's it,' Morton replied, feeling oddly defensive, despite agreeing about the uninspiring appearance of the semi-detached house. He glanced back in his rear-view mirror and caught George snarling, as he stared out of the window.

Jack grinned, craning his neck forwards to see through Morton's window. 'It's exactly how I remember it.'

'Is it the one on the left, or right?' Laura asked.

'Right,' Morton answered, leaving out the crucial information that Margaret lived in the adjacent house.

'Let's go, then,' Jack said.

Morton was taken aback, not quite sure where they were going to go next, when he realised that Jack was unbuckling his seat belt. He copied and stepped from the car, hurrying around to release Grace from her seat, as Jack paused for a moment for a break in the traffic, then trotted across the road.

'Ready?' Jack called from the opposite pavement.

'For what?' Morton asked.

'Go see the house.'

'What are you going to do?'

'See if anyone's home,' Jack said.

Reluctantly, Morton followed, carrying Grace in his arms, with Laura and then George not far behind.

It was with some degree of mortification that Morton watched Jack stride confidently up the fissured concrete drive and press the doorbell. It was something which he never had the audacity to do in his research and, despite harbouring a deep curiosity to know what memories might be evoked by Jack's seeing the inside of this house, found himself actually hoping that nobody would be home. He drew in an anxious breath as a short middle-aged woman opened the door and peered out. She had the look of a retired secretary with thick-rimmed glasses and pinched features.

'Hi,' Jack greeted. 'This is going to sound a little crazy but I once stayed in this house...back in January 1974, when this place was a guesthouse. I'm over with my family on vacation and I sure would like to show them the place. Would that be possible?'

Morton's eyes fell to the floor in amazement at Jack's self-assurance, clearly displaying a trait which he had *not* inherited.

The lady frowned, then glanced quickly at the strange group of people assembled on her drive. 'What is it you want to do, exactly?'

'Just take a look inside—real quick. My room was right there,' Jack said, stepping back and pointing up at a window directly above them.

The lady seemed to soften. 'Well, it won't be the same as it was in the seventies, I can tell you that much.'

Jack laughed. 'We'll be two minutes and it'll make this American a very happy man.'

The lady raised her eyebrows, bewildered at how seeing the inside of her house, with forty years' worth of changes and redecoration, could make anybody happy. She took one last fleeting glance at the group, evidently satisfied by something—perhaps the presence of a baby or lady of her own age—then stepped back and allowed them to enter.

'Thank you so much,' Jack said, leading the way inside.

A sharp tang of frying oil hit Morton as soon as he entered, then he detected other cooking smells—bacon, possibly and onions.

Jack peered around the corner of the first open door. 'This was Mr and Mrs Dyche's lounge. We could only use it until nine in the evening, then we had to go to our rooms,' Jack said with a grin.

The owner smiled slightly, although Morton perceived no genuine interest in her house's previous incarnation as a guesthouse.

'Yup, the kitchen is just the same,' Jack said at the next door. 'Mrs Dyche would make us breakfast every day—some kind of gritty porridge.'

'Well,' the lady said, crossing her arms, 'it's not *exactly* the same; we had a new one fitted in 1994.'

'Is it okay to go upstairs and see my old room?' Jack asked, ignoring her rebuttal.

'I suppose so,' the lady muttered.

As Morton began to climb the stairs behind Jack, Grace started to wriggle. 'Down!' she said, declaring the latest addition to her growing vocabulary. 'Down!'

'You can't get down, Grace. We're just going upstairs.'

'No!' Grace responded, bursting into tears and wriggling more frantically.

'Do you want me to take her outside?' Laura offered, lowering her voice and adding, 'I don't really need to see the room.'

'Are you sure?' Morton asked, wondering whether her reluctance to see the room was because of the implications of what had occurred— possibly *there*—with Margaret, or whether it was the simpler reason of its not being remotely interesting to see a bedroom where her husband had spent six or seven nights forty years ago.

'Absolutely,' she insisted, reaching out.

Morton smiled and handed Grace over to her. 'Thank you. We won't be long.'

'I'll come too,' George said.

Morton watched the three of them troop out of the house, then took the remaining steps two at a time until he reached the top. Jack's voice guided him to a box room at the front of the house. He was standing with his hands on his hips, slowly taking in the room, under the curious gaze of the owner. It was now evidently used for crafting, there being two sewing machines set up on a table to the left, from one of which dangled a garish paisley piece of fabric. On the wall facing the door, framing the window, were dozens of rolls of material, and on the right-hand wall were cabinets with small plastic drawers fronted with obscure labels 'wooden embellishments', 'hessian jute twine', 'rainbow sticky paper', 'clear washi tape'.

'So,' Jack said, stepping fully into the room. 'The single bed used to be here, running right under the window and over here—' he pointed to the sewing machines, '—there was a wardrobe and chest of drawers. And that was it.'

The house owner maintained a fixed, yet clearly disinterested smile.

Morton edged into the room slightly, as if that might help him picture the room better as it would have been forty years ago, when in fact it was so that he could see how Laura was getting on with Grace outside. Grace was in her arms, calmly watching the passing cars, but there was something going on between Laura and George; their body language—hands flicking about and the way they seemed to be interrupting each other—was sufficient without the accompanying dialogue for Morton to interpret it as an argument. Morton shifted his look to Jack to see if he had registered it. He had not, or at least was pretending so.

'Right,' the woman said, clearly bringing the intrusion to a close.

'Yes,' Jack agreed. 'Thank you so much. It's really brought back a lot of memories for me. Thank you.'

Morton turned to leave the room and led the way back downstairs, wondering what memories being back here had evoked in Jack. In the hallway, Morton thanked the owner and opened the front door. Jack shook her hand and again expressed his gratitude. The owner smiled in relief and closed the door behind them.

Jack slapped his arm on Morton's shoulder, as they ventured down the driveway towards the road. Morton glanced across to his Mini, where George was leaning against the boot, staring at his mobile like a surly teenager. It took him a moment to spot Laura slowly ambling up the road with Grace in her arms, as she pointed at things which they passed.

At the pavement, with his hand still on Morton's shoulder, Jack turned, and for a brief moment of mortification, Morton thought that he was being led up the driveway of number 163. Instead, Jack stopped at the symbolic wall between the two properties. 'And that was Margaret's room, up there.' Jack pointed to the window which mirrored the one in which he had stayed. 'Next to her room was your mom and dad's room. It was pretty basic, from what I can remember; they were saving up to get their own place. They were good people—we all used to hang out together.'

304

'Really?' Morton asked, never having heard that Jack and Margaret had spent any time with his adoptive parents. The idea was entirely bizarre and sat strangely in Morton's mind, as he tried to imagine the four of them together. He tried to picture them—Jack and Margaret as they looked right now, his adoptive father as he had looked before his death three years ago, and his adoptive mother as she had looked before her death twenty-eight years ago—but the image was strained and somehow false.

'Oh, sure,' Jack continued. 'We all went to the movies together... went into town. Your dad, Peter, was old enough to drive and he took us to the White Cliffs for a walk... We all got on real well.'

'Right,' Morton murmured.

'I guess they took on a kind of parental role,' Jack added.

Morton was confused. His grandmother, Anna, had died in childbirth, but his grandfather was still around. 'Was Alfred not there, then?'

'Not really, no. I only met him once the whole week,' Jack said.

'Where was he, then?' This new information seemed somehow more significant than Morton could give reason to.

Jack shrugged. 'Away with his job, I think. A regular occurrence, from what I can recall.'

'But he owned a men's clothing shop in Folkestone...' Morton said, thinking aloud.

'Well, what I'm very certain of,' Jack said with a coy smile, 'is that he only stayed home for one, or maybe two nights the whole while I was in town.'

'Oh,' Morton said, realising the implication of what Jack had just told him.

'A long time ago...'

'Yes,' Morton agreed and then, when he saw that Jack was turning back towards the car, added, 'can I ask something?'

'Sure—fire away.'

'What's up with George?' Morton said.

Jack smiled, seemingly not needing further explanation. He sighed and bit his lower lip, as though wondering how to impart whatever the problem was.

'It's fine if it's because he just doesn't like me,' Morton said, not quite truthfully.

'No, it's not that. I don't imagine he's even given you the chance to know if he likes you or not. Last year, after we met up for the first time, Laura and I sat down and had a very long talk, which culminated in us changing our wills to benefit the both of you equally.'

'Oh...' Morton said. Suddenly George's conduct towards him made sense. 'And he's unhappy about it... I get it.'

'Yeah, that's why we kind of insisted he came on this trip—so that he could see what a great guy you are.'

'That's very generous of you to do that,' Morton said. 'You shouldn't have...'

'Yeah, I did,' Jack countered. 'It's in no way trying to make up for the lost years, it's simply that you're as much my son as he is.'

The words meant more—so much more—to Morton than the gesture and his eyes welled. 'Thank you,' he said, pulling Jack into a hug.

'You're welcome, Son.' When they broke away, Jack said, 'The best thing you can do is to ignore it; he'll come around in his own good time.'

Morton nodded uncertainly at the advice, fairly confident that if it had not happened whilst they had been living under the same roof, the intervening four thousand miles between their homes would give little opportunity for George to 'come around'.

'Shall we go get something to eat?' Jack suggested.

'Yes, let's do that,' Morton said, as they crossed back over to his car. While they waited for Laura and Grace to return, Morton pulled out his mobile, intending to send a message to Juliette about what he had just learned, seeing then that he already had a message from her. *'Two officers being sent to B cottage tonight. You'd better be right!'* she had written, followed by a grimacing emoji and pair of kisses.

Phil Garrow was sitting on the sofa in his grey tracksuit, with Katie's laptop perched on his legs. A teatime gameshow was playing on the television in front of him, causing him to shout random words at the screen to the questions to which he knew—or thought that he knew—the answers.

'Jesus, hurry up,' he said to the laptop, as a pixelated map began to load on-screen. He had typed 'Aldington Church' into Google Maps and the computer was now struggling with his latest request to switch to satellite mode. 'Japan!' he shouted at the television.

'And the answer is North Korea,' the gameshow host announced, to a rapturous applause from the audience.

306

'Pretty sure it *wasn't* North Korea,' Phil replied. The map finally loaded, and he zoomed into the farm adjacent to the church. There, among several properties, he found one labelled, '*Braemar Cottage.*' The garden was long and widened out like a fan from the back of the house. He saw what looked from his bird's-eye view to be a greenhouse. Then there was a children's trampoline and a pair of thin wooden sheds. He punched the air with delight when he saw, at the far end of the property, some kind of an outhouse. He centred the building and pushed in closer to it. It appeared to have a tiled roof, which pitched in the centre.

He might just have found the end of the rainbow.

'Blueberries!' he yelled with delight, just as the front door slammed shut and Katie entered the lounge.

'What about blueberries?' she asked, tossing her handbag onto the sofa beside him.

'A kind of berry harvested from the bogs of New England,' Phil revealed.

'Isn't it cranberries?' Katie asked, flashing a look at the television, receiving confirmation of her answer.

Phil picked up the remote control and switched off the television. He closed the lid of the laptop and stood up. 'Can I borrow your car?'

'When?'

'Now.'

'No, I'm going back out. I've got another shift in an hour's time. I'm only home to pick Kyle up from afterschool club. I need you to babysit this evening.'

'You're joking me?' Phil exclaimed.

Katie shook her head. 'That was part of the deal of you staying here *rent-free* that you did some babysitting.'

'Okay,' he mumbled, not really in a position to argue. It did not actually have to be tonight, but he was so close that he could not help feeling disappointed.

The rainbow's end would have to wait a bit longer.

Chapter Twenty-Seven

Morton was sitting at the desk in his study, a low amber glow from his lamp lighting the room. Today had been Jack, Laura and George's final full day and, since the weather had been favourable, they had spent it together, using the miniature railway to explore the Kentish coastal towns of Hythe, New Romney and Dymchurch. Morton had taken several opportunities in the day to talk with George, but each attempt had felt as painfully difficult and strained as speaking to someone with little grasp of the English language. Still, he had enjoyed spending time with Jack and Laura and filling in the backstory of their past lives. Since they would be leaving early tomorrow morning, they had all taken an early night, and Morton had used the opportunity to retreat to his study to work on the Fothergill Case.

Having reviewed all the photographs taken at the National Archives, Morton had printed the key documents, which he was now analysing for any content which might give further clues as to Ann Fothergill's connection to the Aldington Gang. He came to the letter written to the Admiralty by the captain of the *Ramillies*, Hugh Pigot, shortly after the arrests, and read it again: '*18th October 1826. Sir, With reference to my letter of the 30th July last detailing the particulars of the murder of Richard Morgan, first-rate quartermaster, I have the honour to inform you that warrants having been obtained against the parties implicated – the same were entrusted to the execution of Lieutenant Samuel Hellard superintending the Right Division assisted by Jonas Blackwood and Thomas Nightingale, officers from Bow Street – and now have the pleasure in communicating to you the successful arrest of George Ransley and nine of his gang. I cannot abstain from congratulating you upon these men's work, particularly when it is considered that the leader of this ruffian band has defied the whole Civil Power of the county for the last six years. I am most anxious to impress upon your mind my unqualified opinion of the energy, zeal and address and indefatigable exertion upon the present and upon all occasions of these three men. I further beg leave to acquaint you that the tender to this ship, Antelope will proceed immediately to Deptford with the prisoners beforementioned, accompanied by Messrs Blackwood and Nightingale in order to their being disposed of as the case may require. I have the honour to be, Sir, your most obedient, humble servant, Captain Hugh Pigot.*'

Morton studied the letter for a moment longer, before moving on to the next significant letter from Pigot to the Admiralty: '*24th October 1826. Sir, with reference to the attack on the parties of the Coast Blockade, by armed parties of smugglers, and the murder of Richard Morgan, first rate quartermaster, I do myself the honour to acquaint you, for the information of my Lords Commissioners of the Admiralty that, following the investigations of Mr Blackwood, the Bow Street officer, a person named Samuel Banister has had several interviews with Lieutenant Hellard, superintending the Right Division of the Blockade, and offered to give information as to the persons actually engaged in the outrages in question. I most respectfully submit for consideration, that their Lordships may be pleased to authorise their solicitor to send for, and examine Samuel Banister and take such measures as shall be found expedient on any information this man may give. I have authorised the aforesaid Samuel Banister to be supplied with a small sum of money for subsistence, until their Lordships pleasure is known. I most respectfully hope that they may be pleased to direct their solicitor to discharge the same. I have the honour to be, Sir, Your most obedient humble servant, Captain Hugh Pigot.'*

It had taken the Bow Street officer, Jonas Blackwood, little more than two months of investigation to track down Samuel Banister, who had willingly, it seemed, given evidence against his fellow smugglers. But why? The implication, towards the end of the letter, was that the reason had been financial. If Samuel had needed money for subsistence, then receiving the reward pay-out for the conviction of the other smugglers would have been life-changing. He looked back over the notes which he had made at Dover Library and saw that the reward offered for the capture of Richard Morgan's murderer had been a hefty five hundred pounds. An online historical pricing website converted the amount to approximately £429,500: a fairly big incentive for a labouring man who had needed the help of the parish to survive. But that still gave no explanation as to why he would leave his wife and children behind, unless simple greed had been the reason.

Morton's eyes shifted to Ann's name on the investigation wall in front of him, wondering how—or even *if*—she had figured in Samuel's apparent shifting of allegiance. By the time of Richard Morgan's murder, she was well into her tenure of the Bell Inn and he wondered if perhaps the Bow Street investigator had made enquiries there.

He quietly moved around his desk to the timeline at the base of the investigation wall and began to add the information gleaned at the National Archives, feeling somewhat frustrated that no further connection to Ann Fothergill had emerged.

Back at his desk, he briefly turned to the other aspect of the case, to which he had given little time: finding the father of Ann's son, William. He logged in to his Ancestry account and, from among the many DNA tests in his name, selected Arthur Fothergill's. *Lab Processing*, it told him, meaning that the results would not be much longer.

Morton was startled as his mobile ringtone shrieked loudly into the air. He quickly scrambled to hit the silent button, hoping that it had not woken the rest of the house. Juliette's name appeared on-screen. 'Hi,' he whispered. 'You okay?'

'Well,' she began, and Morton knew that he was in trouble. 'They sent a car and two officers to Aldington last night—terrified the residents there, who've got young kids—stayed until daylight with no sign of Phillip Garrow. How sure are you that he's going to turn up there?'

The truth was, he did not know how sure he was; a hunch based on his previous behaviour was all he had, but he knew that Juliette needed more than that. 'Pretty sure,' he answered confidently.

Juliette went quiet. 'Well, they're there again tonight but that's it and that was really only because the people living there were so scared.'

'They didn't park the car outside the house, did they?' Morton asked. 'Or make it obvious they were there?'

Juliette tutted. 'Of course not.'

'They've all gone to bed ready for their flight tomorrow,' Morton said, changing the subject. 'And Grace went down well at bedtime.'

'What are you up to, dare I ask?'

'In the study, working.'

'Okay… well, I'd better go. See you later.'

'See you later.' He ended the call, wondering if he had made a mistake in getting Juliette to involve the police. As he imagined the two officers cooped up in the outhouse of Braemar Cottage, with the frightened residents hidden upstairs behind locked doors, his hunch began to seem a little ridiculous.

Morton continued scrutinising the documents from the National Archives and building up a shortlist of next steps that he would need to take. At the top of the list was a visit to the London Metropolitan Archives to search the records pertaining to the Bow Street officers involved in bringing down the Aldington Gang.

As the evening pushed into night, so Morton began to lose focus. His tired eyes settled on the photographs of his family on the desk and, as he looked again at the picture of Jack and Margaret together in 1974, recalled what Jack had said—that Margaret's father, Alfred, had been barely present during the time of Jack's visit to Folkestone. He typed out a rushed email to Margaret, asking what Alfred's occupation had been at the time of Jack's visit, wondering if he had got it wrong about the clothing shop.

A yawn, long and protracted, was enough for Morton to close the lid of his laptop, switch off the desk lamp and quietly leave the room.

Downstairs in the kitchen, he was consumed by another great yawn and momentarily considered making himself a coffee but reasoned that instead, he should just admit defeat and go to bed. He switched off the lights and headed up to his bedroom. As he began to undress, his mobile beeped with the arrival of a text message. It was from Juliette and read simply, *'He's there.'*

Chapter Twenty-Eight

2ⁿᵈ August 1826, Dover, Kent

Jonas Blackwood stepped from the private chaise onto the side of the road, taking a moment to observe the hectic passing of horses and carts, running to and fro in the busy port. He paid his fare and watched the carriage as it quickly became lost among the harbour traffic.

He pulled out his silver pocket watch and took the opportunity of being seven minutes ahead of his scheduled meeting to take a preliminary look around. Behind him, across from the street and butted into the chalk cliffs, was the Townsend Battery, a station at which the Blockade Service maintained a night sentry with the sole purpose of preventing smuggling in this vicinity. And yet, past the long row of wheeled bathing machines in front of him, several hundred men had gathered here three days ago to receive illegal contraband and, in the ruckus which had followed, a first-rate quartermaster had been murdered.

Today as that murdered man, Richard Morgan, was laid to rest, so it marked the beginning of a new case for Jonas to solve; or, at least the conclusion of an old one. As such, he was dressed in a manner befitting his office: immaculate black coat, top hat and spotless cream buckskin breeches. He had come directly from Bow Street Magistrate's Court in Westminster, holding his tipstaff: the badge of his office, a hollowed tube of wood, capped with a crown. Bearing the most senior rank of police officer, Jonas's power of arrest extended from Westminster to the four surrounding counties of Middlesex, Surrey, Essex and Kent, but despite this authority, rolled carefully inside his tipstaff, Jonas carried the magistrate's warrant of arrest.

Jonas inhaled, then coughed, as the salty air caught in the back of his throat.

'Oh, dear. The sea is supposed to be restorative,' someone said from behind, 'not debilitating.'

Jonas whipped around to see a gruff middle-aged man in naval uniform striding towards him.

'Lieutenant Hellard,' the man introduced, thrusting his right hand forward.

Jonas shook his hand and said, 'Jonas Blackwood, Principal Officer of Bow Street.'

'I am most sincerely gratified that you are willing to offer an insight into the barbarians behind these heinous crimes. Blighting our damned coastline for too many years.'

'Lieutenant Hellard,' Jonas replied, 'you will be receiving more than an insight; you will be receiving the men themselves—in handcuffs. Now, could you take me to the *exact* spot where the murder occurred and give me your version of events.'

'I would be much obliged to do so,' Hellard answered. 'If you will follow me.'

Hellard marched through a narrow space between two bathing machines with the striding gait of someone with a life spent in the military. Having made four or five further paces out onto the open shingle beach, Hellard stopped and pointed at the ground. 'Here.'

Jonas looked down at the area indicated by Hellard's fat extended index finger. Being just a few feet above the seaweed-strewn tideline, the scene had been spared the intervening days' tide changes, leaving an obvious, although minor displacement of the shingle. Jonas crouched down and picked up a stone the size of a squashed orange, the top being covered in the rust-brown glaze of dried blood. He placed the stone back exactly as he had found it and looked carefully around him. The beach, being entirely shingle, contained no footmarks or other identifying clues. Jonas thought for a moment longer, then stood and faced Hellard. 'Tell me what happened, being as precise as you can.'

Hellard nodded, then began his recount: 'Around one o'clock in the morning on Sunday, Morgan had been delivering mail to the Townsend Battery—just behind us here—when he saw a boat coming into land. He fired his pistol to raise the alarm and he and the sentinel on duty, Pickett, ran down the beach, where they encountered a large group of smugglers. Morgan shouted for them to surrender but was fired upon with three shots from long duck guns, which hit him close to the heart, killing him instantly. Pickett tried to assist Morgan, but was clubbed over the head and knocked out. He's woken rather insensibly with little recollection of the night.'

'Surely Morgan's pistol firing brought assistance from other men?' Jonas said.

'It did, but they had to get down from the Casemates–' Hellard turned and pointed to the castle on top of the cliff, '—the tunnels cut into the chalk below the castle. By the time they got here the smugglers and the contraband was all but gone.'

Jonas sighed. 'All but gone?'

'Thirty-three tubs were left on the shore.'

'I'd like to see them. Where are they?' Jonas asked.

'Just over in the Townsend Battery stores.'

'And thus far, you have no further clue where these hundreds of men went to once they left the beach? Not even in which direction they moved?'

Hellard shifted his weight and pointed along the coast. 'They headed west...towards Folkestone.'

'On foot or with carts?'

'Both,' Hellard confirmed.

Jonas nodded, his earlier involvement with smuggling rendering him certain that it was the Aldington Gang who were behind the murder of Richard Morgan. To arrest them, however, he needed evidence. 'And their boat?'

'Cut up and burned,' Hellard said with a grimace, evidently realising that Jonas might have liked to see it.

'Show me those barrels.'

Hellard led him across the street to the battery, a double arch of stone and brick cut into the base of the white cliffs. They walked through a long dimly lit room with a low-vaulted ceiling. On either side were six simple bunks. At the far end was a solid oak door which Hellard unlocked, revealing a short windowless room which reeked of damp.

When Jonas's eyes had adjusted to the gloom, he saw the barrels, stacked neatly on the far wall. 'Bring me a light.'

Hellard disappeared momentarily, returning with a burning tallow candle, passing it to Jonas, who passed it slowly across the barrels.

The ochre light caught on something, giving Jonas cause to still his hand. He knelt down on the floor, feeling a cold wetness seep into his breeches, as he held the flame closer to the barrel. Small faded lettering: *'Delacroix, Boulogne.'* Jonas stood up, pushing the candle towards Hellard's face. 'Does that mean anything to you?'

Hellard shook his head.

'Where am I staying tonight?' Jonas asked, blowing out the candle and plunging them into a darkness which signalled that his work here was over.

'The Packet Boat Inn,' Hellard answered, walking quickly out of the store room, locking it once Jonas had followed him out.

'And I trust that the *raison d'être* for my visit has not been widely communicated?'

'Not at all,' Hellard confirmed.

Outside the battery, Jonas shook Hellard's hand. 'I shall be in touch in due course.'

Jonas entered the Packet Boat Inn via the rear entrance, keeping his top hat pulled down as he dashed up the stairs to his room. He locked the door, placed his trunk on the single bed and pulled it open.

Minutes later, he descended into the public bar, his hair dishevelled and wearing a grubby smock and pair of torn breeches. Despite the brightness of the day, the inside of the place was cool and dim. 'Pint of ale,' he ordered with a snarl. 'And whatever me old friend here be a-wanting.'

The man beside him, wearing a white fisherman's smock, was rolling a near-empty pint on the bar top, his head swilling in rhythm with the glass. He smacked his left hand to the bar to steady himself, as he squinted at Jonas. 'Ale.'

The barmaid scowled but said nothing as she poured the drinks, banging the first down on the bar in front of the man. 'God be looking on you kindly, today, Fred.'

The man, Fred, stepped forward with a light stumble, pushing closer to Jonas's face. Fred widened his eyes again, seeming not to recognise Jonas. Above his dark beard, his burgundy cheeks and wide nose were lined with a myriad of burst blood vessels, Jonas noted.

The barmaid placed another ale on the bar. 'Five pence.'

Jonas passed the money over. 'How you been keeping yourself, Fred?' Jonas asked, taking a large mouth of ale, allowing some to seep from the side of the glass down his smock. 'A plentiful catch this morn?'

Fred nodded slowly and glanced at the fresh pint of ale.

Jonas smiled. 'I be having a job for you,' he said, pressing ten guineas into Fred's hand.

'Oh, and what be that, then?' Fred asked.

'Well,' Jonas said, lowering his voice, 'after what be a-happening on Sunday, we be in need of a new boat and more contraband.' Jonas was trying his luck, assuming that Fred, like most fishermen in the area, was involved to some degree in the smuggling trade.

'That right,' Fred said, backing away and forcing the money back into Jonas's hand.

Jonas did not flinch, did not show that he was slightly taken aback by the man's refusal. Perhaps he had been wrong and this man had nothing to do with the trade. 'It be a bit of a rush. Delacroix in Boulogne have got overstock,' he said quietly, hoping that his nonsensical statement would be lost to the man's inebriation. There was a flicker of recognition in his eyes, so Jonas pushed his luck further by leaning in to whisper in Fred's ear, 'Ransley be sending any number of boats over. We be paying extra…'

'Twenty guineas,' Fred responded.

Jonas smiled.

'You be a-wanting *Rummy*'s yard, then,' Fred had said on the voyage across the Channel.

'That be right,' Jonas had confirmed, not knowing who Rummy was. With the persuasion of twenty guineas, Fred had mustered a crew of eight fishermen and sailed Jonas over on the *Anne-Marie*.

'Where be Rummy?' Jonas said vaguely, searching the shoreline, as the rowing boat struck the shingle beach of Boulogne, as if knowing for whom he was searching, but just could not actually locate him.

'There,' one of the fishermen said, pointing out a thin man part-way up the beach, running a chisel into a plank of wood, while a pipe dangled through his matted ginger beard.

'Rummy!' Jonas called affably, striding up the beach towards him.

Rummy stopped and stared.

'I be in need of a new boat. Last one got cut Sunday night,' Jonas said, drawing close to the man's scrutiny.

'So I be a-hearing,' Rummy said with a laugh. 'Ransley be in need of another, then.'

'Aye, that be right,' Jonas said, receiving his first certain confirmation that the Aldington Gang were involved in Sunday's smuggling run which had led to Morgan's murder.

'And who the bloody hell do you be?' Rummy sneered, his toothless mouth swimming around the words. 'Why b'aint he a-sending Sam?'

'Sam took a musket ball on Sunday night,' Jonas answered, quickly regretting the disprovable lie.

Rummy laughed wildly at this news, then said, 'A boat be ready in three days.'

Jonas nodded, glanced back at the waiting boat of fishermen, then made his way up the beach in the direction of the distant town, hoping that he was headed somewhere close to the right direction.

After some time, and with the help of passing tradesmen, Jonas arrived at a vast warehouse with the sign *Delacroix* above a huge closed door, which was sufficiently wide for two carriages to pass through simultaneously. Jonas banged his fist on the door and waited.

Several seconds passed before he heard the clunk and scrape of what he assumed to be a heavy-duty lock on the other side. Eventually, a short man with a stout black moustache cracked the door open, just enough to peer out. '*Que voulez-vous?*'

'Do you speak English?' Jonas asked.

'*Oui, un peu,*' the man responded, his hard face unchanging.

'I work with George Ransley and Sam. May I come inside?' Jonas asked.

'*Non, certainement pas,*' the man said, slamming the door shut.

Jonas knocked again, much harder this time.

'What do you want?' the man answered.

'Like I say, I work with George Ransley. I've come for more contraband.'

'I don't know who or what you are talking about. This door will close again and will not reopen to you. *Au revoir.*' The door crashed shut in Jonas's face once again.

Jonas grinned. It did not matter. Over the rude Frenchman's shoulder, he had seen the enterprise taking place inside: hundreds, possibly thousands of barrels were being loaded into carts; he had unequivocally found the depot which supplied the Aldington Gang.

What he did not know yet, but was determined to find, was the identity of the man who had pulled the trigger on Richard Morgan.

Chapter Twenty-Nine

7th August 1826, Hythe, Kent

The eleven-mile walk from Dover to Hythe had lifted all but the negative residual effects from the four pints of ale which he had consumed: just a headache and a swelling feeling of nausea remained. He arrived hot, his smock sodden from the odorous sweat trickling down his sides. He was here to follow up a lead, garnered yesterday from the loose tongue of a disgruntled labourer who had been lost in liqueur.

Having made great strides in the first three days of his investigation, Jonas had found that the influence and reach of the Aldington Gang was such that he had smoked out nobody willing to go beyond pointing a broad finger at the gang without naming specific individuals. According to several sources, there was a man who frequented the inn outside of which he was standing, who had bragged of being involved in last Sunday's smuggling run.

Jonas pushed open the heavy door of the Bell Inn and stepped inside. He lumbered to the bar, only slightly exaggerating his exhaustion and ordered a pint of ale from the young barmaid. 'I be a-looking for a man by the name of Edward Horne,' Jonas muttered quietly to her.

'That black-tan over there,' she said, nodding her head to a man sitting alone beside the fireplace.

'And what do he be drinking?' Jonas asked.

'Rum.'

'Pint of that, then, if you please,' Jonas ordered.

Jonas paid for the drinks and ambled over to Edward's table. 'Here you go. A gift.'

Edward's glazed eyes, puffy and bloodshot, stared at him but he said nothing. He was young, possibly in his mid-twenties, with a labourer's dry and sun-baked skin. He wore a short untidy beard that looked as though he had recently abandoned an attempt to cut it.

'You be looking like Ransley had you out again last night,' Jonas said with a light chuckle.

Edward blinked, then scowled, as if only just becoming aware that a stranger had sat down opposite him. He noticed the drink and took a giant gulp. 'What do you be wanting?' he asked, then belched.

'Nothing more than the company of a fellow smuggler,' Jonas said, raising his glass to Edward.

'Certain-sure, I don't be a-knowing your face,' Edward said.

'That be the drink mabbling your mind,' Jonas said, dropping his voice down and leaning forward. 'I be there on Sunday night. One of the tubmen. I be a-seeing, from a way off, like, what happened in front of the bathing machines...'

Edward nodded slowly, keeping his eyes fixed on Jonas's.

'Three shots to the heart be what I heard,' Jonas said, seeing the first signs of acceptance in the man's face.

'So I be understanding,' Edward said.

'Dropped like a stone,' Jonas muttered, taking a long mouthful of drink.

Edward looked around, as if checking who was within earshot. 'I were stood right there! Watched him fall to his death, I did.'

'Hope he suffered,' Jonas mumbled.

'"Lord, look down upon me!". Thems were his last mortal words,' Edward said with a smirk.

Jonas laughed. 'I be thinking the Lord got better things to do than be watching Richard Morgan breathe his last.'

'"Lord, look down upon me!",' Edward repeated, holding his hands to the ceiling with a laugh.

When yesterday Jonas had visited the wounded sentinel, Pickett, he had learned almost nothing about the attack, the man's injuries having severely impacted on his memory. One thing he did say, however, was that Morgan's last words had been "Lord, look down upon me", a fact his addled brain was keen on repeating.

Jonas smiled, wondering how to elicit from Edward the crucial information about who had fired the gun. Unless he was simply boastfully regurgitating something overheard from another smuggler, then he had been present at the time and would certainly know the identity of the murderer. 'I suppose having shot a member of the Blockade Service, he be laying quite low, now.'

'Bit of a ruckle for him, I should say,' Edward agreed, his eyes glazing over once again, before returning to Jonas's. 'What be your name?'

He had been about to answer, with a false name, when he heard a familiar voice. His eyes darted through the open fireplace to the bar on the other side and saw her face. He quickly looked away, hoping that perhaps she had not recognised him.

'Good afternoon,' Ann said brightly, as she approached the table, her eyes flicking constantly between the two men.

Jonas nodded, without looking up. 'Good afternoon.'

'I must apologise,' Ann began. 'I'm not sure which name you be going by today?' She edged around the table and Jonas could see then that she was carrying a small child. She angled herself to address Edward. 'Is he Jonas today? Or William? Or...?'

Edward shrugged, glancing between them uncertainly.

'I should be most careful, if I were you,' Ann said to Edward. 'This man here, he likes to dress up and pretend he ain't himself. He likes extorting folk, then sailing off to God only knows where—so be warned.'

Jonas heard every word Ann had said and he had seen in Edward's face the revelation of the murderer's name slipping away, but what Jonas had been focussing on was the sleeping child in Ann's arms. Having no children of his own, he was by no means an expert, but her baby looked to be around a year old, placing its conception to last summer. 'Is that your child?' he asked, meeting Ann's fiery eyes for the first time.

For the briefest of seconds, Ann seemed taken aback. She looked down at the child then laughed. 'Mine? No fear.' Ann turned towards the bar and indicated the young barmaid who had served Jonas his drinks. 'He's hers. *Illegitimate.*'

'Why do you have it, then?' Jonas pushed, his feigned accent quivering back towards authentic.

'Because she be working for me,' Ann answered.

'What do you mean?'

'This inn—it's mine,' Ann said. The free smile and clear pride in these words made Jonas suspect all that she had said previously about the baby to have been lies. 'Good day to you both.' She started to walk away.

'Ann, wait!' Jonas called after her but he could see her through the fireplace enter the bar on the other side, then disappear. He jumped up and followed her, witnessing a hasty conversation between her and the barmaid, as Ann passed her the baby. It might have been a convincing display for some but for Jonas it held a certain air of rash pretence and subterfuge, which he had witnessed before among the criminal classes.

The barmaid moved into a room behind the bar with the baby. Ann turned to face him.

320

'What are you doing here?' she asked. 'Edward Horne doesn't have a guinea to his name.'

'I can't tell you why I'm here,' Jonas answered, walking the gap between honesty and dishonesty.

'No,' Ann agreed, 'I don't suppose you can.'

'Is this place really yours, Ann?' he asked.

'Yes, it's mine!'

'And is the baby yours, too?' he pressed.

'No, it's not mine and therefore not yours neither,' she said. 'I'd like you to leave, Jonas.'

Jonas nodded, turned and walked back around to where he had been sitting to find that Edward Horne—his best possibility of a witness—had gone. Jonas raced out to the street, looking frantically among the passers-by. Then, he spotted him, sloping off in the direction of Folkestone. He ran the short distance to catch him up, placing his hand on Edward's shoulder as he reached him.

Edward spun around in defensive fear, which changed to a confused annoyance at seeing Jonas. 'What do you be a-wanting from me?'

Jonas straightened up, paused a moment to catch his breath, then spoke in his own voice. 'I'm a Principal Officer from Bow Street Magistrate's Court.'

'I bain't not done nothing wrong,' Edward pleaded.

'I know that, but you do know who shot Richard Morgan,' Jonas said. 'There is a reward on offer—*five hundred pounds*—for information that leads to the conviction of the Aldington Gang.' He could not tell whether Edward had been unaware of the reward before now, or if he suddenly realised that it might be accessible to him, but there was something which had caught in him. 'Five hundred pounds,' Jonas repeated. 'You would never have to do another day's work in your life.'

'But... what if, say, the person who claims the reward, telling all about the gang... what if he actually been doing the same hisself?'

'Smuggling, or murder?' Jonas asked.

'Smuggling,' Edward clarified.

Jonas shrugged. 'Turning King's evidence would give him immunity.'

'I don't be a-knowing...'

'Five hundred pounds. We can even help the person to disappear after the trial—a new life somewhere.'

Edward fiddled with his beard, his eyes darting around the ground, as if following the course of some indecisive creature. 'I can't be a-giving up all those names. They be friends, neighbours...'

'Do you know the name of the man who killed Richard Morgan?'

'Yes.'

'And is he a friend or neighbour?'

'No.'

'Maybe, then, a portion of the reward could be yours if you just give up his name; a short testimony of what happened, Sunday night,' Jonas said.

Edward looked up and sighed.

Chapter Thirty

Phil had a good feeling about this. No—much better than a good feeling—a fantastic feeling. He had learned his lesson from last time and had parked Katie's car more than two miles away and trekked across the farmland, entering the rear garden of Braemar Cottage over a low fence. The outbuilding was right there, close to the back fence, and bigger than it had appeared on Google Maps. To Phil's mind, it looked old enough to have been here in the 1820s: the bricks and roof tiles looked the same as on the cottage itself. There was a bloody good chance that this crappy little outhouse held the solution to all of his problems. As he stood in the cold darkness beside the building, he thought of all the things that he and Clara would be able to do. They could clear all their debts, get a new car, buy a house, have unlimited holidays—never work again! But they needed to be cautious. He had a vague memory of hearing about some bank robbers—or something similar, possibly stealing from the Royal Mint—who were only caught because of their sudden shift in lifestyle. It would have to be gradual, not too obvious.

There was no door fixed to the outbuilding, making Phil's life a lot easier. He ducked down under the low sill and switched on the torch of his mobile phone. Logs. Tons of logs. Luckily for him, they were stacked neatly against the far wall, keeping the majority of the floor exposed. It was a wooden floor, good solid oak planks and he found, banging his heel, that it was hollow beneath.

Phil grinned, pocketed his mobile and switched on the metal detector. He began hurriedly to swing it along the floor, flinching as it beeped the discovery of each and every nail pinning down the floorboards.

It took under three minutes to complete a full sweep of the room. Nothing but nails. But, he wondered, what if the void was deeper than the range of the detector? He got down onto his hands and knees, trying to see if there were any gaps between the boards, but there were none. He had no choice but to lift them up.

Taking a long crowbar from a bag of tools which he had brought with him, Phil checked the floor and spotted a short board right in the centre of the room. Perfect, at least to get a look at what was below.

Balancing his mobile on its side with the light shining towards him, he hammered the thin edge of the crowbar down between two boards, then began to apply downward pressure. An immediate sweat broke out on his forehead at the exertion. The board creaked and groaned and slowly began to yield. Phil pushed and pulled on the crowbar, giving it all of his energy.

The board gave up with a sharp snap, sending Phil tumbling backwards into the wood pile, dislodging a handful of logs. 'Shit!' he said, rather too loudly. He sat up, grabbed the mobile and saw that the floorboard had lifted, but only from one end: he would need to do the same again at the other. What he could do, though, was to lift the board sufficiently high to get a look below. He placed his fingers under the board and lifted it up as far as it would go. It was not much—a couple of inches—but it was enough. He reached for the mobile and held it carefully at the edge of the chasm, illuminating the space below.

'Wow,' Phil said. The void was, he guessed, ten feet deep with brick walls and a brick floor. Against one wall was an ancient wooden ladder with several rungs missing. Directly below him were two large wooden barrels, lids on the floor beside them, revealing their contents.

A noise outside made Phil drop the board back into place, thrust his mobile into his pocket and creep to the door.

He listened carefully.

Footsteps.

Heading towards him.

Somehow, it was Friday morning. The eight-day visit, which he had feared and desired equally, was almost over. Jack, Laura and George were in their respective rooms finalising their packing. Morton was in the kitchen, drinking coffee, watching Grace lift herself up by the table leg and take a few tentative steps, before she would fall backwards with a giggle onto the plump cushioning of her nappy, then repeat.

He leant on the worktop, half-watching Grace and half-thinking about their imminent departure. No further visits or holidays had been arranged, or even spoken about for the future, and Morton could not help wondering if George was at the root of it. It saddened him that, having discovered a half-brother, they could not be more estranged. The ironic thing was that he had received a text message early this morning from Jeremy to say that he and Guy had found a place on Rye High Street, which might fit the bill for their scone shop. Morton was getting closer to his adoptive brother, who was actually his cousin, whilst his actual half-brother was becoming more distanced.

'Morning,' Juliette said in a scratchy voice, appearing at the door. She was wearing an oversized t-shirt and pink tracksuit bottoms. 'Morning, pickle,' she said, bending down and kissing Grace. 'Have I got time to shower and put make-up on before they go?'

Morton shook his head. 'They won't be long.'

Juliette groaned and poured herself a coffee. Her shift had ended at 2am, and she had then arrived home and woken Morton to tell him what had occurred at Braemar Cottage, leaving her just five hours' sleep. She yawned, as if to prove the point.

Morton could hear low whispers at the top of the stairs and went into the hallway to see Jack and Laura with their suitcases, wondering how to get them downstairs quietly. 'It's okay, everyone's up,' Morton said. 'Let me give you a hand.'

Morton and Jack lugged the two suitcases down to the front door, joined moments later by George and his case.

'Well,' Jack began, 'it's time we headed to the airport. I just want to say thank you both so much for your hospitality. We had such an amazing time with you. All the trips out, food and, well, just spending time together... and we're so grateful to have been here for little Grace's first birthday, of course. Really, it's been the best vacation...getting to know our English family...' His words seemed to falter with emotion.

'It's a true blessing,' Laura finished. 'We couldn't have asked for better family to discover.'

'Yeah, thanks,' George said, offering a vague smile. He offered his hand first to Morton, and then to Juliette.

'Lovely to meet you,' Juliette said—a lie, Morton presumed.

'You, too,' he replied, which Morton also took to be a lie.

'Goodbye, Son,' Jack said, pulling Morton into him. 'Thank you so much.' He broke away, adding, 'So, it's your turn to come out and stay with us. I want dates from you soon, okay?'

'They don't need a *turn*,' Laura criticised, 'they can come as often as they like.'

'Thanks. You, too,' Morton agreed, hugging Laura, whilst Jack embraced Juliette and thanked her again.

'And goodbye to the star of the show!' Jack said, bending down to Grace. 'See you soon.' He kissed her on the top of her head, wiped a tear from his eye, then opened the front door.

Morton helped Jack to load the suitcases into the boot, then hugged him again. 'Take care. Thank you so much for coming,' Morton said.

'I wouldn't have missed it for the world,' Jack said. 'I'll let you know we've landed. Then I want the dates of your visit!'

Morton smiled, watching on as Jack buckled up and started the engine. After a flurry of waving, the car crept down Mermaid Street and, in a moment, was gone.

Heading back inside the house, he closed the door to a strange quietness. Not silence, or even stillness, but something manifestly different about the fabric of the house, created by their absence.

'Feels weird to have the house back to ourselves,' Juliette said, having noticed it also.

'Yeah…' he agreed, uncertain whether he liked the feeling or not. He was certainly going to miss having Jack around and regretted what the huge geographical distance imposed upon their relationship. Having spent so many years unknown to one another, now the best for which they could hope were regular video calls and sporadic reciprocal visits. But that was not enough.

'So, when are you off to London?' Juliette asked. 'Can I shower first?'

'Oh God,' Morton said, having forgotten that he was supposed to be heading to the London Metropolitan Archives today. He could easily have postponed the trip, but he had a feeling that, with just a little more work, the Fothergill Case could be brought to a welcome close. 'You've got time to shower. I'll leave when you're ready.'

Morton arrived at lunchtime at the London Metropolitan Archives. The building was relatively nondescript and always appeared to him, on the outside, like a 1950s factory. He entered a large open room on the ground floor and headed to a shiny red desk in the shape of a letter 'C', upon which was written in white letters 'Information'.

'Afternoon,' he greeted the young man behind the desk, as he signed his name and History Card number into the visitors' book. 'Could I get a camera licence for today, please?'

'Certainly. It's five pounds. If you can just complete this short form,' he said, sliding a piece of paper over to him.

Morton filled in the necessary paperwork, paid the fee, then strode quickly to the Visitor Lounge, where he deposited his coat and bag in a locker and placed his laptop, notepad and pencil in a clear plastic bag.

He took the stairs to the first floor, then made his way to the Archive Study Area, where there was another shiny red desk with the word 'Collection' in white letters. 'Hello, I've pre-ordered some documents,' Morton said to the lady behind the counter, who was youngish but with incongruously long grey hair.

The lady nodded. 'And your name?'

'Morton Farrier,' he said, passing her his History Card.

'Lovely.' She spun her chair around, stood and moved to the long run of black shelving behind her. It was divided into neat oblongs, open at the front for delivery to the researcher and open at the back for loading from the holding rooms below. She stood for a moment, pacing up and down the shelving, stopping to check document references, then, when she reached a stack of several tantalising cardboard boxes, turned to look at Morton. 'Any preference?'

He hurriedly withdrew his notepad and scanned down to see what he had ordered. 'Erm… Domestic Proceedings, please,' then, when he received a quizzical look back, read the reference number: 'PS/BOW/05.'

The lady nodded, pulled out a cardboard box from near the bottom of the stack and handed it over with a smile.

Morton thanked her and paused a moment whilst he looked around the room for a suitable seat. He found a spot not too far away, but with good light from the windows and vacant spaces on either side, giving him room to spread out and use his laptop, if necessary.

The box, Morton found, as he carefully withdrew a great stack of sepia paperwork, was arranged chronologically. Each case was separated and bound in the top left corner by a treasury tag. When he had ordered the documents through the LMA website late last night, there had been a warning attached, stipulating that records from the earliest years of the Bow Street Magistrate's Court were incomplete, with some cases or entire years missing altogether. This box contained whatever cases existed from 1825 to 1835.

The first case comprised just three pieces of painfully thin paper. Morton thought it amazing that time, mixed with almost two hundred years of handling by the public, had not reduced them to dust.

His index finger hovered cautiously above the document, as he began to decipher the handwriting.

Date of commencement: *5th July 1825*
Location: *Woking, Surrey*

Nature of investigation: *Rioting*
By whom directed: *Sir Richard Birnie*
Principal Officer(s): *Henry Goddard*
Detail: *To take notes, observe and obtain information as to the names of the authors and ringleaders attending these seditious meetings. Requires silence, discretion and activity.*
Summary: *Having spent fifteen nights in the town working incognito, I acquainted myself with many of the men involved in these riots...*

The description of the case continued onto the second sheet, naming all of the men believed to have been involved in the riots, and with information of the subsequent arrests. The final piece of paper was a breakdown of the £25 bill, the majority being spent on the Principal Officer's time.

The next case, directed by a private individual, Mr John Lister, was for an officer to investigate a suspected arson attack on his home, for which he paid £20 for the privilege of a suspect being arrested.

Morton found himself reading with great interest among the case files—the murder of a parish constable in the Forest of Dean; a bank robbery in Romford; forgery at the Bank of Scotland; defending the King against pickpockets; food riots in Nottingham—to the point that he realised that he had become side-tracked from his actual task.

He needed to refocus and just check the dates and nature of investigation of each case, before moving on.

Working under these new parameters, Morton paced quickly through 1825 and into 1826, unhappily skipping over intriguing cases which the Bow Street Officers had investigated.

He reached the summer of 1826 and sighed with relief; a case file *did* exist for the capture of the Aldington Gang.

Date of commencement: *2ⁿᵈ August 1826*
Location: *Dover, Folkestone, Aldington, Kent*
Nature of investigation: *Smuggling, Murder*
By whom directed: *The Admiralty*
Principal Officer(s): *Jonas Blackwood & Thomas Nightingale*
Detail: *To make enquiries, observe and take notes of sufficient detail to apprehend and bring to justice a barbaric group of smugglers operating on the Kent and Sussex coast, and to specifically identify and bring to justice, the murderer of Quartermaster Richard Morgan.*

Summary: *I spent several weeks on the coast, inhabiting a public house popular with the lower classes, obtaining information on this most vicious group of men. I discovered the location of their suppliers and boat-builders in Boulogne, the names of the principal characters and ringleaders, as well as the place which serves as the nucleus of their operations. Herewith is a fair account of the arrests: At 11pm on 16th October, I proceeded with a party of officers and seamen previously assembled from Fort Moncrief, led by Lieutenant Hellard, and having marched in the direction of Aldington, reached that place about 3am in the morning. No time was lost in making the necessary arrangements, so that every house in which I expected to arrest a prisoner was surrounded by sentinels, nearly at the same moment. I then instantly advanced to the dwelling of George Ransley, the leader of this ruffian band, and was fortunate enough to get so close to his house before his dogs were disturbed, that he had not time to leave his bed. The dogs were cut down, and his door forced, when I rushed in and had the satisfaction to seize this man in his bedroom, having handcuffed him to one of the stoutest men in the party. I proceeded to the other houses, and was equally successful in arresting nine others of the gang, whose names I subjoin. On my return to Fort Moncrief at 8am, I immediately embarked the prisoners on board the Industry, for a passage to the Ramillies. Jonas Blackwood.*

Morton photographed the entry, then turned the page to see the names of the arrested men.

George Ransley, aged 44 years
Samuel Bailey, aged 36 years
Charles Giles, aged 28 years
Thomas Denard, aged 21 years
Robert Bailey, aged 30 years
Thomas Gillham, aged 22 years
William Wire, aged 17 years
Richard Wire, aged 19 years
James Hogben, aged 21 years
Richard Higgins, aged 22 years

Morton read the names several times. It struck him as curious that, even though Samuel Banister had turned King's evidence, he had not even been arrested, despite being the gang's second-in-command.

The next page contained an itemisation of the £55 bill, the lion's share going to Jonas Blackwood, followed by Thomas Nightingale, then the next highest and final amount claimed went to the Packet

Boat Inn, Dover—presumably where Jonas had stayed whilst conducting his investigation.

It was an interesting aside to the case but with no mention of Ann Fothergill, it did little to further Morton's research. From what he could ascertain from the records thus far, Ann had taken ownership of the Bell Inn by this point in time and, quite likely, had little—if anything—to do with the Aldington Gang any longer.

He placed the case notes to one side and continued looking through the box, taking interest in the range of cases which the officers had been called upon to investigate. He checked the rest of the files for anything familiar, pushing through until the end of the box, in 1835. What appeared to be the final surviving case file for Jonas Blackwood and Thomas Nightingale had occurred in October 1826 with their being summoned by one Mr Bull of Ramsgate to investigate a spate of arson attacks. There was no further mention of smuggling, Aldington nor, as he had expected, anything on Ann Fothergill.

Morton slid out from his chair, stretched and then carried the box back over to the desk.

'All finished with that one?' the lady with the implausible grey hair asked, standing from her computer terminal.

'Yes, thank you. Could I have the correspondence file next, please—PS/BOW/B/06.'

She returned to the same spot on the shelving, momentarily checking the reference details of the top box, before handing it over to Morton.

'Thank you,' he said, taking it to his desk. He sat down, pulled off the lid and, as he placed it to the side, noticed the screen of his mobile light up with an email from his Aunty Margaret. He unlocked the phone and read the message: *'Dear Morton. Many thanks for such a wonderful stay in Sussex—it's always such a pleasure to be back in the area. So pleased that we were able to be there for Grace's birthday—such a sweetie! In answer to your question, my dad worked in his shop in Folkestone – men's clothing. Hope that helps. Take care. M xx'*

It was an interesting quirk of his Aunty Margaret's, that since the revelation that she was actually his biological mother, she had taken to signing off text messages and emails with the letter 'M'—as if she were the character from James Bond. It made Morton wonder if it was as close as her restrained personality would allow her to get to writing the word 'Mum'.

330

He re-read the last couple of lines of her email. No, Aunty Margaret, it did *not* help. He could see that he needed to be more specific, and do what he had been loath to do, which was to paraphrase what Jack had told him about Alfred's not being home for much of the week of his visit. Morton typed a response, mentioning what Jack had said, then clicked send.

He flipped his attention back to the box of correspondence in front of him. Taking a cursory glance at the loose letters, he could see that there was no definable logic to their arrangement: he was going to have to wade through each and every letter, scanning it for the usual keywords.

After over half an hour of reading, he had got the measure of the box: the letters were largely appraisals of a case in progress, a kind of justification for the Principal Officer's being out of Bow Street for days or weeks on end at a time. Some were extremely brief, others gave a full itinerary of each day of the investigation. So far, he had found four letters, written by Jonas Blackwood, dating from 1822 to 1825, of decent length to give Morton an optimism about what he might yet find.

It did not take long for Morton to find a letter, featuring the keyword smuggling, signed by Jonas Blackwood. It was short and incorrectly dated. '*Memorandum from J. Blackwood, Principal Officer. Aldington, Kent. 18th November 1821. Please pass word to Mr Proctor that I will see him to-morrow—smuggling case here terminated by client. I shall return to Bow Street to-morrow morning by chaise. Your obedient servant, J. Blackwood.*'

Morton photographed the letter, closely scrutinising the date. It clearly said 1821, but surely that was an error in place of 1826. But then, November was surely wrong, also; the men having been rounded up and arrested in October.

Since the box was haphazardly arranged, Morton placed the letter to one side and continued searching the remaining quarter of correspondence in the box.

Typically, the letter for which he searched was close to the bottom of the pile. He read it once, quickly, then again, taking his time to make sure that he had understood it correctly.

Yes, the letter from Jonas Blackwood, dated 7th August 1826, gave the name of the man he believed to have murdered Richard Morgan.

Chapter Thirty-One

The barren trees under which they marched were touched with a milky blue light from the full moon, and the path through the woods clearly illuminated, despite its being almost three o'clock in the morning. The brightness unnerved the three men leading the expedition. More than eighty armed uniformed seamen were trooping behind them for anyone who happened to be awake to witness and to raise the alarm. Paradoxically, however, it was the very presence of the full moon which guaranteed that the members of the gang, whom they had come to arrest, would be tucked up in their beds and not several miles away on the coast, embarking on another smuggling run.

Jonas, heading the marching men, slowed his pace slightly. Somewhere around here was the invisible boundary line of the village. By the time they would leave the woods on the other side—neatly avoiding passing too close to the Walnut Tree Inn—they would be in the centre of Aldington.

A pleasant autumnal smell wafted up from the decaying leaves, which were being kicked up by the marching troops, and Jonas found himself feeling oddly relaxed. He was certain that, if they could take Ransley alive, and possibly some of the other key gang members, the group would quickly crumble. But he was not expecting the gang to capitulate quietly. During the course of his investigation, Jonas had heard that Ransley had boasted on several occasions that he would never be taken alive.

His mind was drifting over his association with the Aldington Gang, sensing a dichotomy of feeling between bringing the criminals to face justice and his personal experience of the men—working labourers, struggling with basic subsistence—when Hellard brought the troops to a standstill.

'We're almost at the road. Denard's place is just over there,' Hellard said quietly, pointing at the dark horizon.

The plan of the night had been created some days ago and had been rehearsed many times over. As such, one of the senior officers stepped forward without discussion and led twenty men off, a portion of whom would surround Thomas Denard's house, maintaining guard, whilst the others would continue on to surround the home of the Wire brothers, Richard and William.

Another officer spoke quickly to Hellard, then led another large group of seamen off to the houses of Samuel and Robert Bailey and Charles Giles. A further group were led by another officer to the houses of Thomas Gillham, James Hogben and Richard Higgins.

The potential conflict in hierarchy between Jonas and Hellard had been tactfully avoided: Jonas had left all organisation, mustering and preparing of the seamen to Hellard, whilst Hellard had left the investigation and the strategy for the arrests to Jonas; the end goal being identical for both officers. By the end of the night, all being well, the work of the two Principal Officers would be over.

'Ready?' Jonas said with his mouth upturned nervously.

'Very,' Hellard confirmed, passing instruction back that it was time to move towards the main prize.

The men understood the need for discretion. Jonas, up front beside Hellard, could not hear the footfall of a single one of the men behind them, as they continued on to Aldington Frith.

As they neared the top of the hill, Hellard brought them all to a standstill. Unseen, just over the brow, was the Bourne Tap. As they had planned, Hellard and Jonas tucked themselves close to the hedgerow and edged forward until the house came into view. Both men raised their telescopes and spent time carefully searching the property. Fortune was on their side. Not only was there nobody in sight but also the wind was blowing towards them head-on, giving them more time to deal with one remaining problem.

'Dogs,' Hellard whispered, evidently seeing them at the same time as Jonas.

Four mongrels, curled up beside each other, close to the street door of the house, needing dealing with as quickly and quietly as possible.

'I'll do it,' Jonas said. 'You ready the men.'

Hellard slid past Jonas and, moments later, he heard the faint clicking of multiple pistols being loaded.

Jonas stowed his telescope, drew his cutlass, then, stepping just proud of the hedgerow, padded lightly down towards the Bourne Tap, checking the ground before him as he approached.

He was just a handful of yards from the house and the dogs had not stirred. He paused, his heart racing and his breathing quickening. Behind him, Hellard was slowly inching the troops forwards and Jonas could feel the weight of their eyes upon him and the action which he was about to commit, knowing that, if he failed, chaos would break out and Ransley could very easily escape.

Jonas felt a light quiver in his hand, as he took small careful steps towards the sleeping dogs.

He froze as a crunching sound—like a dead branch being stepped upon—pierced into the air behind him, stirring the dog closest to the street door. It lifted its head in the direction of the sound, then sank back into sleep, oblivious to Jonas's standing just five yards away.

Jonas found that he was holding his breath and slowly released it.

He took a final check around him, then looked at the dogs, reckoning that, as it had just stirred, he would take out the one closest to the door first.

It was time.

Positioning his cutlass in both hands, he moved forwards, deftly bringing the blade down on the back of the dog's neck, a spray of blood and brief crack of bone confirming that the deed was done. Without hesitation, he repeated the action on the second and third dog without them even stirring. The fourth raised its head, emitting a low growl before Jonas cut across its throat.

His heart was thudding loudly in his ears as Jonas stepped back to survey the scene. The dogs were dead and the troops were now silently manoeuvring themselves around the property. Jonas caught the moonlit glint of several poised pistols as the men surrounded the house.

Hellard joined Jonas outside the street door, as if they were awaiting an invitation to go inside. Jonas nodded to Hellard, who in turn gave a silent signal to two seamen, chosen for their brawn. The two stood back, lined themselves up, then ran full pelt at the door, their shoulders effortlessly smashing it to the floor inside.

Hellard ran in first, with Jonas on his heels. Inside, the house was pitch-black. They jumped over the two men who had just busted down the door, one of whom was writhing in agony and clutching his arm. Behind Jonas ran a stream of a dozen men—especially selected by Hellard for this task. The men darted in and out of the rooms downstairs, checking for people and shouting that the rooms were empty, before continuing to the next.

A loud female scream came from somewhere upstairs.

'His wife!' Hellard shouted, making for the stairs.

Jonas followed closely behind, leaping up the stairs and, upon reaching the landing, turned towards a room which overlooked the street.

'In here!' Hellard yelled, and there was suddenly the sound of multiple boots on the wooden stair treads.

A soft pool of moonlight streamed in through the window, catching Ransley standing beside his bed in a white ankle-length nightgown. Beside him stood his wife, her arms crossed protectively across her nightdress, as she looked at her husband. His drained facial expression told Jonas that he admitted defeat, that he was not about to resist or plead ignorance. He knew that his time was up and there was little point in protesting.

'George Ransley,' Jonas said, as Hellard handcuffed him to another brute of a man under his command, 'I am a Bow Street Officer and I am arresting you. You must come with us.'

Ransley nodded his head and Jonas felt in that moment, as he stared at his forlorn features, that something much greater than the arrest of one man had occurred this night; something prodigious had irrevocably changed.

Under Hellard and Jonas's supervision, Ransley had been able to dress and say goodbye to his wife. At the street door, he spotted the bodies of his four mongrels and he attempted to stop. The guards to which he had been handcuffed continued, tugging him sharply back to their sides. Ransley shouted, 'Tarnal pigs! Do that really be right?'

'Silence!' Hellard ordered. 'Unless you want gagging?'

'Bastards...' he muttered.

From the Bourne Tap, the body of men marched around the village to where the sentinels were keeping guard, quietly arresting the other nine men. None put up the fight which Jonas had been expecting.

Once the last had been taken captive, Hellard shook Jonas's hand and led the party back to Fort Moncrief.

Jonas had one last visit to make.

Now that he was alone and out of the imposing presence of naval officers, Jonas walked with a much slower pace and a less military-like gait. His heart was beginning to return to its normal rhythm but with that slackening of his pulse came an acute tiredness in his legs and he could not imagine facing the nine-mile return journey tonight. Perhaps he could take a room at the Walnut Tree Inn, then get a post-chaise back to Dover in the morning. But then he remembered what he was about to do: the outcome of this and this alone would dictate the time of his return.

When he arrived, the cottage was unsurprisingly dark. He paused a moment, staring at the pale moonlight on the window panes, as he pushed away the evening's events and focused his thoughts. He took out his pistol and loaded it with shot.

Jonas walked up the path and hammered his fist on the street door. The authority of his role returned, as he pulled in a long breath and puffed out his chest. He rapped again, impatiently.

The door was opened by Samuel, his face embodying the expected mixture of anger, curiosity and sleepiness.

Jonas pointed the pistol at him, stony-faced, realising that Samuel did not recognise him. 'Samuel Banister, I am a Principal Officer from Bow Street Magistrate's Court and I am here to arrest you.'

'What?'

Jonas stepped into the house, pushing past Samuel. He sat beside the dying fire, holding in his euphoria at finally having some rest, watching whilst Samuel shut the door.

'What on...!' It was Hester, appearing with a tallow candle. She saw Jonas, saw the gun and gasped. 'Oh!'

'He be coming here to arrest me,' Samuel said quietly.

'Oh, merciful Lord! What do you be arresting him for?' Hester cried.

'The murder of Quartermaster Richard Morgan on the 30th July this year,' Jonas said.

'They be a-hanging him!' Hester wailed, 'It be just the same as my two dear brothers... What did I be a-telling you, Sam? You be a-heading for the gallows! Oh, merciful Lord...'

Samuel ignored his wife's delirium and, as he sat at the only other chair in the room, Jonas noticed the same sense of resignation to his demeanour as he had just witnessed in George Ransley. All the bravado, all the bluster, gone.

'What be happening now?' Samuel asked. 'Why don't you be carting me off? What do you be waiting for?'

'That all depends,' Jonas said, deliberately cryptic. He placed one leg over the other, set his pistol down beside him and knitted his fingers together, as though himself unsure of what might happen next.

''Pends on what?' Sam asked.

'It rather depends upon what decision you make next,' Jonas said.

Samuel snorted, casting a brief eye towards his wife. 'What choice do I got?'

'You can choose to die,' Jonas said. 'I've got sufficient evidence to see you swinging from the gallows at Newgate... That is one choice.'

Another snort from Samuel and a shaky drawing of breath from Hester.

'Or,' Jonas continued, 'you can live and take a share in the five-hundred-pound reward.'

Samuel closed his eyes, as the realisation of what was being asked of him took hold. 'You be wanting me to turn King's evidence...'

'Correct. I want to bring down the entire Aldington Gang—clean this ugly stain from the coast.'

'Oh, Sam! There bain't no choice here. You got to be a-doing it.'

'And what?' Sam begged, glowering at Jonas. 'You be expecting those men—men what kill anything what stands in his way—to be letting that happen? Sir, you be presenting me with *no* choice, but whether I be leaving this earth whip-sticks at the gallows or longly and excruciatingly, beaten to the last breath in a month-or-so's time. Bain't no actual choice.'

Jonas offered a cold sneer. 'At Bow Street, we help those who help us. If you would volunteer the necessary information we seek, you would be given a new name and identity far from this damnable place.'

Samuel looked at Hester, but his eyes quickly darted away in thought.

'In short, Samuel Banister,' Jonas clarified, 'you leave here with me a handcuffed prisoner or you leave here with me as a free witness.'

He looked again at Hester, this time for reassurance. She nodded and Samuel stood. 'Let me be dressing right, then I be coming.'

Ann heard the street door close from her tentative position on the stairs—not up where they thought her to be and not down—privy to the conversation which she had just heard. Her tongue rested on her lip and she debated what to do. She had come here to warn Sam, to tell him of her shocking discovery, that Jonas Blackwood was an officer from Bow Street and not any one of the various characters who he had purported to have been. Ann felt cheated, violated, even. The complexity and detail of his explanations to her that day in the Packet Boat Inn were astonishing, even to a person such as she, who was so used to warping and colouring the truth; he was exceptional at his job, that much was apparent to her. It had taken weeks of slow enquiries to trace the elusive man back to the offices of Bow Street.

Ann hesitated as to which way she should go but, on hearing a sniffle from downstairs, descended to the parlour, where Hester was trying to regain her composure. The grotesque fury in her eyes was accentuated by shadows cast on her face, drawn and twisted by the candle in her trembling hand.

'You be too late,' Hester seethed, angry spittle fleeing the corners of her mouth.

'I heard everything... He's been given a reprieve—a new life for you all.'

'What you blethering about, girl of Satan? I don't be a-going nowhere. I be having nothing more to do with that man... I be a-hearing the whispers, about what he been a-doing.' The look, so bilious and cutting, told Ann everything.

'You're not so innocent yourself, though, are you, Mistress?' Ann replied coolly, withdrawing a leather purse from around her neck and pulling out a guinea coin, tossing it across to Hester, as she headed to the stairs. 'It might not be too late,' she muttered.

Chapter Thirty-Two

Morton read the letter for a third time. '*Report from J. Blackwood, Principal Officer, Bow Street. The Packet Boat Inn, Dover. 7ᵗʰ August 1826. My investigations on the south coast are continuing with promise. There is absolutely no doubt that the smuggling audacities occasioned over several years in these parts can be attributed to a gang operating from the village of Aldington—some eighteen miles inland from here. Whilst many witnesses will speak freely of this fact, few will identify the individuals concerned. I have secured a key witness from this notorious smuggling fraternity, Edward Horne. I am convinced by this man's account that he was present at the time of Morgan's shooting. He attributes the killing to the gang's second-in-command, Samuel Banister of the beforementioned village. My inquiries into this aspect, as well as the wider surveys into these barbaric criminals continues. Your obedient servant, J. Blackwood.*'

The trial documents now started to make sense to Morton. Samuel Banister, in turning King's evidence against his fellow smugglers, had gained immunity from his own crimes. He had likely received a substantial share of the reward, which he had taken off to some place unknown, leaving his wife and children behind.

In many respects, this document finalised the case for Morton. He had an abundance of information on what Ann Fothergill had got up to in the 1820s, but at some point, prior to taking ownership of the Bell Inn, she and the Aldington Gang had gone their separate ways. Now that Morton was here, however, he felt that he might as well finish going through the documents which he had pre-ordered, despite believing that there would be no reference to Ann. Once he had received Arthur's DNA results through, the case would be closed satisfactorily.

Morton set the document to one side, then began to wade through the final letters in the box. He quickly came upon another, written by Jonas Blackwood, adding a fitting postscript to how Morton was feeling about the Fothergill Case's having reached its conclusion: '*Report from J. Blackwood, Principal Officer, Bow Street. The Packet Boat Inn, Dover. 17ᵗʰ October 1826. Please find attached my final report into the successful arrest of the leading figures in the Aldington smuggling gang, which were occasioned last night by myself, Thomas Nightingale and Lieutenant Hellard from the Blockade Service. The prisoners will be taken today to Deptford, where they will receive individual interrogation whilst awaiting trial. In exchange for his testimony, the main witness has requested to be assisted in his passage to Illinois. The successful outcome of this case means that I shall be returning to Bow Street to-morrow. Your obedient servant, J. Blackwood.'*

Morton suspected that the final report, *not* included with the letter as mentioned, had been detached long ago and was what he had just read in the case file box. So, Samuel Banister had possibly been assisted to a new life in Illinois. Interesting, Morton thought, as he photographed the dispatch.

The penultimate letter in the box was written by another Bow Street officer, Daniel Bishop, and Morton had been about to leave it in place and put the rest of the letters back on top of it and return the box, when he spotted Jonas's name within the text. The short memo was clearly in response to a direct question from Bow Street: '...*I have heard nothing at all of Blackwood nor Nightingale since they embarked on their latest case...*' Although it did not say so, the implication was clear, that Jonas Blackwood and Thomas Nightingale had not returned or made contact when they should have done, at least up to the point when this letter had been written. He quickly checked the date: 30th October 1826.

Something bothered Morton. He quickly leapt up and hurried to the collections counter, where he had to stand behind a doddery old man, who was informing the grey-haired assistant all about something in which she clearly had no interest. Morton coughed loudly, hoping to make clear that he was waiting to be seen.

It worked. The old man told the lady that he would let her get on and promptly shuffled off across the room with a gentle nod to Morton.

'Has the box I just handed in gone back yet?' Morton said quickly.

The grey-haired lady frowned and turned to look to the side.

Morton saw it at the same time as she, being pulled away on a white trolley stacked with finished documents. 'I'd like it back,' he blurted, 'please.'

Though seemingly irritated by his apparent ineptitude, she called out for her colleague to stop and plucked the box from the trolley. 'I'll need the other document back first,' she said, clutching it to her chest, as if he somehow meant to do harm to the contents.

Morton nodded, carefully packed the letters away into the box, aware that he was being scrutinised, then returned it to her. Once it was safely on the desk in front of the lady, she passed the box to him for a second time. 'I just needed to double-check something,' he said, feeling the need to justify himself.

'Shall I keep this one back?' she asked, placing a hand on the returned correspondence. 'Just in case?'

'Not a bad idea,' Morton said, only half-joking.

She arched an eyebrow and settled on leaving the box exactly where it was, whilst watching as Morton went back to his table.

He flicked rapidly through the pile of cases until he reached the report of the arson attacks, which Blackwood and Nightingale had been called upon to investigate, and of which he had caught a glimpse earlier.

Date: *18th October 1826*
Location: *Ramsgate, Kent*
Nature of investigation: *Arson*
By whom directed: *Mr Bull*
Principal Officer(s): *Jonas Blackwood & Thomas Nightingale*
Detail: *To investigate with discretion a series of deliberate arson attacks against the person and property of Mr Isaac Bull, local squire, and to apprehend the culprit(s).*
Summary:

The summary had been left blank, which both puzzled Morton and added to a rising suspicion inside of him. He made a hasty check of the case files which had preceded it: all of them had been completed—to a lesser or greater extent—fully.

Something was amiss.

Morton closed his eyes, shutting out the muffled sound of researchers milling about around him, and the hushed voices, and the watchful stare of the grey-haired lady. In his mind, he took the names, locations and dates of the parts which troubled him, assembling and analysing them, then rearranging them in a different order when they refused to cohere.

A while later, he had created a narrative, which made some degree of sense to him; it was one which needed to be proven or disproven but could not be ignored or left in its current speculative state.

Opening his laptop, he saw that another email had arrived from his Aunty Margaret. Despite the heightened desire to test his new theory on an aspect of the Fothergill Case, he clicked to read the message: '*Hi again. Well, yes, my father was away a great deal with business. He had a large number of suppliers who were out of town and he used to say it was this uniqueness that made his business stand out from the likes of Bobby & Co. It was all we were*

341

used to, but I suppose from the perspective of a stranger it would have seemed odd how often he was away. It caused some problems at home—I remember your father had a big row with him once in the 70s—challenging him on why he'd seen his van parked up in some back street of Sevenoaks! Have no idea now of the whys and wherefores, but there you have it. Soon after that your mother and father moved out and I wasn't too long behind them! Families! Love, M x.'

There was something there, in the part about the argument in the 70s, which he would like to raise with her again, next time they were face-to-face. Whatever the finer detail of the disagreement had been, it had held sufficient depth at the time to have remained in her memory.

He minimized his emails, and opened a web browser, logging on to the British Newspaper Archive, where he ran a search for Jonas Blackwood and Thomas Nightingale. Several results, but the first was the one which he wanted.

'Ramsgate Herald. 5th November 1826. Missing. Two persons by the names of Thomas Nightingale and Jonas Blackwood, who left London on the 17th October last, and who arrived in Ramsgate on the same day, and have not been since heard of. Mr Nightingale is a man 5ft 10in. high, thin faced, dark hair and whiskers, and 33 years of age. Mr Blackwood is a man of 6ft, stout with dark hair, a dark moustache, and 38 years of age. Both gentlemen were wearing black coats, dark blue trousers and black boots. Any persons who will give any information that will lead to their discovery will be very handsomely rewarded, by calling or sending to the offices of the Bow Street Magistrates Court, Westminster.'

The article, Morton noted, was very clear in not articulating that the two men were Principal Officers. Returning to the search results, Morton found further appeals for the two men in many other local and regional newspapers, running for several weeks more.

Morton opened the document of notes which would form the basis of his final report into the Fothergill Case, and saw confirmation of one part of his misgivings. *Ann Fothergill baptised 19th July 1803, St Mary the Virgin Church, Ramsgate to Sophia Fothergill. Sophia married Isaac Bull in 1816. Sophia buried 1817...*

Jonas Blackwood and Thomas Nightingale had disappeared following the commencement of a new case, in Ramsgate, which had been commissioned by a man named Isaac Bull. Around this time—possibly, he had to admit, by coincidence—the bodies of two men were interred in the chimney place of a pub owned by Ann Fothergill. But, the problems with this neat narrative—namely that when the two men had been discovered in 1963, they had been wearing coastguard uniforms—became more troubled when Morton ran a search for the death of Isaac Bull and found that he had been buried just three weeks after Sophia in 1817.

Suddenly, a multitude of possible explanations entered Morton's mind. He sat staring into space, giving each possibility due consideration, before moving on to the next. His previous belief that Ann had parted company with the smuggling group in 1825 now looked much more doubtful and threw a new uncertain light on his research here.

Picking up his mobile, Morton began to re-read the case files and correspondence, which he had photographed that afternoon, reappraising it with the latest information in mind. He stalled at the letter, which had been incorrectly dated as 1821, which Jonas Blackwood had sent to Bow Street. *'Memorandum from J. Blackwood, Principal Officer. Aldington, Kent. 18th November 1821. Please pass word to Mr Proctor that I will see him to-morrow—smuggling case here terminated by client. I shall return to Bow Street to-morrow morning by chaise. Your obedient servant, J. Blackwood.'*

What if it hadn't been incorrectly dated?

Morton hastily ordered the case files for the previous period to that which he had already searched, 1818-1824.

And now came a frustrating wait.

He placed the documents back into the box, and handed it in at the counter, half-expecting, but not receiving some pithy remark about keeping it by in case it should be required again.

He strolled down to the ground floor, unable to prevent himself from working to unravel the threads of the case. He took a weak watery coffee from a vending machine and looked at the digital display board, which gave timings in red LED letters for document delivery.

As he sat at a small table and drank the insipid coffee, his thoughts leapfrogged around the case, ending up at what had happened last night at Braemar Cottage. According to Juliette, two police officers had been waiting inside the property, not, as Morton had suggested, in the outbuilding itself. Phillip Garrow had managed to reach the back of the garden without being detected until one of the police officers had spotted movement down the garden, using a pair of the homeowner's binoculars. They had rushed out to get him, but he had disappeared over the back fence before they had been able to apprehend him. There was still no sign of him.

'And what was in the outbuilding?' Morton had pressed Juliette, expecting the answer to be along the lines of nothing at all, or the usual garden junk which people store in such places.

'Two wooden barrels,' she had revealed.

Morton had sat up in bed, stunned. 'What?'

'Two wooden barrels,' she had confirmed.

'No… Full of gold guineas?' Morton had said. 'Jesus, they were right.'

'Not full of gold guineas, no,' Juliette had said. 'Full of nothing. They were empty. No, tell a lie, there was *one* coin, a single gold guinea, found wedged at the bottom of one of them.'

'Oh…' Morton had said, entirely flummoxed by her disclosure.

The barrels of gold guineas *had* existed but did not any longer. When they had been emptied, it was impossible to say. Any number of previous tenants in the past hundred-and-ninety-odd years could have discovered them.

With a small insignificant beeping, the display board changed and documents ordered half an hour previously were now available in the search room.

Morton dropped the half-drunk coffee into a bin and bounded upstairs to the Archive Study Area, where he was relieved to see somebody different sitting behind the desk: a middle-aged brunette with round glasses and a wide smile of welcome. 'What can I do for you, love?' this new archivist asked.

Morton handed over his History Card, asking for the Bow Street case files and watched with slight edginess, as she marched up and down the shelving until she reached the place where the documents destined for him were contained.

'Ah. Here we are,' she said, reaching for it, then passing it over the counter to him.

'Thanks,' Morton said, returning to his desk.

The case files were arranged chronologically in a similar fashion to those which had followed later. The main problem he had was not really knowing for what he was searching.

He looked at the clock. The building would be closing in just over an hour: he needed to navigate the delicate balance between diligence and haste *very* prudently.

Jonas Blackwood appeared in the second document, working with another officer by the name of James John Smith. The case, Morton read, was about the cold-blooded murder of a shoe-shop owner in

344

Bishop Stortford. He skim-read the remainder of the text, keeping alert for any keywords which might be linked to his investigations.

Further cases of forgery, larceny and burglary were investigated by either Jonas Blackwood or Thomas Nightingale, or a combination of the two, as the years rolled on.

Aware that time was fast disappearing, Morton pushed through the documents at a speed which he found unsettling and unprofessional. It would be very easy to miss the kind of minor anomaly which was actually the very thing for which he was searching.

Without realising it, he had reached the case file to which the letter of 18th November 1821 had referred.

It had not been incorrectly dated at all; Jonas Blackwood had been employed by a private client on the 4th October 1821.

Morton read it, baffled.

Phil was sitting in Katie's borrowed Astra, his head tipped back, fast asleep. He woke suddenly and with a sharp jolt. Recognition of where he was—in a quiet car park just outside New Romney—took several seconds. It took several more seconds to find his mobile, the cause of his having woken at all. Clara.

'Yeah?' he said.

'Where are you, Phil?' she asked. She had been crying, he could tell.

'Just out,' he answered.

'The police have been here, again.'

'Oh, right,' he replied, not in the least bit surprised. He sniffed. 'I'm going to hand myself in in the morning.'

'Really?' she said. He could not tell from her tone whether she thought that a good idea or not, or even whether she believed him. Did she really care if he was sent to prison? He wouldn't be, though. He actually hadn't stolen anything—just been trespassing, really. The most he'd get was some community service order.

'Yeah, really,' he confirmed. He was telling her the truth. In the morning he was going to return the Astra to Katie and make his way to Ashford Police Station.

'So,' Clara began, 'what are you doing now?'

Phil rubbed his face and looked at the time. 6.22pm. 'Waiting. Then bringing forward some money that's coming our way.'

'What do you mean?' she asked.

'Money, Clara, MONEY!' he repeated. 'We need money. We have no money.'

'But what are you doing, exactly?' she asked. 'I don't like the sound of it.'

'Do you want the bailiffs turning up?' he asked.

'No, but...'

Phil sighed, terminated the call and switched the phone onto silent.

He tipped his head back and closed his eyes again, seeing a flash of the empty barrels, receiving another gut-wrenching kick of realisation that the gold—if it had ever existed—was now gone. Some greedy bastard had got there first. And to think he'd spent so much money on that metal detector. Well, that was going straight back to Amazon.

His thoughts began to slow down, as he thought of his new strategy. It did not take long for his contemplations to become stretched and torn, before plummeting into blackness.

It was just gone two-thirty in the morning when Phil climbed out of the car, pulled up his hood and began to jog along the deserted residential streets. He reached the bungalow in fewer than ten minutes. He slowed and changed his gait to one of casual confidence and walked up to the front door of Arthur Fothergill's house. He pulled the key from his pocket, inserted it into the lock and silently pushed open the door.

In the hallway Phil stood, motionless.

The only sounds were a gentle clock ticking from the kitchen.

He moved a short way down the dark corridor. Arthur's bedroom door was shut.

He pulled out his mobile, switched on the torch function and held it to the ceiling. The white beam struck what Phil was looking for: the smoke alarm. A small green LED light flashed rhythmically.

Reaching up, he pulled on a small white flap of plastic, which revealed the internal wiring. He tugged the rectangular battery from its cradle and pulled off the black cap which connected it to the alarm.

The green LED light slowly faded to nothing, as Phil pocketed the battery and closed the flap. Moving into the kitchen, Phil shone the phone around the worktop. He spotted the breadbin, and pulled it open to find a half-consumed loaf of wholemeal bread. He took out two slices and placed them under the grill. Then, he turned the grill up to maximum, sending a steadily growing orange glow into the room.

He glanced around him with a new sense of urgency.

Hanging from a rail beside the fridge were a tea-towel, hand-towel and oven glove. Phil grabbed all three, and placed them on the open door of the grill, before feeding the tea-towel gently in above the bread slices.

It took seconds for the tea-towel to blacken and then quickly catch light.

He watched the flames fanning out, reaching the oven glove and hand-towel.

Phil looked around him and noticed the apron on the back of the door. He pulled it down and placed it on the worktop above the grill, dangling the neck string around the kitchen roll holder.

He stood back, taking in all of the objects on the worktop, many of them highly combustible.

Hot flames were now ravaging the apron, stretching fiery probes sideways to the wooden cupboards which framed the oven.

The flames were now devouring the kitchen roll, seeming to utilise it as a ladder to reach the cupboards above.

There was no way, now, that this fire was going to go out of its own volition.

Chapter Thirty-Three

18th October 1826, Ramsgate, Kent

Jonas gazed out of the post-chaise, as they coursed along the rutted Kentish countryside. Darkness would come early tonight. A black veil, seemingly being pushed down from above, had left just a peculiar thin band of light grey sitting above the distant horizon.

He had not said so, but Jonas would have much preferred a case more localised to Westminster. Having rounded up the Aldington smuggling gang just two nights ago, he was exhausted. The magistrate, Sir Richard Birnie, had handed him and Nightingale this new case, saying that, as often happened, their services had been requested personally.

'What do we know about this case?' Nightingale asked from the seat beside him.

Jonas drew a breath. 'Gentleman by the name of Isaac Bull—a local landowner—has had several properties damaged by arson. He's of the belief that they are protests or revenge attacks and that the identity of the culprit is probably known locally, but he's being protected.'

Nightingale nodded.

Just like the investigation into the Aldington smuggling gang, it wouldn't be especially difficult; it would just take time to gain the trust of the locals. If they could induce Mr Bull into offering a reward, all the better.

They arrived at the Red Lion Inn, on the outskirts of the town, under the welcome cover of darkness. Its location and the obscurity offered from the early evening duskiness suited Jonas; the fewer people who noticed their arrival, the better.

The two men stepped from the post-chaise with their cases and took a cursory glance at the public house. It was a typical affair, detached with Kent peg tiles on the roof and upper storey. The ground floor walls were whitewashed and, through the small windows, Jonas could make out the shapes of movement behind the glow of candlelight. This would be their home for the coming days or weeks ahead, depending on how long the case would take. With the exhaustion, which he currently felt, he was certainly in no hurry to wrap it up quickly and rush back to Bow Street.

'Come on,' Jonas said, moving around to the rear of the property in search of the back entrance.

They stopped at a solid oak door. Jonas tried to turn the ring handle, but it was locked. With a crooked index finger, he tapped four times. When nobody answered, he banged again, this time more loudly.

An irritated man—a good two foot shorter than Jonas—yanked open the door and glowered up at him. 'What?'

Jonas smiled at the greeting. 'Mr Blackwood and,' he said, stepping to one side, 'Mr Nightingale. I believe our appointment, via the tradesmen's entrance, was expected?'

'Aye,' he said, still apparently irked, as he allowed them inside. 'Mr Bull be here soon. He got you a private room. There be a drink each in there, compliments of Mr Bull.' The short man pointed to a closed door to their right. 'In there.'

'Thank you kindly,' Jonas said, opening the door and entering a small but comfortable room. It was wooden-panelled in dark oak, with several lit candlesticks fixed to the walls. A good fire fizzed in the hearth, which, judging by the warmth of the room, had evidently been lit for some time. In the centre of the room were three chairs, tucked under a table which was draped in a white cloth, upon which were three filled glasses.

Jonas set down his case and gratefully reached for the drink. He took a long gulp: rum, water and something bitter, whisky, perhaps. He sighed with the warm pleasure of the liquid running down the back of his throat. He took one of the other glasses and passed it to Nightingale.

'I think,' Nightingale said, 'once we've met with Mr Bull, we should perhaps retire for the night.'

'Agreed,' Jonas said, not sure that he was actually enjoying the drink. The bitterness seemed to increase the more that he drank. Judging by Nightingale's grimace, he too felt the same way.

'Perhaps not,' Nightingale said, setting the drink down on the table. He abruptly ran a hand to his chest and began to rub it. His face suggested that he was in pain.

Then, before Jonas could ask if he was alright, a tightening in his own chest and throat occurred. He released the glass in his hand, sending it smashing to the floor, as he reached out for the nearest chair to steady himself.

Nightingale's terrified eyes met with his, neither one of them able to speak.

As the pain and tightening increased, so his pulse raced out of control, thundering in his chest like nothing which he had ever felt before. His breathing had reduced to a wheezing rasp and he fell to his knees.

The door opened beside him, just as Nightingale collapsed to the floor, his legs and arms jittering around of their own dancing desire.

His hands flailed between his neck and chest as he gasped for one last breath. In his peripheral vision, he saw her standing in the doorway, watching, waiting for the inevitability which was surely seconds away.

Jonas Blackwood's final thought was to wish for the acute thrashing pain in his chest to stop.

Ann Fothergill stepped calmly into the room. Behind her James Carter hobbled on his crutch. She closed the door and ran the bolt across into the hole in the frame.

'Gracious-heart-alive,' James said. 'What in the good Lord's name did you be a-giving those men?'

'Strophanthin,' Ann replied. 'A poison.'

'Yeah, I be a-getting that, Ann.'

'It comes from boiling the leaves of the *Acokanthera schimperi* plant found in East Africa.'

'And where do you be getting such a thing?' he asked.

'My sort-of stepfather was an apothecary,' she said simply, hoping that her answer would provide a suitable enough explanation. The real answer was protracted and not especially interesting. Herbs, spices, drugs, plant extracts came from a myriad of sources: some from the streets of the capital; some from an indirect route across the Continent. This particular plant extract had reached England via a slave ship, returning from Africa laden with tobacco and sugar, and had been dealt to Ann by the dubious gentleman, who had once supplied her stepfather.

They both continued to stare at the two bodies, half-expecting them to begin to move again. But they would not. The dosage, even if they had taken just one mouthful of the drink, had been enough to stop their hearts beating in their chests.

'And you be thinking it might stop the trial?'

Ann nodded. 'If they can't testify, then there's no case,' she answered, hoping to goodness that she was right. 'Let's get them changed, so that, if anyone sees them, they won't have the same appearance.'

James grunted, opened up his canvas bag and tipped two uniforms onto the floor.

'What be these?' Ann said, holding one up to view.

'All I could be finding at short notice,' he answered, avoiding her gaze. 'Two men's outfits you be saying to get… and that be what I did get.'

'It will have to do,' Ann acknowledged, beginning to remove Jonas Blackwood's trousers.

'Do it really be needed to change their costume?' he asked, reluctantly, and with some difficulty, dropping down to the floor beside Nightingale.

Ann spoke as she worked. 'These men will have been seen lots of times. When they don't go back to Bow Street someone will come looking for them with a description of what clothes they were wearing.'

'But we be about to be hiding them beneath a lot of old sacking! What devil be looking in the back of my cart?'

Ann shrugged. 'What about at the other end? When we're unloading them? They need to look like two drunk…coastguard officers, not two dead men wearing all this,' she said, gesturing to the growing pile of Jonas's clothing, 'the very clothes what they left London wearing.'

James snorted, but carried on undressing Nightingale's corpse.

Twenty minutes later, James cautiously opened the tradesmen's entrance to the inn. 'Right,' he whispered into the room.

They needed now to move swiftly, which would not be an easy feat, given that she and a one-legged man had to transfer two hulking great dead men into the back of a cart, unseen. She had paid a vagrant to book the private room and so far, nobody had seen her or James Carter here.

Ann placed her hands under Jonas's armpits and began to drag his dead weight through the doorway and outside. Ann dropped the body down and climbed onto the back of the cart, which James had brought practically to the door.

With some difficulty, James stooped down on his crutch and picked up Jonas's right arm for Ann to reach. Then, with both of them heaving, the body was slowly hauled up inside the cart.

Ann hurriedly pulled a sack over Jonas, then jumped down from the cart, sweating profusely. She entered the private room once again and dragged the other officer outside in a similar fashion.

Within ten minutes, the bodies of the two Principal Officers had been concealed below a layer of hessian sacks in the open cart, and the horse began to pull it away into the night.

Ann sat in the rear of the cart with a piece of sacking pulled up to her chin. The realisation of what she had done struck on her when she felt the press of cold flesh against her leg. With a nauseating shudder, she yanked up her knees.

Ann closed her eyes and closed her mind for the long journey back to Hythe.

The following evening, shortly after closing the bar, Ann poured herself her second pint of rum and water, enjoying the warm lift which it provided, as she sat down beside the hearth and breathed out. It was a lengthy exhalation, which seemed a partial release in itself of all that was burdening her mind.

Beside her, a hot fire was in the process of devouring great chunks of chopped oak.

She gazed through the vaulting flames to the new brick wall behind it, which now separated the two bars. Last night, upon their arrival back from Ramsgate, James Carter had applied his trade and spent the whole night building a dividing wall with a cavity suitable for the perpetual interment of Jonas Blackwood and Thomas Nightingale.

Ann bit her lip, as she mulled over her actions. She could justify them, to herself at least, provided that what she had done had spared the Aldington Gang from the gallows. Specifically, that it could prevent Sam from having to leave.

She thought, with a profound sense of regret, of her little boy, sound asleep upstairs. She did not know down which of the many potential paths in front of her the course of life would now run, but one thing that she did know, was that William was destined never to know his father. She could never even tell William about him or supply him with the simplest of detail—his name—for she did not know it herself; it was one of two men who stood on either side of the giant chasm called the law.

She sipped more from her drink and cried. As the hot painful tears ran down her cheeks, she realised that it had been the first time that she had cried since her mother had died.

Chapter Thirty-Four

1st February 1827, Maidstone, Kent

Despite the freezing temperatures and dusting of snow outside, the inside of the court was unbearably suffocating. Ann loosened her red shawl, struggling to draw breath in the airless room, thick with the odour of dozens of people wanting to be present when the judgement was passed down on the now infamous Aldington Gang. Ann had travelled up to Maidstone several days ago, taking a seat in a private wagon amongst thirteen strangers, all keen to be present at the closing of this famed trial. She had feigned sleep for much of the journey, in order to avoid the almost continual chatter about the smugglers and what would become of them. If the men's fate had lain in the hands of those with whom she had shared the journey, they would all be swinging by their necks. Ann had struggled to find accommodation in the busy town, the trial having drawn people from way out of the town and county. Eventually she had found a room in the Royal Oak, intending to remain in the town until the verdict had been delivered.

Now she was standing, with barely a view of the judge, crushed between two stinking labourers.

'Ransley be sure to hang,' the one to her left said, his breath marginally worse than his body odour. His head was turned in her direction, but he seemed to be offering his opinions to any who might be interested.

Ann craned her neck around, pretending to search the crowds for someone. She looked at the great number of people gathered here. Many were outsiders, come from far and wide to catch sight of the notorious gang; others she recognised from in and around Aldington. Intermingled with the curious visitors were the smugglers' wives and family, along with many uniformed men from the Blockade Service.

At last the judge, Justice Park, a large man whose uncompromising face scowled into the court room, blustered for complete silence. When his instructions had been obeyed, a quick jolty nod of his head to a guard protecting a side entrance brought about the quiet scuffling of boots against the floor and a clinking of metal, as the prisoners were led inside.

Their arrival caused a general stir amongst the crowd; heads twitched from side to side, necks were angled, calves were strained as folk pushed up onto tiptoe—anything for a better view of the gang.

With a slight raising of her head, Ann could see some of the men shuffling in, each wearing a smock-frock, and each having their feet chained together. The men, whom she could see, appeared fatigued in their features, although surprisingly calm.

The judge spoke only to open the conclusion of the case trial which, he stated, would be brief, delivering the men to their fate.

The Solicitor-General, Sir John Singleton-Copley, took the stand. He cleared his throat and set his chin onto a heavy dewlap, before nodding deferentially to the judge and jury. 'My Lord, members of the Grand Jury. The prisoners, having pleaded guilty to the charges brought before this court, have forfeited their lives to the laws of the country. However, it is *not* my intention to offer any evidence against them on the charge of murder. I cannot say that their lives may be spared, but, as my recommendation to His Majesty goes, they should have the benefit of it.'

A wave of incoherent murmurings and mutterings shuddered around the room before the judge demanded silence once again. He paused, then faced the prisoners. 'You have pleaded guilty to an offence of a most heinous nature, the commission of which struck terror into every well-disposed mind. You have assembled in numerous bodies to aid in the running of uncustomed goods, and in so aiding had fired upon persons who were only doing their duty. Your offences were so serious against the laws of man, and a breach of the laws of man is also an offence against the laws of God; and smuggling led to the commission of the greatest crimes, even the crime of murder. If the mercy of our gracious sovereign *were* extended to you, I trust you would receive it with due gratitude, and be still more grateful to your God, whom you have all so very grievously offended.' Here the judge stopped and cast his eyes carefully over the court, before returning them to the prisoners. 'Given that you have pleaded guilty to a capital offence, I have little alternative but to serve upon you all a sentence of death.'

Ann's gasp was lost among a dozen other similar reactions, mixing in with an unholy cacophony of jeers, roars, and shouts for clemency.

'You will be duly executed on the fifth day of this month,' the judge shouted over the din.

All the individual sounds around Ann melded into one deeply penetrating shrill, and she threw up her hands to cover her ears as she looked over to see the reaction of the Aldington Gang to their fate. Ransley turned to Richard Wire, who was standing beside him. The two men looked bizarrely accepting and simply shrugged. Ann leant to her right and saw a look of disbelief on the next man, Charles Giles. His disbelief turned to an angry shout, which was lost in the noise around the court. She was unable to see the rest of the gang and could only imagine their reactions at being told they had less than one week to live.

The men were going to hang. Sam would be sent away forever. Her despicable actions to stop the trial had failed colossally. In fact, the absence of Jonas and his colleague had only merited a minor mention at the beginning of the trial, when counsel for the prosecution had said that, although it was usual for the Principal Officers to deliver their own evidence, the two men had undertaken their investigation with such diligence that the Crown could muster some seventy-three witnesses to testify against the gang.

Ann found herself moving, being pushed along in a mass of unfamiliar faces, towards the rear of the court.

Her jumbled thoughts returned to her last conversation with Sam. He had arrived unannounced at the Bell Inn a week after the arrests had been made, somehow changed. He had looked drained and haggard, his eyes bloodshot and puffy, that much had been clear, but, as he had sat beside the hearth shivering, there had been something more than that, she had quickly realised, something much more profound, like a degradation of his very spirit.

He had sat beside her, clasping a glass of brandy in front of the fire, although the shivering had refused to stop for the entire time, during which he had been with her. He had explained in a low, monotone voice that he had given evidence to a man named Lieutenant Hellard and another man—a solicitor from the Admiralty—of every smuggler whom he had ever known, and of every smuggling run which he could remember ever having taken place.

'I only ever be doing it to keep us from the poorhouse,' he had said several times, staring into the fire.

Ann had not been sure if he had been talking to her or to himself, but she had agreed.

355

Then, Sam had laughed. It was a strange hollow laugh, one that Ann had never heard from him before. 'Do you be remembering that night what we met?'

Ann had nodded. 'Yes, I do. You were feverish, nigh-on dead,' she had said.

'Gold,' Sam had remembered.

'Pardon?' Ann had said.

'Two barrels of gold guineas underneath his aunt's pigpen—that be what old Quested be telling me.' Sam had snorted and drunk more of his brandy. 'What life might've bin were that true…'

'It was true,' Ann had found herself saying, 'but they're gone now—empty.'

Sam had shot her a look of shocked disbelief. 'What?'

'The guineas—there were two barrels full—now they're empty.'

'Did you…?'

Ann had shaken her head vehemently. 'No—not me.'

'Who?'

'It doesn't matter, now…'

Sam had either accepted her flimsy assertion, or had not the energy to counter it, for he had nodded in acceptance and gazed at his dwindling drink. 'No, what matter do it be to a condemned man?'

'You might yet be spared the trial,' Ann had said.

Ann's eyes had darted to the new wall in the hearth, then she had chosen her words carefully, turning to face Sam. 'You don't yet know that there will be a trial—anything might happen.'

'Yeah,' he had said, 'Happen I grow a pair of wings and be flying away.'

'I'm serious, Sam,' Ann had pushed.

He had given her a wooden smile. 'Will you be coming with me?' he had asked.

'Where?'

'Illinois be where I planning on going after the trial be done—I got an old mate out there.'

'But…Hester?'

Sam had grunted. 'She bain't coming.' He had looked her in the eyes earnestly. 'Please, Ann? Nobody be knowing us there, we can be man and wife… New start.'

She had sighed, a long, drawn out exhalation of feeling and then he had taken her hand in his, leaned across and kissed her.

The freezing cold seemed to slap Ann hard across the face, bringing her sharply back to the present. Somehow, she was alone outside the court, her red shawl standing out brightly against the thick falling snow.

Chapter Thirty-Five

As Morton approached Arthur Fothergill's bungalow, he saw the large crowd of bemused onlookers, held back behind a long line of police tape. Among their number, he spotted Clara Garrow, quietly sobbing into her hand.

Morton reached the corner of the bungalow; at least, what was left of it. All that now remained was a scorched brick shell. The roof had collapsed and all of the front-facing windows had shattered. Narrow plumes of grey smoke rose from the indescribable ruins.

He looked at Clara's devastated face, unsure of how to approach her and what he would say, exactly.

He hesitated for a few seconds longer, then walked over to her with a concerned expression. 'Hi, Clara.'

She took a moment to recognise him, then quickly sniffed, wiped her eyes and tried to put on something resembling a brave face. 'Oh, hello… Sorry.'

'No need to apologise—it must have been a big shock,' he said.

She nodded, as she hurried to catch a tear running down her left cheek.

'I just knew…had a feeling from what Phil said to me on the phone that he was going to do something stupid,' she managed to say through her sobs. 'But I really didn't think he was capable of *this*.' She nodded towards the smouldering wreck in front of them. 'I feel so stupid. To think I let him just *steal* my uncle's guinea like that and then sell it on eBay. I feel sick. My poor uncle…'

'Yes,' Morton said, casting his eyes over the bungalow. 'How is he?'

'Bewildered, but absolutely fine,' she said, sobbing. 'The police came and got him after I told them that I was worried Phil was about to do something reckless.'

'And they've got him now,' Morton said, a statement more than a question, Juliette having already given him a summary of what had happened.

'Thank God,' she said. 'They were waiting for him as soon as he left the house, but it was too late to stop the fire.'

A pause stretched out before them, then Morton said, 'I don't know if your uncle is still interested but I've almost finished on the case…' Given all that had happened, it sounded a slightly pathetic and ridiculous thing to be discussing.

Clara smiled. 'Thank you. Yes, he's still interested in it. He wants to know all about Ann and her life. It was Phil who kept pushing those blasted guineas into everyone's face.'

'Okay, well I'm just waiting on the DNA results, then I'll be in touch to arrange a meeting.'

'Thank you,' Clara said.

Six days later, Morton was sitting in the Coach House Coffee Shop in New Romney with Clara and Arthur. On the round table in front of them was a bulging folder, filled with his report and all of its associated evidence on the Fothergill Case. He had just finished giving a brief rundown on the gang and some of their exploits along the coast in the 1820s.

'Smugglers!' Arthur said, clearly delighted with Ann's association with it. 'I've heard of the Aldington Gang! To think that my great-grandmother worked for them as an apothecary. Well, I'll be jiggered...'

'Who'd have thought it?' Clara said, nudging Arthur gently.

'At some point in 1825, Ann took ownership of the Bell Inn—'

'*She* took the gold guineas, didn't she? To buy the pub,' Arthur interjected, receiving a nod of agreement from Clara. Morton guessed that it had been a much-debated topic of conversation between them.

'Well, I'll come to those...*contentious* guineas in a moment,' Morton replied. 'Fast-forward to 1963 when a dividing wall in the fireplace in the Bell Inn was demolished and two bodies were discovered.'

'Oh,' Clara said, frowning at Arthur. 'Ann didn't kill them, did she?' she added with a laugh.

'Well...' Morton began. 'In that file is a great deal of evidence—circumstantial evidence—that suggests that yes, she might have killed them.'

'What?' Clara said. 'I was joking.'

'How can you know that?' Arthur stammered, glancing from Morton to Clara.

'The bodies were certainly put there after 1822. Someone I interviewed, who was there at the time of their discovery, Clive Baintree, said that the bodies were remarkably intact and showed no visible signs of violence. Now, that could mean any number of possibilities, one being that the two men met their end in a non-violent manner, and yet they were clearly murdered...'

'Poison,' Clara intuited.

'Exactly,' Morton said. 'In 1963 it was never established who the two men actually were, but in October 1826, just days after two officers from Bow Street had arrested the main culprits from the Aldington Gang, those same two men—Jonas Blackwood and Thomas Nightingale—were called out to investigate a case in Ramsgate. The person employing them was apparently a man named Isaac Bull. The two officers arrived in Ramsgate, never to be heard of or seen again.'

Arthur curled his lower lip, half-accepting Morton's theory. Clara scowled, clearly not convinced.

'Ramsgate was where Ann Fothergill grew up,' Morton explained. 'Her mother married a man by the name of Isaac Bull.'

This additional information caused both Arthur and Clara to raise their eyebrows.

'So, Ann's mother's husband killed the men, then, surely?' Clara said, sounding as though she was not quite following the story.

'Isaac Bull had died already in 1817,' Morton clarified.

'Oh,' Clara said.

'It's my belief that Ann poisoned the two men in the hope that it would put a stop to the trial and save her friends from possible death, or, as happened, transportation for life.'

'But, you said that these two policemen arrived in October 1826 and that Ann had left the gang in 1825... Why did she go to such extreme lengths?' Clara asked.

'The evidence points to her having a desire to save one man in particular, Samuel Banister, the group's second-in-command. Ann lived in Braemar Cottage with them...'

'Wasn't that where they found those wretched barrels that Phil was after?' Arthur asked.

Morton nodded. 'Yes, that's right.'

'And yet you still say that Ann didn't take the guineas herself?' Clara pushed.

Morton flipped some pages in the folder and spun it around to face Arthur and his niece. 'Take a read of that.'

'Oh, I can't get a word of it,' Arthur said, squinting hard at the page, then giving up and sitting back.

'*4th October 1821*,' Clara read slowly. '*Location: Aldington. Nature of investigation: Smuggling. By whom directed: Mrs. Hester Banister...*' Clara stopped reading and looked up. 'The *wife* of Samuel Banister?'

'Yes. Just a few months after the gang's first leader, Cephas Quested, had died, George Ransley picked up the reins with Samuel

Banister as his deputy. It seems, though, that Hester had other ideas and wanted to put an end to the smuggling business once and for all.'

'That seems a bit overly harsh,' Clara said.

'Yes,' Morton agreed, 'I thought the same thing. After I discovered that particular document, I spent a bit of time looking into Hester Banister. Two of her brothers, William and James, were hanged in 1800 for smuggling and...well, her maiden name was Ransley. She was George Ransley's cousin. I guess she wanted to stop the same from happening to her husband.'

'*She* took the gold!' Arthur declared.

'I believe so, yes,' Morton said. He turned several more pages in the folder. 'Look here, this is essentially a Poor Law record, where the parish have to help those most in need.' His finger settled on the upside-down entry.

'*2nd March 1821,*' Clara read, '*Paid for coal and*—candles, is that?—*candles for Braemar Cottage, requested by Ann Fothergill, lodging there. 8 shillings and 4 pence.*'

'They were poor, below the breadline,' Morton relayed, turning more pages, 'and yet...somewhere...here, just seven months later, Hester manages to settle a *thirty-five-pound* bill.' He shook his head. 'It's unfathomable that the money came from anywhere else. I've checked close family to see if perhaps anyone had died and left them money, but nothing. It's my belief, in the way that Samuel continued smuggling, that he was none the wiser about the guineas. I think, essentially, Hester spent them all behind his back.'

Clara found this last assertion amusing and laughed out loud. 'My goodness!'

'What I can't account for in official documentation,' Morton said, 'is *why* Hester terminated the case. My best guess, though, would be that her husband found out, or that he was so embroiled in the gang that to bring them down would mean sending her own husband to the gallows.'

'Well...' Arthur said. 'Where the blazes did Ann get the money to buy the pub, then?'

'I think she simply saved for it or took out a mortgage: she was clearly an astute woman. Look at what she had in her name when she died. She educated herself, ran successful businesses and raised a son by herself. Frankly, given her upbringing, she's to be applauded.'

Arthur cocked an eyebrow, seeming not to like this modest explanation.

'Overlooking the minor issue of her being a murderess, of course,' Clara reminded him with a wry smile.

'Yes…' Morton grinned. 'In that respect, Ann failed slightly in this inspiring rags-to-riches story. The trial happened, the men *were* transported and Samuel Banister essentially went into a self-imposed exile.'

'Do we know where he went?' Arthur asked.

'Illinois… Never to return. He was given a share of the reward money and I found his passage out of the country two days after the trial ended. He went out under the pseudonym of John Fothergill.'

'Well, what does that tell you?' Arthur muttered.

'That they were much more than just smuggling friends?' Clara suggested with another titter.

'It certainly looks that way, yes,' Morton agreed. 'But, it seems Ann's love life was a little more complex than that. As you know, I was waiting for the DNA results to come through. It took quite a lot of work to separate the various strands of your DNA, Arthur, but, using various online family trees and making links with some of your distant relatives on the Lost Cousins website, I've managed to identify the father of Ann's baby.'

'Well, go on!' Clara encouraged. 'Don't keep us in suspense.'

Morton felt as though he should be asking for a drumroll, seeing the eagerness in their eyes. 'His name was Jonas Blackwood—'

'Oh, my goodness! The Principal Officer conducting the smuggling and murder investigations. So, he was one of the two…bricked up in the chimney…' Clara said.

'Yes, I'm afraid I believe so,' Morton confirmed.

Morton closed his front door behind him with a sigh. He was grateful to be home, and grateful to have closed the Fothergill Case.

Juliette appeared from the lounge with Grace in her arms.

'Dadda!' Grace yelled.

'Watch this, Dadda,' Juliette said, taking a few steps backwards and placing Grace on the floor, standing. 'Walk to Dadda.'

Grace smiled knowingly and, with deep concentration on her face, took six tentative steps into Morton's outstretched arms.

'Good girl, Grace!' he said, planting a big kiss on her lips. 'Well done!'

'Wine?' Juliette offered.

'Absolutely,' he replied.

'No,' Grace said.

Epilogue

Ann ran the bolts across the door, closing the inn for the night. Carrying a tallow candle in her hand, she walked slowly around the bar, extinguishing those candles affixed to the walls, leaving just the dying fire in the hearth. She exhaled as she climbed the stairs, and at the top, she paused outside of William's room and listened for a moment to his soft wheezy breathing. She smiled and continued into her bedroom, where she placed the candle on the table beside her bed, the light illuminating the letter which had arrived that morning. With a sigh, she picked it up and re-read it. *'My dearest Ann, I have found decent lodgings in the city—it be such a different place what can't even be described. I have found work in a gentlemen's stables, earning a decent wage. Ann, I beg you again to bring William and come and join me out here. Nobody knows nobody and asks no questions. There be folk here from all around the world. We could be having such a life here—man, wife and son. Think proper on it, Ann. Could I be asking another question of you, my dear Ann? Before the Great Trial you be saying that the barrels of guineas did exist, but they be long gone. Where do they be and how do you be knowing it for certain-sure? I will close now, dear Ann and say again my desire for you and William to be coming here. Your loving Sam.'*

Ann stared at the letter, which, judging by the handwriting and some choices of words, Sam had clearly asked somebody else to write for him, wondering how she would respond. The answer to the first part—his offer for her to go out to him in Illinois—was easy: there was no way such a thing was going to happen. She felt reciprocal feelings for him and, were that the end of the matter, she might well have gone to him. What she had here, though, her own life and business, was too much to surrender. That, coupled with the secret buried in the fireplace, which she could not risk anyone discovering, made the decision firmer in her mind. Ann also knew that part of Sam's desire for them to join him stemmed from his believing that he was William's father, something which, from the child's appearance of late, she now doubted very strongly. Her actions and the effects of smuggling would forever hold her in the Old World, whilst Sam had a fresh start in the New World.

And what could she say to the second part of his letter, about the guineas? That she had known of their location since 1821? When, in his feverish delirium, Sam had told her and Hester that they had been buried beneath Widow Stewart's pigpen, something which Ann had dismissed at the time as the fantasy of a hallucinating mind. It had only been by chance on the night of the arrests that Ann had seen Hester appearing from the outbuilding at the rear of Braemar Cottage, carrying a handful of gold guineas. Ann had realised that at some point—and God only knew how—Hester had found them and had had them moved to Braemar Cottage. Ann had slipped unnoticed into the outbuilding, discovering two barrels beneath the floor, one entirely empty, the other with just a thin scattering remaining. Ann had taken two coins of her own, as evidence: one she had thrown at Hester; the other she now looked at on the table beside her bed.

She would write a letter to Sam in the morning, but she knew somehow that she would never post it.

She blew out the candle, picked up the guinea and lay on her bed, turning it over repeatedly, wondering at what might have been.

Historical Information

I had known for a number of years that a story about smuggling—so intrinsically linked to the counties of Kent and Sussex, in which this series is set—would be an inevitable addition. Having undertaken some basic research into the various smuggling gangs in operation in the eighteenth and nineteenth centuries, I settled on basing this story around the exploits of the Aldington Gang. Then, when I read in *Kent Smugglers' Pubs* that in 1963 two skeletons had been found during building works at the Bell Inn, Hythe, I knew that I had found my prologue. The story, as expanded upon in several other local history books on Hythe, went that a local builder had discovered two full human skeletons when working on the pub's chimney. The skeletons—identified as Revenue Officers by their outfits—were sent to the local coroner's before being buried locally. However, none of the books referring to the story gave specific details, including the actual date of discovery. So, I undertook my own research, contacting local churches and cemeteries, the coroner's office and making lengthy searches of *The Folkestone, Hythe and District Herald* at Folkestone Library. What I had found by the end of my research was that in late March / early April 1962 the fireplace of the Bell was indeed opened up, revealing a small quantity of beer mugs, keys and pig bones. Unfortunately, to-date I have found no official record of the two skeletons. My findings were later confirmed by a local historian, Sean McNally, who had also been simultaneously researching this curious apocryphal tale.

The Aldington Gang were a real smuggling group, operating a large-scale enterprise which ran from Rye in East Sussex to Walmer in Kent. In its heyday, the group could muster between two- and three-hundred local men. Its first leader was Cephas Quested, who was captured at the Battle of Brookland on the 11th February 1821, as described in this story. The records held at the Kent History and Library Centre, in which Morton locates overseers' help being given to Cephas Quested, are real. His apparent poverty in early 1820 is the likely reason for his seeking extra income from smuggling. I took the liberty of bringing forward the date of his execution. In fact, he was hanged at Newgate on the 4th July 1821. His five-month incarceration was owed to the hope that he might give up the names of the rest of the gang before going to the gallows, which he did not. Following his death, officials wanted to hang his body from chains in Brookland as a deterrent to other would-be smugglers, but, following the intervention of the local magistrate, Sir Edward Knatchbull, he was returned to Aldington for burial in the parish church. A small wooden shoe, carved by Quested, is on display in the smuggling room of Ashford Museum, along with a letter dictated by him from his gaol cell.

Following Quested's death, there appears to have been a short period which showed a lack of leadership in the smuggling runs. From this vacuum rose a new leader: George Ransley, a carter by trade, who built his own home in Aldington Frith, called the Bourne Tap, from where he sold cheap liquor. The place, according to *Scarecrow's Legion,* was '...the scene of many a drunken orgy and became the scandal of the neighbourhood.' From here and the Walnut Tree Inn, Ransley organised his elaborate smuggling runs. The group were prevalent throughout the early 1820s and were responsible for most of the large-scale smuggling in Kent and Sussex at this time. Deaths among both smugglers and the preventative service were common throughout this period.

Dr Ralph Papworth-Hougham, the son of a surgeon-apothecary, lived at Pear Tree House in Brookland and was used by both the preventative service and by the Aldington Gang to assist with medical matters. His first wife, Ann, died soon after the Battle of Brookland in February 1827 and was buried in Brookland churchyard, leaving Ralph with six children for whom to care. In November 1827, he married Charlotte Lee and the couple went on to have further children together. Ralph died in 1837 and was also buried in Brookland churchyard.

Alexander John Spence and Thomas Brazier were arrested in March 1822 for stealing compasses and telescopes from boats along the coast. When the Dover Gaoler and the Mayor's Sergeant attempted to arrest the two men, they were fired upon by twenty-two-year-old Spence. Assistance was then secured by Lieutenant Philip Graham, a Preventative Officer working from the ship *Ramillies,* upon whom Spence fired twice, each ball only grazing the officer and singeing his uniform. The two men were incarcerated in Dover Gaol, but both men managed to escape their cell by breaking through the walls; they were captured in a boat fleeing to France. Spence was hanged on the 9th August 1822 in the town gallows on Black Horse Lane (now Tower Hamlets Road), just in front of the Black Horse Inn (now the Eagle), from where the mayor and other local dignitaries watched the execution. Spence was brought to the gallows in a horse and cart, sitting upon his own coffin, while the hangman sat up front with the rope noose in his lap. Spence either jumped or slipped moments prior to the pulling away of the horse and cart to effect his hanging. He was the last Dovorian to be hanged there and was buried in St Mary's churchyard.

Many of the shops, public houses and businesses used in this story—including Miss Bowler's academy on St James's Street, J. Minet, Fector & Co. bank on Strond Street and the agents Latham, Rice & Co.—existed in 1820s Dover.

Although deaths on both sides were commonplace during the smuggling days of the 1820s, the tide began to turn against the smugglers following the murder of Quartermaster Richard Morgan on the 30th July 1826. His death occurred as is described in the book. He was buried on 2nd August 1826, aged 34, in St Martin's Church, Dover. The transcription of Richard Morgan's headstone at the beginning of this book is correct. The headstone was cleared with the rest of the churchyard in the 1970s as part of the development of York Street and sadly no longer exists. A substantial reward of £500 was offered for information to catch his killer. One of the smugglers, Edward Horne, turned King's evidence and became the main witness for the prosecution.

The day after Morgan's murder Hugh Pigot, the captain of the *Ramillies* wrote to the Admiralty, requesting that they send two of the best officers from Bow Street to catch Morgan's killer. Principal Officers Daniel Bishop and James John Smith were hastily dispatched to Dover, staying at the Packet Boat Inn whilst they carried out their investigations. After 1815, many Bow Street officers were employed assisting with prosecutions outside of London (more than 70% occurring in the south), their fees and expenses being met by the clients for whom they worked. Cases could be expensive and last many days or even weeks, with fees going well over £50. The officers were not uniformed and often wore disguises to aid their efforts in crime detection. The types of cases referred to in this story were typical of those investigated by Principal Officers from Bow Street.

By October 1826, Bishop and Smith had gathered sufficient evidence to arrest the principal members of the Aldington Gang. On the night of 16th October, they, along with Lieutenant Hellard from the Blockade Service, marched from Fort Moncrief in Hythe the nine miles to Aldington, arriving there around 3am. Sentinels were positioned around the homes of seven of the smugglers, whilst Hellard and the two Principal Officers led troops to arrest George Ransley. They arrived unannounced, cut down the dogs and arrested Ransley in his bedroom, before moving on to arrest Samuel and Robert Bailey, Charles Giles, Thomas Denard, Thomas Gillham and Richard and William Wire. The prisoners were marched to Fort Moncrief, then, because of fears that they might be broken out of gaol, if they remained locally, they were immediately escorted on the *Industry* to *HMS Ramillies*. The following day, they were transferred to a gaol in Deptford, where the men were interrogated individually before being transferred to Newgate Prison. Weeks later, came further arrests by Hellard and his men, bringing the total arrested to twenty.

The trial of the Aldington Gang took place before Mr Justice Park at the Maidstone Special Assizes on the 12th January 1827. Richard Wire was charged with the murder of Richard Morgan, with the rest of the group being charged as accessories to the crime. All the defendants pleaded not guilty and, after plea-bargaining between counsels, the charges were amended to smuggling and shooting at Revenue Officers: in all, a capital offence for which the men could still have been hanged. Two men were released and the remaining fourteen pleaded guilty to the new charges. The men were sentenced to death by hanging on 5th February 1827. However, just days prior to the execution, the Governor of Maidstone County Gaol, Mr Agar, received a letter from the Secretary of State informing him that the sentence had been commuted to transportation for life to Van Dieman's Land (now Tasmania). The £500 reward for the men's capture was shared between the three smugglers who had turned King's evidence: James Bushell, Edward Horne, and William Marsh.

The convicted men left Portsmouth on the 3rd April 1827 on board the *Governor Ready*, arriving in Hobart Town on 31st July. Two years later, Ransley's wife and some of their children joined him in Van Dieman's Land. He was pardoned in 1838 and spent the remainder of his life farming in River Plenty, New Norfolk. He died there in 1856.

The story surrounding the movement of large quantities of gold guineas from England to France is true. At the time of the Napoleonic Wars, gold guineas were shipped to France in order to pay Wellington's troops, and, alongside this, an exchange rate crisis in England led to a rise in gold speculation, where, after purchase in London with bank notes, gold guineas were sailed across the Channel and sold on the Continent for a much higher price, with up to twenty percent profit.

I had the idea of Ann Fothergill using the poison, strophanthin after reading about the death of the 'Unknown Man' in Adelaide, Australia. Having died in mysterious circumstances in 1948, the police suspected the use of this drug as it decomposed very soon after death, leaving no trace. When the case reached the courts, the coroner thought the poison so dangerous that he would not say the name aloud, instead writing it on a piece of paper.

The research for this book has been comprehensive, with visits to many churches, archives, pubs, libraries and museums. Some of the most useful were: the National Archives, Dover Library, Ashford Museum, Folkestone Library, Rye Castle Museum, the Walnut Tree Inn and the Kent History and Library Centre. All of the public-domain records, which Morton uses, are real but with sometimes fictitious content, with the exception of the records for the Bow Street Magistrate's Court. Sadly, most records for this period have not survived, although some other later records are held at the London Metropolitan Archives and the National Archives.

Among the books which I found useful in the research for this book were the following:

Beattie, J.M., *The First English Detectives* (OUP, 2012)

Clark, K.M., *Smuggling in Rye and District* (Rye Museum, 2011)

Cox, D.J., *A Certain Share of Low Cunning* (Routledge, 2012)

Douch, J., *Smuggling: Flogging Joey's Warriors* (Crabwell Publications, 1985)

Finn, R., *The Kent Coast Blockade* (White, 1971)

Howe, I., *Kent Dialect* (Bradwell Books, 2012)

Hufton, G. & Baird, E., *Scarecrows Legion: smuggling in Kent and Sussex* (Rochester Press, 1983)

Major, A., *Kentish As She Wus Spoke* (SB Publications, 2003)

May, T., *Smugglers and Smuggling* (Shire Publications, 2014)

Parish, W.D., *A Dictionary of the Kentish Dialect and Provincialisms* (Forgotten Books, 2015)

Philp, R., *The Coast Blockade: The Royal Navy's War on Smuggling 1817-31* (Compton Press, 2002)

Platt, R., *Smuggling in the British Isles* (The History Press, 2011)

Townsend, T., *Kent Smugglers' Pubs* (Pixz Books, 2014)

Waugh, M., *Smuggling in Kent & Sussex 1700-1840* (Countryside Books, 1985)

Acknowledgements

First of all, for their assistance with various aspects of this book, I would like to sincerely thank Trish Godfrey at Dover Library; Susan Leggett for helping with documents at the National Archives; the staff of the National Archives; Dr David J. Cox for his assistance with information regarding the Bow Street Principal Officers; Helen Woolven for answering various questions regarding police procedure.

In my research into the validity of the phantom skeleton discovery in 1963, I gratefully received the assistance of the following people: Sue Goodwin at Hawkinge Crematorium, Annette Jones at Shepway District Council, Hayley Edmunds, Brin Hughes, Mike Umbers, Sean McNally and Anne Petrie.

My thanks to Patrick Dengate for his super book cover and to Julia Gibbs for her proof-reading services.

Thanks to Jens Knoops for agreeing to appear in the book as himself. His hot chocolates truly are the best in the world—a must for anyone visiting Rye!

Thanks, as always to Robert Bristow for once again joining the adventure, being driver, helper, sounding-board, first reader and everything in between.

Finally, I would like to offer my sincere gratitude to my regular readers and ongoing supporters of the series. I have been very fortunate to receive encouragement from many of the most influential people working in genealogy today. In particular, I should like to thank Peter Calver at Lost Cousins; The Genealogy Guys (Drew Smith & George Morgan); DearMyrtle; Scott Fisher at Extreme Genes; Bobbi King and Dick Eastman; Sunny Morton and Lisa Louise Cooke at Genealogy Gems Podcast; Amy Lay and Penny Bonawitz at Genealogy Happy Hour; Andrew Chapman at *Your Family History*; Karen Clare at *Family History* magazine; Randy Seaver; Tina Sansome; Jill Ball; Shauna Hicks; Eileen Furlani Souza and all of the many Family History societies around the world which have run such kind reviews of the series. Your support is truly appreciated.

Further Information

Website & Newsletter: www.nathandylangoodwin.com
Twitter: @NathanDGoodwin
Facebook: www.facebook.com/NathanDylanGoodwin
Pinterest: www.pinterest.com/NathanDylanGoodwin
Instagram: www.instagram.com/NathanDylanGoodwin
Blog: theforensicgenealogist.blogspot.co.uk
LinkedIn: www.linkedin.com/in/NathanDylanGoodwin

Hiding the Past
(The Forensic Genealogist #1)

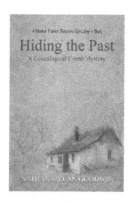

Peter Coldrick had no past; that was the conclusion drawn by years of personal and professional research. Then he employed the services of one Morton Farrier, Forensic Genealogist – a stubborn, determined man who uses whatever means necessary to uncover the past. With the Coldrick Case, Morton faces his toughest and most dangerous assignment yet, where all of his investigative and genealogical skills are put to the test. However, others are also interested in the Coldrick family, people who will stop at nothing, including murder, to hide the past. As Morton begins to unearth his client's mysterious past, he is forced to confront his own family's dark history, a history which he knows little about.

'Flicking between the present and stories and extracts from the past, the pace never lets up in an excellent addition to this unique genre of literature'
Your Family Tree

'At times amusing and shocking, this is a fast-moving modern crime mystery with genealogical twists. The blend of well fleshed-out characters, complete with flaws and foibles, will keep you guessing until the end'
Family Tree

The Lost Ancestor
(The Forensic Genealogist #2)

From acclaimed author, Nathan Dylan Goodwin comes this exciting new genealogical crime mystery, featuring the redoubtable forensic genealogist, Morton Farrier. When Morton is called upon by Ray Mercer to investigate the 1911 disappearance of his great aunt, a housemaid working in a large Edwardian country house, he has no idea of the perilous journey into the past that he is about to make. Morton must use his not inconsiderable genealogical skills to solve the mystery of Mary Mercer's disappearance, in the face of the dangers posed by those others who are determined to end his investigation at any cost.

'If you enjoy a novel with a keen eye for historical detail, solid writing, believable settings and a sturdy protagonist, *The Lost Ancestor* is a safe bet. Goodwin spins a riveting genealogical crime mystery with a pulsing, realistic storyline'
Your Family Tree

'Full of realistic genealogical terms and tricks, this is an enjoyable whodunit with engaging research twists that keep you guessing until the end. If you enjoy genealogical fiction and mysteries, you'll find this a pleasing page-turner'
Family Tree

The Orange Lilies
(The Forensic Genealogist #3)

Morton Farrier has spent his entire career as a forensic genealogist solving other people's family history secrets, all the while knowing so little of his very own family's mysterious past. However, this poignant Christmastime novella sees Morton's skills put to use much closer to home, as he must confront his own past, present and future through events both present-day and one hundred years ago. It seems that not every soldier saw a truce on the Western Front that 1914 Christmas...

'The Orange Lilies sees Morton for once investigating his own tree (and about time too!). Moving smoothly between Christmas 1914 and Christmas 2014, the author weaves an intriguing tale with more than a few twists - several times I thought I'd figured it all out, but each time there was a surprise waiting in the next chapter... Thoroughly recommended - and I can't wait for the next novel'
Lost Cousins

'Morton confronts a long-standing mystery in his own family—one that leads him just a little closer to the truth about his personal origins. This Christmas-time tale flashes back to Christmas 1914, to a turning point in his relatives' lives. Don't miss it!'
Lisa Louise Cooke

The America Ground
(The Forensic Genealogist #4)

Morton Farrier, the esteemed English forensic genealogist, had cleared a space in his busy schedule to track down his own elusive father finally. But he is then presented with a case that challenges his research skills in his quest to find the killer of a woman murdered more than one hundred and eighty years ago. Thoughts of his own family history are quickly and violently pushed to one side as Morton rushes to complete his investigation before other sinister elements succeed in derailing the case.

'As in the earlier novels, each chapter slips smoothly from past to present, revealing murderous events as the likeable Morton uncovers evidence in the present, while trying to solve the mystery of his own paternity. Packed once more with glorious detail of records familiar to family historians, *The America Ground* is a delightfully pacey read'
Family Tree

'Like most genealogical mysteries this book has several threads, cleverly woven together by the author - and there are plenty of surprises for the reader as the story approaches its conclusion. A jolly good read!'
Lost Cousins

The Spyglass File
(The Forensic Genealogist #5)

Morton Farrier was no longer at the top of his game. His forensic genealogy career was faltering and he was refusing to accept any new cases, preferring instead to concentrate on locating his own elusive biological father. Yet, when a particular case presents itself, that of finding the family of a woman abandoned in the midst of the Battle of Britain, Morton is compelled to help her to unravel her past. Using all of his genealogical skills, he soon discovers that the case is connected to The Spyglass File—a secretive document which throws up links which threaten to disturb the wrongdoings of others, who would rather its contents, as well as their actions, remain hidden forever.

'If you like a good mystery, and the detective work of genealogy, this is another mystery novel from Nathan which will have you whizzing through the pages with time slipping by unnoticed'
Your Family History

'The first page was so overwhelming that I had to stop for breath…Well, the rest of the book certainly lived up to that impressive start, with twists and turns that kept me guessing right to the end'
Lost Cousins

The Missing Man
(The Forensic Genealogist #6)

It was to be the most important case of Morton Farrier's career in forensic genealogy so far. A case that had eluded him for many years: finding his own father. Harley 'Jack' Jacklin disappeared just six days after a fatal fire at his Cape Cod home on Christmas Eve in 1976, leaving no trace behind. Now his son, Morton must travel to the East Coast of America to unravel the family's dark secrets in order to discover what really happened to him.

'One of the hallmarks of genealogical mystery novels is the way that they weave together multiple threads and this book is no exception, cleverly skipping across the generations - and there's also a pleasing symmetry that helps to endear us to one of the key characters...If you've read the other books in this series you won't need me to tell you to rush out and buy this one'
Lost Cousins

'Nathan Dylan Goodwin has delivered another page-turning mystery laden with forensic genealogical clues that will keep any family historian glued to the book until the mystery is solved'
Eastman's Online Genealogy Newsletter

The Wicked Trade
(The Forensic Genealogist #7)

When Morton Farrier is presented with a case revolving around a mysterious letter written by disreputable criminal, Ann Fothergill in 1827, he quickly finds himself delving into a shadowy Georgian underworld of smuggling and murder on the Kent and Sussex border. Morton must use his skills as a forensic genealogist to untangle Ann's association with the notorious Aldington Gang and also with the brutal killing of Quartermaster Richard Morgan. As his research continues, Morton suspects that his client's family might have more troubling and dangerous expectations of his findings.

'Once again the author has carefully built the story around real places, real people, and historical facts - and whilst the tale itself is fictional, it's so well written that you'd be forgiven for thinking it was true'
Lost Cousins

'I can thoroughly recommend this book, which is a superior example of its genre. It is an ideal purchase for anyone with an interest in reading thrillers and in family history studies. I look forward to the next instalment of Morton Farrier's quest!'
Waltham Forest FHS

The Sterling Affair
(The Forensic Genealogist #8)

When an unannounced stranger comes calling at Morton Farrier's front door, he finds himself faced with the most intriguing and confounding case of his career to-date as a forensic genealogist. He agrees to accept the contract to identify a man who had been secretly living under the name of his new client's long-deceased brother. Morton must use his range of resources and research skills to help him deconstruct this mysterious man's life, ultimately leading him back into the murky world of 1950s international affairs of state. Meanwhile, Morton is faced with his own alarmingly close DNA match which itself comes with far-reaching implications for the Farriers.

'If you love a whodunnit *The Sterling Affair* is sure to grab your curiosity, and if you enjoy family history you'll relish the read all the more'
Family History magazine

'The events of the book are as much of a roller-coaster ride for Morton as they are for the reader. If you're an avid reader of Nathan Dylan Goodwin's books you won't need to be convinced to buy this latest instalment in the Forensic Genealogist series - but if you're not, now's the time to start, because *The Sterling Affair* is a real cracker!'
LostCousins

CPSIA information can be obtained
at www.ICGtesting.com
Printed in the USA
LVHW031548020521
686266LV00002B/80